D1713886

IN THAT ENDLESSNESS, OUR END

GEMMA FILES

GRIMSCRIBE
PRESS

New Orleans, Louisiana

Grimscribe Press
New Orleans, LA
USA

grimscribepress.com

CONTENTS

THIS IS HOW IT GOES

*L*AST NIGHT I had that dream where I was washing my face, and after I ran the cloth over my shut lids, I opened them again, and one of my eyes fell out—my left eye. Right eye? No, it was definitely the left; the sinister one, with all that that implies. And underneath where my eye used to be there was another eye, someone else's eye. So, there I was, standing there like an asshole, and there *it* was, looking out at me from the bathroom mirror. And the worst part was, it could *see* me. And I didn't *want* it to see me.

I'll tell you this much: I really want not to have that dream anymore or any of my other recurring dreams. Or not to dream at all—that would be good, too. Better, actually.

This is how it goes, these days. Stand by.

This fucking city, man, *this* one, right here. I don't know about any other, not for sure; whole rest of the world could be a lie made from stock footage, for all I know. For all any of us really ever knew.

Ah, but that's not true, is it? Because—

I was on the phone with my Dad when it started to happen, facetiming long distance, from Toronto, Canada to Hobart, Tasmania. Three in the morning my time, seven at night his time; they're fourteen hours ahead, which makes stuff weird. It was his birthday, or it had been, and I kind of felt like I owed him more than an e-card, given he was turning eighty. But his girlfriend came in halfway through our usual once-a-year mutual update, frowning at her iPad, and when he heard the note in her voice he rang off, saying he'd get back to me—which he didn't, but I don't blame him for it.

Sometimes I wonder what I would have seen, if I'd been able to keep watching. Something pretty much like what it turned out she was watching at the time, no doubt. I couldn't have known that, though.

Not yet.

It was roughly twenty-four hours before the Split hit Toronto, and I was back online, where I spent most of my days then. I worked from home, my mom's basement—a virtual telemarketing job, Skype-routed from my home number through a call center in New Delhi and back again. Half my calls required being fluent in Hindi and Urdu, the other half being fluent in accent-less English, so I was set for life, if I wanted to be; don't think I would have really stayed with it much more than two years, though, since the burn-out rate was amazing. I was processing one call roughly every minute and a half, and even my completed calls took less than five minutes, tops. In all the time I worked "there," I don't think I made more than fifty legitimate sales—the rest were all hang-ups or carry-through on previous calls made by other operators.

The content? Offering regular Marriott Hotel customers the chance at a "free" cruise, which required them to travel to Mississauga, listen to a presentation on time-shared beach-front cabins, then take part in a draw. One winner per draw, out of twenty to thirty applicants. It's truly amazing, the amount of time we used to waste trying to get something for nothing, isn't it?

The job suited me, because at that time I was still suffering from fairly extreme episodes of anxiety, bad enough I'd been forced to drop out of university halfway through the second semester of my five-year Biology program. I took it because I had immediate bills to pay but also to save enough money to try again, probably not the next semester but the one after that. Since my initial breakdown, however, I'd gone on a cocktail of prescribed drugs which made me both agoraphobic and overweight, a bad combination in terms of socializing, even after I felt well enough to want to, so the Internet had become my only friend—my enabler as well as my employer. I "knew" a lot of people online, people I spoke to and interacted with every day, but in most cases, I'd never even seen their photos, let alone met them in person.

Telemarketing can be mind-numbing work, so I distracted myself as much as I could while still being able to keep up to standard. Which is how I happened to have three screens open that day, one of them being a continually refreshed view of my favorite General Weird Shit thread on CreepTracker.org, and how, in turn—simply by clicking on a seemingly random link, posted without any sort of explanation—I became one of the first wave of people to view the initial upload of what would eventually become known as the Snowtown Dupe Vid.

Snowtown, a small village outside of Adelaide, South Australia, had up to that point garnered a slight amount of global infamy as the location of a series of homicides committed between 1992 and 1999, culminating in one of the longest, most publicized criminal trials in Australian history. I'd never been there, but the video certainly made it look familiar: Just one more bus-stop in the Bush, a big slice of wide open street with the horizon showing if you squinted, plus an exposed brick wall under a dripping awning—possibly that of a convenience store, given the large glass window and the faintly visible reflection from a neon sign above. Winter for them and their rainiest month, so the street itself was one big puddle, sky above full of lowering, thunderhead clouds. A shit day to be out, but whoever took the video—low-res, probably done on a cell-phone—seemed to be enjoying themselves, just like the kid they had their lens pointed at. Some young dude in jeans and a t-shirt, both equally soaked, drinking a Coke and complaining about the downpour, until...

Until.

Unless you've seen someone doing it, or done it yourself, you'll never know how bad being Duped looks when it happens. One second you're fine, bodily integrity at one hundred percent, totally normal. The next—

"Mate," a voice says offscreen, sounding worried. "You all right? Said, Y'all right, mate? Gaz? C'mon, stop it. Stop arsin' around. Mate?"

So there's poor Gazza, looking out at the rain, laughing and shooting the shit with his friend, who probably must've been standing almost right next to the store's front entrance, because when he saw what was starting to happen, he steps back far enough to set the automatic doors off and just stays there, frozen. So there's this Star-ship *Enterprise*-type sound of glass and rubber swiping back and forth for the entire rest of the whole vid: Whoosh-THUNK, whoosh-THUNK, whoosh-THUNK. Not that the friend really notices, riveted as he is on what's happening right in front of him—like me, that first time, or anybody else who's ever seen it, since. Like *everybody* was, 'til the Split finally ended up moving far enough around the world to hit them, too.

My man Gaz, totally happy and nonchalant, just one more bro spending bro-time with his best bud, rain and all. But then he suddenly jack-knifes, folded up, vi-brating all over—makes this weird face like he's been punched from the inside, again and again, just not stopping. And this... ripple, would be the best way to describe it... passing over him from head to toe, deforming his outline. Just seemed like a glitch at first, some bad pixilation, like the recording was sticking and jumping or something—

—but no, that wasn't it, not really. It was *him* you saw next: His flesh, his skin, puffing and peeling, bulging and ripping; tumors breeding everywhere, fast as pop-corn. Collarbone skewing, a bump detaching from his neck, yawning open and grow-ing eyes; ribs cracking apart like a hinged box-lid, to let a slimy copy of his torso shoul-der its way out from inside; a damn third hand coming straight up through his back, even, ripping right through his shirt. Something else—some*body* else—tearing him-self free, shedding Gaz like a spasming skin, with no regards whatsoever to the ruin he left in his wake.

Yeah, and blood, too—plenty of that, by the end. Blood spraying up every-where, even faster than the screams.

"Oh my *God*," the guy keeps on yelling, camera-phone waving back and forth like he was trying to semaphore. "Holy Christing fuck, who IS that, *who*? Who *is* that, mate? Mate? *Gaz*?"

And Gaz, grabbing his own newly-Duped throat with both hands, snarling in atavistic pain and hatred; Dupe-Gaz, grabbing back, just as committed to killing the person it's pulling itself out of. *There can be only one!* The two of them hanging on for dear life, tearing and snapping at each other like some horrible flesh cartoon, even as the nameless guy with the phone starts to cough and groan himself, starts to crack and squish and roar. Even as his blood splashes up (or down?) across the phone's skewed screen, as the phone slips from his hand and cracks against the ground, face down. Yet still, somehow, recording. Still streaming.

No reply and no more images either, just those terrible sounds. And that just goes on 'til it's gone in turn, 'til *he* is. Both of them or all three or all four. 'Til somebody involved survives that particular body horror mêlée or doesn't.

And that was it.

I hung up, cashed out, told my supervisor I was sick, that I was going to puke—food poisoning, whatever, I couldn't stick around. He wasn't happy, to say the least. Suggested strongly how I might not have a job by tomorrow, but I was fine with that, surprisingly; maybe I sensed which way the wind was blowing, so to speak. Then I IMed a friend of mine, instead—this guy in L.A., claimed he did Second Unit work on TV. I cut and pasted, shared the link, asked him what he thought.

> *See that there man?*
> *yah ridic, as if*
> *Soooo a hoax, is what your sayin*
> *course its a haox man what else? rlly think sm guy split down th/middle like a fukcng amoeba beat himself up run off? cmon dude check urself i do that shit daily, cgi out the ass*

I sat there for the next... six hours maybe, tracking the vid as it made its way round the world, passing through time-zone after time-zone, drawing comments like flies; ate in front of the screen, barely got up to piss, then fell sideways and rolled into bed. It was time I should have been spending upstairs with my mom, with my stepsiblings, her dead second husband's kids. But I wasn't to know, any more than it would've occurred to me to think I'd wake up next morning feeling like I'd pulled my guts out through my throat while trying to kill myself with my own bare hands, not at *all* metaphorically.

Here's what happened over here, meanwhile, when it all started to fall apart—it got hot, real hot. And still, too, the light outside all gray except for some kind of flicker along the horizon, heat lightning maybe, like just before a storm breaks. Then the power went out, then the Wi-Fi, then the rest of the amenities. Subway trains crashed into each other, all up and down both lines; planes coming into the Billy Bishop Toronto Island airport crashed instead of landing, skipping off the coast of Port George VI Island like stones, right into Lake Ontario. One apparently went so deep it broke through the roof of the channel tunnel between check-in and arrivals/departures, drowning a bunch of potential passengers who'd opted to walk instead of taking the ferry across.

All this while I was asleep, obviously. I've picked the details up from various other survivors, the ones I trade with or pay tribute to, the ones I sometimes have to hide from. The mad, the broken and the desperate wreckage-sifters, just like me.

TTC streetcars went dead in the middle of the road, creating convenient breaks for pileups that probably would have happened anyhow. The underground PATHs beneath the main buildings of Toronto's downtown business and shopping district all went dark at the same time, sparking panic, a wild upward rush for fresh air and sun that soon broke into site-specific riots, leaving the previously pristine tiled floors covered in bodies, some walls splashed with blood up to their ceilings. Not that the sidewalks above looked any better, by the end of the day—or my own condo's hallways, for that matter.

I had a friend once who happened to get caught in New Orleans during Katrina. "First time you turn on the tap and nothing comes out, things go downhill pretty fast," he told me. And he was right.

I don't know where he is now—lived out near Niagara Falls, last I heard, with his husband and their kids. They were okay the day before, far as I could tell, at least from Facebook.

But a whole lot of things have changed, since then.

No one left to clean up, afterwards—no one who gave enough of a shit to try, anyhow. Which is why downtown seems to be so full of birds now, more than I ever remember seeing in what none of us knew was our last decade of civilization: pigeons flocking and seagulls swooping everywhere, sparrows and starlings and red-winged black-birds, even hawks and crows. Not to mention former pets gone feral and the so-called vermin nobody bothers to cull, some rabid, most extremely well-fed—raccoons, skunks, rats, squirrels, foxes. Insects too, which can be surprisingly beautiful, in their season.

I walked through what used to be David Crombie Park yesterday, foraging for edible weeds near where the lavender once merely planted to edge banks of cultivated flowers has grown wild into a blossoming tangle almost four foot square, only to find it buzzing so loud with bees I could hear it down the block and absolutely covered in a fluttering black-and-orange cloud of Monarch butterflies. Those were declared extinct, back before the Split; nice to see we were wrong about that, in the end. Along with so much else.

I hardly ever see any corpses, to speak of. Bones, yes, here and there; scraps and leavings, dried to a fine brown leather. Most of the worst of it covered with grass, vines, greenery, though—and garbage too, of course, its toxic-bright colors sun-faded, covered in dust.

Human beings are full of garbage, like any other type of vermin; if animals eat us, they eat our filth, our madness. They go mad, in turn.

Birds and bats and butterflies, drunk on so much carrion, so many suddenly opulent food-sources. Ghosts of the towers of silence, of the vultures who are used to eating corpses, to being *allowed* to eat corpses. Of having them prepared for them. Some downtown people really have started exposing their dead on the tops of buildings, disjointed: Sky burial. I've seen it. Like they're trying to appease the mad birds' ghosts.

I remember looking down at that fat brown girl, the one who would've looked so much more like me if she'd been wearing both halves of the pajama set I went to bed in instead of just the one, torn haphazardly down the middle—or if she'd only had my face to go along with my hair, the purple streaks I'd just put in it still intact, a single earring dangling from one torn lobe. But she was dead, her head caved in. Her eyes were inside her mouth. And my hands were gloved with blood, up to the elbows. Not all of it that poor dead girl's, either; surprise surprise, beating someone to death with your bare hands *hurts*.

I had to pick a molar out of one my knuckles later on—the shattered remains of one. Worst infection I've ever had. The human mouth is a disgusting thing; my nail turned black. Eventually, I had to get a doctor who lives in my building to cut the finger off, along with the one next to it, so I didn't lose my whole hand.

Adrenaline could have explained not noticing that pain while it was happening. Nobody's ever explained why the Split itself blots out most of your memory and all your volition; nobody's ever remembered thinking clearly enough to try to stop, or flee instead of fight, or even just yell something like, *Hey, you're me!*, or *Where did you come from?*, or *Why are we doing this?* Just agony, nightmare fugue, and then a corpse. If you don't have a handy artificial marker somewhere—piercings, tattoos, whatever—most people can't even take a guess whether the survivor is dupe or original. Because memory's duplicated too, you see. So not even the survivors know who they *really* are.

I heard stories about people who killed the dupes of their loved ones, before everyone realized that. Some of those people killed themselves, after.

I didn't face that decision. I went upstairs and found the house trashed but empty, except for the bodies: my step-siblings Maggie and Phil (or their copies)—Phil with a kitchen knife in his chest and Maggie smothered in a plastic bag—and... something gray, warped and bloody that looked more like a John Carpenter film prop than anything once human. I fled, but more in blind terror than grief, not even really understanding what I'd seen.

Halfway down the block, I suddenly realized the gray thing with too many limbs must've been my mom. She'd died mid-Split like most of the elderly or the sick, the children too young to survive the trauma. Which was everything I'd need or want to know about my Dad and his girlfriend, as well, in the end. Not that I'll ever be able to find out now.

For a century or so, the world was small enough not to be afraid of. It got smaller and faster and faster and smaller, 'til you could hold it in your hand. 'Til you could watch it from morning to night without ever having to go anywhere.

That's never going to be true again.

At any given point during the Split, as the initial wave passed through Canada, scientists have determined (to the best of their ability, given present circumstances) that as much as one third of the population must have been either duping, already duped, or entering the full-bore throes of dupe-on-dupe death-combat. No one was immune, not even twins, who you'd assume came sort of pre-duped already. The blows to our infrastructure were so hard and immediate, we've hardly begun yet to clean up that first mess, let alone the messes which followed. It was a full-bore ecological landslide, a global tsunami... and the very funniest part of all, in context, is that even though the only thing that changed was us, that was more than enough, because we *infested* this planet, like any other virus; we were already literally everywhere, doing everything.

Except now there were suddenly so many, many more of us than usual, and we were all doing our level best to murder each other.

The worst stuff I heard, the *very* worst... that was all after, from people I swapped junk, food and stories with. Which makes sense. During, we were apart, trapped in our own little slices of frenzy, our very specific orbits; right after, we clung together just to keep everything—everyone—else out. Just a day and a half, two at the most, and suddenly we were cut off like we hadn't been for decades: no coms, no radio, no TV, no energy, no phones, no Internet. What else could we do but sit in the dark and tell stories? Confess to each other and hope for absolution?

So, anyhow: there's this guy, and his wife is pregnant, like out to here—maybe nine months, maybe a bit more. They're going to get an ultrasound, to see if they have to induce. And in the time he parks his car, the time it takes him to get out and go 'round to her side, she starts screaming; falls out when he opens her door, right onto the street, like she's having a fit. He manages to get her up and walk her inside. And when they go to put the gel on her, her stomach is all jiggling around, stretching violently like it's going to tear open, bruises appearing from the inside. They can't even get a look, have to sedate her and go in for a caesarian, quick as humanly possible.

But when they open her up, what they discover is that she'd left the house with one baby, then all of a sudden, she had two—they'd duped, right inside of her. After which they attacked each other, like dupes do; stuck in there, all dark and close, it must've been like waking into hell. And one of them killed the other, but the dead one gave as good as it got, so the one who won didn't live for long, either.

The mother, when she saw all that, she just went insane. Killed herself, before she even had to dupe.

The father too, eventually, poor bastard.

That was how it started for me, like that was how it ended, for them. And at the time, when I heard about it—I thought they were lucky, sort of. Luck*ier,* I mean. Because at least they were out of it, right? They had that, if nothing else. At the *very* least, they wouldn't have to see whatever fresh new horror came along next.

Not like the rest of us.

One member of our enclave told a story of something that had happened to his brother—or was it his roommate? Anyway. Our guy had been walking along the Bloor Street viaduct with the other guy when the Split hit, and the dupe-fight ended with one of those lottery-win flukes: one of them threw the other off the bridge into the

Don River... except, according to Our Guy, the Other Guy's dupe was *still alive*. Our Guy says he could see the dupe still flailing about in the water as the current bore him downstream, before he vanished; Other Guy was too injured at that point to try pursuing, so Our Guy brought him back home and patched him up as best he could. And then, still understanding nothing, he'd asked: *Should we, like... try to find that guy?* And Other Guy said, *Fuck no. I see him again I'm gonna kill him.* Which was surreal enough, said Our Guy, but what made it even weirder was that Other Guy was a big ass pacifist. Hadn't ever raised a hand to anyone in his life before that day.

Weirdest of all, though, said Our Guy, looking round the fire to each of us, *was... I understood what he meant. I hadn't even duped yet. But just thinking about it made me so, so...* angry. *Like puke-your-guts-out pissed off. Like finding out your kid's a crack dealer or your wife's been fucking your best friend, except even worse. Something that's just—not supposed to* happen. *You know what I mean, right?*

We all did.

Humans are amazingly adaptable creatures, which seemed like more of a compliment before I realized, post-Split, it was an equally apt descriptor for rats. But—astonishing as I found it—the government *did* have disaster recovery plans in place for scenarios as destructive if not as weird.

A day or so after Toronto stopped working, emergency military units rolled in, burning the gasoline reserves they must have had squirrelled away somewhere, setting up camps and sending round jeeps with megaphones and instructions. Communicating via radio, they corralled survivors, distributed emergency rations, cleared travel routes, counted and named the dead. I spent a few weeks sleeping on a cot in the John Innes Community Center gymnasium. Never had any trouble getting to sleep either, despite knowing full well I probably wouldn't get my anxiety meds back for months if not years. *Might be true after all,* I remember thinking as I drifted off one night; *once you know the absolute worst actually* has *happened, you really can relax.*

Or maybe my blood sugar was just bottoming out. The disaster rations kept us from starving, but nobody ever had quite enough. Which described pretty much everything else in those weeks, for that matter. Enough power for critical functions, from careful, intermittent generator use, but nothing that broke the silence of phones, TVs, iPads. Enough water to quell thirst, never enough to get clean. Enough routine to hold back panic, never enough to feel safe.

Enough recovery to promise hope. Never quite enough to convince.

We were all surprised, when telling our stories later, to realize just how many cultures had a word for it. The *ka*, in Egyptian myth. A witch's fetch. *Vardøger, etiänen, doppelgänger, Ankou.* "Twin strangers," social media called it; Artem said there'd even been a website, Twinstrangers.net, where you could upload a photo and use facial recognition software to search for your own double. We laughed at that, tiredly, until Artem made the mistake of trying for more laughter. *Maybe that's where the Dupes came from, eh? The harbingers got onto the Web, went all high-tech mass production.* He pounded his knee and guffawed but stopped when he saw none of us smiling.

Ryuji, who'd been a physics student, had a different idea. *The Many-Worlds theory says every decision creates a separate universe,* he'd explained in his soft voice, as we went from apartment to apartment in an empty condo building, looking for cans of food. *I think perhaps someone at CERN ran the Supercollider too hard and broke down the barrier between us and another of these universes, probably the very closest one. The violence is the result of the mind trying to exist simultaneously in separate overlapping realities and resolving the conflict the only way it can—by eliminating it. That's why it's only people who Split, not objects or animals. We're the only ones who make choices.*

So, if we ran this collider thing in reverse, could we stop it happening? I'd asked, mostly to keep him talking. I was pretty sure Ryuji didn't return the way I felt at all, but I still liked being near him, listening to him. But the question had backfired, wiping the smile off his face.

I don't think it works that way, Aditi, he'd finally said, looking at nothing in particular. And shut up after that except for absent little grunts, until we were back in the group's squat.

He made the mistake of going out alone on his next scavenging run. When we found him a week later, most of the meat had been carved off him.

You may have guessed the next part from the fact I said, "*stop it happening,*" i.e., present tense.

Within a week it was obvious the Split was still going on, just much less frequently—maybe one person in a hundred, every three or four days or so. After the first few times, people started trying to jump in and restrain the dupers, which only got *both* of them to turn on the interlopers and as often as not racked up four or five corpses instead of just one. Finally, the soldiers worked out a protocol where they'd haul the dupers apart while a doctor sedated them both into oblivion, then drag them off somewhere to do... something. Fix them, experiment on them—grind one of them up for more food, for all we knew; it was fresh protein literally out of nowhere for free, after all. The only certainty was no one ever saw them again, except for the officers in charge, and they weren't talking.

But somebody must have found *some* way to do something about it. Electroshock therapy, the right drug cocktail, or just keep dupers far enough apart for long enough. Because the day it all went to shit for the second time, that day in the John Innes gym, I was paying attention. I saw when some of the soldiers suddenly turned on the rest of them, opening up with their guns; I hid under a table, watching for a few seconds before Artem grabbed me and hauled me away.

I'm still pretty sure I was the first to realize that the men shouting orders on each side of that battle had the same face.

The most horrible part—or what part of me thinks *should* be the horrible part, any-way—is that the world's actually gotten more beautiful, to me anyway. More peaceful. Not just physically, with green sweeping over everything, the end of engine noise, hy-drocarbon stink and contrails in the sky, but almost spiritually somehow. Like the planet's undergone the same vast unclenching I've felt inside me, at the realization I'd been off my meds for weeks and hadn't missed them. And the knotted tension I've felt as long as I could remember—the constant ache of trying to figure out what a stranger's politeness does or doesn't hide, the gnawing fear that at any moment I'll let my social mask slip and suddenly wind up once more outcast, hated, ridiculed, for no reason I've ever been able to understand… that's finally dissipated. For good.

Apocalypse as psychotherapy: effective, but expensive, I've joked to the others. Eve-rybody laughed, especially Artem. But sometimes I think it might not be a joke. Some-times I ask myself how someone can be—not happy, exactly, but *relaxed*, in what must be humanity's last days. Content, even. Is it just all the problems of life going away? No more carbon footprints, no more taxes, flame wars or credit card debt, no more asshole bosses?

Or… does something else happen, in the Split? Does part of us—maybe the part we've always wanted to kill—die in that fight, with whichever half loses?

I'd like to think that, sometimes. That somehow, I'm better for what I've gone through. But it's easier in the afternoon and evening, when I've forgotten the dreams. When I can forget that I'm only alive because I was able to kill a version of myself… a version which might be back, if I Split again. Which might remember losing, for all I know, and fight that much harder—

—no, not if. When. *When* I Split again.

This is how it goes these days.

We've been talking about trying to head south, especially since it's going to be a lot harder here once winter comes. I walked down to the Lakeshore the other day and wondered how many boats there must be abandoned, both on this side of the harbor and on the Islands. At least one's got to have enough room for eight people. None of us have ever sailed before, but we've had to learn to do harder things.

The sun on the lake water was beautiful. You can drink it now, if you boil it first.

Getting enough food down to the harbor while evading the other scavenger groups will be hard. Especially since, to some of them, we'll *be* the food. And if luck goes against us and one of us Splits while we're on the water, that could get us all killed if the fight does enough damage. But we'll figure something out.

Or we won't. I couldn't have said anything like that so calmly, before. But when you finally grasp that you can't count on anything, you either worry about everything or you worry about nothing, and I've already tried one of those.

I think I'm going to stop recording now.

This is how it goes. Stand by.

Bulb

Lucas Brennan 1:41 PM (4 hours ago)
to me ▼

Ian,

I wish you'd told me to listen to your recordings first, because I just wasted ninety fucking minutes on editing your intro script first. There's absolutely no way we can use this interview, Ian – this isn't what we're about, it isn't what our listeners want, and it isn't what we sold anyone on or what our advertisers want to be connected with! I hate being the heavy here, but you've put the rest of us in a truly bad position – I can either pull Jen and Oshi off the May 17 episode to try putting together a half-assed substitute or we can screw over our listeners with a rerun, and either way we're almost certainly gonna lose audience clicks, which means we lose ad clicks which means we all lose revenue.

I'll let you know which way we go. In the interim I'd do yourself a favor and stay offline for a day or two. I'm not the only person on the team who's pissed about this.

—L.
Sent from my iPhone

Ian Dossimer Apr 20 (1 day ago)
to Lucas ▼

Hey Luke,

I've enclosed the first whack at the intro script for the May 3 episode; sorry it's a little late but I think we've still got time, especially given how little editing I think the interview portion's going to need. Text me or call me with any questions! — Doss

"GRIDLOST" — EPISODE 22 MAY 3
Proposed Title: "Leaving the Light Behind"
Intro Script

Good morning, afternoon or evening, everybody, whenever you're listening; I'm your host Ian Dossimer and welcome to another episode of "GridLost", the podcast where we interview the new pioneers of the 21st century, people looking for ways to build themselves a space of privacy and safety in an increasingly technology-polluted world. We've got something of exceptional interest today, so I hope everybody has time to sit down and listen to things straight through, because I can promise you—this story isn't like anything you've heard on "GridLost" before. It isn't like anything we've *done* on "GridLost" before.

The first and most important thing I have to tell you today is about our guest. Because her name is... not something we know, in fact. That's right, for the first time in our show's history we're conducting an anonymous interview. The only contact information I have for this woman is an Internet forum handle and a phone number that I was assured belongs to a burner phone she plans to discard pretty much the moment she hangs up on us. Some of our more devoted fans may recognize this handle if they frequent the right websites: she goes by the alias "Harmony6893", and she's posted on Prepperforums.net and Survivalistboards.com, among others.

If you do recognize that alias, you'll also probably know why this is something of a coup for us: unlike a lot of our subjects, Harmony6893 hasn't just disconnected from the central North American power network, she has (so she claims) completely abandoned the use of *any* kind of electrical technology or telecommunications device. She has no cable, no Wi-Fi, no smartphone, no solar panels, batteries or wind turbines, not even an emergency generator – in fact, she only posts to the 'Net every two weeks when she visits a not-exactly-nearby town to use their Internet cafe. More controversially, some say dangerously, she's doing this all completely alone; she has no family or housemates in her property, wherever it is. If there is an ultimate off-the-grid story, this woman is it.

The next thing I have to warn you about is the nature of Harmony6893's story. As you'll know from our other episodes, the reasons people choose to unplug are as varied as the people themselves; some want to recapture a childhood that modern technology is destroying, some are preparing for an EMP attack or any of half a dozen other kinds of disaster, some want to help bring about political decentralization by creating the infrastructure for social decentralization. But in my first phone call, when I asked Harmony6893 to explain the reasons for her self-imposed isolation, she told me that it wasn't any of that. That it was something utterly unique to her, something she was utterly sure nobody else would understand or believe. And after listening to what she has to say... well, I'm not sure she's wrong. But I do think it's something that our listeners deserve the chance to make up their own mind about.

Harmony is, in fact, so cautious that during our interview, she was obviously using some sort of commercial sound distorter on her phone to disguise her voice – just to explain why it sounds so odd. Please don't blame our tech guys! Without further ado, then, let us introduce you... to Harmony6893.

harmony-interview-apr-18.mp3

* * *

INTERVIEW TRANSCRIPT
Q: I. DOSSIMER, "GRIDLOST", 04-18

A: "HARMONY6893"

Q: I want to thank you again for being willing to take the time to do this.

A: (PAUSE) "Willing" might be a strong word. "Attack of conscience" is probably more accurate.

Q: Well, *that* sounds ominous.

A: If you're not going to take this seriously, I'm hanging up.

Q: No, yes, of course, you're right, I do apologize. Let's begin with the standard introduction: So… you're currently known only as Harmony6893 on a number of Internet forums.

A: You already know that.

Q: And your real name is…?

A: None of your business.

Q: Well, that creates just a bit of a problem for us, especially in terms of, you know, fact-checking whatever it is you're going to—

A: Mmm-hmh, yeah, I don't care. If that's some kind of deal-breaker for you, then I guess we're…

Q: No, no, it's okay, it's all right! How would you prefer we refer to you, then?

A: Um. (PAUSES) Bronwyn, that's always been a name I liked. Call me that.

Q: All right, Bronwyn. How long have you been off the grid, at this point?

A: Almost a year and four months. Since January of last year.

Q: And you've gone completely non-technological? Like, back to the nineteenth century?

A: Hardly. When I need to buy tools and supplies, I buy modern machine-shop versions. I don't hand-carve my own butter churns. (BEAT) But I do *have* a butter churn. (CHUCKLES) That's one of the reasons I started posting to prepper sites, in the first place—I had to learn a lot of the old techniques just to stay afloat, and people in the survivalist community put big value on skill-sharing.

Q: And yet you also live completely by yourself as well, we hear. One thing a lot of our other interviewees have said is that total isolation is actually dangerous – not just in case you find yourself hurt and without help, but because humans aren't really meant to live that way. Community's a key part of sanity. Why forgo it?

A: (PAUSE) I'd have to call that a matter of conscience, as well.

Q: Meaning you don't want to tell us? It's all right, if you don't. We always respect the defined spaces of our guests' privacy.

A: No, I'm *going* to tell you. It's just that explaining it is going to take a while. And enough of your listeners are going to think I'm a psycho by the end of this anyway.

Q: You might be surprised. We're pretty open-minded around here.

A: We'll see.

(PAUSE)

Q: So, we may as well start from the beginning: Had you always been interested in disconnection as a lifestyle, or was it a sudden change?

A: You could call it "sudden." (BEAT) The truth is, up until last January, you would probably have pegged me as the last person you'd have imagined doing this. I was a stockbroker—or, as I liked to tell people I thought would think it was charming, I tricked suckers into throwing away their money trying to cheat the system out of more for a living. I was one of those people you see powerwalking along Bay Street with a Bluetooth in her ear and her nose in her smartphone, checking on Bloomberg and the

TSE[1] for the latest buying and selling movements. That's how it all started, in fact—I got a promotion and a pay raise that meant I'd finally be able to live downtown on my own salary, so I started looking around for a condo within walking distance of my office. And in December, I thought I'd finally found it. It wasn't a new unit, just a one-bedroom plus den job belonging to a guy who flew back and forth every week between Hong Kong and... and where I used to live, so when his job suddenly changed and he didn't need to be there anymore, he was more interested in unloading it fast than in gouging potential buyers. Not a lot of room, but all the space I needed for my office, plus a lot of shelving and a really nice northern view with lots of natural light. And there was this beautiful line of track-lighting in the main room, one of the best I'd ever seen—bright bulbs, understated fixtures, on a dimmer switch. I remember looking up at it while the realtor was nattering on and thinking, "Wow, that's *really nice*."

Q: So, what you're saying is, it was really nice.

A: Yeah, well, I think ultimately, that lighting might've been the primary reason I agreed to buy the place. So I go through all the paperwork, wait for my buddy to move out and head back to Hong Kong, and I move in three weeks later and... the lighting is gone. He took it with him.

Q: You mean he actually removed the entire fixture? Not just took out the bulbs?

A: Yeah, that's what I mean. There wasn't anything left in the ceiling except this S-shaped row of plastic nodules where it must have been attached. I don't mind telling you I was really pissed off about that, especially when the realtor said she couldn't do anything—if the guy put it in, he had the right to take it out.

Q: Was this some kind of unique hand-made brand, or something? I wouldn't think it'd be that impossible to replace a set of lights.

---

[1] The references to "Bay Street" and the "TSE" make it likely that Harmony/Bronwyn is Canadian, specifically from Toronto, Ontario; "TSE" in context almost certainly stands for the Toronto Stock Exchange, and Bay Street runs through the downtown finance core of the city, making it the Canadian equivalent of Wall Street in Manhattan.

24

A: You wouldn't, right? But no. I mean… getting a new track and bulbs wasn't the problem—didn't look exactly like what'd been there before, but at this point, I was willing to settle. The *problem* was when I got the lighting tech in to hook everything up, and he just couldn't get it to work.

Q: How do you mean?

A: I mean he couldn't get a current out of any of the wires running into those sockets. And even weirder? He couldn't even find the goddam *switch* that worked that particular fixture. The dimmer and all that shit? Well, my realtor couldn't remember where it was supposed to be, and neither I nor the lighting guy could find anything like it. Sure, there was a switch inside the door for the hall light, one for the kitchen—guy-o didn't take *that.* A switch inside the john, for the vanity lights above the sink. But no switches anywhere else except right next to the in-suite washer-dryer unit built-in, and you know what *that* turned out to run?

Q: The washer-dryer?

A: Got it in one.

Q: Okay, I admit it, that's a little weird… You're sure you saw these lights actually working, when you were first looking at the apartment? When the realtor was there?

A: *Yes*, for fuck's sake.

Q: Uh, we'd really rather you didn't—

A: Whatever. (ANOTHER PAUSE) And then I went downstairs, talked to the concierge, wanted to know what the lighting setup was in all the other apartments with the same layout—they wouldn't tell me. Cited privacy, can you believe that? So I tell them what's happened and how I just want to figure out how to put in lights that'll turn on so I don't have to light the whole place with floor-lamps, and they're like, well, we can't help, can't even get in touch with the Hong Kong dude, because he changed his phone number, and it turns out they never even had his email. And my mortgage agreement says I'm the one who's basically responsible for everything that happens inside my walls, anyhow.

Q: So, it was the, um... annoying, frustrating, no doubt expensive unreliability of this system which prompted your eventual... lifestyle change?

A: No. Not that. (ANOTHER, LONGER PAUSE) Have you ever thought—I mean, I guess you kind of must have, considering this show you run—but have you ever *really* thought, like in *detail,* about just how much we all rely on things these days that almost *none* of us actually understand?

Q: You mean, technologically? Like—

A: Yeah, that too, of course. But... not just that.

Q: Well, a lot of the people we interview do make a big deal out of how much we take for granted. How our whole society runs on these... tides of energy going back and forth: electricity, cellular signals, microwaves. Invisible presences that we all work with, constantly, and only a tiny minority of people actually know how to build, or control, or fix. I remember one bloke talking about how he'd taught himself practical electrician's skills as part of getting his lodge set up, and he did some handyman work for his friends and neighbors in the meantime; what always amazed him, he said, was how mind-boggled everybody he helped was. "It really was like I was some kind of wizard or magician," he told me. "Wave my screwdriver, say stuff that made no sense, then everything works again. I mean, it felt good, but it was also kind of unnerving, you know?"

A: Wow, it's like you do this for a living. Though I guess it's probably not much of one, right?

Q: Well, we get to do what we enjoy; most of us think that's worth the trade-off.

A: Yeah. Well, my way of dealing with stuff like that was always to pay other people, like your friend, to do it for me. As it happened, I was dating a guy at the time, who was—lucky for me—both an engineering student and *not* a dickhead, surprisingly. It was early days, we'd met in a club and liked each other, I brought him home, and he looked around and said, "Why do you have all these floor lamps?" So, I told him the story, or a truncated version thereof, and he said, "Oh, I can fix that for you." I didn't say, *I doubt it*, largely because I still wanted to sleep with him, but his pitch was that he'd had a light meter at home, which he'd used before for similar things, so it would be cheap, and we could enjoy each other's company while he did it.

Q: He was well fit, I take it?

A: Very. Very... well fit. (PAUSE) So a couple of days later, he comes over to my place, and I buzz him in; he's got his toolbox with him and a vest on with all these pockets where you can stick things, like he's dressed to go into battle, and he's got what look like bandoliers of shotgun shells slung across his chest. They weren't, obviously; they were batteries and lightbulbs, all the different kinds he thought he'd be likely to need. I say, "Great," show him the empty fixture sockets, the light switch and where everything was, including the fuse box, and he gets to work. Well, he can't get anything out of the wires either, any more than the other guy did; I'm standing by his stepladder holding the light meter up over my head, and he keeps asking me, "Did you see it jump? Is it jumping now?" to which I just kept saying, "Nope." I honestly thought the meter was broken, and for a minute so did he, until he tested it with one of the floor lamps and proved that it wasn't. Then he gets into the fuse box and manages to turn everything else in the apartment on and off at least once but still can't find anything that looks like a working light circuit in the ceiling outside the kitchen and the front hallway. And he's like, "Well, *that's* weird." And it *was* weird. To be frank, it was kind of starting to freak me out at this point, and I was perfectly willing to tell him to stop. But you know how guys get; he had this look on his face like he was taking it personally. Like "This is pissing me off, and I'm gonna *beat* it." So he took the light meter from me—he was a tall guy—and he stuck it up right up near the ceiling, maybe ten centi-meters[2] away, started going back and forth across the ceiling from the fixture, doing this sort of—like he was sweeping a field for mines, you know? Or using a metal de-tector to look for treasure, and I was like, *Oh, this is ridiculous.* But eventually, he was almost to the main window, and he was making a sweep to his left, and suddenly... the pointer on the meter twitched. He stops, says: "Look at this!" Further he went towards the corner, meanwhile, the more reaction he got, until finally it was reading as though there was an active socket there.

Q: But there couldn't have been, was there? Or you'd have seen it.

A: Correct. There wasn't even a power point. I never even put a floor lamp in that corner.

Q: Why not?

A: Because... I didn't like that corner. It was always cold there. I mean, it was always going to be a little cold, because it was winter; plus, an additional downside to floor-to-ceiling windows that slide open is that if you want to be *able* to open them you can't caulk them up. But this was—colder. Off-puttingly so. So, I just avoided putting any-thing in there, because I didn't want to *be* there.

Q: What was it like in summer?

A: I never made it to summer. (PAUSE) So he asks me, "Was there *ever* a fixture here?" and I tell him I have no idea. And he looked at me, and I looked at him, and then he said, "I'm gonna try something." Gave me the light meter and took out one of the light-bulbs by the—what do you call the metal part on the bottom, the part that screws in?

Q: That's the cap.

---

[2] Four inches.

A: Right, yeah. So, he held it by the cap, just this standard 100-watt incandescent and lifted it up closer and closer to the ceiling… and as he got further and further up, the filament began to glow, and then, suddenly, it turned on. Full brightness. It was… it was horrible. Unnatural. I mean, anything unnatural is horrible, right? Like a preaching dog or a singing rose, that kind of shit? Somebody said that.[3]

Q: I guess. And, uh, your boyfriend – how did he react?

A: Oh, he was delighted. Very impressed with himself. He started to laugh. He had his arm straight out at shoulder height, and he was moving it all around watching the light brighten and dim, like it was the coolest toy in the world. It must have been really hot, but he didn't seem to notice; maybe he had calluses on his fingers. And then, basically just by accident, he brushed the wall with the metal base of the bulb—and it *stuck* there. Like, it actually pulled out of his fingers and stayed behind on the wall, sticking right out like a, I don't know, like a fucking *tumor* or something. A fucking glowing tumour. And he shook his hand, fingers snapping like he'd just figured out how close he'd just come to almost burning them, and he goes: "Whoo! *That* was something!" Me, I just stand there with my mouth open, not knowing what the hell to say. But then he's peering closer at it, until finally I can't stand it anymore, and I just tell him, "Pull it off. I don't want it there." He starts going on about how there must be something magnetized in the wall, and this is a complete cock-up that I could probably sue the building over, and I say, "I don't *care,* I want you to *get it off my wall, please!*" So, because he'd have to grab it by the hot part of the bulb this time, he put on a pair of work gloves and took hold of it—very gently—and starts trying to pull it off the wall. And it won't come off.

Q: Was he right? Had something been magnetized in the walls?

A: I have no fucking idea, but I *really* don't think so. Anyway, he's like, "I don't know what to do at this point, I don't want to break it," and I'm like, "*Break* it, man!" So, he

---

[3] Arthur Machen, in the prologue to "The White People." Paraphrased.

tries to pull it from the cap this time, hauling on it harder and harder, and then he slips a little and the bulb *slides up* the wall, and we both suddenly realize he can move it *upwards*. Towards where the reading is coming from.

Q: The cold spot.

A: Yeah. I hadn't thought about it like that, but—that's what it was, wasn't it?

Q: Like in a haunted house?

A: You tell me. (PAUSE) So he keeps pushing it up the wall, closer and closer to the cold spot—the "source", he's calling it—and it gets brighter and brighter. And I didn't really realize this at first, but it was as if, while the bulb was getting brighter, the rest of the apartment seemed to be getting... dimmer. Like it was about to flicker; I'd seen that before, plenty of times. Normal stuff. Even brand new, very expensive condos have power fluctuations.

Q: Well, if the bulb was that bright, it would have made everything else *look* dim, wouldn't it?

A: Exactly. Brighter, and brighter, and then—it popped. Not just burnt out, I mean the whole bulb actually exploded, and it was only because my guy already had one hand up shielding his eyes against the light that he didn't get hurt. And we both jump back, and we're left with nothing except the cap and a little jagged rim of broken glass around it stuck almost right in the top corner of my ceiling. And we look at each other, and I tell him, "Okay, I think we're done with this tonight," and I go to get the broom and dustpan and start sweeping up the broken glass off my lovingly-installed hardwood floors. But, you know, there's gotta be more to it. So, he takes out the highest-wattage bulb he has—spotlight-quality halogen, it looks like—puts on a pair of fricking polarized safety glasses, for fuck's sake, and says: "Let me just try one more thing." Well, how was I gonna stop him? He holds up the bulb, pointing it away from me, and the same thing happens as he lifts it closer and closer to the cold spot: Filament starts glowing, ramps up as he lifts, until the cone of light it's throwing is so bright the colors on that side of the apartment look almost completely washed out. And I turn away, shielding my face, which is the only reason I see it happening.

Q: See... what happening?

A: How every other bulb in the place really *is* dimming down now, *very* visibly: kitchen, hallway, bathroom—and before you ask, this isn't just my vision adjusting to one bright light source, I can *see* them browning out. And it's getting *colder* in the place, too, like the window and front door have both been thrown open and a cross-breeze is sucking out all the heat. Except everything's still closed. And then Joe—my... my friend—I hear him yelp, like the sound you'd make if somebody startled you by slapping your hand. He staggers back from the corner, and he's just staring at the bulb hovering there, and the look on his face is finally about as freaked out as I've been for the last fifteen minutes. So, I hurry over to him, asking what's wrong, and he pulls me almost right against the window so I can see what he's seeing. The bulb isn't stuck to the wall. It's floating there right in mid-fucking-*air*. And smoke is curling and hissing off the plaster overhead, except the stain spilling across it isn't black, it's... "white" isn't strong enough. It was like someone photographed a heat-scorch and then flipped it into negative, so black becomes white, except it's this blinding purplish-UV glow that—I can't describe it; staring at it *hurt*, like someone was squeezing my eyeballs, like the world's worst case of glaucoma, and after a second I had to hunch over with my palms in my eye sockets. But Joe, he's got his glasses on so I guess it wasn't hurting him to look at, and he was just staring up at it, his mouth open a little, almost smiling— like he was so amazed, he was happy. Like he was seeing God. Then, under the sizzling sound of my ceiling cooking, there's this rippling wave of sharp cracking, banging sounds, and the plaster splits open all around the bulb, shooting out in all directions from the corner—along the ceiling, down the wall, towards the windows. And more glowing shit spills out through all these cracks, except this isn't light or smoke or fire; it's more like... Ever seen one of those phosphorescent jellyfish they have in aquariums? Like the wall at Ripley's Aquarium, the one they shot part of *The Handmaid's Tale* pilot episode in front of? They're all made of, um, goo, right, even the biggest ones...

transparent, like slime, or mucus that isn't infected. Invisible, really. Until you shine a light behind them. (PAUSE) I'll assume you have. Anyway, imagine that, but with the wall's brightness amped up to eleven, almost as hard to look at as the bulb itself. And I can't even *see* the bulb anymore, only the place in the corner where the light is brightest. And this horrid blinding incandescent shit coming in through the cracks, that fizzling, spitting sparkler of a fissure between here and—somewhere else starts... *weaving* itself out in all directions, dropping these wet viscous tendrils onto the floor, throwing them out at the walls like the support lines on a spiderweb. Oh God, and just the way it *sounded* made me want to puke, and the smell was like ozone and rotten seaweed and rancid fat. But even while it's doing all this, making itself *manifest* like somebody—fucking cutting themselves apart so their entrails fall out, or whatever—it's still cycling through every color you can think of, and it's fucking *beautiful*, like staring into a ten-foot-tall kaleidoscope. The bell forms, then filaments, then tentacles. Mucus and spines spread all over Joe, cocooning him—he's up to his waist in this swamp of oozing, spiny tendrils, and I'm standing in a puddle of oil-slick glowing crap that's inching its way up my ankles, like I'm sinking into the floor. If I hadn't already had the broom in my hand I really don't think I would have gotten out of there, but thank Christ, I did. I don't even remember being angry, or frightened, just... wired. Like I was buzzing. Like a signal going through me. So, I stumble forwards with my eyes closed and start flailing with the broom at the corner of the ceiling, the cold spot. And I can feel the sickening, wet way all this slimy guck gives way under it when I'm swinging and jabbing, but then—somehow—there's this solid *crunch*, and the light goes out, with this... it isn't a *sound*. It's like a feeling in the air. This silent, agonizing trembling all along my skin, like a thousand dog-whistles all screaming at once. I broke the bulb, and that's all it took. Right then, anyhow. So. All the shit that's wrapping up Joe falls apart with this disgusting squelching noise, and Joe goes over on his side, which is when I grab him up with both hands, trying to haul him to the door—where I thought the door used to be. Because it was *dark* in there, man, super-dark; dark plus. I've never seen dark like that, before or after. Must've looked pretty funny, in retrospect: there I am, dragging—attempting to drag—this huge, cut young dude twice my size, slapping his face and yelling hysterically at him, desperate to get him to wake up. Couldn't see much, but I remember his arms felt slimy, and patches of his skin almost seemed...

soft, like if I squeezed too hard it would just slide right off his arm. Overcooked meat, that was the feel. (SOFTER) God, I wish I hadn't remembered that. (PAUSE, THEN NORMAL TONE) Okay, so. I get him past the kitchen counter into the vestibule, still fumbling around, and my hand falls on the door handle, at fucking *last*. Jesus! It was like a miracle. And I open the main door, so I can finally *see* again in the light coming in from the hallway—which is exactly when the thing in the apartment suddenly bursts into blazing light again, even brighter, but I can *still see what it's doing*. It kind of... *pulses*, first inward and then outward, and opens up like a gigantic umbrella, a vampire fucking squid, with red and purple teeth all ringed round inside and dripping. Tendrils shoot out and they wrap 'round Joe and haul him back in, so fast and hard I don't have time to let go. Next thing I know, it snaps shut on us both: all of him, me just to the wrist, the right one. Joe's just—gone, swallowed. And my hand is stuck inside the peak of the thing, and it's *burning,* like I stuck it in a beehive, or a vat full of acid. Like I'd stuck it through a hole, right into somebody else's stomach. I must've been screaming, but I don't remember. Just hauling as hard as I could 'til my hand peeled free and throwing myself back out that door, slamming it shut behind me.

Q: (AFTER A MOMENT) Joe?

A: (SOFT) No. I didn't—I don't... I don't *feel* good about it. But... I didn't...

Q: You didn't know him well enough to die for him.

A: Thank you for saying it. (ANOTHER LONG PAUSE) By the way, when I say "peeled", I mean literally. Large patches of skin on my hand just melted away, exposing layered patches of fat, visible veins and tendons. Nauseating, and painful as *shit*. I wound up having to have most of the rest of the epidermis debrided so the skin would grow back evenly, and I still don't have any mobility in my right ring or little fingers. By the time I got to the nearest ER, I'd been making a fist so long they had to sort of prise, sort of cut it open, because it'd already started healing shut. Human body's an amazing thing, man. When they got my fingers uncurled, a bunch of stuff fell out: goo, pulp, faintly pinkish. Things that looked like bones, but soft—bendy. Like they'd been digested and shit back out. And something else. It was a Ryerson University Engineering Department ring. So yeah, nobody ever found much else of Joe. Just this... layer of sludge all over the apartment, unidentifiable, biological in origin. Just cracks in the ceiling and two broken bulbs lying in the far-left corner, right by the window. Adding insult to injury, the condo corporation tried like hell to blame *me* for the damage. They only gave up when I got a lawyer smart enough to point out that just publicizing the legal battle would tank sales in the entire building. That's how I got out of my mortgage with enough money to do whatever I wanted, after that. But by that point, I already knew what I had to do. See, after that day? I couldn't turn on an electric light anywhere—couldn't even get near one—without hearing this... *buzzing.* Incandescent, CFL, LED, doesn't matter. If I listen hard enough, like really, *really* hard, I can even hear it coming from computer screens or smartphones. And the buzzing... once you listen long enough, it sounds like—a voice. Whispering. I can't ever make out *what* it's saying, but I know it's saying something. You know, how you can always tell? And once it starts sounding like a voice, I know whose voice it is. Has to be. So. (LONG PAUSE) I quit my job. I bought a farmhouse—all stone and wood, not a bit of metal in it. I took up growing my own vegetables, raising my own chickens—they really are amazingly stupid birds, by the way. I made goddamn sure they ripped out every piece of wiring in the building. I cut my own firewood, I buy oil supplies for lanterns and candles. Reading is the only entertainment I have. And when I'm too tired to read, I shut off the lantern and I sit in the dark, and the quiet, until I can fall asleep. Because the grid is a web, a network of energies. Of ghosts. And things live in it, waiting for food. Hunting. Like spiders. I mean, maybe I'm being paranoid. Maybe that thing was as ass-dumb as a chicken itself. But if it wasn't... if it remembers there's stuff here to eat and at least one meal escaped... it might come looking. And I don't want anybody else to die like Joe, eaten just because I wasn't fast enough to get him to safety in time. That's why I live alone. That's the "conscience" part. That's why I'm telling you this story, now. Because if it happened to me, it might happen again. To someone else. (LONG, LONG PAUSE) Hey. Did I lose you there, Doss?

Q: No. No, I just... um... I'm not sure what to say to all that. (PAUSE) I mean, I assume this is the reason for the anonymity and the alias. And the burner phone, too.

A: Bingo. (PAUSE) So how crazy do you think I am, now? C'mon. Scale of one to ten.

Q: Bronwyn, we don't—look, that's not—

A: Relax. I've heard your show before. You did an interview last year with those guys who're waiting for the shapeshifting space lizards to reveal they control the world, remember?

Q: Well—yeah, but as long as they stuck to talking about building shelters and hunting schedules, they *sounded* sane. Maybe... maybe you could tell us a little more about your daily routine, the skills you use as part of your off-grid life...

A: Nope. I've already been on this phone too long.

Q: Wait, Bronwyn—one last question. If you're afraid that this—thing, whatever—that it might come after whoever talks about it... should *we* be careful? What kind of... of risk would we be taking if we release this interview?

A: If you *do* think I'm crazy, then obviously none. Right?

Q: Bronwyn—
(DIAL TONE)

Oshi Takamura 4:53 PM (1 hour ago)
to me, Jen ▼

Hi Lucas,
Listened to Doss's file, and I have to say I agree—don't care about people's crazy reasons for living off-grid, but our shows have to talk about actually *living off grid*,

because that's what people tune in for. It's also not long enough—we'd need at least another twenty minutes to round out a full episode.

Try not to be too hard on Doss, BTW. I'll have to pull an all-nighter to catch up, but it's still a couple of weeks before exams.

Oshi

Lucas Brennan 5:21 PM (30 minutes ago)
to Oshi, Jen ▼

Hey Oshi,
Dude, you're way too forgiving. Doss should have damn well known better before he wasted all our time on this. This is not the same as spending three out of forty-two minutes on a conspiracy theory, this is Stephen King nightmare crap. If Doss wasn't our biggest audience draw I'd be seriously tempted to fire his ass. I'm deleting that file and I'd strongly recommend you do too.

If you're OK with the all-nighters, Oshi, then I'm going to go ahead and pull the May 17th episode material forward to the 3rd – make sure you update the home page sidebars to match. Jen, I've reworked the interstitial scripts to pad them out a little; if you could review the attached files and do a couple of rehearsals on your own, then be ready to go for a recording session on the afternoon of April 25th, that'd be great. Let me know if either of you have any problems.   —L.

From Reddit.com, posted May 13th:

Lost episode of "GridLost"

submitted 11 hours ago by DossalFinn

74 commentssharesavehidereport

harmony-interview-apr-18.mp3

[-] **offbroadwaychaos**

anyone got a screenshot of the GridLost home page? i wanna see if this was ever scheduled.

permalinkembedsavereply

[-] **HyperJoan**

I've attached a .gif from Wayback but it just says "Special Guest Star coming". Which could be this Harmony chick, I suppose.

Permalinkembedsavereply

[-] **svalbard43**

Don't get it. Is this supposed to be a late April Fool's joke or what?

permalinkembedsavereply

[-] **MichaelTwyla50**

No, I listen to GL all the time and this is the guy, this is Doss. + on the May 3 show the producer did come on and apologize for a shorter-than-usual episode, which would completely make sense if they chickened out of releasing this. + Harmony6893's a real person, I've read some of her posts on prepperforums.net

permalinkembedsavereply

[-] **ChocoBot14**

I've posted a transcript of the file here if anyone's interested, with a few annotations.

permalinkembedsavereply

[-] **RagingManticore**

Okay guys: read transcript and phoned up the Toronto police department. theyve got a missing persons case still on the books from January 2017 for a ryerson engineering student age 22 named joseph macklay, last seen near a condo off adelaide west, fifteen minutes from downtown bay street. local real estate records say theres a corner one bed plus den unit still listed hasnt sold since. sooooo either a *really* well-researched creepypasta or ???????!!!!!?????

Permalinkembedsavereply

[-] **KevlarTuxedo**
lol youre a tool – links or its bullshit
permalinkembedsavereply

From a subforum on www.prepperforums.net, *posted June 5:*

Hello everyone.

I've been drafting this post for a couple of weeks now, after my last trip into town, when I realized that my interview with the "GridLost" people had gone viral. Honestly, I never expected them to release it in any form. I just wanted to tell myself I'd told *somebody*. I still don't know if I haven't made a really big mistake. But there's nothing I can do about it now.

That's why this is going to be my last post to these forums or any other. I'm cutting the last cord. I want to thank everyone for everything I've learned here, and I hope I've given as much as I've gained. If I came into this community out of fear, I think I've found something like peace, and I couldn't be more grateful.

Some of you are probably going to ask why I'm not trying to make more out of this. I mean, if you believe me, then you accept I saw something that proves everything people think they know about the world is wrong or at the very least horrifically incomplete—and when there are millions desperate for *any* reason to believe there's something out there beyond the 9-to-5, beyond iPhone lineups and Netflix, why would I not trumpet it everywhere I could? Some people would say even a universe full of horrors is better than a universe full of nothing but us.

To that, I say: Wait until *you* meet one.

If we do live in the bubble I think we do, then the single best thing I can do is not poke more holes in it than I have to. Maybe it's temporary and futile; maybe the bubble's going to collapse anyway, one day. Maybe we'll all become nothing more than parts of the same EM spectrum we're living off of, energy reduced to its lowest thermodynamic denominator, constantly preyed upon, consumed without ever being destroyed. And in that endlessness will be our end, an ouroboros knot, forever tied and untying—no heaven, no hell. Just the circuit, eternally casting off energy, the sparks that move this awful world.

But not today. Not if I have anything to... *not* say... about it.

This is Harmony6893, signing off.

THE PUPPET MOTEL

OMETIMES, IF WE don't watch out, we might slip inside a crack between moments and see that there's an ebb and flow under everything we've been told is real, a current that moves the world—the invisible strings which pull us, spun from some source we'll never trace. Sometimes we can be forced by circumstance to see that there's a hand in the darkness, just visible if we squint, outstretched towards us: upside-down and angled, palm and fingers curved to flutter enticingly, waving us on. The universal sign for *come closer, my darling, come closer.*

And sometimes, when things get particularly bad, we may suddenly find ourselves able to hear the steady hum under the world's noise, an electrically charged tone far too light to be static, yet too faint to be a crackle; a thin bone whistle reaching through the walls, almost too faint to register. Rising and falling like the breath behind words you can almost make out, if we only try.

That out flung hand, beckoning us on; that unseen mouth, smiling. All the while telling us, without words, its voice the merest whisper in our singing blood: *come here, love—my sweet one, my other, come. Don't be afraid. Come here to me, to my call.*

That tone—that beckoning—is one I've heard far more often than I'd like to admit, mainly because I just keep *on* hearing it, even though I don't want to. It's louder than you'd think, especially once you're no longer able *not* to concentrate on it... so much so it makes it hard to sleep or work or dream. Sometimes, it gets so loud I'm afraid I might actually start wanting to answer.

If you ever hear that sound, or even suspect you're about to, then my advice to you is simple.

Just. Fucking. Run.

Everything you can think of is true, somewhere, for someone; is now, or has been, or will be. And proof, for all our demands, has never been more than the very least of it.

For example, my father sometimes talked about this thing that happened to him when he was a kid, but only because I wouldn't stop bothering him about it. How he took the wrong path at the campsite by the lake, walked straight off a cliff, a sharp downward slope. How he fell and fell, mainly through mud, 'til he hit the bottom and cracked his forearm on a rock, buried a hand's-breadth deep. How he stayed down there for what seemed like hours, calling out weakly, hoping his family would hear. But it was Dominion Day, night already falling, fireworks going off. The campsite was a zoo. He couldn't even tell if they'd noticed he was gone.

He lay there, staring up at the cliff's rim, willing somebody to look over. Until, eventually... someone did.

So, he started to yell, louder than ever before: *Down here, here I am,* please! Waved his good arm, pounded on the ground, tried to pivot himself 'round one-handed to get the watcher's attention. But the watcher just stood there, bent over slightly, as though it didn't quite know what it was looking at. After which, slowly— very slowly—it stepped over the ridge and began a careful descent. And Dad was happy, ecstatic, up 'til the very moment the person finally got close enough for him to see it wasn't really a *person* at all.

What was it, then? I'd ask; *I don't know,* he'd reply, every time as baffled as the first. *I don't... I just don't know.*

(Its head was too long, too wide, and it moved—backwards, he said. Too care-ful, like its feet were all wrong, like it had to think extra-hard about where to step in order to avoid falling. Like it didn't have toes.)

When it was close enough they could have touched, it leaned down. And when he saw its face he started to scream again, *hard,* scrabbling back like a crab and fall-ing straight on his bad arm, the awful, gutting pain of it so sudden he blacked out.

He woke up in the hospital two days after, broken bones encased in plaster, mouth dry from painkillers and sedatives. The nurses said he had no other wounds, though when they gave him back his clothes, his underpants weren't there. Had to be burned, they told him.

Why? I always asked; *Because,* was all he'd say. Except for one time, when he looked down and added, softly—

They told me they were full of blood.

Everyone has a story like my Dad's, I've since come to realize. The only surprising part, in hindsight, is that it took so comparatively long for mine to find me.

The summer I first heard what I later came to call the tone, I'd stupidly agreed to manage two Airbnb sites for a friend of my then-boyfriend, Gavin—let's call him Greg, a guy I barely knew in real life, though I was already more than familiar with the fact that if you ever made any sort of statement on Facebook which disagreed with popularly received nerd culture wisdom, he'd suddenly show up out of nowhere to "debate" it into the ground, whether you were actually prepared to argue the point with him or not. But I needed a job for a certain amount of time (June through August, just in time for me to go back to school), and he was offering one, so how bad could it possibly be? Never ask, that's my policy... or always had been, previously.

Not anymore, in case you wondered.

Both sites were fairly close to where I lived back then, give or take. One was at 20 George Street, ten minutes' walk away, the same condo this Greg and his wife Kim planned on moving into once his current contract managing I.T. for a South Korean insurance company ran out; the other was a twenty-minute streetcar ride down to King Street East and Bathurst, a brand-new apartment in a building that had just gone up the previous year. Of course, that was twenty minutes at *best,* when nothing went wrong, but how often does that happen? Re-routing, accidents, construction, shitty weather—everything and anything.

One time Greg booked check-ins at both sites within a half-hour of each other, and I had to tell the guests at King to go wait in a nearby coffee shop until I could get there to let them in; while I was enroute, a thunderstorm blew up so badly that the neighborhood transformer was struck by lightning and all the power went off, forcing the coffee shop to shut down early. By the time I got there, I had a family of five from Buffalo, New York who were standing angrily on the corner next to a streetcar stop with no roof, soaked through. "Why didn't you take a damn cab, moron?" the father demanded, to which I could only smile and shrug, trying to look as inoffensively apologetic/Canadian as possible.

In principle I knew I'd be reimbursed for any expenses incurred on the job, up to and including sudden taxi rides, but that assumed I *had* the cash on hand to lay out for said expenses in the first place, and much of the time I just didn't. I was already living hand to mouth, bank account overdraft withdrawal to unplanned-for credit card charge—that was why I'd needed the job in the first place, for Christ's sake.

I called the place on George Street the House of Flowered Sheets; I think Kim had probably picked out all the linens, which were universally covered in patterns made from peonies, roses, tulips or geraniums. It was small but airy, the floors laid in fake blonde wood, with large windows facing Front Street that let in as much light as possible and fixtures of chrome and white porcelain. It got hot sometimes, but the overall air was functional, welcoming; big closets, a high-plumped double bed, cosily archaic furniture, free Wi-Fi in every room. There was a guard on the front desk who nodded back when I nodded to him every time I used the fob to get in and plenty of fake-friendly, nosy neighbors. This last part eventually turned out to be a bit of a drawback—but we'll get to that later.

The unit on King Street East, on the other hand, I called the Puppet Motel, because it was creepy, like a Laurie Anderson song. Because it was different, squared. Because it made me feel... not myself. And honestly, after only a couple of visits, I couldn't imagine how anybody could possibly want to *live* there after they'd seen it. Not even for a day, much less two or three.

Like I said, the building was new, a boxy-looking modernist monstrosity arranged around what had to be the world's saddest concrete-and-stone park, complete with fake Zen garden sandlot, which doubled as ineffective camouflage for the parking garage's entrances. In a way, since the property had two addresses (the other was on Bathurst Street, allegedly more convenient for guests driving in from Toronto's Pearson International Airport), each with its own front door/mail-room/security desk/elevator access set-up, you could say the place really functioned as two separate buildings somehow shoehorned one inside the other. Greg's apartment was on the mezzanine level, only accessible from either one specific elevator (off King) or one specific set of stairs (off Bathurst), and there was nothing else on that level except a garbage chute, a gym and mirroring apartment, seemingly unoccupied.

The Puppet Motel's windows looked inward, down onto the courtyard, so light was limited at best, a situation not helped by the fact that the entire place had been decorated in vaguely differing shades of black and gray. The bathroom fixtures were all black marble, even the tub, while the bathroom itself was tiled with granite—gray shot with black, like they couldn't decide what would pick up less light. It didn't matter much, anyways, because the main fixture in there didn't even work; the place was lit by vanity mirror fluorescence alone. Some sort of electrical short. Greg kept promising he'd get it fixed, but he never did, not even when guests routinely started complaining about it on Yelp. The ceilings, meanwhile, were so high that I had to climb on a teetering stool to replace the track-lighting bulbs whenever they blew, which was often. They'd go gray, then pop quietly—an implosion, as if the sound itself was being swallowed whole by that creeping pool of darkness lurking in every corner, poised to rush into any space the light no longer touched. I could feel it always at my back as I moved around, raising my neck-hairs, shortening my breath.

After the first day there, I realized just how easy it was to lose track of time completely, hypnotized by the vacuum's drone or the dryer's atonal metallic hum; I'd gotten there at noon, done what I thought was a few loads, then glanced up to suddenly see the central shaft engulfed in shadow, with nothing outside the windows but oncoming night. From then on, I set my phone's alarm for twenty minutes a pop, trusting its old-school rising beacon trill to snap me out of... well, whatever it was. Oddness, at best, a fugue of disconnection; at worst, a physical queasiness, like

I'd stepped through some unseen mirror into a weird, dim world, a cracked reflection of normalcy. On some very basic level, it just seemed *off*.

One day, on impulse, I took a marble out of the big glass vase full of them that decorated the breakfast island and set it down near the far wall, then watched it roll in a slow, meandering zig-zag across the apparently level linoleum to gently *pock* against the inside of the front door. Can you say non-Euclidean, boys and girls?

And there was a tone in there, too. It crept up on you, underneath everything. Sometimes it seemed to be coming out of the fixtures, shivering inside the lamps like an ill-set fuse, a lightbulb's tungsten filament burning itself out from white heat into stillness like some glowing metal pistil. Sometimes I felt it coming through the floor, vibrating in my soles, making my toenails clutch and the bottoms of my feet crawl. It set my teeth on edge.

The longer I was in that place, the more I wanted—with increasing desperation—to be anywhere but.

Not that I cared enough to ask, but by the end I was convinced the only reason Greg had bought this unit, in this building, in the first place—the only way he *could* have—was that he'd never actually been there himself; that the entire exercise, from review to mortgage to signing, had been conducted online through virtual tours, remote bank branches and faxed paperwork.

That was the twenty-first century for you, though, bounded in the proverbial bad-dream nutshell. So supposedly interconnected on a global level that you could buy a place to live in a completely different country, without ever having to see for yourself—in person—just exactly what made it so... utterly unliveable.

When people ask me what I do for fun, for a hobby, here's what I often want to say: that there's a scream that moves around the world, and I follow it. That it's always been there, buried under everything else, all that static and noise and mess we call ordinary life—blowing high and dim, a wind no one else around me ever seems to hear.

Except, of course, that every once in a while, somebody does.

So, I do my research, find the clues, the names and dates and places; I seek those people out, ask my questions and listen carefully, note it all down. Just the facts, if "fact" is ever the right word for something like this—rumor become anecdata, an utterly subjective record of experience, impossible to doubt or verify. Then I input what I learn, reformat it slightly and post it on my webpage, throwing comments open underneath. Leave each story just hanging there, an open question, after which I retreat to the shadows of anonymity and watch to see who might turn up, who responds with reactions that read like answers.

Every story starts and ends the same way, no matter who tells it. *Remember that strange thing that happened, that one time? How it went on, 'til it stopped? How we never knew why?*

I tell through these instances, rubbing each one in turn, a black bone rosary. They're tiny doors I open and then leave open, so others who've heard the same bleak call can peep through. And it's like I'm mapping the edges of something invisible, something which exists on a completely different wavelength, an inhuman frequency; I'd never catch a glimpse of it otherwise, except through compilation, running the numbers. Just trying to figure out what it's not by grasping at whatever I can, however briefly—a blind woman theorizing, modeling the world's most nebulous elephant, and not even by touch. More by rumor.

It lives in the dark, alongside us, not with us. Impinges on us occasionally—or is it the other way around, maybe? We want to believe we're the point of any exercise, after all, but maybe we're not. Maybe we never are.

Collateral damage, spindrift, spume: we're what's left behind, the wake made flesh. Its tendrils blunder by us and scrape us raw, like shark's skin. And I'm just trying to build a community, I guess, to pare the loneliness down before it cores us clear through—cores *me*. Not as though anything actually gets solved in the process, but at least by the time it's over, we no longer assume we're all crazy.

"I just didn't know who else to talk to," they (almost) always say, and I nod, understandingly.

"Me neither," I reply.

Back in April, when my original plans for moving out of Dad's place for the summer had fallen through ("flatting" with school chums who suddenly decided to tour the world over the summer instead, in true Aussie fashion), Gavin had impulsively offered to let me share his apartment until Fall; wouldn't even have to chip in on the rent so long as I got a job and paid for my food, he said. In hindsight, this was one of Gavin's bad habits—he was a chronic over-promiser, always on one manic deadline or another—but I was too overjoyed to put two and two together, though we'd never even talked about sharing a place before then. That this pissed Dad off even more than the previous plan just struck me as an extra bonus at the time.

In practice, Gavin's no-bedroom unit turned out to be way too small for two people, especially when the host was a neat freak and the guest tended to overreact to anything that felt like nagging. Didn't help I already felt indebted, resentful about it and guilty about that resentment, all of which only played into Gavin's increasingly passive-aggressive attitude. Distracting ourselves in bed worked for a while, but not long. Greg's job seemed like a lifeline, as much for the excuse just to get out of the apartment as for the money, and I can't really make myself believe Gavin didn't sense that.

The general routine went like this: Greg booked residents online, then emailed me with the details of when they were supposed to arrive, at which point I went over and cleaned the selected apartment as sparingly as possible, trying to make it look "welcoming" for his guests. This involved garbage and recycling removal, cleaning all sinks and surfaces, running the dishwasher and washer-dryer, putting fresh sheets on every bed, opening windows and spraying Spring Fresh scent everywhere, plus light dusting. I charged fifty dollars an hour for housekeeping, clocked it, then sent Greg the receipts for any household supplies along with the rest of my weekly invoice.

Eighty dollars to check people in, eighty to check them out; I handed the guests a set of keys the first time 'round, took it back the next. Sometimes they were late, but I didn't get paid for waiting around, so I'd ring that up as part of the housekeeping. Sometimes *I* was late, and they just left the keys on a table by the door, closing the apartment door behind them—I worried about it initially, but it was never a genuine problem. People don't really tend to try other people's door handles, not even when they're neighbors.

The money was welcome and arrived fairly regularly, but the job itself ate up far more of my time than I'd thought it would, especially when you factored in what Greg liked to call "floating duties." As the only person the guests ever dealt with face to face, I was essentially playing concierge at a non-existent hotel, often getting texts in the middle of the night from people who thought that paying to squat semi-illegally in someone else's apartment entitled them to treat me like their maid. One woman demanded I come over and re-clean the Flowered Sheets bathroom at 2:00 AM, because it was so "unforgivably filthy" it was keeping her awake; another demanded I babysit her children for free, because I'd "misrepresented" how kid-friendly the area really was. I remember a father and two brothers who booked the Motel over a long weekend, at the beginning of July, apparently for the express purpose of getting solidly drunk together for three days straight; when I came in on Monday, I found they'd already been gone for hours, leaving behind three teetering multi-levelled pyramids made from beer bottles and a stench that didn't disperse until I propped the front door open and set fans in front of all the windows.

Like any public washroom, people do things in hotels they'd never do at home. They specifically come there to do them, because they expect someone else to clean up after them.

Naturally enough, this soon led to a constant series of Variations on a Collapsing Relationship, repeated riffs on *You're never around anymore, Loren* and *I'm* working, *Gavin*—because what else could I do except trust him to understand? After all, we were rowing the exact same leaky financial boat, essentially: him with his unpaid internship, his under-the-counter graphic design contracts, versus me with my two equally illegal jobs, killing time and racking up the dough 'til I could go back to Brock University and live on campus. The both of us robbed and left twisting like the rest of our generation, unable to rely on anything but the post-Too-Big-to-Fail world's inherent unreliability. With nobody else to take out our stress on, our arguments grew bitterer and bitterer, repetitious, discordant as bad jazz:

If the job's giving you that much grief, why don't you just quit?

You know I can't.

I know you *won't.*

You were the one who said I had to pay for my own food.

Fine, but can you at least stop talking *about it all the time?*

What the fuck does that mean?

It means that if you won't do anything to fix a problem, then there's not much point in complaining about it, Loren. So, I'm sorry, but shit or get off the pot. Please.

Didn't help that Gavin was a skeptic by nature—I'd tell him about all the weirdness at the Motel, only to have to listen to him break it all down, carefully, 'til it barely convinced *me* anymore. *It's badly laid floor tile, poor design choices, horrible ventilation,* he told me. *Sick-building syndrome, that's all. And hotel guests behave badly everywhere, nothing needs to be "wrong" for that.* All of it only more infuriating for not being anything I could really argue with.

One evening in mid-July, I finally came home with what I thought might be direct evidence, shoving my phone at him the minute I got through the door. "I've got something you need to hear," I told him, "but first, I have to tell you what happened with these last two guests."

"The women you checked in on Monday?" Gavin asked, and I had to give him this—even if he never took anything I said seriously, he did at least listen, and remember. "From Barrie, kept calling it their 'Big-City-cation'—you said you thought they might be a couple."

"Yeah, exactly. Well, I go by today to do checkout and the shorter one's sitting in the kitchen with her head down, looks like she's been crying. Tells me she and her friend had this horrible fight, but she can't remember about what; anyhow, she stormed out, then came back to find her friend was gone. Hasn't been able to reach her since."

Gavin scoffed. "They wouldn't be the first people to fight on vacation, Loren. Probably just turned her cellphone off and went back by herself."

"Yeah, that's what I told her." I sat down on the couch. "But after she left, when I was cleaning, I found an empty vodka bottle in the trash, and the place was also a lot cleaner already than it usually is, like somebody'd gone over it already. Plus, there was a smear of something that looked like blood on the edge of the bedroom door."

Gavin put his hand over his face. "*Jesus,* Loren. I mean, how are you even sure it *was* blood, exactly? You packing Luminol in that kit of yours?"

"Oh please, fuck the fuck off with that CSI bullshit, okay? 'Cause while I may not have air quotes-worthy 'formal forensic training,' I *have* had a period every month of my life since I was eleven... so yeah, Gav, I do think I know a bloodstain when I see it, thank you very much."

Hadn't meant my voice to be quite so acid, but I was pissed, and it showed; Gavin flushed, like he'd been slapped. "Fine, then—say it *was* blood. So what? Could just have been from one 'em whacking her head on the door by accident, especially if she was drunk. 'Cause if you've got *any* sort of firm evidence it was anything else, you should be telling the cops, not me."

I wanted to punch him but settled for gritting my teeth. "Just listen to the damn file, all right? Tell me if that room tone sounds *normal* to you."

It had taken nearly an hour of creeping around the Motel, holding my phone at wrist-straining angles with its volume jacked to absolute max, but finally I'd found a place where the noise that constantly harassed me seemed both louder and steadier, as if it might be the actual spot it was emanating from directly (today, anyhow). The result was twenty-three solid seconds of ululation, near inaudible without earbuds, which I offered.

Gavin sighed, screwed them in, activated the .mp3; I held my breath, watching as he listened, but his expression didn't change, except for the faintest frown. 'Till he closed his eyes, at last, took the buds out, shook his head. Telling me, as he did: "Loren, that's nothing, literally. It doesn't sound like anything."

I tried not to blink as the wave crashed up over me, sheer disappointment turning my voice harsh again. "So... I'm just crazy, I guess."

"Did I say that?"

"You didn't have to."

We stared at each other for a moment, before Gavin finally turned away. "I'm going to make some dinner," he said. "You sound like you need a break." He went into the kitchen.

The moment he was gone I grabbed the phone back, shoved the buds in my own ears and hit "play." And there it was—that same note, wavering just underneath the hiss of empty air, making my jaw thrum, my fists clench, scowl sliding to wince. How could he *not* hear it? Were his ears just that *bad,* or...?

(*Or. Or, or, or.*)

That night I dreamed I was pulling hair out of the Motel's all-black bathtub's drain, whole sodden clumps of it melted together by decay, reduced to their ropy, extruded skin-cell components. It wasn't mine, and it smelled bad, worse than bad—terrible, terrifying, sharp enough to make the back of my throat burn. Like glue on fire. Like mustard gas.

With that *tone* there too, obviously, behind everything—behind, beneath, whatever. That same unseen filament twisting, sizzling, burning itself out; a call from far off, filtering down through great darkness. That shadow, mounting, yet barely visible: five fingers separating on the Motel's master bedroom wall, angled outwards, sketched charcoal gray on gray.

That open, beckoning hand.

The next morning, I kissed Gavin goodbye as he set off for work, putting a little more energy into it than usual, hoping that would revitalize things, agreeing to vague evening plans for dinner and a movie. Then I came back after cleaning the House of Flowered Sheets and checking somebody in only to find my packed suitcases outside "our" apartment door, a note taped to the handle of my laptop case: SORRY, THIS ISN'T WORKING. TRIED TO TELL YOU BUT COULDN'T. LOCKSMITH CAME WHILE YOU WERE OUT, PLEASE THROW KEYS AWAY. I'M GONE FOR TWO WEEKS, NO POINT CALLING. DON'T HATE ME.

"Fuck *you,*" I told the wall, hoping he was actually lurking behind it, his coward's ear pressed up close to hear my reaction. And left.

Gaslighting, my friends would have called it—he was making me question my own reactions, my own perceptions. But I was doing that anyways; the fucking

Puppet Motel was gaslighting me, not Gavin. Gavin didn't matter enough to gaslight me, and maybe he knew it. Maybe that's why he dumped me. Maybe I would've dumped me too, if I'd been him.

(But I wouldn't have, I know that already. Not when I already knew where I'd inevitably have to end up, after.)

"What are you going to do?" my mother asked me, when we met in our local Starbucks.

"Your place is out of the question, I guess."

To her credit, she looked genuinely unhappy. "You know I *would*, sweetheart, but there just isn't enough room." She knit her hands around her cup, as if for warmth, despite how muggy it was. "And I won't even ask about moving back in with your father, given he's just as stubborn as you are."

"Thanks for that."

"Honesty costs nothing. Seriously, though—you don't have *any* other friends to stay with?"

"They're his friends, mostly," I admitted, "so not crazy about asking. Not that I know who'd have the space, anyway..." I trailed off, realizing the obvious answer.

After mom left me, I pulled out my phone and checked the time-conversion app I'd downloaded a month and a half before, back when I first took this stupid job; it was just coming up on seven a.m. tomorrow morning in Seoul—Greg might still be at home, hopefully already awake. A quick text later, I had my answer: George Street unit's free for 2 wks - yrs if u need it

I slumped, so relieved that I didn't even realize until later that it was as much for *which* unit he'd offered as that he'd offered one at all.

I was so out of practice at dealing with real people, the friendliness of my new neighbors at George Street caught me by surprise. One middle-aged housewife a floor up from me made a point of dropping by to "welcome me to the building," acting so amiable I found myself talking to her when I didn't have to. And, ultimately, telling her a little about my situation—before learning she was actually head of the condo committee.

The very next day, that security guard I usually nodded to handed me a thick manila envelope, telling me the building's by-laws explicitly forbade sub-letting without the proper paperwork—none of which, of course, Greg had ever bothered to fill out. The envelope contained a cease-and-desist letter I was instructed to forward on to Greg as soon as possible, and I was told to be out by eight a.m. next morning, or they'd call the cops. Panicked, I used Greg's own landline to call his Seoul office directly.

"Oh, that," he said, maddeningly unimpressed. "Yeah, go ahead and send the paperwork, but don't worry; the corporation never bothers following up, it's not worth the legal expense. Just lay low whenever you come in to clean and don't talk to anyone, it'll blow over in a week."

"Does that mean I can stay?"

"Uh..." The cheerfulness faded. "No, better not push it that much. King unit's empty tonight, though; I've got a booking in there day after next, but I can switch them over to George, so you'll be good for a week. Don't worry, Loren. We'll figure it out."

The stifled beat of my own rage got me across town, into the Puppet Motel and halfway through unpacking my first suitcase before the place's eerie quiet started to sink in. I looked around, throat suddenly gone tight. It still reeked of old beer, somehow, with even less pleasant things lurking beneath—a filthy alley stink, antithetical to the cleanser I'd personally coated every inch of it in. Probably seeping in from the garbage chute outside, I told myself, through the windows I left constantly open; this place wasn't old enough to have accumulated its own decay-funk yet, and Toronto's summer streets were nobody's idea of perfume. But it was either deal with the smell or live in a sweatbox.

I paused in the middle of the living room, listening hard—straining, almost—but heard nothing aside from my own breath, the pulse and rush of blood in my ears. No tone; not yet. That was a mercy.

That night, I did something I don't usually do: slept naked atop the bedsheets with a fan on high at my feet, carefully-calibrated brown noise playing through my phone's earbuds, trying to tilt myself into what little breeze the windows let in. It was like I was deliberately breaking my own rules because I wasn't used to being alone anymore, making everything strange, so the underlying weirdness wouldn't stand out so much. And it even seemed to work, at first—I fell asleep quick and hard, then slept deeply, without dreaming.

Waking, however, was a different story.

"I don't understand the question. Can you try again?"

It was my phone's voice-activated A.I.—familiar even though I never used it, that skin-crawlingly pleasant Uncanny Valley monotone—speaking out of nowhere into my earbuds, jolting me awake. I groaned and rolled upright, the ringing back in both my ears, like tinnitus, and yanked the earbuds out. After a beat, its voice went off again, plastic-muffled, probably repeating the question, words inaudible but the intonation unmistakeable. I could see "her" readout twang across the screen, back and forth, an electrified rubber band.

I fumbled my way to the settings screen and turned the A.I. off, then checked the time: half an hour before my set alarm. I lay back, eyes rolling up, a palm clapped shade to either eyelid; maybe I could get at least a little more sleep, if that fucking amorphous, ever-present *tone* eased up...

"I don't understand," the A.I. repeated, so loud I actually yelped. *"Please try again. Please—specify."*

Everything in me locked stiff for an instant, like tensing against a punch. I'd never heard that too-calm no-voice pause before, as if *thinking*; the very implication burnt my throat, froze me all over. I stared down at the inert plastic rectangle lying next to me, muscles tensed for fight or flight, my whole scalp crawling—but fight what, flee where? What was—

"Okay," the A.I. said. *"When can we expect you?"*

The Motel's tone was almost inaudible now, but that didn't help; I felt it in my jaw, my teeth, my tongue, realizing for the first time how it wavered up and down when it hit this particular pitch, arrhythmic-random. A mouthful of ants, itching against my palate.

"*Oh, I see. That's very soon.*"

Abruptly, the tone seemed to steady once more, pausing; waiting. For what? An—

(*answer?*)

"*Her name is Loren,*" the A.I. told whatever it was responding to, helpfully— and that was *it*, motherfucker: enough, no more, gone gone *gone*. When the phone buzzed next, I was already in motion, jackknifed to standing, thighs and stomach twisting painful as I grabbed my shit and ran butt-naked out into the hall. Some- body (me, I guess) was making a noise like an injured dog, all terrified whimper. I slammed the door shut behind me, fumbled the key in and jerked it 'round, hearing the bolt squeal; had my shirt up over my head with no time for a bra, one arm al- ready inside and the other sleeve dangling empty, hauling my leggings up like I was trying to lift myself high, crotch-first. Not quite fast enough, though, to prevent the A.I.'s voice from telling me I had a *new message* from *unknown caller* even as I scrab- bled backwards, hit the stairwell door and wrenched it open then half-fell headlong downwards, towards the open air.

I erupted out onto Bathurst, shoeless and panting, only to spend the rest of the day riding streetcars from coffee shop to coffee shop, denuding myself of change in pursuit of company, Wi-Fi, noise. For upwards of five hours, I barely calmed down enough to pee. Didn't even find the nerve to turn my phone back on 'til the end of the day, at which point I immediately retrieved five messages: three from the George Street renters, demanding help with various chores, plus two from Greg, urging me to call. Nothing else in the file, A.I.'s promises aside—not even a hang- up.

But the tone stayed with me, all day, with no respite. It rang through me tip to toe under any music I put on, no matter what the volume. And always deep enough to hurt.

"What in the hell's wrong with King Street, exactly, Loren?" Greg demanded, when I finally FaceTimed him back; the barista who was the only other person left in the Second Cup had already told me they were closing in fifteen minutes, which I figured gave an excuse to bail if things got too acrimonious.

How long you got? I felt like asking but chose to play it dumb/diplomatic. "'Scuse me?"

"Check out the listing, on Airbnb.com. No, I'm serious, do it now. I'll wait."

Once I did, I could see why he was pissed. All but two of the votes were down, and not a single posted review was positive. A few were just the normal stupid shit— "they told me there was a crib but there wasn't" (there was, in the guest bedroom closet, the person just hadn't looked hard enough) or "kitchen PowerPoint doesn't work" (which was why there was a label over the wall switch saying DO NOT TOUCH, which people routinely ignored). The rest, however, were... odder.

Most've the weekend went okay, but the bathroom light doesn't work and the door kept blowing shut when I was showering, so I'm standing there naked in the dark. I complained and they said they'd fix it, which was total B.S., they never did.

I always felt like somebody was watching me.

My alarm clock stopped working, so I missed half the stuff I had scheduled.

It was really hard to get to sleep, and REALLY hard waking up.

All we wanted was to just get drunk and watch some sports, but the TV kept crapping out and my Dad and my brothers wouldn't stop arguing.

I heard somebody crying, it sounded like it was inside the wall. It went on all night.

I had a big fight with my girlfriend, left to cool down, and when I came back, she was gone. I thought maybe she just went home, but I've been back for three weeks and nobody knows where she is.

It smells funny and looking at the walls gave me a headache. Second night it got so bad I got a nosebleed and had to go to Emergency.

Went to bed and woke up with my best friend having sex with me, and neither of us can explain why it happened. It was like he was sleepwalking. Now he won't talk to me.

My ears haven't stopped ringing since I stayed there. My doctor can't figure out what's wrong with me. DO NOT book this place.

"See what I mean?" Greg demanded, soon as I picked my phone back up.

I was still staring at the laptop screen, surprised by how much it disturbed rather than validated me to be finally confronted with proof I wasn't nuts—that I definitely hadn't been the only one who found the Motel's atmosphere toxic. Up 'till then, the only real mystery I'd encountered directly (aside from my own reactions) had been the Case of the Missing Barrie-ite—and there she was, right in the middle, six complaints down. Yet much as I hated the Puppet Motel itself, the idea that so many customers had apparently left the place I was "responsible" for feeling equally unsatisfied and creeped out was strangely insulting.

"Yeah," I finally said, "that's all pretty weird. Not really sure how they can blame *us* for stuff like the accidental gay experimentation, though—"

"Well, sure, obviously. But what about the rest? If I didn't know any better, I'd think they were talking about sick building syndrome, or whatever—bad wiring, transformers, gas leaks. Some kind of contamination." As I hesitated: "I mean, *you* haven't felt any of this, have you?"

Only every fucking time I've been there, I thought, but didn't say. "It... can be a little off-putting, yes," I agreed, at last. "Might be the color scheme."

Greg hissed. "Well, that's not *my* fault. The place came like that."

"Uh huh, that's what I assumed. Could be an idea to repaint, though, at least."

That seemed to calm him or at least make him think twice about whatever rant he had brewing. "Okay, all right, I'm sorry. I just—this place is supposed to pay for itself, you know? At the bare minimum. Optimally, it's supposed to provide a second stream of income for Kim and me, a nest egg to build on for when we come home... but it *isn't,* and I guess now we know why. I mean, I get that that's not your problem—but what it means is I *can't* redecorate right now, because I don't have the funds."

"I understand."

"I mean, it's not like they built the place over a damn cemetery and only moved the headstones, or anything; the company walked me through full disclosure, right before we signed. Nothing's *ever* happened there, Loren. Not in that unit, not in the building."

"Not 'til I started moving people in, huh?" I ventured.

He snorted. "I'm not blaming *you,* if that's what you think. This is nobody's fault."

I nodded, not sure how to answer. "So," I said, at last. "What do you want me to do?"

"Nothing *to* do, I guess." The early morning sunlight behind him made it hard to read his expression. "Ride it out. I'm back in two weeks, and you're back at school, so I'll take over then—Kim'll be joining me once her contract's up. And then... we'll just have to see, I guess."

"Okay," was all I said, and hung up.

I knew at the time I was being passive, if not passive-aggressive. And in hindsight maybe I *should* have told him everything, begged him to let me go back to the House of Flowered Sheets, pressured him into putting me up in a hotel: *Yes, I have all these exact same symptoms; yes, your awful condo gave them to me; yes, it damn well is somebody's fault, and you'll do for lack of anybody else. I've lost time too, felt the dislocation, heard the same ringing. I'm hearing it right now.* But—

—I think the whole thing with Gavin had kind of slapped that particular impulse out of me, at least for the moment. Like Greg said, however bad things got, there was a set time limit to all this, a clock ticking down: I could deal with that. I was an adult. I could take it.

These are the sort of stories we tell ourselves when things get bad, of course, hoping they'll stop them from getting worse. Even though, as we all well know, they so very seldom do. Still, I did the socially acceptable thing, for whatever the fuck *that*'s worth: kept it to myself, all of it—then, and for years afterwards. Not anymore, though.

Obviously.

Greg was right about the building's history, or complete lack thereof. So far as I could find out, there'd never even been a medical emergency here—like most downtown condos, it was full of young singles and couples, some with babies, more with pets. I couldn't tell if any of the babies or pets started crying outside the Motel's door, because I simply didn't get any traffic, other than the ever-more-intermittent guests. It occurred to me that since I must have personally met every single person who'd ever slept under this roof, I knew damn well none of them had died here, mysteriously or otherwise.

Although one *had* disappeared, at least according to her friend. Or "friend." Or... whatever.

It wasn't until I'd finished my cleaning chores over at Flowered Sheets, hours after hanging up on Greg, that I realized the Motel's lingering tone was finally gone—as if the automatic, repetitious, thoughtless movements from appliance to appliance, vacuum and kitchen and washer and dryer, had ritually cleansed me as well. And it stayed gone, didn't reappear even when I went back into the Motel itself after midnight, turning the key the weird way you always had to: widdershins, then opposite, reversing your own natural instincts every time.

The light in the place was still bad, but the air was quiet, and the smell was mostly gone. I swept the floors, had a cool bath, changed into a sleep shirt and lay down, only to realize that despite my exhaustion, I was still buzzing far too much to doze off. So I booted up my laptop instead and surfed around. On a whim, I Googled environmental tinnitus causes, vaguely hoping to find a nice, simple explanation. Made an interesting sidebar into the realm of low-frequency or infra-sound—the kind that's lower in frequency than 20 Hertz or cycles per second, placing it beyond the perceptible/"normal" limit of human hearing, found to produce sleep disorders and vestibular stimulation even in people who can't consciously perceive they were hearing it. In various experiments, listeners exposed to infrasound complained of feeling sea-sick and emotionally disturbed, prone to nervous bursts of revulsion and fear—they even experienced optical illusions, brought on because 18.5 Hertz is the eye's basic resonating frequency. Because these symptoms presented themselves without any apparent cause, scientists believed that infrasound might be present at allegedly haunted sites, giving rise to odd sensations people might attribute to supernatural interference.

See, Loren? Gavin's voice chimed in, smugly, inside my head. *No ghosts, no goblins—there's your "'something wrong,'" probably. Just something resonating around 20*

Hertz or less, creeping you out, making you think you hear things, feel things, see things. Making you afraid you might *see things, at the very least.*

Which did make sense, of a sort. And yet.

So further down the Google click-hole I plunged, until forty minutes later I was wide awake and hunched over my keyboard, speed-reading my way through a website belonging to some guy named Ross Puget who specialized in "esoteric networking," jam-packed with hosted articles about shit like "psychic reconfiguration" and "bioenergetic pollution." The latter, all filed under "*Hauntings Without a Ghost?*", were about locations featuring the usual array of paranormal crap—orbs, cold spots, time fugues, visual and auditory hallucinations—but lacking one key ingredient for a classic paranormal experience: an actual human story, death or what-have-you, to set it all off.

Three months ago, it would have been good for a few laughs or an enthusiastic discussion with Gavin, before falling into bed together. Now, all I could think was *god, oh god,* because almost everything I'd experienced at the Puppet Motel, everything the guests had *implied* they might have experienced—it was all right there, in front of me. In cursor-blinking, eyestrain-saving black on white.

The site linked to Puget's Facebook page as well, and the guy had a startling number of friends—maybe "esoteric networking" was bigger business than I'd thought. Since he was online right now. I opened the site's messenger app, typing: re hauntings w/out ghosts – questions ok?

Sure, go ahead. I should tell you up front, though, I don't provide services myself. I just put you in touch with people who do.

Fine, I typed back, just need info, rn. I gave him my name, then described the Motel situation, as quickly as I could. Finishing up, I typed: wwyd?

What?

What. Would. You. Do.

Define "do." What's your goal here?

Make place ok 2 live in.

Situations like this are difficult to resolve cleanly, or safely. My advice would be to leave and not go back, but I'm assuming that's not an option.

N. Nt really.

All right. In that case, what I'd try to do is get a recording of any phenomena you can, audio or visual, and send it to me. I can review it, and maybe put you in touch with someone.

Omg, thank you. Thank you sm. Can send smthng rn.

Great, go ahead. Hope it all works out.

Me 2, I typed, and signed off.

I sent him the .mp3, waited, got no reply. And then... I must've fallen asleep some- how, because the next time I surfaced I was out of bed entirely, standing staring at the primary guest bedroom wall, swaying slightly back and forth with my hand— the left, my un-dominant side, even though I'm very much right-handed—uplifted, raised halfway, like I'd caught myself in the act of deciding whether or not to touch that dim, dark gray surface. To find out exactly what it'd feel like under my naked fingers, all smooth and cool and only slightly rough, paint over plaster over base- board over steel, concrete, the naked dollhouse pillars from which this hell-box of a condo'd been conjured...

Without thinking, I snatched my hand back as if from an open burner, stom- ach roiling. Then, for the second time in two days, I hauled my shaky ass out of there—more slowly than my first retreat, managing to finish dressing this time, but heart hammering and my throat dust-dry all the same, eyes skittering around like I expected the walls themselves to start clutching at me. And with a lot more dignity, though that deserted me pretty much the second the stairwell door almost hit me in the ass.

Halfway down, my phone's A.I. shook awake and spoke, voice echoing in the concrete stairwell, loud enough I almost screamed. *"Someone wants to talk to you, Loren. Don't be rude."*

Another bitter lesson learned that very second: doesn't matter how hip, self- aware or trope-conscious you think you are—when shit gets weird, your instincts take over, fight or flight and nothing but, all pure shivering prey-instinct. They can't not.

"*Who?*" I shrieked at the phone in my hand, as if the *really* upsetting thing here was having been called rude by a hunk of sleek plastic for not being willing to speak with a ghost. "*Who* fucking wants to talk? *Who?!*"

Must've come out far louder than I'd thought it would, because my throat hurt, by the time I was done. The text message alert chimed. Hands shaking, I swiped the messaging app, saw UNKNOWN at the top and had just enough time to think *of fucking course* before the message itself appeared, halfway down a blank white screen:

help me

I stared at it, panting. After a few seconds, the three rippling dots of an incoming message followed, and then the same two words again, stark and bleak: help me

Sheer reflex took over. I typed back, "keys" clicking: Who R U?, then, Where R U? Hit send, then waited. The seconds stretched out, my rough breath the only sound in the stairwell under a faint buzz of neon. Finally, the "incoming" dots rippled once more.

inside

Inside where? Name? An even longer pause, this time, and my patience snapped. NAME, I typed. Or fuck off. Breathing even harsher now, as much with anger as fear.

The reply appeared without warning, as if the "incoming" signal had been turned off. Inside, it repeated. U NO WHERE.

Then, dropping back into lower-case, as if exhausted: help me

I'm nowhere? I thought, for a second, before realizing what that space between O and W meant: *You know where.* Which was bullshit, of course; how was I supposed to know anything? Except—

—I did.

No, I thought, mouthing it, unable to find the breath even to whisper it. *No, I'm sorry, no. Not me; not this. Not my job.*

please, appeared on the screen, in its rounded gray box. Then after a longer pause: please. And once more: please. My screen gradually dimming even as that beat between each word kept on becoming longer, exponentially, like each new message was burning through my phantom correspondent's own store of energy and draining my battery at the same time: iPhone as Ouija board, a process impossible to explain, or sustain. Until one last word appeared, gray sketched on ever-darker gray, simply reading—

loren

Behind me, I heard the door to the stairwell rattle once: firm, distinct, imperative. And—

—that was it. The tipping point. Where I instantly knew, in every cell, that I was done.

I leapt to my feet and power-walked to the King Street TTC stop, hands completely steady, deleting the entire message chain as I did. I no longer cared about proving anything, to anyone. Then I called my mother.

It took quite a few tries to wake her up. Ten years ago, she'd have been answering a land line, and I had no doubt she would've been supremely pissed. But technology smooths stuff like that over, these days: she already knew it was me, so a mere glance at the clock was enough to tell her something must be wrong—family doesn't call after two a.m. for anything but an emergency. "Loren?" she asked, half muzzy, half frightened.

I opened my mouth and burst into tears.

If you're looking for closure here, you won't find much. These stories I collect now are only alike in their consistent lack of completion or explanation, their sheer refusal to grow a clear and satisfying ending—is any story ever "finished," really? Not until we're dead and maybe not even then.

That's why telling the story or being willing to listen to someone else's version—this story, or ones just like it—can sometimes feel like enough, though mainly because it has to be; because there's simply no other option. Because what I've learned is that our world is far more porous than it seems... full of dark places, thin places, weak places, bad places. Places where things peer in from whatever far larger, deeper darkness surrounds us, whatever macro-verse whose awful touch we may feel on occasion yet simply can't perceive otherwise, not while using our sadly limited human senses.

Because this is the basic trap of empirical knowledge, after all—just one of a million million traps we're all born into, pressed like a fly between two sheets of this impossible cosmic amber we call time: the "fact" that if all data is essentially, inherently unreliable however it's gathered, just as we ourselves can never be more than both imperfect and impermanent, our ideas of the world must always be taken on faith. Even if we have no template for even pretending to view what we come across through faith's lens, because "faith" is just a word to us...

... not just faith in God, mind you. But faith in *anything*.

I slept on my mom's fold-out couch for close to ten hours, not waking until after noon. Several messages from Greg were waiting on my phone. Again, I deleted them all, then wrote him an email that said simply, *I quit*, which I sent without even signing. I half-considered adding *Sorry*, but couldn't bring myself to type the word. So maybe not so much better than Gavin was to me, in the end. At least I had way more excuse for being brusque, in context; that's what I told myself, anyway.

Mom made me some soup and toast, watched me eat, then cleared her throat. "Honey," she began, "forget what I said before—you can *absolutely* stay with me 'till you go back to school. I don't want you to worry about that, okay? But we should probably at least go get the rest of your stuff."

I shook my head, trying to will my voice calm. "No, that's okay, no point to that—like, at all. It's not a big deal. I... don't need it."

"*Any* of it?" I shrugged; she sighed. "Well... even so, you do need to leave Greg's keys there, right? For whoever he hires next. That's only fair."

There wasn't anything to say to that except yes, much though I didn't want to.

So back we went to Bathurst and King, in a cab, with Mom visibly struggling all the while to *not* ask exactly what had convinced me I was no longer able to physically occupy that particular space anymore, in the first place. I ran the prospective conversation in my head as I sat there, trying it out, but there was no version of it where I didn't end up sounding frankly insane. *But does it matter?* The memory-Mom in my head replied, logically enough. *Whoever sent you those messages clearly knows who you are, where you live—*one *of the places you live. Might have followed you to the other. That's reason enough to quit right there, without all the rest.*

(I'd left my phone behind, at Mom's, just to be safe—no messages from beyond to interrupt as we blew in there, got my crap, got back out. I'd drop the keys on the breakfast table and be done with it. Just fifteen minutes more, maybe ten, and I'd never have to see that fucking place again.)

Then the *tone* came back, right outside the door, worse than ever—like a punch, or a skewer through the ear. It seemed to happen just as I slipped the key into the lock and cranked it widdershins, in the very second before making the decision to turn it and actually doing so; loud enough I felt the click instead of hearing it, so bad I barely kept myself from losing balance. I hugged the doorjamb as it opened in order to keep myself from doubling over, free hand slapping up to shield my eyes, and cursed like a sailor.

"Are you okay, Loren?" Mom asked, from behind me, as I made myself nod, somehow. "Fine," I replied, skull abruptly on fire, unable to stop my words from slurring—fresh silver agony everywhere on top of the usual pulse in my bones, my jaw, my eye sockets, a chewed tinfoil drone. "Less juss... do this quick, 'kay? Don' wanna be 'n here... longer'n I have to."

I know Mom could hear the tone too, if only a little; I could tell from the way she suddenly stopped and stared, almost on the Motel's threshold, as though reluctant to move any further inside—hell, I sure didn't blame her. Once upon a time, simply being able to demonstrate the Motel's awfulness to someone who hadn't already paid to stay there would've been unspeakably satisfying, but I was way beyond that now. From the corner of my eye, I saw Mom knuckle her ears like she was trying to get them to pop after a long flight. "Jesus," she said, voice caught somewhere between disgust and amazement. "This is... ugh. Has Greg ever *been* here, in person?"

"Dunno," I replied, staggering forward to wrench the guest bedroom closet's sliding doors open. "Color's not his fault, though. Came this way."

"*Ugh*," she repeated. "So, this was *deliberate*?"

She helped me pull out my suitcases and toted the first one out into the hall while I flipped the other open, stuffing everything I'd left behind haphazardly back inside without any sort of regard as to whether or not mixing used toiletries with lingerie was a good idea. Some lingering sense of professionalism drove me to check that the fridge was empty and the trash cleaned out, but it didn't take long; Mom was already coming back in as I zipped the second case shut. "Done," I called, voice wobbly, my whole head twinging like a wound. I remember feeling as though if I opened my mouth too wide, my teeth might fall out.

"Great," she called back. "Mind if I just use the toilet?"

"... 'course not," I lied.

And here is where my memory always starts to bend, the way things do, under pressure—where it speeds up and slows down at once, stuttering and swerving. I remember putting the case near the door and turning 'round, hearing Mom call through the washroom door, sounding slightly ill: "No *wonder* they complained about the lights." I think I actually might have laughed at that. And then there's a weird skip, a time-lapse, some sort of missing piece, an absence: a hole in my mind, a scar or flaw, something either too bright or dark to look on directly. The pain dims; the tone dims. I can't hear my mom anymore. I can't hear anything but my own breath, my own heart.

I'm back in the guest bedroom, standing in front of the wall. Bright sunlight outside, falling through the concrete shaft like rain. Floating motes of dust lit up like sparks against a gray-black wall.

Loren, a voice says, inside my head. *You came back.*

My knees give out. That's never happened to me before, not even when I'm drunk, and I think I've always thought the idea of your knees "giving out" was just a turn of phrase, an exaggeration. But no, apparently it can happen, because it does: boom and down, my ass hits the floor as my teeth clack together, so hard it hurts.

And the tone comes back up, so high it's all fuzz, a horrible blur through every part of me at once, yet the voice, that voice—it cuts through. It's barely a whisper, but I hear it, so clear the words seem to form themselves against my eardrums. So clear it's like I'm *thinking* them.

Help me.

You have to help me.

I'm a guest.

The *tone*, louder than it's ever been, raw and primordial, wobbling like mercury. Each word vibrating as if a thousand different voices are saying it, at a thousand slightly different pitches. As if the *world* is saying it.

Some gigantic clamp vises my head, forcing it to look upwards once more, at the wall. Too far away to touch, now, but my hand—my *left* hand—reaches for it anyways, pulled as if on a string, a fishing line hooked where that blue "Y" of a vein humps across its back. My vision derezzed out to the point that the wall looks like nothing but a swirling cloud, a roiling cumulonimbus storm-head; it's crumbling, disintegrating, just like me. The wall pixilating like static then beginning to clear, its atoms getting further apart, becoming intangible. And at the heart of all that roiling gray I see something else, something new forming: pale, surrounded by darkness, a monochrome infected wound coming up through colorless skin. It stretches its arms out to me.

But no, not it. Her.

Poor little missing Miss Barrie, come for her now-endless Big-City-cation. Staring out at me from the solid wall, from whatever lies on the other side of all solid walls, with blind, milky eyes and her flesh bleached like cotton, wavering in and out, an illusion of solidity. Her hair floating upwards, mouth stretching horribly wide as some abyssal fish's—a bad parody of a smile made by something that never had, the very opposite of welcoming.

And that voice again, inside me, deeper yet. I felt my lips move as it spoke, pleading.

Caught hold of me, it won't let go, I can't

Are you there?

Help me, please, just reach in

Reach in and pull me out, I'll help

Just help me, please

That fetid, acrid smell back too, so thick, my lungs rigid with it. And then I was up on my feet again, far too close, unable to remember moving; if only I reached out a little further, I'd plunge effortlessly through solid matter, like gray and filthy water. With Miss Barrie reaching back for me, her fingers almost touching mine, their too-pale tips already emerging from the wall's miasma, making my neck ruff with some sort of itchy, awful, sick-making anticipation—

That's when I see them, all around her: tendrils, trailing. Black strings in blackness, gray-shadowed. These weird strings at the corners of her mouth going up and back into the darkness, pulling and tweaking, twitching her lips, opening and closing her jaws. Plucking at her mouth's corners, hauling her limbs into place, raising her slack, soft, drained hand. Her tongue is working the wrong way for the words she's "saying," and it looks dry. Like she's being played long-distance, like a Theremin. Like a spider's web-filaments, tugged on from afar, tempting in a fly. Like some invisible puppeteer's strings.

Time started working the right way again, then: I wrenched back, just in time to see the blackness just above—behind her—move. There was a sort of a stain on her left shoulder I'd thought was just my eyes failing, trying to translate something nobody should ever see into visual signals a human retina could read. But no: as I watched, it rippled, mimicking some much larger wave. A matching mass of utter lightless black reaching out for me, one single finger longer than any of Miss Barrie's limbs first pointing, then wagging slightly—*Oh, you! Always so difficult*—before turning over, crooking, in clear invitation. Curling up and back, then down, then up and back again.

Beckoning.

Come closer, my darling, come closer. Let me touch you, the way I'm touching her. Let me know you. Let us be... together.

Loren, come.

At which point I did exactly what I told *you* to do, if you ever see something similar. Threw down Greg's keys, so hard they bounced, and just.

Fucking.

Ran.

Mom found me back down on the street, eventually, shaking, cases in hand—looked like she wanted to rip into me at first, for leaving her along in that hellhole, 'til she saw I was crying again. Days later, I got an email back from Ross Puget with an attachment that proved, in the end, not much more informative than any of his site's articles. He talked a lot about liminal spaces, about ownership and possession, the idea that when a space is left empty for too long—especially intentionally—it might tend to drift towards the "wrong sort of frequency," one that renders it easy to... penetrate. The Motel's tone, he said, might likely be a sonic side-effect of this collision between existential frequencies, the same sort of tension vibration seismographs pick up from continental plates grinding against one another; people theorized the same kind of fraying might explain what he called "apports," objects mysteriously disappearing and reappearing at particular locations, sideslipping through space from weak point to weak point. If I was still interested in trying to do something about it, he said, he could recommend a few names.

I never answered, which I feel more than a little bad about, these days. I did, however, forward the email on to Greg, with a brusque postscript: *If you can't sell the place, burn it out and collect the insurance. I'm serious.* Then I blocked his number.

Sometimes I dream of my time in the Puppet Motel and wake up heart-sick, breathless, hoping against hope I'm not still there. Sometimes I get texts from an unknown number and delete them unread. Sometimes my phone's A.I. tries to talk to me, and I turn it the fuck off.

I still do hear it call to me, sometimes, though—it or her. Because that's the only real question, isn't it, when all's said and done? Was Miss Barrie only ever what she seemed, a drained shell run long-distance, a mask over something far worse? Or is she still hanging there in darkness even now, two or three plaster-layers down, waiting in vain for a rescue that never comes?

Does something have to be human—have *been* human—to be a ghost? Ross's articles could never quite agree. And that thing I saw, that barest fingertip: malign or just lonely?

The woman inside the wall, she's a ghost, now. I'm almost sure.

Still. I hear that thin, terrible voice, forever pleading with the empty air: *Loren, Loren, help me.* And see myself forever backing away, hands waving, like I'm trying to scrub all trace of my occupancy from the Puppet Motel's polluted atmosphere. Thinking back, as I do: *Stop saying my name, I don't know you, I can't. I* can't. *I don't know* you.

That's a choice, though, to believe that. It always was.

Like everything else.

So, I track these stories on my own time instead, and whenever I think I've identified those who might be able to tell me about what happened, I arrange to make myself available. It doesn't always pay off, of course—some are jokes, or pranks; some are mistakes, honest or otherwise. Sometimes, I've found, people try their best to persuade themselves of supernatural influence in order to re-frame their own errors, to cast their own (entirely human) demons as things whose actions they couldn't possibly bear any responsibility for.

But for myself, I know when a tale is true because when I hear it, that *tone* will start to resonate inside me once more, piercing me through from ear to jaw to bowels, ringing at my marrow like a struck bell. I can't stop it, can't help it. I just… can't.

So, I do the next best thing and listen. Record, maintain. So that future seekers—people caught in the grip of something they struggle to understand, just like I once was—will have a place to go, to learn. To understand.

This world is full of weak places, after all, where dark things peer through. Beckoning. One of which knows my name now. And I just have to live with that.

I always will.

COME CLOSER

A PATH OPENS IN the trees before you, and you have to tread it. You *have* to. It's not a decision. It comes from somewhere else, outside of you. It's not the sort of call that can be ignored.

That's what we tell ourselves, sometimes, when we're about to make a mistake. Or when we're already halfway through making one.

The first time you take its picture, the house is on another street entirely, around the corner, up towards the underpass. By June, it's on your street.

By October, it's next door.

You're keeping a dream diary the day you notice the house, just like Dr. Batmasian told you to, back when you still thought your insomnia was fixable. That morning you dream you're in what you feel absolutely sure is your home, but in hindsight is a completely different apartment—a compilation of other people's, maybe, larger, and with spaces you've never used because they don't exist. It's the sort of dream where you think you're awake and start going through the motions of an ordinary day... taking dishes out of the dishwasher, in this case. Except every time you're "done," you go to shut it and suddenly find it's full again, with a different set of dishes every time. And all the while you're thinking: *This is wrong, this isn't right. This has happened before, over and over.*

At which point another version of you entirely walks in, dressed in what you only now recognize as your father's clothes. *I think I'm dreaming,* you tell her, and she simply nods, replying: *Yeah, you probably are. So, you should do something that'd really hurt in real life, and if it doesn't, you'll know you're asleep.*

Which sounds logical, so you step back a bit, sigh, tuck your hair behind your ears, and slam your head face-down onto the granite counter-top. And since you do indeed barely feel it, you just go ahead and keep on doing it again and again until you wake up at last—kick your way to the surface between various peeled-back layers of sleep, up through untold fathoms, out into the real world once more. Until you come to back in your own bed, your own condo, exhausted and sticky and alone.

Annoyingly mundane, but as recurring dreams go it certainly beats the one where you're desperately trying to kill somebody with a sharp object, stabbing them 'til your hands are sore while they just stand there laughing at you. Not to mention giving you reason enough to at least get you upright, dressed and clean and through the door, so you can make it to work on time for once and thus leave comparatively "early"—i.e., at the time you normally would if you ever bothered to get there when your contract specifies you should in the first place.

Spend all day copying and filing on demand, handing out mail, making coffee; it's a glorified intern's job, if this place could actually afford to pay interns, or anybody actually ever took unpaid internships anymore. You got it by virtue of having a degree in Library Sciences, hoping one day it'll get you the job you really want. But if the day's a grind, there's always the evening: twilight in the Distillery District, magic hour, everything touched with cool blue and gold, making even the most degraded objects pop like they're Pixar-painted. And then, right there on your way over to the weekly meet-up with Joe and Anjit, there's the house.

"Take a look," you say maybe ten minutes later, plopping your phone down on the restaurant table between them. "Either of you ever remember seeing this place before?"

"Nope," Joe says, without even looking, but Anjit narrows her eyes. "Is this one of those post-war bungalows?" she asks.

You shrug. "Might be, I guess—I don't know much about architecture. Looks old enough to be, though."

Anjit agrees, peering closer. "Where *is* this?"

"Just 'round the corner from my place, like halfway up the block. Almost to the China Lily Soy Sauce factory."

"Oh God, yes; that place is so gross. Like... right near that little bridge, the underpass?"

"That's the one. Weird how I never really saw it before, though; must've walked past it a million times, right? Maybe it just never registered how there was an actual *house* under all that other crap."

The other crap in question is however many years' worth of overgrowth, *Life After People* style—ivy everywhere, weeds to the waist, a drooping chestnut tree that probably hasn't been cut back since Dutch Elm disease blew through Toronto. The house is a classic one-story with a later addition slapped on top, a box on top of a box, the second floor only slightly smaller; there's one of those eye-shaped windows at the front, half-blinded by leaves. Whole place is in obvious disrepair, if not quite ruin; windows dark with dust and cracked to boot, paint peeling leprous.

Artificial, not natural, and yet—the house looks like it grew up out of the ground, like roots. It looks... immutable.

Maybe it's all the green.

You tap the phone's screen, asking: "Okay, improv time, bitches—who you think *lives* here, just off the top of your head?"

Joe snorts, still not looking. "Nobody, Lin, Jesus. Not for a *long* damn time."

A passing waitress: "Serial killers, for sure."

Anjit studies it a moment, then glances back up, grinning. "*Witches*," she suggests, then whoops as you high-five her, signaling the waitress as she swings back around. "One more for my friend!" you yell, finally getting Joe's attention, at least momentarily.

"I'll have whatever they're having, and make it a double," he tells her, before going back to editing his Grindr picks queue.

That night, you dream you find a tiny box, no longer than your finger, no wider. But when you open it up, it turns out to be a window, and when you put your eye to it, you see an entire landscape, some gray-on-gray moor under a stormy overhanging sky, moonless, pelting rain. Strange grasses occupied by dark motion, hidden eyes, the wet bones of long-dead things. And an overwhelming fear comes washing up over you, this sudden dread that you might somehow slip through, end up stranded in that bleak field under that same lowering thunderhead, trapped in another world entirely—unable to glimpse the way back into your peaceful room, your familiar bed, except through that tiny, lidded rectangle. Always and forever from then on at the mercy of any stranger who might decide to slam the lid shut over your only way back out.

A week passes, or maybe a couple; you can't help seeing the house out of the corner of your eye as you go by, even when you're not looking for it. Which is how, slowly, you start to notice it isn't in the same place anymore.

"That house is moving," you tell Anjit, eventually, after your usual weekly hook-up. The two of you are lying in bed, sharing a joint; Joe's in the shower, sponging away sex-traces and singing loudly along with Marvin Gaye, but that place between you where he most often lies is still warm, still slightly depressed. "The vine house. You remember."

She inhales, holds the smoke in her lungs a moment, then blows out a little plume of it, miniature dragon style. "The one on your phone," she says, black eyes cast up and shining, watching the last of her toke dissipate into darkness. "Yes, well, that's... what do you *mean* by that, Lin, exactly?"

"That it's not where it used to be, when I took the picture. It's—somewhere else, now."

"Another part of the city?"

"No, still on that block, just... closer to the corner, I guess. A lot closer. Like it's about to turn onto my street, or something."

Anjit turns on her side, frowning. "That really doesn't seem possible, though, does it?"

You shrug, not really able to disagree. "Took some more pictures, if you want to see," you offer, reaching for your phone. And by the time Joe comes back out, humming, you and Anjit are sitting cross-legged together poring over the evidence, swiping back and forth to run it forwards or back, the world's slowest little movie.

"The hell're you doing?" he demands, then snorts when you try to tell him. Scoffing: "Oh Jesus, *that* thing again? You need to get yourself some Netflix."

Anjit shakes her head, hair flipping. "What I don't get," she says, to you, "is what happens to the house right next to it, when it does move. I mean—look at this, here, and here: house, house, *the* house. And then, in this next one..."

"...it's where the second house was," you finish, nodding. "But there's nothing behind it, nothing new; that other house where it used to be hasn't been pushed on like beads on a string or switched around. It's just *gone*, supplanted."

"Yet here, in this next one—the previous house is back, but on the other side, switched from left to right. And now it's the house that *used* to be in front of our mystery bungalow—the *previous* right-hand house—that's gone."

Joe stands there naked, arms crossed in annoyance, yet swinging free; you catch sidelong sight of him and snicker, which probably isn't the effect he was looking to have on you. "Well, that's impossible, obviously. But either way, who cares?"

"Lin," Anjit tells him, eyebrow hiking. "Equally obviously. And why the hell not?"

Joe strikes a pose and makes himself jolt, abruptly tumescent, like he's pointing at her hands-free. "'Cause it's rude to turn down a Greek bearing gifts?" he suggests, theatrically, and watches her dissolve into giggles.

"He does have a point," you concede, which just makes her laugh all the harder.

A week later, you round the corner onto your street, only to find the house waiting for you.

"So, when does it move?" Anjit asks, a few days later, when you show her the latest snaps; "I don't know," you reply, resisting the urge to shiver, automatically, while at the same time swiping through with your eyes kept peeled for ones pretty enough to maybe fix up and post. "When I'm asleep, maybe."

"And you don't see it doing it, obviously."

"Never. It creeps, the same as ivy."

"Apt." A beat. "So, what happens to the other houses, you think, while they're gone? I mean... do they look any different, when they come back?"

You frown, considering this. "Kind of, yeah," you say, at last. "When the houses reappear, they seem more decrepit—drained, reduced, empty. Like everyone just left in the middle of the night, and somehow you just didn't notice until now. And meanwhile, the vine house itself seems bigger every time, as if it's absorbed part of the house it replaced: a cornice or a floor or a room. It seems more *inhabited*."

"Inhabited how?"

"Oh, I don't know, it just... like sometimes I'm walking by, coming home late at night, and there's music inside? Weird music. Weird music, plus weird lights." You pause again. "I mean, no surprise there. 'Cause everything about that damn *place* is weird, inside and out."

Now it's Anjit's turn to frown. "Thought you said you hadn't ever been inside."

"Oh, I haven't. It just—strikes me that way."

Anjit nods. But: "This is ridiculous," Joe breaks in, finally, impatiently dismissive, as if neither of you ever had that exact thought. "You're both stuck on this damn thing, Lin, and it's eating up your brains. We need to—"

"Need to *what*, Joe? What do 'we' need to do about it, exactly?"

It comes out snappish, perhaps more so than you originally intend it to, since it definitely seems to slap him across the face a bit, as—from across the room—Anjit raises her eyebrows; takes him aback, if only for a second. Still, rotating bedroom-centric polyamorous circuit show he co-stars in aside, Joe's never exactly been the kind of guy to take that sort of thing lying down.

"Okay, then," he says, at last. "Not we, so much; me. *I'll* do something."

"Again, like what?"

"Watch and see."

Which is how the three of you end up back on the street at roughly 3:00 AM, approaching the house in question sidelong, like a sleeping dog of uncertain provenance. As if you somewhat expect it to wake up and come for you, teeth bared and barking.

The vines seem fresher, full of bright new growth; the path to the house slopes gently downwards through a "garden" of weeds, dusty, unscuffed, blank. There's a black-barked tree almost at the bottom, its groin bulging with tumorous roots, next to a gate without a fence that stands there alone and ridiculous, a concrete metaphor—just a post and a latch on one side plus a post and hinges on the other, pewter-colored, decorously locked against intruders. Joe snorts, then steps around it, while you and Anjit hover uncomfortable on the other side.

"You coming up, or what?" he demands.

"No, thanks," Anjit shoots back coolly. "Honor's *all* yours."

You think about agreeing, but don't. There's something about this place, the sudden nearness of it, that dries your mouth out. You swallow instead, hearing your throat click.

Weird music, weird lights, figures moving behind shades; your own words come back to you, tone ironic, like a stranger's. None of the above tonight, though—just the windows' black, cracked gaze, eyeing you sidelong. Just that disapproving mouth of a door, pursed shut.

Joe stomps up the path, leaving visible prints. "Hey," he calls. "Yo, serial killers, witches. *Nobody.* Anyone home?"

You hiss, abruptly mortified, voice a strangled stage whisper. *"Jesus,* Joe—keep it down, for Christ's sake! It's the middle of the fucking night."

"Uh huh, middle of the night, downtown Toronto. Where everybody's perfectly free to call the Neighborhood Watch anytime, not that I notice it happening."

"Well, you wouldn't, would you?" Anjit points out, helpfully. "Not until the cops got here."

"Oh, I'm setting my watch."

He's up the path's top now, almost to the vine house's grayly sagging bottom step, its water-stained middle rucked like lichen. Just two more steps and he'll be up onto the tiny porch, barely more than a verandah-topped portico. No knocker, but there's a doorbell's button-topped, plastic rectangle half-hidden underneath that empty patch where the mailbox used to hang, its outlines faint-sketched in dirt, now all but indistinguishable from the rest of the house's gangrenous paintjob or its encrusting foliage, the leaves' shifting shadows.

"Don't you dare ring that," you warn him, and Joe gives a five-year-old's grin, hand already in mid-reach with the pointer finger extended, like he's looking to get caught. But before he can make contact, something rings out, from deep inside— not a chime, so much, as a tone, a drone, a breath. An exhalation.

Joe hears it and perks up; Anjit hears it and blanches. You hear it and think of... what? Something distant, something cold, plucking at the very edges of familiarity. A hoarse wind-blown from far off rattling across the window-frames, making them moan. A glass harmonica touched after midnight, its waters murky, singing with disease.

(There are instruments made of human bone, you've heard, in places like Tibet; they play them in temples, to frighten away evil spirits. But this doesn't sound like that, not exactly. This sounds more like—

—something you play to *welcome* them. To call them closer.)

And now there's shadows, too, set against light, making the drawn shades flicker, same way a dreaming man's pupils do behind shut lids. "See?" Joe announces, to no one in particular. "Normal-ass people, exactly where you'd expect to find them—inside, listening to music, watching... TV, or something. Like *normal.*"

"Doesn't sound much like music to me," Anjit murmurs, from behind you. To which you'd probably agree, if that exact moment didn't happen to be right when the front door suddenly snaps open.

Afterward, Joe claims he couldn't see anything, that the door simply flung itself wide too fast and briefly for any additional details to register, then slammed in his face. But both you and Anjit know that can't possibly be true, because—*you* saw it. Both of you. Because Anjit described it unprompted, using exactly the same words you would have, long before it ever occurred to you to ask her to. Because she did it haltingly, between gasps: described the door's inner edge, worn and seemingly tooth-worried, gray as a dead man's wound; described the tiny slice of lintel thus exposed, the bare, unpainted post with its worm-track hieroglyphics, its flayed and peeling lip of general decay.

And that thin, thin hand reaching forth to stroke itself down the side of Joe's face, quick and gentle—barely resolved, an almost subliminal image, aside from the simultaneous suggestion of far too much bone cut with far too few fingers.

All this followed by Joe, stumbling back, sitting down with a thud on the curbside as if he couldn't physically go any further, sitting there shivering. Joe's skeptical eyes rolling helpless, a spooked horse's, thrown back again and again towards the house only to skitter away like a flinch, helplessly tethered; his hands both fisted, drumming on his thighs, face sweat-slick and pale. Like he'd have given a million bucks to get up and walk away if he'd had it, let alone been capable.

"What happened?" you demand, as he stares back and away, back and away; "Nothing," he claims—*lies*—angrily, before literally biting his lip, hard enough to bruise. But: "Oh Joe, that's *so* much crap," Anjit interjects, equally pissed, before you can. "Who was *in* there? You must've seen—"

"No one. Nothing. I don't..." Joe trails off. "I just don't want to talk about it, okay? *Ever.* Wasted enough of my time on this shit as it is, goddamnit. I mean, *fuck.*" And without giving either of you time for further words he rolls to his feet, power-walks away, still muttering curses under his breath.

You can't get him on the phone the next day, which isn't surprising, not at first. But—you can't reach him the next day, either. Nor the next, nor the next after that, not any. Not you and not Anjit either. Not at his home, at work, on any of his phones... not at all.

Then again, it *is* August. Vacation season. Maybe he just went to Cabo.

Maybe.

Come away with me, Lin, Anjit keeps suggesting, as the house creeps closer; *up North, just until it passes by. My cousin has a house outside of Bracebridge, right on the river.* And eventually you give way, mainly to make her happy, or so you tell yourself—because what the hell do you have to be afraid of, anyhow, after all? You live in a damn condo.

The river is beautiful, though. Quiet. The pine trees whisper. There's just something about being near water, watching it ripple, rise and fall, current bearing everything steadily away, forever...

When you step out of the Uber with Anjit at your side, you study the street up and down as she settles with the driver, afraid of what you'll find. But the house is nowhere to be seen—not up, not down, not left, not right. You make her walk around the block with you, exploring the side-streets further and further, like you're mapping the area. You don't think you've ever paid this much attention to where you live before, barring that time somebody got shot down the block.

It's gone, entirely, no trace left behind. Such a relief. Like a headache you've had for years is finally over.

The vine house is *gone.*

Anjit and you order in, have a nice dinner together, after which you see her off with a kiss and go to bed early—alone but not lonely, having already taken a long, lavender-scented bath, washed and oiled your hair then wrapped it securely enough it won't stain your pillows, just like your mama taught you to. You're so deliciously tired by the time the whole routine is done, you almost have to remind yourself to turn out the light. You fall asleep, humming.

You either don't dream or don't think you do, falling from dark to dark. But you do wake up, eventually: still alone, on the floor, someplace so dark you can barely tell if your eyes are open. A place you've never been, and never wanted to be—elsewhere, elsewhen. Other, with a capital "o."

You already know where, though. You can tell without looking, without having to. You can tell it by the smell.

Lie there in the dark, planks stretching your back, making your hips displace and your pelvis feel like it's cracking open, aching in every cold bone at once. Lie there with your skin crawling, your muscles bunching, a feverish chill making your stomach bunch and your cheeks burn. Lie there sick and scared, horrified far beyond your own capacity to fully feel it, with nothing but the same four words running through your brain—emphasis shifting each to each before looping back around forever, again, and again, and again, and again.

This *isn't my house.*

This isn't *my house.*

This isn't my *house.*

This isn't—

And then, right then, that's when the very worst thing of all happens: you realize you can hear your friends calling to you, desperate, the both of them here in this awful house as well. Anjit's screams appear to come filtering vaguely down somewhere to your right, probably from up on the second floor; Joe's seem to echo closer yet simultaneously further away, thrumming through the wall nearby, the very floor you're sprawled on. You can feel them inside you, knotting around your heart, tugging hard.

I did this, you think, knowing there's no way in hell you possibly could've—no way, Jesus, that's fucking *insane*; that's *crazy.* And yet.

I did this to you, me, you can't stop yourself from thinking. *Just by noticing. By making* you *notice.*

Oh God, I did this to all of us.

You're up, then, knees popping, almost falling—lunge forward, grabbing for the wall, the door. Find it, or what you think might be it. A knob in your hand; you twist it, yank. It opens. You propel yourself through it, into the space beyond. Choke out: "Joe?" and hear your throat creak with it, a strangled whisper running to whimper, like you've been throat-punched; God, everything just *hurts* in here, for no reason. It's so *cold.*

"Lin?"

Someone stumbles into you, hands clawing at your arms, burying her face in your neck—you know that perfume, those sobs. It's Anjit. "Where the hell is Joe?" you ask her, feel her shake her head, skull grinding painfully against your collarbone; "I don't *know,*" she weeps back. "I don't, I just—I thought he was here, next door. I thought he was with you."

(That's what it sounded like, anyhow.)

Which is when Joe starts screaming again, of course, from above or below, you'll never be able to tell; as if he can hear you too, as if he recognizes your voices. As if he's being torn apart with somebody's bare fucking hands, piece by goddamn piece.

"HELP ME, YOU GUYS HAVE TO HELP ME, *CHRIST!* I'VE BEEN HERE SO LONG, SO *LONG,* OH JESUS, *PLEASE*—"

You join hands, knit fingers 'til your knuckles crack, Anjit dragging you headlong in her wake from room to room as she howls Joe's name back at him, barely pausing for breath: *Oh my God Joe, just hold on, we're here, we're here!* But you already know you'll never find him, either of you. Just all these other people, more and more through every new door, catching and clawing at you like you're their only possible means of escape, their last shred of hope. Some of them young and some old but all in pain, the same terrible pain *you* feel, borne incalculably longer—long enough for them to be uniformly insane, caught inside a shriek, their lungs raw from constant screaming. These mad, moon-blind bastards, pleading for something you can never give; how long can they have they *been* here, for God's sake? If God even applies...

Almost none of them seem to speak English, but it's the last who finally calls out in Hindi, startling Anjit into answering—he gives a shout and rushes you, rips you apart, drags her backwards by her hair screaming *Lin, Lin, LIN!* And you go after her, of course you do, but—

—the next room's smaller, and the next, and the next. Smaller and more silent. You're getting further, not closer. You can't hear her anymore, or Joe. You can't hear anything but your own heart, banging at your ribs like a crazed bird caged in bone. Feel its claws, it's beak: that's your fear, made flesh. It's going to eat you alive, from inside-out.

You turn or try to. Fight your way from a room into a corridor, a nook, a cranny. Open the last knob onto what seems like barely a closet, then pivot to find the door has nothing inside it at all—that there *is* no door, no frame or hinges, barely a seam. The plaster simply sealed over behind you, *around* you, like a fold of scar, a cocoon.

There in the dark and cold, held rigid, unable to move an inch; your skin gone sub-zero, so bad it almost doesn't hurt anymore, like the nerves are dying all at once. That's when it takes hold of you at last, the house's true occupant: hugs you close, breathes into your mouth with gentle, loving ease, as if it's trying to infect you. As if it wants nothing more in the whole wide world than to keep you alive, just as long as it possibly can.

So glad you came, it tells you then, smiling, its teeth against your lips, tongue printing yours. *So very, very glad.*

A path, and this is where it ends. A mistake, unfixable, made without even knowing you did.

A fenceless gate, forever left open.

CUT FRAME

Old movies are the dreams of dead people.

—Niall Quent to Barry Jenkinson, *CanCon on CanCon*

(1995, First Hand Waving Press)

Transcript of file recorded 12/05/18 by R. Puget / T. Jankiewicz

Filed under Case #C23-1972, Freihoeven Parapsychological Institute, Toronto

Reported: Intern L. Jankiewicz 11/17/18

Cross-saved at www.noetichealth.org/interviews/torcdusk.mp3

RP: —test, test, test. Excellent. This is Ross Puget for Noetic Health, here with Dr. Tadeusz Jankiewicz of Toronto, who's consented to be interviewed at the encouragement of his granddaughter Lily, our favorite intern. Say a few words into the mic, doc?

TJ: Like this?

RP: Perfect. I don't suppose you had a chance to sign the paperwork we sent you yet?

TJ: Yes, all done. I'll admit I was surprised at the number of releases you require. Lily made this sound very much a... hmmm, what? Hobby, I think is how she put it.

RP: I'd use the word "vocation," myself.

TJ: Have you had legal troubles before?

RP: (PAUSE) Nothing significant.

TJ: And you'd like to keep it that way, right? It's okay, Mr. Puget. I've had patients be... unpleasant, from time to time; a little posterior-covering never goes amiss, eh?

RP: You're very understanding.

TJ: Well, this isn't a story I would have told if I was still practicing. I should also warn you, the material I *can* show you doesn't offer much proof of... anything. Not as much as I'm guessing you'd prefer.

RP: Well, we'll get to that when we get to it.

SUPPLEMENTARY NOTES

Subject:
Dr. Tadeusz Jankiewicz
(*Photograph attached: 5'8", 172 lbs, Polish-Caucasian, white hair, blue eyes*)

Bio:
D.O.B. 2/15/1941, Morges, Switzerland
Emigrated to Toronto with family August 1943
Graduated U of T Faculty of Dentistry June 1965
Retired April 2008

Location:
Subject's residence, 132 Fermanagh Avenue, Toronto, Ontario

Notes: (*Transcript of voice recording, R. Puget*)

Home looks like it was built in the '20s, but really well-maintained. Floors mostly hardwood. Front parlour's been converted into a single-patient dental treatment suite, apparently no longer used. Wall décor's very much film buff paradise: instead of paintings or photos, framed lobby cards, posters, alternate artwork—the classic concept art poster for *Star Wars* is here, some modern Hitchcock reworkings, looks like a complete run of Cronenberg's '70s and '80s stuff... one bookshelf's full of film reference stuff, too—books by Ebert, Kael, all three of Danny Peary's *Cult Movies*— wow, he's even got *Weird Sex and Snowshoes.* Bet it's been a while since anyone took *that* down. Oh. Just noticed—one spot on the wall outside the dental suite looks like a frame's been removed. Remember to ask what that was.

Transcript torcdusk.mp3 *continued:*

RP: We should probably start with the basics. You're the primary investor and only currently living producer credited on IMDb for *The Torc,* directed by Niall Quent and released in 1973.

TJ: Sounds impressive, doesn't it? All it meant was that I signed cheques and got to visit the set, wherever it was that week.

RP: How did you become an investor?

TJ: One of my patients at the time was a producer, a real one, and he'd worked with Quent before. My practice was becoming successful enough that I was thinking about tax-protective investments, and Oleg told me the film industry was an excellent place to park my money.

RP: This was the beginning of the tax-shelter era of Canadian film, of course. I saw your collection in the living room.

TJ: Ah, well, that's all 20-20 hindsight, isn't it? I have to admit, even at the beginning, Oleg was telling me all about the ways I could hide even more money if I'd wanted to, at a hundred percent return, so it didn't surprise me when it all came crashing down in the '80s. Did you know that of the sixty-six feature films officially produced in Canada in 1979, more than half of them were never released at all? And this was the year before their internally notorious "Canada Can and Does" campaign, at Cannes—the one that Lawrence O'Toole wrote about in *Maclean's* (article referenced can be found by searching under June 2, 1980, at http://archive.macleans.ca), under the headline "Canada Can't." A hundred percent became fifty, and all the Hollywood North types ran back home like their, eh...

RP: Asses were on fire? Wow, no, I did *not* know all that. This Oleg sounds like he was a real, um—

TJ: Oh, he was a sleazebucket, without question. Not that my own motives were more honorable, I suppose.

RP: The tax returns.

TJ: Only partly. The rest... that was for *her*. Tamar.

RP: Tamar Dusk. (BEAT) Did you ever get to meet her? Maybe on set?

TJ: Once. But I'm getting ahead of myself. It's important that you understand things as I came to understand them. The—situation. Have you ever seen *The Torc*?

RP: Yes, actually. I probably didn't have the intended audience reaction; I just remember that booming narration, and the catchphrase—"*Don't! Put! On! The Torc!*" (LAUGHS)

TJ: (LAUGHS) Well, don't feel too bad. I'm not sure even Quent knew what reaction he was going for. That wasn't his, what's the word, his *process*. Oleg once told me Quent's method was simply to film as much as possible with "any recognizable American," as he said it, and then to do the pick-up shooting afterwards—and only *then* would he figure out what the film was "about." Sometimes, Quent wouldn't even have much more than a title, or even a poster—nothing so coherent as a script.

RP: And this didn't put you off? It sounded like a good idea?

TJ: It was the only film I'd ever been personally involved with. It still is. I wasn't a director; I was a dentist. And a fan.

RP: Of Niall Quent?

TJ: Of Tamar Dusk.

SUPPLEMENTARY NOTES: TAMAR DUSK

TAMAR DUSK
From Wikipedia, the free encyclopedia

Tamar Dusk, born[?? confirm] **Tamar Janika Duzhneskaya** (January 6, 1917 - ????), is a Slavic-American actress best known for her "exotic" roles in several <u>noir</u> and horror <u>B-movies</u> between 1936 and 1960, all directed by <u>Nicholas Ryback</u>, as well for the controversies surrounding her personal history that emerged during the era of the <u>Hollywood blacklist</u> and, in later years, apocryphal rumors about the "<u>Dusk Curse</u>". This controversy has continued in part into the modern day following Dusk's last appearance in the little-known Canadian horror film <u>*The Torc*</u> (dir. <u>Niall Quent</u>, 1973), after which Dusk and her husband began an extended campaign to render

Dusk's personal information as legally inaccessible as possible, to the extent that even Dusk's date of death cannot presently be verified. Her most well-known roles include Mara in _Under the Bridge_ (1937), "The Woman" in _Woman Without A Name_ (1940), Ingrid in _Kiss of the Succubus_ (1945), Eriska in _Blood Mirror_ (1953), and Mrs. Larkwood in _The Whispering Widow_ (1957), all directed by Nicholas Ryback.

<<Attached file: Tamar-Dusk-1953.jpg>>

<<Attached file: BLOOD-MIRROR-poland-1953.jpg>>

From IMDb.com:
"I never had the opportunity to work with Tamar myself; there is no doubt that her refusal to work with anyone other than Nicholas Ryback did her career no favors. I was lucky enough to meet her once or twice, and if there is any substance to the 'Dusk Curse' rumors it only proves how any beautiful, yet remote, woman can provoke destructive obsession in others simply by existing. She had the remarkable gift of making you feel as if merely by joining her company you had rescued her from some great sadness, yet when you left her, you took some of that sadness with you— and it seemed a gift. Had she chosen to work with any other director, she would have been one of the great tragic actresses of her generation."

—_Alfred Hitchcock_

"Dusk had talent. Can't argue with that. Her problem was, she never really stopped performing. That's nothing unusual in Hollywood, but she took it over the top. The whole business with only shooting at night, hiding her real name, her home country—she let the press make too much out of it, probably to get the publicity, and it shot her in the foot. She was no more a Communist than my cat. But between all the questions she wouldn't answer and her lack of friends, it didn't surprise me how it ended. She put all her eggs in Nicky Ryback's basket. Once his eyes were gone, so was she."

—_Elia Kazan_

"I do not talk about myself, because I do not consider it a subject of appropriate interest. The audience is here to watch the characters I create. My task is to disappear."

—*Tamar Dusk*

Transcript torcdusk.mp3 *continued:*

RP: Tell me about the first time you saw Tamar Dusk.

TJ: On screen? It was 1955, I was twelve. One of my friends had persuaded his big brother to act as the "accompanying adult," so we could all go to a late-night showing of *Blood Mirror* at a repertory theater. I remember the smell of the popcorn—too much fake butter—the feel of the velvet cushions on the seats. If I close my eyes, I can still see all her scenes.

RP: Do you remember which version of *Blood Mirror* you saw?

TJ: You're thinking about the lost final scene, aren't you?[1] No, I'd never heard about any of that; like I said, I was a fan, not a film student. Not that it would have made a difference. Young men are never put off by stories like that, are they? Rather the reverse.

RP: Some of the books say Nick Ryback deliberately spread the rumor about a lost ending, to make up for the fact he didn't really *have* an ending. The blacklist was

---

[1] The only Hollywood director with whom Tamar Dusk ever worked, Nicholas Ryback (born Nikolai Rybakov in Petrograd in 1922), was known for pre-screening his films to small, private audiences before general theatrical release, often conducting final and sometimes radical edits alone after this feedback. *Blood Mirror* (1953) in particular was rumored to have had its entire final scene removed and destroyed after the studio saw it in rushes, with a replacement denouement supposedly assembled from already-cut segments. Apocryphal reports pop up from time to time of the intact original version being broadcast late at night on local television channels, but this is considered to be an urban legend.

into full swing by then, he was already getting pressure over working with Tamar at all, and since he was a Russian émigré himself, he wasn't in any place to protect anyone else.

TJ: But better bad publicity than no publicity? That sounds much more like Quent, to be honest.

RP: You know, some people believe Tamar Dusk literally never worked with anybody but Nick Ryback in her entire career. The idea that she'd come up here and make some crappy CanCon project, with Niall Quent of all people...

TJ: Well, she *did* only work with Ryback in Hollywood. But this was Hollywood North, one time, for one picture. Quent counted himself a very lucky man, in that respect.

RP: And what was he like, to work with?

TJ: Hmmm. Well, I didn't speak with him a great deal, on set or off, but he didn't strike me as, let's say, the most organized of men. At the time, I thought he was just as star struck as the rest of us. I remember being quite angry about it, in fact—he was hogging Tamar, her presence. Getting the chance to meet her was the entire reason I became involved, but whenever I brought it up, Quent always had a reason why it wasn't a good time. She was feeling under the weather, she had a meeting and had to leave the moment shooting was done, they had to review script changes...

RP: You thought he was bullshitting you? Pardon my French.

TJ: Well, I didn't have proof. It was all very plausible. She was not a young woman; she'd gone through her share of tragedy. Her career had mostly ended around 1960, when her director friend, Ryback, contracted retinal cancer and had to have his eyes removed, and then her first husband died—supposedly due to alcoholism, they say, but...

RP: Yeah, the rumors were all that it was suicide via OD. Pathological jealousy.

TJ: Indeed. And her second marriage wasn't exactly... oh, let's tell the truth and shame the devil, why don't we? She married for money. He was a decade her senior, a financier who owned a chain of fur and leather coat warehouse outlets throughout Ontario—I don't remember the name, I think they're out of business now. That was how she came to live up here. He built her a private cabin of her own somewhere in Muskoka, the size of a mansion, fully staffed, all the luxuries. Even an in-house movie theater. Though... I don't think she ever watched anything there. (PAUSE) I don't think she could have.

RP: What do you mean?

TJ: We'll come to that. This has to be in the right order, Mr. Puget.

(PAUSE)

RP: So... what was it about her, exactly? Back in the day?

TJ: Huh. (LAUGHS) Have you *seen* her?

RP: In pictures, sure. Photos, stills...

TJ: But the films?

RP: I've seen clips.

TJ: Not enough. You had to see her in motion, but, um—also everything around her, all the rest? Ryback built his whole film to show her off, like a... jewel-case. A stage.

You needed to see how other people looked at her, how they reacted when she wasn't there anymore. Even all the empty places where she might eventually be— it was a kind of suspense. She might turn up anywhere, any moment. It was like, eh... scratching a raw place just after the scab comes off, so sensitive, a memory of pain. All the nerves on fire, half-healed, but still wounded. Like an itch. You were always looking for her, desperately, even after the movie stopped. Besides which, she was *sexy*. I didn't even know that word, the first time, but I felt it. In *Blood Mirror*, she was that first figure of complete, untrammeled eroticism every young boy en-counters sooner or later—the person, the face and body you can't even *think* about without, ah... reaction, decades later. Will you think less of me if I admit that every woman I've ever been with, even Lily's grandmother, looked like her, to some ex-tent?

RP: Well, uh—I guess everyone has a type.

TJ: I've made you uncomfortable; I apologize. But please believe me, this isn't just prurience; I was far from the only man to have that reaction. One of the elements of the so-called "Dusk Curse" was the fact that Tamar had so many, they call them "stalkers" now, I think—far more than a comparatively minor B-list actress should have had. Security on her movie sets was eventually something like twice the indus-try norm. Which you'd think would make for good headlines, but most producers recognized the increased expense and insurance risk as counterproductive—only one mistake, one mad fan, and they'd have a disaster on their hands. That was the real reason she worked exclusively with Ryback: he was the only one willing to un-derwrite her costs. Which most people never think about, but when your own funds are at stake, that sort of research becomes critical. Film runs on cash. Once you've seen for yourself how money affects literally every decision in the process, you learn how to follow it.

RP: Is that why she married the rich Canadian guy? For money, security?

TJ: Difficult to say. I think he did make her feel safe... safer. She needed that.

RP: Because of her stalkers.

TJ: [SIGHS] We think we understand how bad things can get, because we lived through the 1960s, the 1970s... I remember someone inviting me and Lily's grand-mother out to *Deep Throat*, you know? Dinner and a movie, like a double date; "high-toned," mainstream pornography. We sat there holding hands, trying to look any-where but at the screen, as our hosts dry-humped each other next to us. Or your generation, growing up with the Internet—every one of you saturated in blatantly sexual imagery, from childhood on. But, nevertheless... try to imagine being Tamar Dusk, as a young woman, in 1936. To be, without effort or even intent, a figure of such raw attractiveness that more than half the people you speak to become stupid with it, while far too many of the rest turn vicious, jealous, petty, spiteful, suspicious, resentful. You think things might get better if you go to a place so full of other beau-tiful people, surely some of them can perhaps see past that glamor and be friends with who you *are,* instead of obsessed with what you look like; it doesn't, though. Because the people there still just want to use you, to package you like a drug and sell you to addicts. So, what you thought would be your salvation becomes, instead, just another marketplace, another pit full of dogs eating each other for the same scraps. Another hell.

RP: Doesn't sound all that unusual so far, for Hollywood.

TJ: No. Most people on the same track, though—Greta Garbo, Hedy Lamarr, Rita Hayworth, Merle Oberon, Dorothy Dandridge... no, not even poor Marlene Die-trich, fleeing Germany one step ahead of *her* biggest fan—

RP: Hitler, right?

TJ: That was the rumor. And Garbo liked girls, and Lamarr swam nude but wanted to practice science; Merle could pass but Dandridge couldn't, and Rita was a Mexi-can dancer too young to drink alone, who had to have her hairline raised with elec-trolysis so no one would know she wasn't Irish. But none of them had to deal with what Tamar Dusk had to deal with, for which I'm sure they thanked their various versions of God. Or *should* have thanked Him.

RP: Wait a minute. Are you telling me the Dusk Curse was *real*?

TJ: What everybody *thought* was "the Dusk Curse" was only a side-effect, essentially. The truth of it, the full phenomenon, is what I promised Lily to tell about you today.

SUPPLEMENTARY NOTES: THE "DUSK CURSE"

TAMAR DUSK
From Wikipedia, the free encyclopedia

The "Dusk Curse" [edit]

Following public backlash after Dusk's testimony before <u>HUAC</u>, rumors about the existence of a "Dusk curse" began to circulate among film crew who had worked on Ryback's productions with Dusk. Much like the "<u>*Exorcist*</u> curse"[14] or "<u>*Poltergeist*</u> curse"[15] of later decades, where a statistically unusual concentration of on-set misfortunes were attributed to supernatural influence supposedly arising from the subject matter of the films, any accident or disruptive event was retroactively blamed on Dusk's presence, even on days where she had not been on set. However, film researchers during the 1960s documented and verified a number of statistical oddities in the history of Dusk's productions[16]:

> • Incidence of <u>suicides</u> among on-set crew, averaged over the body of Dusk's work, was approximately 25% higher than normal (the median range).

- Reports of <u>violent behavior</u> and assault on the part of crew members were nearly 50% higher than normal.

- Incidence of <u>divorces</u> among on-set crew was approximately 40% higher than normal, with an exceptional pattern—over 75% of proceedings were initiated by the male partner.

- The number of on-set crew who later went into therapy for significant psychological problems, ranging from <u>major depressive disorder</u> to <u>drug addiction</u> and <u>antisocial personality breakdown</u>, was approximately 30% higher than normal.

Skeptics have explained this discrepancy by noting Ryback's production company was known for saving money via deliberately waiving industry hiring standards, something for which Ryback faced several union sanctions in his career.[17] It is also true that despite the supposed danger of Dusk's presence on set, very few staff ever resigned from a Ryback production once principal photography had begun; the statistical patterns observed above did *not* hold true for anyone actually performing on camera during the production, whether they shared scenes with Dusk or not. Nonetheless, rumors of a "Dusk curse" have continued to circulate ever since filming wrapped on Dusk's first major role and persist to this day.

Transcript torcdusk.mp3 *continued:*

RP: You say it was a side-effect? A side-effect of what?

TJ: Tamar didn't have a word for it. If I had to come up with the kind of term you'd use on your website, Mr. Puget, I'd probably call it "psychosynthesis" or something like that. But even that's misleading, because it suggests that what was happening was natural for her. It wasn't.

RP: What are you talking about?

TJ: The effect she had on other people, and the effect that... other people, their attention, their... worship... had on her.

RP: Okay. Which was?

TJ: (SIGHS) That what they wanted from her inevitably ended up making her into something else, something which would fill a very particular hunger. Something... inhuman. (PAUSE) Less so in person, or so she said; if she'd only been a theatrical actress, then perhaps the effect might have—scattered amongst the crowd she evoked it from, somehow. Dissipated. What really changed things, however, was the camera's lens, the camera's *eye*. The camera's ability to fix her image as a sort of... moving idol to be played and replayed at will, as a literal object of worship.

RP: Worship. For who?

TJ: Her fans, of course, and the filmmakers who fed them. People like Ryback, like Quent—though I don't think Quent really knew what she was cooperating with, whereas Ryback knew *exactly* what he was doing. (ANOTHER PAUSE) People like them... or like me.

RP: And—I'm sorry, I'm lost. *How* did you know about all this, again?

TJ: Tamar told me, of course. (BEAT) Ah, I've buried the lede... that's the term, yes? Lily's grandmother always told me I couldn't ever keep to the point of a story. (ANOTHER BEAT) Give me a moment, please; I'll show you the proofs I was saving for the end. When I finally got Quent to agree to a set visit, I went out and bought myself a Polaroid camera. I was hoping for some shots of myself and Tamar, of course, but I was genuinely fascinated by everything else, too. You said you'd seen *The Torc*; you should recognize a number of the faces.

RP: Wow. There's Quent—holy crap, he looks young. This guy played the lead, right?

TJ: Steven Paulson, yes. And Bill Walker, he played the villain, the would-be modern-day Druid—"busiest actor in Canada," they used to call him, for a while. That's Claudette Beecroft, the love interest. This was the day we filmed in High Park. Look at the skyline.

RP: No CN Tower, Jesus. So weird. Wait, is that—?

TJ: Yes. That's her.

RP: Are you sure? I'm sorry, it's just—she looked a lot younger in the film.

TJ: I took that shot when she arrived, at the start of the evening's shooting. I was lucky enough to catch her again when she left, later that night. Let me find it. Here—there she is, getting into her town car.

RP: (PAUSE) I don't understand. Didn't she bother taking her makeup off?

TJ: That's what everybody assumed. But I was the principal investor; I got to look at the budget, their production schedule. There were two American films shooting in town, and they'd already gone through five D.O.P.s—directors of photography. People just kept quitting, jumping ship. They had one makeup assistant, plus barely enough money to cover basic blood effects. Nowhere near enough time, or skill, to shave forty years off someone's face, not even for the ostensible star.

RP: What are you saying?

TJ: I'm saying that when Oleg knocked my camera off a table and broke it next time I visited the set, it wasn't an accident, and we both knew it wasn't an accident. Which was why I didn't bother buying another one.

RP: Did Quent know?

TJ: Honestly, I don't know what Quent knew or didn't. Or when he figured it out for himself, if he did; he had his own problems, lots of them. Re-writing the script every night, for one. Feeding Tamar her lines from behind the camera. But I watched and I learned, and one evening I came by when both he and Oleg were away, just in time to overhear one of the P.A.s saying Ms. Dusk's dinner had arrived. I jumped in and said I'd take it to her in her trailer, and nobody saw anything wrong with that. I remember that when I lifted my hand to knock on her door, I could actually see it shaking... my God. I'm shaking now. She looked up when the door opened. She smiled at me. I don't think anyone else in my entire life smiled at me the way Tamar did, not even my wife on our wedding day. Does that sound terrible? It should. I expected her to be different, in person. But she wasn't. She wasn't different, at all. Things... bent, around her. All the light in the room went in her direction. Like a halo. But her eyes... her eyes. So dark. I don't... I can't possibly...

RP: (AFTER A MOMENT) Doc?

TJ: Yes. I'm sorry. I served her, like a waiter. She told me to sit down. Took a bite, chewed it, swallowed. Then she looked back up, and said, in that husky voice, "You know, don't you?"

RP: Know what?

TJ: That's what I asked. She just shook her head and sighed. Said something like, "No, it's better that way. Even suspecting protects you for a little while as acting out the story protects me, and them—the other performers. The flow only ever goes one way, Nikolai told me; those who feed can't be fed upon." I asked, "Nicholas Ryback, you mean?" and she said, "Yes." Was that why she'd only ever worked with him? And at this she actually laughed, and I would have felt stupid, except by then I had no room left to think of myself. She laughed again and said, "He knew before I did. They were the ones who told me where I come from, what I was... Nikolai and the little secret church he belonged to, back in Los Angeles. That city is full of cults, always, like Rome before the fall. All the names they gave me—*nocnitca, gorska majka, plachky, mrake.* They told me what I would become, what they *wanted* me to become, but Nikolai only went along with it so far. He knew a good thing when he saw it, after all; he had plans for me, for himself. So, he taught me how to use the movies to stave it off, slow it down. Suspend it, perhaps, even for good."

RP: ... what?

TJ: I think you heard me, Mr. Puget.

SUPPLEMENTARY NOTES: TERMINOLOGY

(from the Freihoeven Institute files, compiled and written by Dr. Guilden Abbott)

Nocnitca (Polish), *Gorska Majka* (Bulgarian), *Plachky* or *Kricksy-Plaksy* (Slavic), *Mrake* (Croatian)—the night flyer, night moth, night hag, night maiden. All versions of this archetype seem to trace back to the phenomenon known as night terrors, the *Mara* or night-Mare, an apparent confusion in the hypnagogic stage of pre-R.E.M. sleep, during which the conscious mind snaps awake but the body remains functionally paralyzed. Very specific hallucinations will then ensue, along with a literally pressing sense of dread, anxiety and immediate physical danger. Sufferers often speak of a dark figure standing over them, a woman who trails her long hair down their bodies, a beautiful but faceless figure whose appearance shifts from attractiveness to awfulness almost at random.

Sometimes, in its "night moth" form, the *Mara* is seen to hover above the sleeper, borne on filmy, insectile wings which also appear spun from her own hair. At other times, it crawls on the floor like a caterpillar or larva, rising to suck at the sleeper's face with a circular mouth full of lamprey-esque teeth. Sometimes, in its "night flyer" form, the *Mara* unfurls itself ritualistically from a standing cocoon whose outer skin is often described either as stiff and peeling, much like the bandages of an Egyptian mummy, or soft and folded in on itself, yet knotted at the top, like an Elizabethan-era burial shroud. In this last form her face is "blank as the moon yet set with two great black jewels for eyes, its expression impossible to read and her hair a glittering swarm about her, floating in every direction like a mist." (Hélas Manzynski, *Grandmother's Tales* [Hope & Gershwin, 1922], translated by Morden Jegado.)

Theosophically speaking, the moth is both a psychopomp and a symbol of the soul. Similarly, just as the moth was once said to subsist on tears sipped from the corners of sleeping nightmare-sufferers' eyes, the *Mara* is said to both siphon off and inspire its victim's dreams. A secondary stream of mythology suggests that— night terrors aside—these dreams can't possibly be entirely nightmarish, since the point of the exercise is to keep the sufferer as much asleep as possible while still allowing the *Mara* to conjure the emotions she supposedly feeds upon. This clearly seems to align the *Mara* with stories of incubi and succubi, first found in Roman tradition—male and female daimons who lie full-length upon sleepers of the opposite sex, arousing them with fantasies of passionate activity, then sucking out the resultant yin/yang energy. Repeated visits from an incubus or succubus will eventually bring about deterioration of the sleeper's health and mental state, or even death; in *The Hammer of Witches*, Medieval tales have been collected which imply these creatures can shift form from male to female at will and vice versa, sucking sperm from male victims in order to impregnate female victims with parasitic phantom babies.

In some tales, the *Nocnitca* is known to visit when one sleeps on one's back, hands folded on the chest (a position allegedly called "sleeping with the dead"). According to some folklore, night hags are made of shadow, may also have a horrible screeching voice, and might allegedly also smell of the moss and dirt from her forest of origin. Finally, a stone with a hole in its center is said to be protection from the *Nocnitca*, since she can only be glimpsed while awake by looking through such a lens or frame. Otherwise, she will remain perfectly invisible, subsumed into the body of her unlucky mortal host.

RP: So... Nick Ryback was in a cult. A Hollywood cult.

TJ: So, Tamar Dusk said.

RP: I mean—there's a lot of those, right? Tom Cruise, that kind of—

TJ: Oh, you're thinking of Scientology? Nothing that recent. I think she meant older things, odder things. And as to whether or not Ryback was *in* the cult or simply associated with them somehow, well—I think he had been, yes. That he might even have been looking for someone like her, for them. But when he found her, I think things must have changed for him. I can't see how they wouldn't have. At any rate, when I asked Tamar what she meant, her face went through a... transfiguration, is the only word. All her mouth did was turn down the slightest degree, and suddenly I had to fight to keep from sobbing, even though her own eyes were absolutely dry. And she said, so quietly I could barely hear her, "I am a person, still, you know. Like anyone else. I want to live, to love—but it is hard, so hard, to do either. And when an alternative is offered, no matter how deeply you may suspect it is might be a mistake, you *have* to try. You cannot... not." And then it was as if she'd woken up, and she looked at me and said, "You are Oleg's friend, the dentist. The one with the money." And I said yes, I was, and she leaned forward and grabbed my hands—I literally lost the ability to breathe—and she said, "If you love me, take the money away. Stop paying for this. If they cannot pay the crew, they cannot finish." And I said I'd given my word, and she said, "It is not you who will pay the price for keeping it. I beg you. Go." And then her expression changed again, and her voice got deeper. And her hands were moving in mine. And—somehow, I don't know how—she was suddenly speaking perfect Polish, with the accent of my parents. And she said, "If you need another reason, I can... encourage you." And she was leaning towards me, closing her eyes, and I was closing mine, and— I don't know what would have happened if the P.A. hadn't knocked on the trailer door right that second. Logically, why would I have been in danger, after all? She had just begged me in sheer desperation to do something only I could do. Doing anything that might... damage me... would have made no sense, and yet. I got the feeling that she was not entirely in control of herself, in those last moments. That something, some—instinct—had taken her over. And when the P.A.'s knock broke that trance, I don't even remember fleeing. I only remember finding myself in my own car, shuddering and gasping, like I'd climbed out of a bath of ice.

RP: Jesus.

TJ: (PAUSE) The next day, I called Oleg. I told him I was pulling my funding. That he was no longer welcome as a patient at my practice. Well, he was extremely unhappy and made some unpleasant suggestions about how he could change my mind, until I pointed out that I'd been his dentist for a year and a half and could make sure the police learned everything they'd need to know to find him, right down to his Social Insurance Number, his birth certificate, and his dental records. And that was the end of my involvement with *The Torc*, the last time I ever saw any of them in person.

RP: But it didn't work. The movie came out anyway.

TJ: (DEEP SIGH) I know. I went to see it; I was one of the few who did, in its very brief and limited run. Somehow, Quent had found just enough resources to produce that final sequence, along with whatever interstitial material he needed to fill in the gaps to his satisfaction. I suspect he did most of the final photography himself.

RP: What makes you say that?

TJ: Well, it's pure speculation, at this point. But... in epidemiology, the term "natural immunity" refers to people who are born with the antibodies to a particular disease already in their system. There are people who are tone-deaf, who literally can't hear the difference between music and noise; there are those who can't tell red from green, and those who can't see color at all. So, it has always seemed to me that if certain... influences existed, certain... methods of exchanging metaphysical energies, let's say—then some people would also be naturally insensitive to those, as well. Whatever... effect Tamar had on most around her would simply roll off them.

RP: You think Ryback might've been like that?

TJ: Oh, I don't know. I don't even know if what happened to him was related to Tamar at all; people do just get cancer. But if he was—and if Quent was another one—it would explain why Quent was able to finish the film without any... issues. Especially if he did everything himself.

RP: (PAUSE) But he couldn't have, could he? Not if *The Torc*'s final sequence wasn't shot until after you left the production. There's too much F/X work in that scene for it to be a solo job. Too many extras, for that matter—there's like, what, thirty, forty people in the glade, not including Tamar? No way Quent did the aging makeup on all of them himself. Or the lighting, for that night shoot. And Tamar herself, the perspective changes, the distortions, the way he makes her look, like, twelve feet tall near the end, that's not— Jesus. Oh, you're not—Doc, tell me you aren't serious.

TJ: Like I said, Mr. Puget, pure speculation. Still. I've been an amateur student of Canadian film for over forty years now; I've read dozens of articles about Niall Quent and seen all his interviews. He's not a man shy of talking about himself. Yet *The Torc* is one film he's never discussed in detail. He's never even said much about working with Tamar Dusk, beyond the usual rote phrases about what an honor it was, how wonderful a person she was, all that... bullshit. (PAUSE) If you play this for Lily, can you cut that out?

RP: No. Look, Doc, if what you're talking about really happened, how the hell could Quent—and Oleg, I guess—get away with it? Forty people dead or disappeared? I don't care how much money you throw at something; you can't cover that up!

TJ: Can't you? This was the early '70s, no cellphones, no Internet, no GPS satellites or surveillance drones. And when I stopped the funding, Quent and Oleg lost any obligation to report production expenses to anyone, let alone involve ACTRA or the CLC. If anything, I think about how *incredibly* easy it would be to find a few dozen young, hungry people on the streets of Toronto, people with no families or re-sources, desperate dreamers who'd do anything to be in an honest-to-God *movie*...People who wouldn't balk at being driven out to someplace in the Ontario backwoods, so long as they went together. Perhaps the buses were hired by Tamar's husband, a man who'd find it a lot easier to hide a few under-the-table payments than an official production investment he'd have to claim on his tax returns. A man who's since spent the rest of his life erasing as much record as he can of himself... *and* his wife. After all, Mr. Puget, consider how much strangeness you yourself have seen, in all the stages of your work. Your vocation, you said to me. Strangeness that others have reported, eyewitnesses with no evidence of madness, no reason to lie. Your Institute has photographs, videos, sound recordings—a veritable library of the stuff. Yet people, in general, *still do not believe.*

RP: (LONG PAUSE, THEN) Look. Ectoplasm and psychic decontamination is one thing—even death, when it happens. But there's a *body*. There are *records*. People *know*. You're telling me that over forty years ago, one of Canada's most respected filmmakers not only participated in an act of fucking mass human sacrifice to turn a retired B-list actress into some kind of pagan night goddess, but *filmed* it and *re-leased* it? As a goddam *feature-length movie?!*

TJ: Why not? Some secrets are far easier to keep than others, Mr. Puget. Some are so incredible people will simply laugh them off; others are terrible enough that no one *wants* to believe them, if given any choice at all. And some are so ghastly that by the time you are certain of them, they have already tainted you for good—drawn you in so deep you cannot betray them without being destroyed as a co-conspirator, a fellow monster. Tell me you haven't seen proof of this, not just yesterday but right now, in so very many places.

RP: (PAUSE) That's different.

TJ: Of course it is. But as I said, this is all just inference. Filling in the gaps. Like astronomers, spotting planets not by looking for the light, but for where the light disappears. By thinking not about what's *in* the film, but what's been cut from it. And why.

(LONG PAUSE)

RP: The film keeps right on playing, though, right? Canadian Content regs keep it in circulation, even if it only ever shows in the middle of the night. People keep on watching it, and... nothing happens.

TJ: Apparently.

RP: Why?

TJ: Maybe... you just had to be there, physically. No taint seems to have attached to her earlier films, after all, beyond a certain—very specific—sexual allure. But whatever her films did for Tamar, however the psychic attention of viewing them sustained her, I believe that stage of her... existence is over at last. Her husband lives in her presence, alone with whatever she's become; maybe it laps him in, keeps him forever asleep like Endymion, forever alive like Tithonus, frozen in a halo of dream. I don't know whether or not to envy him, really. If there's any danger left in her image, however, I think only lies whatever the viewer brings with them while viewing it.

RP: So... that's why you took down the picture outside your office suite, right? Because it was of her. A portrait, a film poster, something.

TJ: Yes. (PAUSE) She fought so hard to remain as human as she could, for as long as she could—even marrying a man for whom she felt nothing, thinking that would make them both safer. If there is anything left of who she was, I cannot think she is happy.

RP: How would you know?

TJ: Exactly.

[TRANSCRIPT ENDS]

SUPPLEMENTARY CORRESPONDENCE

DATE: January 9, 2019
TO: drgabbott@freihoeveninst.ca; ross.puget@freihoeveninst.ca
FROM: andrew.sorenaar@geography.utoronto.ca
RE: Geolocation request

Dear Dr. Abbott and Mr. Puget,

Apologies for the delay in responding; most of my grad students were away for the Christmas break. I'm sorry to say that we weren't able to find a single conclusive candidate location for the terrain images you provided—there simply wasn't enough detail in the shots. However, based on reviewing the vegetation visible in the frames, and factoring in the information you were able to provide about likely distances from the Toronto core and accessibility to motor vehicles, we were able to isolate three possible coordinate sets—and fortunately for you, they're all relatively close to one another, up in the Lake of the North district. With a good all-terrain vehicle, you should be able to visit all three in one or two days. GPS coordinates and map routes are attached. (If you do travel out to visit these coordinates, I advise caution; these locations are all very remote and emergency assistance would be very long in coming.)

Hoping this information is of use to you,
Dr. Andrew Sorenaar
University of Toronto, Faculty of Geography & Planning

FROM A NOTE FOUND IN THE EMPTY HOUSE OF DR T. JANKIEWICZ:

Dear Mr. Puget, Lily, and Dr. Abbott:

Though it perhaps goes without saying, let me nevertheless make things clear: I apologize for misleading you all. As you noted during our interview, I had removed one of the lobby cards made for *The Torc*'s initial screening from a display on my wall—a cut frame from the film's climax, the ritual conducted at "druidic altar" supposedly located just outside the rather literally-named fictional small town of Night Worship, Ontario. You will no doubt recognize it as one of the geolocations Lily showed me, as part of our own final conversation.

The fact is that even after withdrawing my money from Oleg and Quent, I made sure to continue paying certain lesser crew members to keep me informed on all aspects of *The Torc*'s production, including location scouting. As you will no doubt have figured out by now, the particular site where the climax was filmed is located on what Overdeere residents refer to as "the Dourvale shore," near the location of the Sidderstane family's original canning facility. It was chosen because of the central feature, a gigantic root mass growing up through the ruins of the cannery's central hub, forming what appears to be a single massive altar fashioned from weathered stone and living wood. At the time the lobby-card picture was taken, the root system was covered in fungal growth of a type that Quent wasn't able to identify.

In the years since, I've tried to match the photograph to existing species and found that it most resembles a combination of two types of jelly fungus: "black witch's butter" and "yellow brain." Since these are most commonly found on either the dead branches of deciduous trees or living hardwoods, you wouldn't normally expect to find them on a living root system, even one as ... exotic ... as this one. Looking closely, however, you'll see that the gelatinous mass darkened gilding the roots spreading outwards from the "altar" very clearly contains sprinkled blooms of orange-yellow, in distinctive fleshy outcrops. You can also see a clear layering of folded, lobed dark orange fruit-bodies underneath both types of fresh "butter," indicating that the growth has been flourishing and dying off cyclically for some time. It's an amazing effect, and I remember the location scout describing Quent's clear pleasure at having discovered it. The only thing they had to do in order to "dress" it before shooting was to add candles and dishes of spirit, which were set alight to provide ambience during the climactic sequence.

Near the end of our interview, after you had already turned off your recording equipment, I made sure to suggest that this altar must have been an improvised construction of black yarn and hastily painted Styrofoam. The geographic experts you consulted would therefore have searched, assuming it to be no longer there, which is why all three of their possible candidate sites could not fail to be wrong. By the time you read this, you will have visited them all and found nothing, while I will have gone straight to the correct site.

I leave you the lobby card, since you evinced a clear interest in it.

I don't know why I assume whatever has become of Tamar might still be there. I do not know what I will find at the site, nor whether what I find will be what *you* might have found, had I allowed you, Lily, and your Dr. Abbott to go there as planned. One way or the other, however, I believe, perhaps selfishly, that I am doing you all a favor—Lily, most specifically. I certainly know I am probably doing myself one.

To die without seeing her again, you see, at least once... would have been— anti-climactic. To say the very least.

I remain, yours truly,

Tadeusz Jankiewicz, DDS

P.S. Lily, my sweet girl, I am so sorry. Please believe that I did not mean to betray your trust. It is only that my interactions with Mr. Puget reawakened an old addiction inside me, and when I saw a way to indulge it, I took it. I love you, child, as I loved your grandmother and mother. I will miss you always. Goodbye.

Sleep Hygiene

$\mathcal{S}$HUT YOUR EYES, let your breathing slow. Then follow the map, from any direction, and you will find you are there now, in that place—*your* place. Look to the horizon; something is coming.

A short list of things you may do when it comes:

Cry.

Scream.

Flinch.

Shut your eyes again.

Find yourself unable to shut your eyes.

Find yourself short of breath, or unable to breathe entirely.

Hear your own heart in your ears.

Hear absolutely nothing.

See absolutely nothing.

Feel your face go blank.

Feel your mind go blank.

Watch everything cloud over, then go black.

Find yourself elsewhere, discovering you've lost time.

Think: "I must have fainted." Have no proof this is true. Have no proof otherwise.

Wake up. Fall asleep once more. Dream. Lose yourself. Wake up. Repeat.

Repeat, repeat, repeat...

...until, one night, you never wake up again.

"I need you to make a map of whatever landscape you find yourself in, next time you're there," Gracie Hollander told me, to which I frowned; "Keep a dream diary, you mean," I replied. But she just shook her head.

"No, I don't," she said. "I mean—do that too, obviously. But this is something different."

It was only our second consultation, officially. My regular GP had recommended her to me, after I finally admitted I'd gone a month and a half without sleeping more than a third or quarter of the night: fallen asleep at three, or four, or five, always knowing I'd have to be up again before eight. Sometimes I'd steal a nap in the afternoon, then pay for it—get the bulk of my day's work done between seven and eleven, feel mounting fatigue suddenly permeate me like a drug injection and brown the fuck out, sleep from noon to two before waking again with groggy surprise to my iPhone's warbling alarm tone, mouth gummed and cheek sheet-printed, hair sweat-stuck up in horns. And when midnight finally rolled around, I'd start the cycle all over again: take a bath, brush my teeth, lie down whether I wanted to or not and force myself to keep my eyes damn well shut while I took long, slow breaths through the nose, willing my monkey-mind silent: *let go, let go, let GO.* Could count on one hand the times that worked, as a strategy, but it didn't ever seem to stop me trying.

At least I live alone, I often caught myself thinking. *Nobody but myself to inconvenience with this sad, stupid shit.* Still, this was no sort of comfort at all, in the long run; the way I lived—endured, existed—probably wasn't that different from the way anyone else around me did, except for the fact that they might be dealing with it better. Because loneliness is this century's true disease, with every other problem just a symptom of the same.

Anyhow. My doctor had told me I couldn't go on much longer this way without damaging myself irreparably, and I agreed, having no other option. So off to Gracie I was sent, for lessons in what her employers at the Sleep Habits Clinic apparently called sleep hygiene.

"Think of sleep as a destination," she said, sketching free-hand with a soft charcoal pencil on the paper she'd placed between us, after already ticking off the usual checklist of pro-somnolence habits to cultivate: don't eat after six PM, drink nothing caffeinated, start a wind-down routine that involved turning off all my devices, taking a bath, making sure my bedroom was light-tight. "A place, securely located in time and space, with fixed coordinates. Like if you could only find your way back there twice in a row, you could re-trace your steps the same way forever, and never get lost again."

"Program it into my mental GPS," I suggested, not actually trying to be facetious. But she shot me a pointed glance, so I fell silent.

The resultant map was divided into quarters and the path she drew meandered through all four in roughly circular fashion, spiral-form, like the world's easiest-to-beat maze. The terrain itself was intentionally generic—upside-down Vs for mountains, looping scribbles for forests, a dashed white space for grasslands with wandering lines for rivers, a tiny shaded-in lake and a wooded island in the middle—but came out with a weird vividness, nonetheless; either Gracie was a born artist, or she'd done this so often she had it down to a skill, an idea I found somewhat troubling.

I was no stranger to the concept of lending supposedly important tasks only a portion of my full attention, after all. Though that was less a choice on my part, by this time, than a simple necessity: the only way I knew of to preserve what was left of my mind as the wall between waking and sleep grew ever more flexible, bulging darkly with the shadows of things that might lie beyond and stretching my life out recklessly around the damage that left behind, like some slow-forming, paratemporal bruise...

"...based mine on Strawberry Island, up in Lake Simcoe," Gracie said, indicating the central island with her eraser, as I belatedly forced myself to focus in on her voice once more, recalled to myself from yet another one of those increasingly-too-frequent microsleep episodes, apparently by the sharpening ring of her tone alone. "I used to go there as a kid so it's extra-easy to summon, a great little anchor. You might want to use someplace closer, a point on the Toronto Islands maybe, or whatever works for you—the key is, it has to be a location that's an overall *pleasant* memory, yet has some clear element of separation from your normal life. What kind of places do you normally dream about?"

I shrugged. "Honestly, I don't remember. When I sleep at all, I'm *out*—completely inert. Maybe I don't see anything."

"Unlikely. You'd have other symptoms, if you really didn't dream." Gracie tapped her pencil against her teeth. "Can you remember faces?"

"What? Yeah, sure. Of course."

"Okay, good, then your brain probably isn't damaged." *Probably?* I furrowed my brow at her as she went on. "True complete dream loss is associated with focal, acute-onset cerebral harm—hemorrhage, thrombosis, trauma. Charcot-Wilbrand syndrome, specifically characterized by visual agnosia and loss of ability to mentally recall or 'revisualize' images: face-blindness, in other words, which can be triggered by lesions in the parietal lobe or the right fusiform gyrus. What you have sounds more like being so tired overall you just forget your dreams as soon as you wake up, which is a far better deal, because we can fix that."

"...how?"

"Oh, by using memory tricks to build you a personal dreamland, one worth the exploration; the more attractive we make sleep as a process, the longer you'll want to spent there, so we make it into a reward, not a chore." She gave me a smile. "I know it sounds like mumbo-jumbo, but trust me, it really does work—so long as you don't use skepticism as an excuse to be half-assed about it."

"I have no plans in that direction," I said, dryly.

"Excellent." She scribbled something on her prescription pad. "I'm also prescribing a drug regimen, short but sweet, just to help kick things off—a mild sedative combined with a *very* mild hallucinogen, so you won't have to work too hard. Stop by the pharmacy on your way out."

Me being who I am—born and raised in a paved-over former Paradise turned current parking lot—I opted to make my own dream map strictly urban, not rural. I picked the quarters of Toronto I knew best, then strung them along a mental subway-loop, from least to most interesting: Rosedale, the Yonge-Dundas downtown core, Distillery District, Queen West Village, the Annex. A favorite used bookstore became my anchor-point, the end of my quest; it was the place I felt most relaxed and comfortable in real life, so why not? Good as any other.

Remember, this was all theoretical at this point. Remember, too, how I didn't really expect that to change anytime soon.

Gracie studied my map for a moment, frowning slightly. "You may not end up where you want to, following this," she told me at last. I shrugged again.

"I'm not sure I expect to end up anywhere, to tell the complete truth," I replied. To which she eventually quirked an eyebrow and smiled.

"We'll see," she said.

That night, I lay down after taking my first pill (one nightly and no more, thirty minutes before bed, absolutely *no* mixing with alcohol) and shut my eyes, expecting nothing but the usual: a shallow handful of hours spent knotted in on myself, teeth grinding, hands fisted. Light leaking in from outside, gradually bleaching my eyelid-darkness red. Morning's familiar despair.

Before Gracie, my idea of "good sleep" had been simple darkness at worst, nothing at best—a glitch, a blink, lost time. Followed, if God was good, by a refreshing sense of physical renewal: laxness without lassitude, no aches or pains, no hangover. I had some vague idea that once upon a time, long ago in distant childhood, I'd almost always woken up happy, sharp, ready to jump up and get at it, whatever it might be. That had once been my *natural state*: the rule, not the exception. But it seemed so frankly impossible these days, I barely spared the matter a thought anymore. Just composed myself yet again, ready to suffer.

Instead, without any clear sense of how it even might have happened, I found myself abruptly... elsewhere.

People I'd overheard talking about their dreams always claimed they couldn't tell they'd been having one half the time, except in hindsight. Interactions with dead relatives, talking animals and singing flowers, surreal landscapes, ordinary objects suddenly converted to starkly awesome fear-totems, flying while falling, falling while flying—it all just got taken in stride, somehow; the abnormal, normalized. Some put it down to simple neurology, a side effect of their brain's effort to protect itself proactively against a wholesale invasion of the uncanny, installing filters, building walls. The mental flinch before the equally mental bruise, improvably skull-shrouded, invisible even on MRI or x-ray.

Whatever you see behind your shut lids must still come from you, *though, right? I mean, where else? And that's why it always seems so familiar, even when it's anything but.*

Suddenly snapping conscious—or seeming to—and finding myself foot-sore yet upright, Achilles tendon stretched out and calves trembling slightly, wavering heavy-ankled in the center of an open, roughly circular, eerily quiet block of wilderness: thick grass, scattered trees (elm, birch, maple), hummocks, hills and ivy-draped cliffs. Nothing unnatural, literally, yet all of it strangely regular, as though laid out on a grid. All of it with a very slight touch of design.

Above, the sky hung striated, red and green and gray. The air smelled of ash, furze underfoot coarse as hair, dew-greasy. I wasn't wearing any shoes in the dream, so when I stepped forward, I felt something hidden jut up under my toes—hard, uneven. The submerged cobbles of a long-dead street thrust apart by dirt and overlaid with mulch, then furred over by crop after fallow crop of wind-blown seeds.

Peering around, eyes narrowed, feeling the sun on my face, the wind at my back, a fresh cool breeze with the mounting chill of deeper shadow barely hidden underneath. And thinking, while I did: *I know* this place, *though I very palpably do* not *know this place, not in any way, shape or form... feel deep in my soul that I've been here before, even as I know for a fact that I've never been here at all.*

Ridiculous. No one had ever been there, I realized later, back in the waking world. Because that place didn't exist, had never existed. I was—

—almost sure.

Some people claim they can make themselves wake up the moment they understand they must be dreaming, but I hadn't been aware of my nighttime explorations long enough to learn *that* trick. The only viable alternative plan, I decided, was to pick a random direction and simply start walking until something stopped me, so that's exactly what I did: vaguely right, sort of diagonal, possibly south. I followed the dead road's corkscrew track wherever I found it, trying not to trip, as the cartoon sky roiled above me.

No insects. No animals. No human noises, however distant.

Eventually, after who knows how long, a particularly sharp turn snagged me, and I stumbled, almost going down on one knee; my hand met the largest chunk of cobblestone thus far palm-first, wetting itself with what I thought at first was blood until I wiped it on my pants—too dark, too shiny. Oily asphalt and gravel with a forked line of white paint scored down one side, like the broken pieces of roadway you see around every pothole in Toronto during the summer roadwork season. And with that, the whole scene snapped into... not focus exactly, but clarity, the picture hidden inside the illusion.

This *was* my city, it turned out. Or it had been.

That flat green square off to my right, great mounds of grass-covered rubble on every other side, intersected by waving, urine-colored stands and sprays of weeds: it was Yonge Street and Dundas, the junction, but reduced to long-empty wreck and ruin, digested by wilderness. I turned slowly in place, three hundred and sixty degrees, overlaying Toronto's downtown on top of this wasteland and seeing it match, point for point. Even then, I don't remember feeling horror, grief or any of the other things you'd expect. Simply a vague confusion. Senseless; no sense. Nonsense.

I only saw the temple once I'd completed my full circuit.

Set in the far corner of the flat sward that had once been Yonge-Dundas Square—and I was absolutely certain it hadn't been there when I'd first looked around—it appeared more like an amphitheater than anything else, a sunken cup surrounded by concentric walls with an empty space down in the middle. There was nothing like an altar: no signs or images, no icons, only a circular hole in the center like a beehive turned inside out. But by the time I was standing in it—

(*and when the hell had I done that? Walked over, stepped in? Why was I there now?*)

—the silence became even deeper: cathedral, funereal. A low gray hum. Cold air breathed from that black gap at my feet, whispering up the broken steps I saw spiraling down into it; discolored wine-vomit splotches ringed it, sunk deep into the stone, the stains round a dead drunk's mouth. And here I felt my stomach clench for the first time, coldly filling in with fear, or its dimmest echo. Thinking dully: *Please. Not down there.*

Of course, I went. Trudging down the steps into the cold, the black. Down and down and down, until I was too exhausted even to imagine turning around to climb back up. Which might well have been why I didn't scream when the stone vanished under my feet, when I fell face-first into the dark. Why I only screamed when I dimly began, at long last, to see exactly what I was falling *towards*...

...but here I lost it, memory falling from my mind to shatter like a dropped dish, as I jackknifed awake with hammering heart, burning eyes, and raw-rasping throat. I clenched my hands before me, pressed to my breastbone, gulping down air, hunched amid twisted, sodden sheets. The awful color of the light that had swelled around me—some horrid, poisonous shade of yellow-green lingered on my retinas like the after-flash of a strobe.

Thinking: *Something coming. Something is. Coming.*

(*What?*)

"Jesus," I croaked aloud, half-wanting to weep. Yet not able to, not then. Not now either.

Gracie was silent for more than a few seconds after I told her all this the next day.

"Well," she said at last. "Let's focus on the positive. Even with the interruption, you got a total of eight hours sleep last night, for the first time in... how long?"

"That was the *antithesis* of 'restful,' Gracie," I said flatly.

"Yes, but it's an amazing improvement for your first night. And it means we can write off the possibility of brain injury."

"Really? 'Cause if this is the cure, I think I'd rather have the damage." I leant forward, prodding the map between us with my finger. "I don't ever want to go back there, map or no map. I *won't*."

"Then you don't have to." Gracie held up her hands, palms out. "Don't like this map? Draw another." She shuffled it into a nearby file folder, grabbed her pad, and scribbled a few notes. "I'll tweak your 'scrip, too—we may not need the hallucinogen as much as I thought."

"That's it?" I demanded. "Aren't we supposed to, like, go over the dream? Figure out what it means?"

Gracie shrugged. "We could, if you want, but... honestly, that strikes me as a distraction." She closed the pad and leaned forward again, looking earnest. "Alex, I know this is difficult. But believe me, it'll all be worth it in the end."

I let out my breath in a sigh. "Fine," I said, picking up the sketchpad and another pencil, and turned to a blank page.

This time the map had been chronological rather than geographical: I'd sketched out all the houses I'd ever lived in, from a tiny apartment out in Brampton with my father through various Torontonian townhouses and converted, semi-detached units, to the current condo. When I shut my eyes and found myself standing in the marble-tiled lobby of my own building, I folded my arms—the mental semblance of them, anyhow—in deep satisfaction.

It was only when I passed by the open door of the building's coffee lounge that I caught a glimpse of grass with a tell-tale flash of stone hidden under it, heard the low gray sound of a hollow wind. The shock hit me in right in my stomach, like a punch; I actually wobbled on my feet, then turned and ran.

Maybe if I'd had more experience dreaming, I'd have known not to expect that tactic to work. Or maybe not—people do seem to keep on trying to extricate themselves from repetitive nightmares, however useless it always proves. One way or the other, the effort proved fruitless: after what felt like a quarter of an hour spent crossing the lobby, I hauled open the main double doors and staggered out, only to find myself right back onto that flat plain, which looked even wider this time, stretching from horizon to horizon like images of the prairies in winter. Yellowish-gray corn stalks, harvest's detritus, whipping in the wind; gangrene-colored clouds, racing by overhead.

I spun, and my building was gone. But the temple was there instead, of course, slap-bang in the middle of the flatland. Ring of gray stone, a black crater at its heart, cold air perceptibly welling up from the dark, the cup, the well. And the stairs, going down.

Oh God.

Don't know if I said it or thought it; didn't help, either way. Tried to run once more in the other direction, 'till I was gasping and dizzy, only to look up and find the temple back in front of me again. Tried yet one more time, closing my eyes, not stopping until I stumbled over that gap and nearly fell down the stairs, clinging to the side with both hands. At which point it frankly just didn't seem worth fighting any more.

Muscle memory led the way, unprompted and unwanted, as I tested each step with my feet, just barely able to pull back from the point where the stairs vanished, plastered against the stone wall as I stared down into the abyss; a tiny speck of light glimmered some unimaginable distance below me, the same nauseating yellow-green as before, gut-wrenching even at a distance. My grip was uncertain. The stone felt soapy under my fingers, slippery, as if fat-coated.

Far away, in the back of my head, I could almost hear a woman's voice singing some fragment of a plaintive miner's lament, Appalachian style: *I'm down... in a hole... I'm down... in a hole... I'm down ... in a deep, dark hole...*

I don't know how long I stood there, if that even means anything. All I remember is that sick, spine-shaking jerk of my foot slipping on the stone, shooting out from under me as I tried to the very last not to move, cold air burning my face as I fell. That ghastly light coming at me like a hammer, throat bursting with screams, as I finally saw what was in it: there, then gone, an empty space. A hole inside a hole inside a hole.

For all that forgetting should have been a good thing, surely, I shook awake feeling like I'd just witnessed a death foretold—my own, maybe. And knowing, now, *knowing...*

... there was no way on earth it wouldn't happen again.

Something's coming.

A week, then two; seven nights, fourteen, more. Eight hours a night, sometimes more, but when I looked in the mirror, all I saw was the blue-gray shadows under my eyes, steadily deepening. Hygienic as my sleep cycle might have seemed from the outside, I was still *tired*, to my very bones, in a way that only looked likely to get worse. I felt caught in a loop, a snare. I couldn't see my way out.

Before you ask, meanwhile: yes, I stopped taking the drug. I stopped taking the drug about five nights in. And no, it didn't help.

(I woke up in yet another field, in a ravine, in a crevasse. The first time I thought it was a hangover, prescription still making its way out my system. But there I was, following the crevasse along, tracing a trickle of muddy river, only to turn a sharp corner and find myself at the place where the temple's door should be, the very threshold. The very next night, meanwhile, I started off inside what looked to have been a parking garage, two floors below street-level, so I deliberately turned and went down instead of up, found a door, opened it—right into the temple's stairway, the grim, fading light, those steps leading down, down, down. Into the Well.

And yes, again: The name came to me there and then in the dream. I've never thought of it as anything else, since.)

"This shit is worse than homeopathy!" I complained to my GP, two and a half weeks in, not feeling like facing Gracie again; I was slumped back against the wall, still in my paper gown, too exhausted to stand. "I mean, at least that doesn't do *anything*; Gracie's map-drawing crap is actually making a bad situation *worse*."

She'd just given me an all-over exam, entering the initial results as she sat there nodding, one eyebrow cocked. "Not according to your numbers," was all she had to say in return, at last, angling the page towards me so I could see for myself, like she really thought that proved anything. The only good part of which, I guess, was that it at least made me mad enough to force myself back upright again.

"Yeah, okay," I managed, grabbing for my clothes. "But riddle me this: what do you really know about Gracie Hollander, anyhow—what can you *attest* to? Professionally?"

My GP thought that over. "Well," she said, at last, "I know her methods work."

"Always? For *everybody*?"

Like it was gospel: "Always."

"... better start working *soon*, then," I muttered, momentarily defused.

Sometimes, all I can think is that nobody believes in the assumed social contract between and doctor and patient quite as much as doctors themselves do. Which is good, I suppose; really, they sort of have to. Seeing how it's all that keeps them from abusing their authority 'till it bleeds.

So, yeah: I don't know whether I thought Gracie was mishandling my case deliberately, or what. By that point, frankly, I could have been thinking all sorts of crap. I *was*. On paper, physically, I was well-rested and firmly on my way to recovery, but my *mind* didn't feel that way at all. Even if that *was* happening with my body, provably, there's no way my mind believed it.

Three days on, though, I sat in Gracie's office once more, my own file open in front of me. I'd spread the sheaf of discarded maps out, then had the strange impulse to lay them overtop each other, stacking them clockwise; the paper was thin enough you could see them form what looked like one huge, circular chart.

"Like a whole other world," Gracie remarked, her tone oddly admiring. As she stared down, eyes never leaving the map-made-from-maps, studying its multiple-choice fan-shaped destiny of paths for all the world as though, on some level, she was beginning to recognize them.

Each route made a sliver of a quadrant, filling the whole thing in. I pointed to the result, and she studied it, eyes narrowing—because done this way, it seemed fairly undeniable how no matter where they might have begun, all roads did indeed lead to Rome: the fallow field, the temple, the hole. The Well.

"What made you choose to call it that, you think?" Gracie asked, gaze still held fast, doodling a series of unintelligible notes in her scratch-pad's margins.

"No idea," I replied. "But you do see it, right? The pattern?"

"I see what looks to *you* like a pattern, yes."

I snorted. "Then look again, goddamnit." Tapping the papers, as she did. "No matter where I start out, I always end up *there,* every time. Does that seem… normal, to you?"

She smiled, eyes crinkling adorably. Pointing out: "Normal's a fairly negotiable concept, Alex."

I shook my head sharply, neck sparking, impatience fierce as rage.

"No, but seriously: 'distraction' or not, why would I keep on *doing* that to myself? Why the temple, the Weh—the *hole*? Why those endless fucking stairs? All night, every night. What's the goddamn point of it all, exactly?"

She was frowning slightly now, pen still going a veritable mile a minute. "In dream language, the well is a very primal image," she allowed, at last. "Basic shorthand, the place where Jung and Freud meet; it can symbolize change under pressure, sometimes forcible, beyond your control. More shallowly, it could stand for anything which opens inwards: a mouth, a door, a grave… your own vagina, even…"

"Pretty sure it's not *that*," I snapped back, annoyed.

"… but my *point* is," she continued, overtop, as though I hadn't even spoken, "*most* people in general dream of wells, even repeatedly; it's not just you. A lot of my other clients do it, too."

"Wells or *well*?"

"I don't know what you mean by that, Alex."

I tapped the ream of paper between us. "Like, *this* well? That's what I mean. Do most of your other clients also dream of *this* well, maybe?"

"That's… ridiculous."

I could hear the words coming out of my mouth but didn't seem able to stop them; it was like I'd finally been pushed beyond my limits, so far my internal censor had popped a fuse. Like something inside me had simply burnt out, leaving me as naked in daylight as I felt during the dark, down the Well, clinging to my unreliable perch as I teetered in the bare instant before the fall. Forever hovering between fear of the unknown and whatever unknown thing I feared.

"Oh yeah, I'm sure," I snapped back, before adding, far too brightly: "But could I really trust you to tell me if they did?"

This is where my research phase would surely have started, if this was another sort of story—plunged myself into the Internet, found myself some sort of magic keyhole giving me access to other people's medical records. Where I would've waited until Gracie went home and broken into her office using my mad lock-picking skills, the ones I'd picked up osmotically by watching an ass-load of *CSI: Crime Scene Investigation* holiday marathon installments; where I would've been able to find exactly what I was looking for on the first try, just by glancing through her filing system. Some sort of paper trail or pixel trail. Some patient—or colleague—who'd bonded hard with Gracie, volunteered to prove her theories correct, then disappeared up her own repetitive dream cycle forever, leaving no forwarding address. Some Case Zero that would prove I was right in my frankly demented suspicions about Gracie's methodology, about the reasoning behind her continually pushing me to keep doing exactly what I'd been doing thus far, yet act as though I truly expected a different result, however many times I might have had to try before that happened, like some goddamn crazy person.

(Which I probably was, by now. True sleep-deprived, hallucinating... yeah, I can see it from the outside, the way I couldn't back then when I was in it neck-deep. The way no one ever can in similar situations.)

In hindsight, the only sort of sight I have to reckon by, this is what I realized I must have been looking for, afterwards. But no, that's not the way it went. Because when it comes to solving your own dreams' puzzle, the only investigative tool available to a person in my position is a willingness to do things personally, confrontationally; take a leap of faith, however potentially damning. Take the challenge between your mental teeth and run.

I went home, took a bath, lay down, closed my eyes. Let the nightmare enfold me yet one more time. Welcomed it with open arms.

Just lay down in the dark and let whatever was going to happen... happen.

Something is coming, the voice whispered once more under that cold wind, but the Well itself didn't move, ever. Remained the fulcrum, the still point at the center of this otherwise fluid world. And: *Am I the thing that's coming, then?* I wondered, before finally relinquishing that last step—plunging downwards into darkness, voluntarily, for once. *Was that always* me?

Only one way to find out.

The green light came at me bullet-fast this time, as I felt a wrench that cracked my whole dream's spine. Felt things around me splinter, split and branch, cracks extending fractally in every possible direction, like roots from some invisible tree. They reached upwards, spiking into the shimmering shadows of what seemed like a hundred brains at once, scattered country-wide, yet all asleep and dreaming the same dream; a hundred other sleepers, presumably linked by Gracie's therapy and/or prescriptions, all making their slow way across a hundred different landscapes towards the exact same destination. Not a habit, not a chore: a ritual pilgrimage, infinitely shared, bleak and black though it might be. A method of worship.

Around me, the Well flipped itself front to back to inside-out, becoming a tower—a beacon. Descent into ascent, stairs down into stairs up, though still hammered haphazardly together from the same crumbling, greasy stone, each cobble a puzzle-piece only lightly intertwined, a relic from some age before mortar. And at the top—

—at the top, laid open to that glaring, gangrene-colored sky whose stars were nothing like the stars we see from Earth, someone waited.

(Who?)

I didn't know their name, even now, even here. I never expected to. But... I knew that voice.

(*... in a hole... I'm down... in a deep, dark hole.*)

Cast herself down the Well, just like me, I thought, not knowing why. Then: *Just like me, oh God, oh God. Oh, Jesus fucking* God.

(*Just like me.*)

And here it spoke, that same too-familiar voice, skull-resonant even masked under the Well's low gray din. The ruin-echoed blood-slosh of some long-dead ocean, on some long-empty world.

Gracie? It asked, apparently to the empty air. *Is that you? Did you come back for me... to find me? Has this been long enough?*

I drew you a map, but I went too far. I lost it.

Can I finally come home?

Oh, what the hell.

I swallowed, hard enough something seemed to scrape, suddenly dry from lips to esophagus. My tongue felt numb, stinging. "I'm not Gracie," I told it, finally, wincing at how weak my voice sounded in that unhallowed place.

As I spoke, the person—more a thing, really; greenish-black on greenish-purple-red, more an absence where someone once used to be, an echo, rather than the person themselves—shifted its attention onto me fully or appeared to. Stood watching me from afar but not quite far enough. And though I couldn't see its eyes, not even at that distance, I *knew*, somehow... it recognized me.

Could almost feel the words graze me all over like snakeskin or a poison tongue: a lack of voice, almost too alien to organize itself into words. Yet hearing them nonetheless, if only in some highly primitive way—tasting, *smelling* their most basic meaning, borne on a burnt-skin stink-wave. Reading them out loud and translating from a foreign language, even as they carved themselves, stroke by cauterized stroke, into my mind's soft meat.

Oh, oh yes. So, it's you, finally.

(At last.)

Did Gracie send you after me? It asked, after an aeon.

"Not... as such."

Then why are you here? How did you—?

I shrugged, helpless.

"I don't know," was all I could say.

We stood there a minute more—several, crawling like fossils, like erosion, shale tectonically crushed against shale. All the slowest moments of the earth.

I was someone before I got here, the thing told me, almost sadly. *Now I'm something else. No one can stay who they are here, not for long.*

I nodded, trying not to breathe. Not that it seemed to need my agreement, exactly.

If I let you leave, it began again, slyly, *will you go see her, Gracie, when you—wake up? Will you tell her what you found?*

If? Jesus Christ. My stomach clenched against the very idea, knotted itself off like a bag, burning bile. But I wouldn't let the implications faze me, not for long. I couldn't.

"If you do, then... yes," I replied, carefully.

Of course I will. No sense not. Neither of us get what we want if I don't.

I agreed, not trusting my words any longer, in silent dumb show bowed my head, spread my hands. Pinched a helpless smile and felt—rather than saw—it, bare broken teeth at the spectacle, half amused but all angry, colder than death and twice as raw.

Thank me for that, Alex, it suggested.

"... thank you."

Tell her I want *to go home, but I don't know the way. Tell her... I need a map.* The map.

I nodded. "The one you drew. Right?"

No. The one she *drew for me. She knows which.*

"All right."

Be very sure to tell her, Alex. Or we'll see each other again.

Another clutch, body-wide this time, running me like a gamut from top to toe. I had to wait just a few more beats to have any hope of self-control, let alone avoid dying of sheer, existential terror before I got the chance to answer.

"I don't think either of us want that," I said at last. And felt the thing give something not at all like a laugh in return, resonant with the universe's anti-rotation, so awful on a cosmic level that simply acknowledging it risked madness.

Just the touch of that laugh killed something inside me, some capacity I hadn't known I had until then. But by that point, frankly, I was glad to feel it go.

When you ask me where Gracie Hollander can possibly have disappeared to, officers, you must therefore take the preceding as my very poor stab at an explanation. Or not. I'd absolutely understand if you didn't.

You tell me she had a partner once, long ago, and I nod. You tell me that partner helped her develop her methods, as well as the drug regimen that bolsters them. That this woman disappeared as well, years back, with similarly little trace left behind; it was as though she slid off the world's surface, slipped through a crack, to somewhere underneath. As if she'd tripped, unseen by anyone else in her life, and fallen down a deep, dark hole.

You say this, and I nod. No other response seems suitable; it all sounds extremely plausible indeed to me. But I don't have anything else to tell you, unfortunately, beyond what you've already heard. I simply can't remember.

I'm not capable of it.

I'm back to not dreaming at all, thank Christ, though I maintain the hygiene of my sleep habits zealously. Of course, the brain damage has a lot to do with the former, if not the latter. My GP thinks it might have been a series of small strokes brought on by stress in the wake of my insomnia. All I know is that since I woke that last time, I've basically been unable to picture anything visually inside my head at all; if I didn't have this document to remind me I'd once been able to, I'd be tempted to assume everyone around me is lying or joking whenever they claim they *can*. Not classic prosopagnosia per se, but I do have a lot of trouble telling one person from another, unless I use certain tricks—recognizing voices or knowing where people are likely to be at any given time or categorizing people by their accessories, their favorite t-shirts, the color of their hair, eyes, skin.

It sounds bad to say, for example, but because there are only so many black people I *know,* if somebody with dark skin comes up to me using my first name and acting like we're friends, I'll always give them the benefit of the doubt. I actually thought one of *you* might be a friend of mine when you first walked in, but by now I've certainly spoken with you long enough to understand I must have been mistaken. The minute you leave, however, my ability to remember you will go straight back down to zero. I'll reset like a bad alarm system, waiting for the next person to set me off.

The worst part is my family—they can't understand why I can't tell, say, my own mother from any other woman on the street, and I can't blame them for that. But there's nothing to be done, and by now, I'm used to it.

My nights are neither long nor dark anymore. They pass in a blink. I wake refreshed, remembering nothing. If something still lurks behind my eyes, dug deep into that interior landscape I can no longer map, then it's invisible to me—completely, utterly, safely so. I'll never see it coming.

I prefer it that way.

If you'd been where I have, you would too.

Always After Three

THE LAST TIME you lived alone was in another condominium, five blocks from where you and Kyle live now. One room and a kitchenette, bathroom attached—you slept in pretty much the same place you ate, if not exactly the place you performed every other bodily function. Ten years in the same apartment, and you barely ever remember passing your neighbors in the halls, let alone knowing any of their names. As far as you were concerned, they might as well not have existed.

That's how it always is, you eventually came to realize, here in the city's heart: you know nothing, and you're basically happy to, as if you think your own shell of semi-wilful ignorance protects you from having to worry about the bugs in the walls as opposed to the ones which occasionally crawl out of the drain, the man who might be slowly losing his mind behind that door across the way as opposed to the very obviously crazy guy who capers each morning on the corner of your street. Not to mention whether that cheerfully drunk lady in the unit to your right, who you see fumble with her keys every evening, will doze off one night with a lit cigarette in her hand and burn the whole fucking building down.

Best not to buy trouble, like old aunt Ida used to say, the one you were named after: don't look too close, don't question; you might not like the answer. There's always a story if you stop to listen, always a thread winding around things if you stoop down to look more closely, trailing off into the distance, ready for you to follow. Always a hand just waiting to take yours whenever you reach out in darkness, to grab on fast and hold on tight, never letting go. To yank you headlong out of your comfort zone and strand you somewhere else entirely, forever.

It's the same way here, too, of course. You walk by quickly with your eyes politely averted even as you check the corners for potential trouble, gaze carefully ever so slightly out of focus: see nothing, know nothing, business as usual. Until, one day...

... it isn't.

The night it starts, you find yourself snapping awake, nose wrinkling, thinking: *What the hell* is *that?* Beside you, Kyle's asleep and snoring; the clock on the bedside table says 3:04 a.m., then 3:05. The smell seems to come out of nowhere, pungent and penetrating, an invisible stranger's hot breath, right in your face. You can't immediately place *why* it's so disgusting, and yet.

Rotten mushrooms, you think, as you lever yourself up and bumble around in the streetlamp-lit half-dark, trying to figure out where it's coming from. *Asparagus piss, drunk psycho sweat, dead skunk.* Marijuana's legal in Canada now, especially for home consumption—there's two dispensaries within walking distance, one to the north, the other to the west, but this isn't that. You've smelled enough weed in your time to know that weed would be pleasant by comparison.

Granted, the apartment reeks in general these days, just like the rest of the building. Maybe half a year ago the condo board voted to renovate; this just happens to be the month they finally decided to strip and replace the old wallpaper, switch out the hall carpets, re-paint all the trim and every unit door. The stench of glue and paint i's so constant you barely even notice it anymore, which means this new smell must really be something.

"So, I search, and I search, and eventually I narrow it down," you tell Kyle in the morning. "Know where the worst of it was? The baby's room."

He frowns. "In it or coming through the wall?"

"The wall."

"That's unit #770, right?" You nod. "Okay, well—what do you want me to do about it? Talk to the concierge?"

You sigh. "Ugh, maybe not... I mean, it's gone *now*. Of fucking course."

"I'm sorry, hon."

"Not your fault."

He shoots you that same look he's been giving you almost every morning since you finally watched your usual weekly pregnancy test turn blue, the one that says: *You look like hell, Ida, how much sleep did you even get, exactly? Maybe that's all you really need.* Because while other people spend their first trimester battling morning sickness, what you've ended up with is more like morning, afternoon, and evening sickness cut with a lovely side order of insomnia: nauseated exhaustion during the day and a grinding inability to do much more but doze fitfully at night. You're not really showing yet, but your anxiety is up because you had to go off your meds the minute you made the decision to stay pregnant. And since Dr. Spring confirms there's no other real option but to stick it out, that's what you're doing—suck it up, smile, keep yourself occupied. Imitate a good attitude, if nothing else.

Maybe this isn't the greatest ever time to have a kid, either, given the state of the world—that avalanche of bad news you're trying your best to block out and mainly succeeding, especially since you deleted your Facebook app. But then again, when would it be? *Babies make their own luck,* your mother-in-law likes to say, comfortably; *guess we'll see,* you all too often find yourself thinking in return, trying to keep your breathing steady.

Shit like this truly doesn't help, though. For Christ's sake, you can't even drink coffee anymore.

Kyle's checking his phone now, swallowing the last of his oatmeal; you're holding him up, and you know it. "Oh man, gotta go. You sure it wasn't just the chemicals they're using outside, to strip the floors? The ones that melt the glue from the old carpet?"

"I kind of think I know what carpet-glue smells like, Kyle, at this point."

"All right, sure—so we'll wait, see if it happens again, all right? And then, we'll... figure something out. Okay?"

Nothing to do but nod, so you do, attempting some bad version of a smile. "Yeah, thanks for listening. Have a great day at work. Love you."

"You too."

So, you pull the blackout shades and fall back into bed, trying to block out the dueling noise of construction from the street and renovation from the hall while this oh-so-elaborate *process* going on inside your body sucks you down yet again, mind blanking by degrees, a wiped Etch-a-Sketch screen. Then it's evening, and Kyle i's home, enabling you gently through your routine: dinner, bath, pre-natal vitamins, TV, an hour or so of lying in bed with the lights down, hugging. He drifts off to sleep, you don't.

Eventually, it's just after three in the morning again, and... there it is, right on time, that smell, just as strong. Just as bad.

Worse.

You shake Kyle, who surfaces quickly (thank Christ), arms and legs flexing like he's ready for a fight: "Uh, um—I'm up, I'm here. Is it back?"

You gulp in a swallow of air, resisting the urge to spit. "*God,* yes."

He does the same, then grimaces. "Ugh, okay, I see what you mean. Jesus! Coming through in the same place?"

"I haven't looked yet. Maybe."

"All right, you stay here. Leave it to me."

You trail along behind him, all the same, as he heads over to what used to be "the nook," a catch-all office space next to the front door; you've walled it in and stuck that crib his parents gave you inside, ready for when the clutch of cells you're nurturing turns into a squishy larval human being viable enough to survive outside your womb. Once inside, he sticks his face as close to the wall as he can and takes a long, deep sniff. "I don't... no, it's not in here, not anymore. That's weird."

Of course, it isn't in here now, you think, but don't say. After all, he's up, isn't he? He's a good guy that way; believes you even when it sounds crazy, the way a thousand others wouldn't. Which alone makes him better than you, by far.

Don't say stuff like that, Ida, he'd reply, if you let it slip. *Unmedicated or not, you're my wife, right? Light of my life, mother of my child...*

Excuse me, our child.

Same difference.

Kyle follows his nose back out into the living room and makes a careful circuit, eventually homing in on the air conditioning vent above the television screen. "I never knew this connected with #770," he says. "But—yeah, this is where the smell's strongest, so it must. Take a whiff."

You swallow again, stomach rumbling. "Pass," you manage. "Is that enough to go downstairs?"

"One more night, maybe, or two—three at the most. We really do need a clear pattern if we're going to sell the building on doing something about it." As you groan: "Look, just sit down for now, okay? It'll be all right, I swear. I'll make you some ginger tea."

So it goes: always after three in the morning, and not exactly like clockwork— sometimes it's 3:08, sometimes 3:10, sometimes even as late as 3:18. But not *every* night in a row, annoyingly, and never after three-thirty. Once you twig to the pattern, however, it's impossible to un-see it; you find yourself sitting up rather than lying awake in the dark, waiting, head cocked like a pointer's. The smell ebbs and flows, sometimes higher, sometimes lower. Sometimes it comes through another wall entirely: the kitchen, the bathroom, down from the ceiling. The Saturday after you and Kyle start trying to keep a record it rises straight up like it's welling out of every inch of the floor, fresh roadkill-reeking until finally it converges with your condition, driving you headlong to retch your guts out into the toilet.

Kyle's still asleep when it starts, but even though he's previously managed to stay dormant through both fire alarms and fender benders, one thing you've always been able to count on is that he'll jolt upright at any hint of distress from you. So, he stumbles into the bathroom to hold your shoulders and wipe your face with a damp washcloth, and only after flushing away the aftermath does he finally notice what you've been dealing with. "Holy *shit*," he blurts, his whole face twisting. "That is freakin' *rancid!*"

"Uh huh," you mutter, light-headed. Your tongue feels bile-burnt.

"Okay, that's it. We're going downstairs now."

"Gimme a minute. Please."

He nods, but continues, like he just can't help himself: "I mean, *God*—any-body'd have a right to complain, and you're pregnant, for Christ's sake..." Here he trails off, though. "... is that music?"

You listen for a long moment, then shake your head, carefully. "Can't tell," you reply, at last.

Down at the front desk, the security guard looks sympathetic, but you get there really isn't much she can do, at least right now. "I can text the concierge," she offers, "but he'd probably tell you to just go back to bed. I know for a fact he isn't going to sign off on me calling the cops, not this late. Not over a smell and some music."

"I thought you had noise disturbance by-laws," Kyle says.

"They're more like standards. Besides, you said you didn't even really know where it's coming from."

"Either #766, #770 or #678, if it really is coming up through the floor. That's just logic, right?"

She shrugs, helpless. "Have you... spoken to any of the people in those units? Before this, I mean."

"Isn't that *your* job?"

"Um, not really? I'm just here to accept packages and patrol the halls, then note stuff down in my log so real people can deal with it, you know? I can't just go around banging on random people's doors, not in the middle of the night." She pauses. "Why don't you record it?"

"How the hell do you record a smell?" Kyle demands.

"No, I meant the music. It's loud, right? Loud enough to wake you up? Play it for the concierge. That might help."

More freaky than loud, but it's not a bad idea.

Having made this commitment, it only makes a sort of sense that three more days go by before anything worth recording actually seeps through the walls: first a low beat whose rhythm skips like a diseased heart's, more felt than heard, followed by strings run through a resonator so their notes bend and warp together (sawing, thrumming, skirling) and a vague suggestion of woodwinds underneath, breath-huffing. You're alone on the living room couch, waiting; Kyle manfully fought to stay up the first two nights with you, but his fatigue the next day got him a dressing-down from his manager, so you've closed the bedroom door on his heavy snores.

Right, left or hall? The stench seems to point you forward, towards the window and the street below, which is ridiculous, but you grab up your phone and fumble with it, nonetheless, triggering the recording app—then pause, realizing there's a *voice* woven in with the noise, now. Not quite singing, not quite chanting, but definitely human speech, if not any language you can recognize. Although...

Pressing both ear and phone to the wall, holding your breath to keep out the stink. If you could just hear a *bit* more clearly, then maybe you could figure out why there's a pause every minute or so—the voice repeating itself, chanting similar syllables with rising intensity. Angrier? More frustrated? You close your eyes and lean in, straining to make sense of it. Just repetition after repetition, a loop or round, some sort of experimental project gone wrong: John Cage by way of Yoko Ono, or one of those ten-hour-long white noise performance videos people post on YouTube.

Something coils inside of you, draws taut, seem to *squeeze*. Is that a kick? Too early, you'd think; last ultrasound showed the creature you sometimes (though only to yourself, in your head) refer to as "Ida Junior" flipping around like some transparent minnow, all head and tail, a bare sketch of potential humanity. But—

—here you fade out for a moment, then blink, forcing your eyes to focus; the phone's display says ten minutes've gone by, more than enough to be getting on with. So, you close out, save the sound-file, plug the phone back in to charge before curling up in the crook of Kyle's arm. Sleep comes down on you hard, all over, like turning off a light switch.

It's not 'til your phone's trilling ring drags you up out of the black that you realize just how tired you must have been; when you're able to get it to your ear and answer, it turns out to be Kyle, already waiting downstairs with the concierge, so you shove yourself into clothes and stumble out the door to join him. Halfway to the elevator, you look around and nearly fall, disoriented almost to the point of fresh nausea: where the fuck *are* you? You don't recognize anything. The doors have changed, the carpet's changed, the lights all have new shades...

Oh, right. The renovation. Fuck. You have to shut your eyes again and take a deepish, centering breath, trying not to choke on glue fumes.

In the concierge's office, Kyle recaps the situation while you open up your recording app, pressing play at his nod. For a second, nothing happens, sending a spike of cold through your gut—maybe you dreamed the whole thing, and the file contains only dead air. But no, thankfully: it's all there. Eerie, atonal music and unintelligible ranting fills the office while Kyle and the concierge sit bolt upright simultaneously, both looking poleaxed. "Holy Toledo," Kyle says, after a beat. "The singing's new."

"Sounds more like an argument to me, except there's only one voice. And it goes on for almost fifteen minutes," you tell them.

The concierge stares at the phone, finally shaking his head as if snapping awake. "Okay, enough—stop it, please." Takes a couple of tries, but eventually the racket falls silent. "And you've been hearing this every night?"

"Almost," Kyle corrects him. "And always after three. Right, Ida?" You nod. "First the smell, then the music. Now this."

The concierge's eyes narrow. "But you can't tie down the exact point of origin."

"Not really. It... seems to move."

"Well, *that* doesn't make any sense."

No, eh? you think, but don't say. Hearing the echo of that weird babble resonate through your head as though the file's still playing, that note of almost... pleading? Begging? All authority discarded in a moment, gone from slave-master issuing orders to a tearful groveler, urgent but servile, almost hysterical: glossolalic prayers vomiting out in a gush, hot with guilty regret. A supplicant worshiping in vain at some empty, silent church.

Answer me, oh answer, please. Don't leave me here, all alone. Please, please, please, please.

The concierge rubs his forehead, wincing. "All right, at any rate—disturbing though that is, until you can identify the apartment, there's a limit to what we can do."

Kyle frowns. "What? Why?"

"The units are the owners' property, not ours—we can't go in without permission unless it relates specifically to pre-contracted maintenance or verified property damage, any more than a cop can go in without a warrant or exigent circumstances. Unless you've heard anything that sounds like someone actually being injured... no?" He raises his eyebrows; you feel your face heat. "I'm sorry."

Kyle lets out a sharp, annoyed breath. "Could you at least have the night guard walk our floor around three a.m., or something? I mean, if *we* can hear all this, it's *gotta* be audible outside. I'm surprised nobody else has complained, considering the last tenants' meeting memo said every unit's been filled."

"All the units are *sold*," the concierge corrects him. "Not everyone's taken up residence yet—some people are holding off until the renovations are done. And no, I can't tell you which units are empty and which aren't. Security policy."

"So, what *can* you do?" you finally demand.

"I can help you fill out a complaint form."

"Four hundred bucks a month in maintenance fees, and this is what it gets us," Kyle grumbles, making you some more ginger tea. "I mean, what the hell? You need sleep, for Christ's sake. You're *pregnant*."

Like I need reminding, you think—but he's frustrated, you get it. Which reminds *you,* in turn, of how you felt at the very end of last night's recording session, listening to your freaky neighbor's invocation wind up or down: that coiling squeeze, that phantom kick. Ida Junior lies quiet under your seeking hand now, as you fumble your phone back out and skip forward to the part of the sound-file the concierge didn't want to hear, the part you lost when you fell asleep. You tell yourself it's to see if you can hear anything that might help identify the point of origin, but really it's just the same impulse that slows drivers down at traffic accidents, an inability to look away whenever the civilized world's paper-thin scrim of safety strains and tears, even just a little.

You watch the file numbers count down to the end, the voice decaying into a wavery, barely audible rasp that stops about ten seconds before the music itself does, seemingly on the verge of weeping. Kyle puts two steaming mugs of tea on the coffee table and sits down beside you, listening in silence 'til it's done. "'Such a quiet fellow, all the neighbors said,'" he announces, at length, and sighs. "Jesus. Guess they can't exactly vet for mental health before they rent to people, though, can they? And everybody has to live somewhere."

"I'm not so sure—whoever that is—is crazy, though," you reply, without planning to. Then add, embarrassed, as Kyle's eyebrows shoot up: "I just… if it was OCD, or some kind of mania, it'd sound different, wouldn't it? More disconnected, autonomic." You hold up the phone. "This guy *means* what he's doing. He's got a reason for it."

"And… that would be?"

Without warning, a new noise suddenly intrudes—a muffled yell, sharp enough to make you both jump. The file wasn't done, after all. Then there's a beat, a gasp followed by choking coughs, followed in turn by a laugh: loud, but not at all unpleasant. Delighted, actually; almost gleeful. The kind of sound somebody makes when at last, after long, frustrating effort, something *works.*

It trails off, peters out. Thirty seconds after that, the sound file finally does end, for real.

You and Kyle just stare at each other over the resulting silence, mouths open.

The apartment's empty when you wake. Sunlight's flooded the place, high and warm; it must be close to noon, if not after. You squint around for your phone, which has slid from your hand down to the couch. A red circle on your messaging app's icon announces a waiting text—Kyle, sent around seven-thirty. *Tried to wake you*

before I left and couldn't, it says. *Figured you needed the sleep. Text me back when you get this. Love.*

You yawn, stretch, and realize with some surprise that for once you actually *don't* feel like complete crap; a few aches from the poor posture, sure, but the ever-present fatigue and nausea are almost completely gone. You feel more alert and clear-headed than you have in weeks. Which, of course, sets off its own spiral of worry: don't stroke victims sometimes get a sudden rush, just before the blowout? You think you remember reading that somewhere, you're almost certain—

Jesus, Ida, get a grip.

Was this a skip night, then, or did you actually sleep through the cacophony, for once? At the idea, disquiet settles back onto you—maybe this is your new normal, the smell, the music, the raving. That infectious craziness, seeping through your walls at random. But then again, how different would that really be, when think about it? Nowhere's 100% safe, not really; nothing's guaranteed. People get shot in high-end shopping malls; kids wander away in their underwear on winter nights and freeze to death right in the middle of downtown. Somebody with all the privilege and opportunity in the world can turn to black magic one day, decide to kill strangers because an angel appeared in their brain and told them to, for no reason but neurological meltdown. And the only thing you *can* predict is that their neighbors won't ever see it coming, because they simply can't conceive of it.

My *child won't grow up in a world like that,* you swear to yourself, knowing full well that she—or he—most definitely will. Knowing there's basically shit-all point nothing you can do about it, except in the tiniest of all possible increments. And so:

"We have to *find* that guy," you tell Kyle, the minute he walks through the door at the end of the day. "Like, tonight. If they can't do anything then it's obviously up to us, before it's too late. Yes?"

"Um..."

"Say 'yes,' Kyle."

He looks at you, pauses, then nods—uncomfortable, yet resigned. He can see your face, after all. He knows your mind's made up.

"Okay, Ida," he replies.

Three again. Always after three. The time of night when most people die, isn't it, or at least have heart attacks—when the blood pressure drops lowest; that's the rumor, anyway. Or maybe that's 4:00 a.m.

But tonight, it ends, you think, words shaping themselves bravely, not having the least idea how to make them come true.

"What do we do when we find the guy, if we find him?" Kyle asks, as if reading your mind.

You shrug. "Knock," you reply. "Ask him to stop."

"What if he won't?"

A long pause. "Then at least we tried," you say, at last.

You wait what seems like a surprisingly long time until the smell's bad enough to track, then follow it carefully all around the apartment until you have a clear consensus: from the south, this time, through the front door, which Kyle carefully locks behind you both. "You really think somebody's going to rob us in the middle of the night?" you ask.

"Weirder things have happened."

True enough, you guess. They're happening right now.

You haven't been out all day, so it's not as big a surprise as it might otherwise be to realize they finally must have laid down the new carpet. What *is* somewhat surprising is the way it looks, however—white lines on black, Doppler effect weirdness like a tangle of dying neurons rocketing off into nowhere. It makes the halls seem twice as long, the corners sharper, oddly slanted. The pile's so soft your feet make no sound.

You knock on #770. Nothing. #766 has TV noise coming out of it, obviously disturbing the ever-barking dog in #765, which sounds like it's about to choke on its own spit. #771, nothing; #767, nothing. That's your end of the hallway done, your immediate circle of neighbors.

"Should we go further?" Kyle asks, frowning. "I mean... how could we even smell it, if it's coming from that far away?"

"Because it's always been coming through the building's main vents, not from next door at all? You tell me."

"I don't know."

"Yeah, me either."

Which is when the music starts, of course, dim (and far away?) enough that you can barely hear it—more feel it, registering inside you like another heartbeat, diseased and erratic. A series of chords so wrong they make you want to vomit.

"It's *worse*," you exclaim, and now it's Kyle's turn to nod. "How can it be *worse*?"

"I don't know, Ida."

"Oh, my God. Where's it even coming from now?"

"Uh... over there?" He waves vaguely. "Want to check it out?"

"Want" would be a strong word. But he's already moving, just as the sound of chanting, ranting, adds itself to the mix. That goddamn *sound. Didn't get what you wanted the other night, huh?* You wonder, not knowing in the least who you're supposed to be addressing—not yet anyhow. Is there more to do? When's enough ever going to be enough?

Oh man, just stop, *all right?* you suddenly find you want to call after Kyle as he slips around the corner up ahead, disappearing from view, hopefully only momentarily. *While you still can. Stop, before it's—*

(too late)

But on he goes, and on you do too, accelerating 'til your lungs hurt. 'Til your real pulse overcomes the music's at last, rising and lodging in your throat, making it hard to breathe.

"We should go back," you say, out loud.

"Why?"

"Because... shit, Kyle, this is taking too long. I don't even know where we are." You glance around, scanning for anything you recognize, and failing. "I mean— have you ever been here before?"

"On this part of our floor? No, but who cares? It's always been here. We just live on a different piece of the exact same place."

"Is it? It doesn't even look like our building anymore."

"The renovation just hasn't reached down here yet, that's all."

"Kyle, it doesn't even look like it *used* to look. It doesn't look like anywhere."

"Well…" He stops, glances. "… no, that's dumb. We passed our garbage chute, remember? Right back there."

"Before we went through that double-door?" He nods. "Okay, but how long ago was that?"

"I don't know."

"Me either."

You both stop, staring at each other, breath ragged. For a moment, you can see it on his face: he gets it. He wants to go back, he just can't say it—so you have to, show fear, get hysterical. Freak out, the way crazy pregnant women are expected to. Just push hard enough, he'll give in.

Then the fucking music starts up again, making his eyes harden. Making him look like a stranger.

"I'm done with this," he tells himself. "I'm *done,* I can't… no, this is it. Just stop it, goddamn it." Raising his voice: "Just fucking *stop,* you fucker!"

You grab his sleeve. "Kyle, I'm scared, please don't—"

"Ida, c'mon! We can't live like this. You *have to sleep.*"

"*Stop telling me what I have to do.*"

It comes out like a growl, in a voice you don't recognize: coarse, worn, suffused with grief that reads like rage. That sounds more like, more like—

(that one)

(right in there)

(that voice behind that door)

That door, there, at the very end of the hall, the *dead*-end cast in half-darkness, beyond where the lights start to flicker and pop and buzz. That door painted red, when every other door you've passed so far has been first fresh new black, then tired old blue-gray, then bare blank wood scarred here and there from paint remover, stripped to the skin and waiting for primer. That door, from which that *smell* proceeds like a wave, like a wall.

Kyle's face lights up when he sees it; he takes two big strides forward even as you recoil, heaving, hugging your belly for comfort. He's almost close enough to touch it now, fist lifting, poised to hammer—

But before he can, it just *stops,* all of it. The music, the noise. Even the smell seems to twitch away, impossibly fast, there and then not. You'd think it'd make you feel better, but it doesn't.

The new normal, you remember, annoyance abruptly gone. Feeling your entire body shudder all over instead, hit in every part at once with a single massive, crashing wave of cold fear. Thinking, as what sounds like a series of locks begins to open, slow but steady, utterly deliberate: *That's it, all right, you asshole—oh, shit. Now you've gone and done it!*

"Kyle, we have to go," you tell him, already turning and yanking his arm hard enough to hurt as you do, not waiting for protest. "*Jesus,* let's *go,* now—"

"What?!"

"Just fucking GO, Kyle! Run run run *run*—"

And you do, thank God, back past the unfamiliar part of this floor, back through those double doors, back through the un-renovated portion and into the newly finished sections, borne by your own furious momentum. Slamming into walls hard enough to bruise, rounding corners so sharply they graze your hip, half-falling at least once as your legs go out from underneath you, only to be jerked back upright with Kyle's arm 'round your waist. Past three separate sets of elevators (one more than usual) whose doors jolt gently back and forth as if jammed, interior lights red-filtered, distant alarms piping in through static-clogged speakers. The air coming out of the AC vents licks you like a ghost-tongue, hot and gross; the fans judder and shake, groaning painfully, hitting the same notes that—*person*—behind the red door's music used to, back in what you couldn't possibly have known were far simpler times. And everything drumming, inside and out; you can't tell what's your body, your ears, your mind. You can't tell where you are, or how you got there.

Here, Ida, we're here, let me just get my key—don't black out! Stay awake, Ida, we're almost back inside... we're home, honey, I swear to you. We're home, at last...

A stitch in your side tightening, just begging to be ripped wide open. The baby kicking, for sure this time—just once, like knocking.

Your door opening, soft as a kiss, before Kyle can even touch it, and oh, but it's dark inside. Darker than it's ever been.

"Come in," a too-familiar voice tells you, that same laughter in every word, so happy it could cry. "I've been waiting for you, you know—a long, long time. Waiting for someone to hear, to care enough to come. And now I'm glad, *so* very glad..."

... you finally came to meet me.

THIN COLD HANDS

*T*HOUGH IT'S A long time since I've lived in a house, I still have memories about what that used to be like, which work on me constantly, mainly subconsciously. When I dream, I open a door into a composite domicile cobbled together from bits and pieces of all the houses my parents passed through during my childhood, dragging me behind them. And while I suppose it's strange how I never seem to dream about where I live right now—this apparently safe little condominium apartment with its security guards, its concierge, its maintenance crew, its entire fee-fed infrastructure—that's just how it is, how it's always been. How it always will be, probably.

Instead, night after night, I shut my eyes and drift off only to discover I'm back in the dark, the dust, that symphony of too-familiar noises: scratch of claws through wood shavings as my long-dead rat skitters around in his cage, exercise wheel whirring against the bars; weird clang and hoarse, throaty hum of the furnace starting up, down deep in the basement's bowels. Hot air exhaling through the vents, rank as some sleeping monster's breath.

It feels like being swallowed, always, still alive. Swallowed but never digested.

Living in a house is defined, to some degree, by the process of accidentally finding places in your "home" you can't remember ever having seen before. In my case, this was often aided by the fact I was still young enough I didn't mind getting dirty, nor was my "ew, gross!" reflex fully formed, making the treasures I found while exploring a mixture of the genuinely interesting and the merely disgusting. There's a story my Dad used to like to tell, for example—before he left us—about how he once went looking for me down in the basement of a particular place (13 Hocken Avenue? 33?) only to eventually discover me crouching behind a huge piece of plywood leant against the back wall, covered in dirt, absently sucking on a dead mouse's tail.

Sometimes, when I concentrate hard enough, I can even almost remember what doing that felt like, if not dissect what weird turn of toddler logic led me to make that particular decision: conjure how soft the mouse was in the middle but how stiff at either end, the feel of its dusty fur under my stroking fingers, the taste of its tail in its mouth, that sharply angled little corpse-curl pricking my tongue. Familiarly unfamiliar, a mere memory-sketch filtered through someone else's version of it, someone else's story. Because the past really is another country, and all children lunatics, in their very different ways.

I can testify to that last part for certain, especially now I have a child myself.

I don't remember giving birth, just waking up afterwards, dazed from drugs. The feeling when they folded my slack arms around her, pressing her face to my breast. Her mouth gone round against my warm skin, seeking ring of lips so soft yet oddly cold, latching on tight; an instinctive sense of predation, of something being stolen. And then, as she started to suck, that sharp, prickling pain.

I gasped, whimpered; tears came to my eyes. It was a moment before I could find my words.

"*Hurts,*" I told the nurse, when I was able. "Babies aren't s'posed t'have... *teeth,* right?

The nurse stroked my slick hair, comfortingly. "Most don't, no, but some do; no worries, it's perfectly natural. She's a very forward-thinking young lady, your daughter."

Nothing for it, after that—I didn't have the strength to do anything but lie there and let her drain me, never letting go. They had to pull her off me at last, blind crumpled face avid and a red ring vivid around those still-pursed lips, of blood and milk admixed.

"Greedy girl!" the nurse called her, affectionately. "Well, you'll both have to work it out, I guess, eventually. Once you take her home."

I nodded or thought I did. Before slipping back into sleep, my wounds salved, this vampire thing I'd birthed still clutched to my chest.

But almost six years later, I still can't say that's ever really happened.

I don't remember how old I was when I first figured out that if I slid aside a basket-woven screen on one side of the front deck, I could crawl underneath the house. Indeed, I don't even really remember which house it was, though it must have been one from the part of my childhood after Dad left, since the property in question had both a porch and a garden, as well as a back yard. In the crawlspace it was dim and cool, soil soft beneath me and stone joists on every side like squat little pillars, holding up the walls, the floorboards, the house itself. I had no idea of danger, only that elation which comes with exploring, scuffling around on my hands and knees like a badger in shorts. I enjoyed knowing what I thought nobody else knew, seeing what I thought no one else could have seen.

And it was down there, at last, that I found the grave.

I don't know what attracted me to *that* spot, exactly: a slight hump under my hand, faint but unmistakable, like reading braille. I looked down, squinting, but could more feel than see it. Mapped *out* its dimensions with that one-handed reach my piano teacher always told me she envied, middle finger stretching elastically, thumb rotating in its socket, so the nail pointed to my elbow. It was my full reach long and three slightly spread fingers wide—pointer, middle, ring. It narrowed at the top and bottom, like a seed pod, so eventually I simply dug my thumbs into the middle and peeled it open. Milkweed fluff spilled out, dirty white silk, along with a flood of bones I picked out one by one, reassembling them there in the part-light. Once painstakingly pieced back together, the bones reminded me of any classic fossil, crushed like an insect between two rock-beds... but not quite. Two arms, check; two legs, check. One skull, snoutless, eyes forward-facing, nude grin full of delicate needle-teeth. The remains of a spine, yet nothing that looked like a tail. A ribcage, mostly intact, though with its second and third rib down on (my) left-hand side wrenched and cracked out of shape by that rusty four-inch iron nail stuck in between them—I removed it so they'd lie flat, slipping it into my pocket. Wishbone slope of a pelvis, half-cracked, a socket-hole on either side for a pair of delicate, too-sharp hip bones. An unstrung spray of what could only be finger-joints scattered at either end of its out-flung radiae and ulnae, tiny as caraway seeds.

And oh, but they were cold to the touch, all of them—*so* damn cold. Cold enough they crisped and pulled at my skin like freezer-burn.

Light as a bird's yet impossible to break, with two more things spread out like huge, dried oak-leaves left at the very bottom, frayed but intact. And though I couldn't possibly have known what they were back then, whenever I think about them now, they look just a bit... just a little bit... like wings.

Tinkerbell, I remember thinking. *Someone murdered Tinkerbell.*

But even as I stroked those bones a light began to kindle at the heart of them, icy-colorless, traced thin as a thread along where the vertebrae should have been strung. And I thought I heard a thin ringing like a half-full glass's rim being toyed with begin, almost at the same time, somewhere off in the distance... or no, maybe not; far closer, maybe, though muffled by my own skull's echo-chambers. A sick, dim bell tolling out from deep inside, fluttering like some insect mired in wax and cartilage alike. The very idea, in turn, coming with an image attached, so sharp I could almost see it: a flashbulb going off behind the curve of one ear to show the culprit caught inside, fluttering between hammer and drum, silhouetted to its delicate little black leg-hairs.

None of which I much liked, so I recoiled instead, knocking my head on the boards above—scrabbled back, feeling blind behind me for the screen, afraid to avert my eyes; missed it not once but twice before I found it again at last, wrenched it breathlessly aside and spilled back out into sunlight, my hair full of dirty cobwebs.

Before Mom heard me scrambling around in the grass and threw the back door open, yelling, "You better not be under that goddamn deck *again*, Emme, goddammnit!"

That night, in the bath, I watched dirt sluice off me down the drain, turning the clear water gray; waited for my mother to come tell me to get dressed, brush my teeth, turn that light off too, because we weren't made of money—and thinking, as I did (glimpsing it briefly between the lines of my own mind, pretty much, in the very fuzziest, least explicit of ways) how everything I did, everything I was *allowed* to do, was only ever at someone else's sufferance. Since that was always the scrambled background signal lurking behind all my childhood memories, same as everyone else's—the part I, like them, only grew to understand later on, when I was finally old enough to put a name to what I'd never been able to recognize before. That constant feeling of helplessness, of misunderstanding, that everything was decided for me, that I had no control...

Because I just didn't, ever, from birth almost to the moment I moved out. Because some would say I never had more than the illusion of control even after that.

Thus, all the small rebellions, small sins, small betrayals which make up every coming-of-age narrative: cruelties practiced on me versus cruelties I didn't yet know better than to practice on whatever other, weaker things I could get a hold of—kids, animals, objects. The first blunt, sticky stirrings of sexuality paired with an equally itchy feeling of being *not yet fully formed,* both equally impossible to do much about. And knowing, on some level—not accepting, just knowing—that all those unslakable aches are only ever half the problem.

I found the iron nail in my pocket when I threw my jeans aside and fell asleep holding it, clutching it between two fingers. Hours after, meanwhile, I jerked straight up in bed with no earthly idea what I might've heard to wake me, 'til it came again: a drone pitched somewhere between cicada's whine and bumblebee's buzz, so deep it almost read as a moan. No sleeping through *that,* so I crept to the door instead, heart in my throat—cracked it, stared out, took a pair of shaky steps into the hall, nail raised like a cross with its sharp end pointed towards that noise, angling further up the louder it became. Then watched the same sort of wintry light I'd seen beneath the deck begin to form at the corridor's other end, moving ever-closer, casting a flickering, fluttering shadow against the wall... but when it finally drifted 'round the corner, that's somehow all it was: just empty light, a fire without a fly.

The shadow projected on top of it, though, self-lit to twice natural size—it was a hovering figure whose outline reminded me of that body-bag pod I'd found while rooting through the deck's cool dark turned inside-out, its silhouette half down, half dirt. Spread finger-claws like two bundles of pins against lace-leaf dragonfly wings, not two but four (or maybe six), all blurred and trembling with motion; profile deformed by bulgy beetle-eyes and a gothic pair of mandibles, those horned jaws spread as if to speak, though any pretence at words stayed caught in its invisible throat's curve. And all with that glass harmonica buzz soaring ever higher, painful enough it made my eyes cross, my sight winking out so fast I barely felt the floor hit my face—

My mom still tells the part of the story I have no clear access to, sometimes: how she heard a thump and got up to investigate only to find me passed out in the hall with my pants urine-soaked, my forehead bruised and some sort of weird rash 'round my mouth, lips digestive-acids puffed like I'd puked myself unconscious. How my throat hurt too much to talk. How I'd also fallen on my own wrist, bending it underneath me at an angle, full body weight coming down on it at once; they found a hairline fracture at the hospital, casted me up and would have sent me home, but I had a panic attack when I heard that so they let me stay a few days more. In the intervening time, Mom arranged for me to go visit my Dad out of season, and by the time I came back she'd not only sold the house, but already found another one.

The fastest move we ever made, and I wasn't even there to help.

Sometimes I go into my daughter's room, all pink and sparkly, and look at her while she's asleep. While her eyes are closed at any rate; she's very good at lying there, flat chest going steadily up and down. I look at the pillow she clutches in her arms and wonder how fast I could rip it away, press it to her face—if I could trust myself to be fast enough, strong enough. To not slacken for once. To stop believing in the lies that are her life.

Other times I wake to find her standing in my room, looking down on me. Her eyes give back the light, even with my blackout blinds pulled down.

"I love you, Mommy," she tells me, smiling. "Just like you love me."

"Yes," I agree.

"All mommies love their children, and all children love their mommies. Isn't that true?"

"Yes."

"That's why the fairies used to steal the real children, you know, and replace them. Because they didn't have any mommies of their own."

I swallow. "Then why didn't they steal the mommies, instead?"

She tilts her head to one side, not quite smiling. "Now that I don't know. What do *you* think?"

Because they like to lie, I think, but don't say. *Because they're old and evil and cruel. Because they wanted it to hurt as much as possible when the mommies found out what they'd done. Because they didn't think we were capable of doing anything about it, 'til they found out better.*

Ah, but then they figured out another way, some of them—or only just the one maybe. Long after we'd already killed them all.

I look up at her, my daughter, saying none of this. Because she *is* my daughter, after all; half of her, or even a little more. My flesh and blood, my only. And that thing squished down inside, it can't really be *most* of her, can it? There has to be something else, another percentage—a little more, a little less, whatever. Some parodic variety of human soul, even with that shard of something else stuck inside of it—those delicate skeleton wings too flesh-pinned to flap, shadow-bones caught in a calcium cage. Disease and cure born interlocked, zero sum, each forever at war with its own potential.

What she was before, I'll never understand. And what she is now—

Something that can change, now it's enough like us to be able to, I think. *She's changed already, after all, just to become herself...*

(whatever *that* is)

"Those are just stories, though," I tell her, trying my best to believe it. "Right, honey? You know that."

"Of course, mommy."

I open my arms. "Hug me, please," I tell her, to which she nods, and does. The way she always has, oddly enough, from the very first—something I never predicted, not ever. Something I never thought I'd grow to need.

But she always lets go first.

"Good night," she says, turning her back on me, as I feel all my empty parts turn cold once more. That hole inside me where she once hid, folding back upon itself again; this scar yet unhealed, never-healing, gaping wide under my stomach-set hands like that grave beneath the deck.

So, from a childhood rooted in nightmare, I grew up, liking myself a little better with every passing year. It wasn't that I'd been *actively* unhappy, by most standards, but it was never my favorite thing, either—the loneliness, the social weight, the dependency. Being dragged from one place to another, having rules set and re-set apparently at random, never fully understanding why. Being unable, yet, to see the adults around me not as infallible authority figures but imperfect human beings like the one I was flowering into, just as trapped in their own roles as by their own mistakes.

Some people talk about the golden light of childhood, call it "the best time of [their] li[ves]," but those people must have been lucky at best, stupid at worst. Whatever they felt, I didn't.

Then again, whatever I *saw, they* didn't.

"Why *do* you find people so exhausting?" my mother asked me once, when I was still in university. "Is it because you think they'll judge you? You shouldn't. My friends all think you're charming. '"Emme's so easy to talk to," that's what they tell me."

I laughed. "You do get that I *work* at that, right? I have to watch myself all the time—make sure I don't talk about anything real. Just let them talk about themselves, and act like I'm interested."

"So... you're not? Is that what you're saying?" She paused. "What about with me?"

"I'm always interested in what you have to say, mom."

"Well, how can I believe that *now*?"

Just forget we ever had this conversation, I didn't suggest. Because if she couldn't see how important she was to me by now, how she had pretty much always been the *only* person whose good opinion I truly wanted to keep, then I certainly didn't know what more I could do to convince her.

But that was how it'd always been for me since that day under the house, that night in the hall, though it rarely occurred to me unless I stopped long enough to feel it: how sometimes I felt so utterly false, an empty mask over a hollow, echoing shell. Or how other times—more times than I liked to admit, in fact—I felt anything but.

I graduated, got a job, and did it diligently enough not to be fired, making no enemies, yet forming no attachments. Mornings I arrived early, a smile on my face; nights I went straight home, watched TV, slept dreamlessly. Nothing changed or not very much. Nothing changed until it did.

Until it *all* did.

The building I lived in that year was a 1970s-era tower of furnished bachelor and one-bedroom rental suites, the best I could afford until I got my CPA certification. The elevators broke down a lot, and the stairwells stank. I learned to recognize people by their faces, even if I never knew their names—the gaunt, too-young hooker I sometimes passed down on the street at night, loitering next to the Neighborhood Watch sign in nothing but a Maple Leafs jersey and short-shorts; a flannel-jacketed guy, black beard so thick you could barely see his mouth; a heavyset lady with a

Jamaican accent I only ever met coming out of the mailroom, who always told me exactly the same three stories about her grandkids. I was counting days and dollars towards a telecommuting job I'd already interviewed for and a different apartment, so I kept my head down, nodding politely at anyone who approached me.

The basement laundry suite was technically closed after nine p.m., but the lock had been broken since I'd moved in and nobody cared if you ran loads at night, which was useful to an insomniac whose days were spent cramming tax law. More often than not, I found it easier by far to fall asleep to the washer-dryer's rhythmic susurration than I ever could in bed. I was drifting off that night, head down on my arms, when the door suddenly slammed open: Blackbeard stood there, mouth working as though he was chewing taffy, staring just past me (the closest he ever got to eye contact with anybody).

Excuse me? I think I thought about saying; my own mouth might have opened, at least part-way. But it was already too late.

"You're... very rude," he blurted, before I could. "It's not right to be—like that, you don't have to ... You don't feel, don't want—it's fine, that's fine, it's okay. But you don't, you don't just get to—fucking *IGNORE* people!"

No warning at all before that last shouted word or the punch he slammed past my ear, right into the cement wall behind. Any potential scream choked off short, a hoarse gurgle; my gut spasmed like a full body standing crunch, as Blackbeard shook his bloodied fist in my face. "You shouldn't get to—you *don't*. Get to *do* that."

Oh, Jesus, I remember thinking, through a buzzy, electrical blur. *This isn't supposed to happen. I'm moving out in five weeks... four? I don't, I don't, I can't—*

Mimicking his own words without thinking as if he'd actually managed to hit me, so hard he'd gotten inside my head. And then, and then: the light fuzzed out as Blackbeard pushed in, eyes still averted but his other hand lashing out, anything but gentle. I felt his fingers grip my jaw and twist, thumb digging into the hinge; felt the muscle spark, my scalp heave upwards, like it was tensing to jump off my skull. Followed by pain—not the kind you're expecting, though. Or me either.

From within, like thin cold hands inside my throat, clawing upwards; sharp wings along my tongue, scoring the muscles so my scream dropped even as it broke my voice-box, hoarsening, blood-hot. I lurched forward, spasming, to loose a gush of bile right at his feet... saw him jump back from the hot splash, exclaiming, even as something far more solid rocketed its shimmering way out along with the rest. I remember Blackbeard spinning to stare as it whipped around the laundry room, eyes wide, like maybe it was the first thing he'd really ever *seen* in his life, his own mouth wide—

Shut that, for Christ's sake, I might've told him, if I'd only been able to speak. Not even knowing why I would've wanted to warn him in the first place, aside from the simple fact that he was human, like me. Like we both were. Like that *thing*... wasn't.

(Still isn't.)

I knew that light, you see, long before I recognized the noise that came along with it. That dim, sick, wax and meat-clogged insect trill. Dead Tinkerbell's ghost risen from the grave and not some long-gone feverish trauma nightmare after all: first in the dirt under the deck, then in the dusty upper hall, then inside me, then him—but not for long.

It plunged, straight between his lips and down his throat. I saw his neck bulge, heard his breathing clog, choke as he fell back against the wall, sank down, clawing his Adam's apple. Saw the bulge disappear through his collarbones' gate while he threw his head back, trying to scream. Saw blood burst upwards, thick and raw, like he was a blender someone'd turned on after forgetting to close the lid. I watched him spasm and drum and buck and bleed and *shrink* as if being deflated, consumed, a plastic bag in a fire—face slack, eyes collapsed, from dying frenzy to motionless corpse in an instant. Watched a blood-outline briefly limn the linoleum beneath him before quick-drying Hiroshima-style to black, to gray, to dust.

I clung to the nearest dryer, still warm but no longer rumbling, sobbing for breath and trembling far too much to stand; I think there actually might have been tears on my face, though it's not like I had a hand free to check. The silence stretched on: one beat, two. Two and a half.

Then: Blackbeard's throat swelled once more, jaw hinging back open. Something clambered out of him, glistening fiercely; something gaunt and tiny, that same dimly ringing clot of light now stained purple by a coating of gore, bright red over bluish white. Something with hands like microscopic spiders and joints hinged high above its back, leaf-wings blurred like a hummingbird's hazing the air, flicking the very last of him away with each successive beat—crimson, then pink, then clear, faster and faster, an explosion turned halo. Sparks falling upwards, scarring the eye like solder.

And right in the center, brightness-wreathed the way the sun looks through ice-slicked petals on a frozen flower, a face reminiscent of nothing so much as the skull I'd once touched turned inside out was angled my way: black bug-eyes, mandible-set jaws, teeth like tiny bone needles. Seeming to grin in sheer delight now it could finally see me again first-hand after all those years stuck down inside my chest, fluttering there in the wet, red dark like a second beating heart.

This time, it was one of my neighbors who found me, passed out cold on the laundry-room floor next to a pile of Blackbeard's empty clothes, left balled up in his wake as if he'd simply evaporated out of them. The cops they insisted I call really only briefly considered me a suspect in his disappearance, especially after his mother let them into his room and they discovered that weird half-worshipful, half-threatening stuff he'd written about me all over the walls. I took advantage of the attack by using it as an excuse to move out far sooner than scheduled, packing up so quickly I think I might have left that last load of laundry behind me. One way or the other, I'd been in my new apartment for at least two months already before I woke up feeling nauseous.

Four positive home pregnancy tests and a doctor's trip later, I found out why. Mom wanted me to get an abortion, assuming Blackbeard had to be the father, but I told her he couldn't be—I'd had a rape kit done as part of the police investigation, taken the morning-after pill just in case, the whole nine yards. I claimed I'd had a one-night stand during my recovery period and just hadn't wanted to admit it, but that I was more than ready to raise the kid on my own, if I had to.

Given the circumstances of my daughter's not-so-immaculate conception, I think Mom's first guess was more likely true than not, in some insane way. But it isn't as if she looks like him, thank God, any more than she looks like me.

Or anyone else.

And now, years later, I lie here thinking how neatly the thing she used to be must have re-folded itself into my body, having finally fed enough to be seen clearly—a bright red streak down my gaping throat, knife to sheath, stuffing the scream back down. How she must have curled into my womb, nesting, waiting for me to quicken.

Knocking at the inside of my yet un-cracked pelvis to be let out into this world, so she could occupy it in what passes for her version of flesh, the way her long-dead former self surely used to.

These days, along with my usual work organizing other people's money, I also make jewelry and sell it on Etsy. It's stress relief and a second stream of income combined, something to keep my hands busy as I watch the same bunch of too-young movies over and over just because my daughter likes them: Miyazaki's *My Neighbor Totoro*, classic Pixar, anything Disney. Just sort and string, string and sort, match color to texture to pattern—let each necklace grow organically, intuitively, in the spaces between my own long, slow breaths. As a form of self-comfort, it's cheaper than booze or anti-depressants, and better for the complexion; as a form of meditation, it certainly helps the hours pass. And assembling the components helps me plan my free time, too, now that my daughter's old enough to ride the subway on her own, surrounded by that floating gaggle of girls whose names clog the smartphone she's had since she was six. Now that she has her own devices she can leave me from and I can leave her to—all the interests I tried to distract her with when she was undeveloped enough that something old and odd and hungry still occasionally seemed to peep out through her eyes: dance lessons, art lessons, drama lessons. The skills she uses to construct a mask of humanity no one will take notice of long enough ask questions.

Her teachers like her, apparently; everybody does. Her marks are high. She has social cred I could only dream of at her age. And sometimes the other mothers on my playdate phone tree chide me gently about the amount of freedom I allow her, how I'll often just hand her a twenty and my Metro Pass, telling her to go have fun. She knows to text me if she wants to stay out later than discussed, for all I rarely answer. I suppose, on some level, what I'm waiting to see is exactly how long I can go without talking to her before she simply decides to never come home at all.

It's a dangerous world, Emme, they say. *Think how you'd feel if you lost her.* To which I simply smile, sometimes having to physically restrain myself from replying: *I should be so lucky, ladies.*

But I've never been that lucky.

Last night she was out with her besties, probably chaperoned by Linda's mom (or Rosie's, or Ning's, or Gurinder's—anyone but me, obviously). I sat in front of the TV with my nature shows on and my bead-box out, wondering why it ever surprised me to consider that the world might once have been full of whatever ended up buried beneath my deck, whole shining swarms of them, fluttering schools flocking like starling across the skies in search of prey and singing their pale, trilling songs, their creepy ghost-insect buzz: bioluminescent, poisonous, each one a miracle designed to latch on and bite deep, tearing free chunks of human-meat with their tiny lamprey mouths. Each one spinning silent yet deadly through the air like sparkler-drift, like acid snowflakes, like glass bells lit from inside and thrown high 'til gravity pulled them back to ground, wounding on contact.

Feeling around in the box, I felt my fingers touch something familiar and pulled it out, frowning: the nail. I hadn't remembered I still had it. So, I polished it with oil, knotted it on a length of rawhide and tied it around my neck like a pendant, tucking it away under my shirt. And when my daughter came home at last, she opened her arms for a hug before flinching away when that rusty iron length of it touched her chest, even through a layer of cloth: "That *hurts*," she said, with just a hint of surprised dislike. "Wow, Mom—what *is* that, down there? Ugh."

I tapped my own chest, drawing a circle around the nail as it swung, angled down, pointing the way to my Caesarian scar. "Just something new, repurposed. Want to see?"

Her eyes widened slightly, strangeness flickering just beneath the surface, an anglerfish's phantom lure. "Pass, thanks. What's for dinner?"

I'd made her favorite earlier, liver and bacon, no onions. She ate it with her hands, licked the juices from her fingers, then waited until she thought I wasn't looking to tip up the plate for the rest. After her bath I saw her standing in front of the mirror, frowning, a hand over her breastbone. "I can still feel it," she complained. "That *thing* of yours. Mom, you have to get rid of it."

"Of course," I agree. "Did it scratch you?"

"It burnt me. Look."

She fanned her fingers, showing me a small, red mark between the nubs where her breasts still hadn't quite grown as yet. She's not shy, my daughter, but I know it annoys her that other girls already have boyfriends, or the middle-school version thereof. Tall and slim she might be—taller than me, soon—but she reads like a child, an orphan princess, a wanderer through wooded places. She won't let me cut her silky hair, which falls to her mid-back. Her hands are long, good for piano. No one can tell me what color her eyes are, so large and odd, sockets like an owl's.

I am at the wide world's mercy, those eyes say, always. *No one is like me, not exactly. Come closer, don't be afraid—see me, pity me, help me. I need you. I need.*

When she goes to hug me again before bed, she finds she simply can't: the iron's just too disturbing to her, even hidden inside my fist. It makes her brows furrow. And I want to be strong, looking at her—hopefully, this will be enough to make her leave, eventually. Hopefully I'll never be weak enough to take it off again.

From the way I talk about my mom sometimes, you'd assume I hate her, though the opposite is true. But I never write about the parts of my life where she and my dad were together, when I was untaintedly happy, or thought I was. I can barely remember what it was like to be that person.

I mean... in high school I fell in love with a boy, and every time we were together it felt as if we were wrapped so tight, we lived inside each other, a strange knot of bliss, always tightening. The actual time we spent enmeshed was relatively brief, but it remade the world. And the minute we broke up it was like none of that ever happened—there was no point in remembering any of it, because all it meant was that at the time I just hadn't realized yet that it didn't mean anything except how stupid I'd been not to see the end of it all coming, to think I'd actually been loved.

He was very upset when I told him that. "Well, it meant a lot to *me*," he said. "Obviously not," I replied. "Considering you broke my fucking heart."

So that's what it's like for me: my parents broke my heart, and after they divorced none of my "happy" childhood meant shit. I've enjoyed the adulthood I've eventually been able to have with my mom, and (to some extent) my dad. But that right there, the holidays, the photos, all those hugs and kisses, those goodnight stories? That was a lie.

I just didn't know it yet.

I know how that realization felt, how it hurt—but now, years later, a mother myself, I finally know how it must have hurt my own mother to see me suffer. Because that's the other side of it, of course, the sting in the tail. So, when I look at my daughter and think that I don't want to break her heart, it isn't just because I don't fully understand what she might do if I did. It's because even if I don't think there was ever a time when I believed she was fully human, I know there must have been a time when *she* did. When *she* didn't know any better.

Is that just another trick, another lie? I don't know. I can't know.

I don't think I ever will.

Will she search the rest of her kind out when she leaves me at last, one by one, wherever they're buried? Will she teach them to snare humans of their own, playing on them the same sort of trick she played on me? I hope not, and not just for our sakes.

For hers as well.

One day, a long time from now for me—but maybe not for her—she'll go away one last time, forever. And even now, even *now,* I still can't tell if that prospect makes me happy or not. Only that it'll happen either way. That it's beyond my control and always was.

Be different, I want to tell her, explicitly, before she leaves me. *Be yourself, whatever that is—not was,* is. *Make your own path.*

Fly away, stranger, and don't come back.

I think, but I don't say; I hope, more and more. I try not to pray. While she looks at me now and then, her strange eyes throwing back the light, not quite smiling. And I hear her voice inside my head the same way I once did, so long ago: like a glass bell, a distant ringing. Like the buzzing of some monstrous fly.

But how can I leave? It seems to say. *I'm yours, after all, like you're mine. Your very own.*

Thin cold hands reaching down again, tightening around my heart. Squeezing 'til I feel they fingerprint embed on the tissue, 'til the veins bulge and the chambers contract, resentful love pumping out like blood.

You are home, mother.

My home.

VENIO

WATCH OUT.

I'M going to tell you about something, and then... you'll know. You won't be able to *un*-know or forget why you should want to. And even if you decide you don't believe it now, you'll still have thought about it long enough to make that call, so it'll still be too late. Because now it knows you know, it'll be able to find you. To home in on you.

Just like it did with me.

Sometimes, a door is enough, open or otherwise. Or an empty moment, an empty page.

An empty head.

I remember the night my group and I first played the game that led us here, the Shut Door Sessions. It was all about imagination, or the lack of it.

We were writers, you see, supposedly. Desperate to be. And yes, I know the received wisdom, thank you very much—how you can fix *bad* writing, but you can't fix *no* writing. How nothing you put down in words is ever going to match that gleaming, awe-inspiring thing you glimpse at the back of your head, so you might as well just let it come as it comes and try to make it better later. Try not to fixate on how the gold you had just before you started trying to hammer it into words somehow seems to have turned entirely to shit, an alchemical working in reverse: albedo up out of nigredo and back on down into nigredo again, hi ho, hi ho.

Always seeking the same goal, all of us, with no real hope of achieving it: something fresh, something new, something real—*unique.* The impossible fucking dream.

We'd all been there. We'd all spent most of our writing lives there, high school awards or university chapbook-publishing aside. And we'd still be there now, still stuck on the stories we weren't qualified to wrestle from dream to page, if we'd never started playing that game.

Christ, how I wish we'd never started playing that game.

Here's how it works: you each get a piece of paper—blank, lined or unlined, depending on what works best for you. You each get a pen. It can't be your own pen or a piece of paper from your own notebook, if you have one; the work must be done physically, not electronically—no tablets, no laptops, no phones. *And I don't give a shit about how your ADD means you can't spell without spell-check, Trevor. This isn't* school. *I'm not taking marks off for presentation.*

Four people around a four-person table, the sort made for family dinners. One person per cardinal direction with just enough elbow room to scribble without hurting each other, assuming you're all similarly-handed. And at the top of each page, you draw a door, any sort, so long as it's shut.

Draw a door, a shut door, locked if it must be, and look at it. Look at it for as long as *you must before you can write down exactly what'd be behind it, if it opened.*

And which of us was it who first got the idea that grew into this weird-ass prompt-turned-ritual? Oh, that would be Leah, obviously. Little Ms. "The Voices in My Head Aren't Talking to Me Directly This Week" herself, the queen of pants versus plot, always puking out stuff in seemingly unrelated chunks before stringing it together afterwards and telling people her characters told her how to do it. The woman whose whole idea of outlining is to basically throw a pack of Tarot cards in the air, turn them over at random once they hit the ground, and see what happens.

Leah and I had once been together in the sharing-a-bed sense, as opposed to the simply sharing-an-apartment one: met in first year, moved in together by third year, then broke up the year after graduation only to discover there was nowhere to move within public transit distance that wouldn't cost twice as much rent as we were already paying. Which is how we still came to be "together" when she started the Shut Door Sessions, two roommates turned exes pretending we could actually be some variety of friends even after what happened... happened.

Such a cliché, too, all said and done, especially for two people so deeply engaged in trying to avoid clichés like the plague. One of those uncomfortable breakups where you don't really want each other's company anymore but have far too much in common to avoid each other without making a scene. I mean, nobody *wants* to be the Crazy Ex from Hell, do they? The bitch, the asshole, the one who ruins things for everyone else. Don't want to make your other friends unhappy, assuming you have some. So why throw the few friends you've already got away over something as negligible as mere post-physical entanglement heartbreak?

Just play along, guys, okay? No matter how silly it seems. Look at your door, let your eyes unfocus. Relax. Breathe deep and open yourselves up.

Just open yourselves up and wait to see what comes through.

Leah's voice in Yuri's living room that first night, excited enough to turn just a bit breathless, the way I'd heard it so many times before, albeit under very different circumstances. Which maybe explains why I was not only willing but eager to go along with this ridiculous plan of hers—chase the monkey down the monkey-track one more time, in hot pursuit of a truly inventive creativity I already suspected I had never really possessed. I'm talking about the ability to see something lurking inside a block of mental marble and free it with just a few pen-strokes. Craft a sentence clean as a bone over and over again, then hook them together into the skeleton of something never seen before.

My door was featureless, graphic, almost hieroglyphic—I'm a writer, not a visual artist. A bare rectangle with a small circle inside, halfway down the right-hand post...a handle, probably smooth brass, or maybe one of those old glassine diamonds with a bit of paint-slop left down around the part that rotates, turning left to pull tongue from lock and open inwards to reveal—

"The part that rotates," hell... I really should know what that thing's called, right? Considering my profession.

The door, and what's behind it. What's behind your door? See it, guys. Write it down. Write it down, then tell me.

And now you want to stop, I'll bet—to pull out before you go much further, let alone the whole, full way with me. But you can't, can you? You need to know what you won't be able to stop thinking about, if you do.

Besides which: it's already too late, really. I mean, you've already read this far. Haven't you?

Here's what I wrote that first time:

> *A dark road, or what looks like one. No moon and no horizon. Hard to see where the ground blends with the sky, but as it comes towards the door-frame it starts looking porous, tactile. Tiny holes or tiny stones? Gravel? A bed of gravel on either side of two long, dull gray lines with lighter lines between them like a ladder on the ground or maybe train-tracks, away into the distance. Trees on either side? Shadows, spiky, overhanging. They switch back and forth on the tracks, no noise but if there was it would be rustling. Distant. A high and a lonely wind. Nothing else.*

Breathing in, breathing out. Resisting the urge to check my watch. Listening to the scratch of other people's pens around me—trying not to picture Leah with her tongue-tip caught between her teeth, bottom lip a little furled to show darker pink inside pale lipstick. Trevor scribbling hard, like he's fighting the alphabet. Yuri humming. Trying not to recognize the tune.

> *The posts are darkening, shadow spreading outwards. A black thickening at the threshold, like drool.*

(I wanted to stop then too, believe me. That early on. Before I'd even seen... anything.)

Another tick, a half-breath, barely tasted. And then—

> *Now a sense of something changing in the furthest section: a dot, dark separating from dark. Thinning as it moves closer, paced like a man's stride, not quick, not slow. Steady. Taller now. The track isn't completely straight like it seemed, there's a rise, and he's moving up it, cresting it. Very tall now, very, in a long dark coat like the song. Head down, hood up. Movement around the knees, pump of muscle and flutter of wind. The coat is black. His face is pale, obscure. Pitted? Hair down across the eyes? Chin pointed?*
>
> *Nothing to stop him. Nothing that <u>can</u> stop him.*
>
> *I don't know where he's going. Coming.*
>
> *Coming <u>HERE</u>?*

My hand formed the word, the question mark, <u>HERE</u> plus a squiggle above a dot. Underline swooping up into two-part quirk done so fast it scarred the page, barely separated, ink bleeding into ink.

Shut it again, and fast, I remember thinking, breath hissing back out like a stomach-punch, *just do it slam it lock it. Just shut shut shut the fucking door.*

"Annnnd done," Leah chimed in overtop, cheerily. "Pens down, guys. Let's see what we've got."

I remember sitting back, flipping my paper as I did so, like I was afraid what might come out of it. Then seeing Leah point at Trevor, who winced, and started reading.

"Behind my door, um, what I see is, like... a long, dark road," he began, flat and halting, eyes squinched as if having trouble with his own words. "Or a bunch of train-tracks? One track, going off through a forest, uh... and it's really hard to see where it goes because the trees are all, like, jam-packed in on either side—"

Across the table, Yuri snorted. "You fucking kidding me?" he asked, glaring at Trevor.

Leah, still breathless: "Uh—no crit until we're all finished, please..."

"Oh, seriously? When joker here just read mine upside-down and copied it, instead of making up his own? *Real* mature, T."

Trevor flushed. "Am I supposed to know what the fuck he's talking about?"

"Guys," said Leah. "*Guys.*"

But Yuri was off again, as he so often was during these workshop attempts: he was an old-school Asimov fan who believed anything other than Ass-In-Chair-Hands-On-Keyboard was self-indulgent time-wasting and didn't think much of Trevor's too-obvious eagerness to try anything Leah proposed. Nor had he ever stinted at saying so, bluntly. If anything was a surprise this time, it was the uncharacteristic ferocity with which Trevor came back at him, for once; within minutes both were on their feet yelling at each other, with Leah shrinking between, her feeble efforts at mediation completely silenced.

Nobody noticed me, at the time, picking up Trevor's page and scanning it. Then Yuri's. After which, I got up and left, leaving my own scribble on the table without saying anything.

I don't think anybody noticed that for a while, either.

"Kris?" Hand on my shoulder, light, tinglingly familiar. It took some effort not to roll towards the touch for a kiss. "You awake?"

"Am now," I muttered. The bedroom was dark, but it wasn't like Leah needed the lights to know her way around. "Sorry. Should've said goodbye."

"No, no. I understand." The hand withdrew; a small, compact weight settled itself on the bed, carefully distant. After a moment, paper crackled. "I, um—I thought you might want this." And there it was, thrust without warning in front of my face. My Shut Door Exercise. I had to stifle the urge to rip it from her hands and tear it into shreds.

In hindsight I don't think that would have helped. But I still wish I had. Instead, I just took it, levered myself upright and slipped it into my bedside table drawer. Leah watched, wide eyes glinting in the dark.

"Is that really what you wrote?" she asked.

"What do you think?"

I hate how you do that, I remember her shouting at me. *Dodge questions by asking more questions. You always put everything back on me!* But she surprised me. Not saying anything, she shuffled close enough to reach the bedside *lamp,* turned it on, then gave me another piece of paper. I stared at her. She just nodded at the paper and gazed back.

Her door was pure Leah: a neat little sketch of opened gates with arching tops and angular runes above them, Tolkien's Mines of Moria entrance in miniature. Below that, her handwriting reeled across the page in the familiar chicken-scratches. Reading it had always, always been an effort in squinting patience and guesswork... until now. *Railroad tracks off into the dark,* it began. *I see them through the trees. A night with no moon, and he comes walking. . .*

I didn't need to read the rest, any more than you need to read it now. All sleepiness was gone, though I couldn't have told you what replaced it. Fear didn't seem like the right word. It felt more like prickly queasiness. Like nothing I'd ever felt.

"Trevor didn't copy Yuri," I said, roughly. "Neither did you. Right?"

Leah shook her head. "I—I thought, for just a minute, that he might have. I mean, if he was really desperate enough to impress you, then maybe he—"

"Impress *me?* I thought he was hung up on you."

That got a smile I hadn't seen in a long time; something caught in my throat. Leah shook her head. "God, Kris, you never could pick up on that kind of thing."

The smile faded. "No, he was too angry. Which means it was real. Which means..." She let out a shaky breath. "I also got this word in my head," she said, without segue. "Like I was hearing it from far away. An echo of an echo. Something—something Latin, I think."

"I didn't know you knew Latin."

"I don't, it just—sounded that way to me. Like a Roman name from *Asterix*, or something." She stopped by the door, arms folded, half-turned away. I couldn't see her eyes anymore.

"Are you okay?" I blurted, before I caught myself. We'd stopped asking each other that sort of thing. But all I got was a dull shrug.

"Sure." A deep breath; a sidelong look. "I don't think the exercise worked tonight, though."

"Probably... better not to do it again, then," I answered carefully.

"Probably."

So much that could have been said, in that look. None of it anything we could say. Nothing that would have made a difference, even now.

"Good night, Kris," she said, and left.

Not a forest this time. Flat, open prairie, an achingly wide night sky overhead; stars like spilled salt, crusting purple clouds. I stood amid swaying, whispering plants that might have been corn, or wheat, or savannah grass. A black shadow painted a depthless rectangle before me on the plain; I could smell the barn's wood mold and wet hay, undercut with dead mice and desiccated cow shit. A road cut across the plain past me, straight as a laser beam. The full moon blazed.

Made it all the easier to see.

The walker was farther away, tiny, only a smudged speck of moving black where the road disappeared into the invisible horizon. No way to tell where he was looking, though his shape inched slowly but evenly down the road's dead center, as if he was staring straight ahead. But I knew he knew I was there. Just as I knew why he wasn't hurrying. What need? He knew I couldn't move.

It should have taken a long time for him to reach me. Maybe it did. Time slips around in dreams, we all know that. But he didn't change course even as he approached. Hooded, black-cloaked, nothing but shadow under the cowl; his head didn't angle towards me. He wasn't even particularly *tall*—maybe six feet, if that. And the cloak draped and flowed like a perfectly normal human was wearing it. Even his movement looked like an ordinary walk. A steady, slightly-too-rhythmic walk, but a walk.

And... he was passing me. Not even turning to look.

I had half an instant to feel a surreal mix of giddy relief, bemused shock and even something like indignation, like part of me wanted to yell *Is that* it?! But then—

I want to tell you the word he told me: the word that sounded right in my ear, despite the distance between us; the word spoken at a nearly normal volume, calm, quiet, without rancor, without haste. But the explosion of sheer terror it detonated inside me erased it even as I heard it—a trauma so huge it blotted itself out in the instant of its own creation, the way the mind discards any pain too huge to process. Like when a tooth's pulled without freezing or a bone breaks; when you knock the wind out of yourself, when you get a concussion. You know it happened, and you know you never want it to happen again, but... that's all, that's it. Nothing else.

Just the scar where it's been.

At some point I realized I was awake. My mouth and throat felt dry, and dizziness lingered; I must have been hyperventilating. Had I screamed? Leah would have come running to check on me if I had. Unless—I checked the alarm clock and groaned. No, she was long gone to work by now. I made myself get up, shower, and get dressed, even though my shift at the bookstore didn't start for hours.

The apartment was unnervingly quiet. I did what little busywork I could find, which didn't take long. And then, without letting myself think about it, I went into Leah's room and sat down on the bed.

I hadn't allowed myself to do this in nearly two years. This had been the room we'd shared while we were together—I'd taken the spare bedroom afterwards because I had far less stuff to move out; I'd never collected anything like her vast array of kitsch, knickknacks and tchotchkes, like the horde of ceramic monkeys still taking up an entire shelf or the rows of unused Sacred Heart candles littering her dresser. Boxes and boxes of odds and ends, strewn along the windowsill. The closet stuffed to bursting with clothes. And her smell, still in the air, without any need to press my face into the pillow.

You had to look close to see what was missing. Beside the stereo, the stack of CDs was half the height it had once been. A sparsely-filled bookshelf, slightly bent, as if it had long held up a much heavier weight. A protruding nail on the wall where a picture had hung, the sort of thing everybody reminds themselves to get around to removing and never remembers. But if you didn't think to look, you wouldn't notice. You might think nobody else had ever slept here.

Maybe it was anger that made me get up and go to the second box from the right on her windowsill, the only one you needed to know the trick to open. Fingernails in the right hidden slots: slide, twist, press, *click*. I dug out the notepad and pencil that Leah had showed me, the pad where I knew she wrote down her dreams. And for the first time in two years, I sat down and started reading.

Nothing about me, which was both a relief and a disappointment. The usual surreal nonsense. One surprising scene about Yuri, of all people—I'd always known Leah's tastes were wider than mine but hadn't thought she felt anything for him beyond friendship. Journeys, conversations, images clearly plucked out and set aside for some future poem—

I turned to the last page and stopped. She'd written something down here... but it had been utterly obliterated by a black charcoal smear scribbled so forcefully onto the paper that the sheet itself felt warped under my fingers. I tilted it back and forth under the light, trying to make something out, but gave up when my eyes started to hurt.

Then a better idea came to mind. I flipped to the next page, took the pencil, and began delicately shading light gray over the paper. The impression of the word bloomed up in white against the gray, gouged into the pulp; almost, but not quite, too faint to see.

(*Like I was hearing it from far away. An echo of an echo. Something Latin, I think...*)

On her desk, Leah had left her computer open and running, as she always did. One Google search, and the answer was there in front of me. It was, indeed, Latin. My face felt numb.

Venio.

I am coming.

I begged off sick from my shift, waited for Leah to get home and told her what I'd found. I was a little surprised she didn't get angry—violation of her privacy was one of the few things that normally set her off—but I guess both of us knew we were beyond that now. We called the guys. Trevor, surprise surprise, was perfectly willing to meet tonight even on this short notice; Yuri took some persuading, but finally agreed, and even offered his living room again.

Once Yuri had finally gotten it through his head that no, this wasn't some kind of practical joke, he practically went berserk; it was the most excited I'd ever seen him. "Don't you *get* it, Kris?" he raved, striding around the room. "We've actually achieved something *paranormal* here! Subconscious telepathic communication, at least—or maybe we actually *contacted* something! A spirit, a ghost, whatever..."

"Well, you know, it could also be—" Trevor began.

Yuri didn't listen. "We have to do this again. Now we all know what to concentrate on, maybe we can make contact consciously. God! I should record this. Let me get my phone." He sprinted out and was back in a second, setting up his phone on a sideboard by the dining room table. Trevor looked at me helplessly.

"Yuri. *Yuri.*" I had to raise my voice. He blinked at me. "Yuri, we didn't do this to convince you to keep going with it. We want it to *stop.*"

Yuri stared. "That's ridiculous," he said after a moment, in a perfectly level voice. "That's *stupid*. That's like Alexander Fleming throwing out his moldy petri dishes without checking them first. Look, we're not calling up Captain Howdy on a Ouija board here. We're confirming whether we're sharing the same mental experiences. That's *all*. Besides, if you want it to stop, doesn't it make more sense to finish it? Wrap it up, bring it to a conclusion, whatever it is?"

Trevor cleared his throat. "I, um... I gotta say, I kind of don't want to leave it hanging either. You're... you're supposed to face this stuff, I think. That's what Dr. Tallan always says."

I turned to Leah for backup. The look on her face was like a slap. My fists knotted. "Fuck's sake, don't tell me you're buying this," I said.

She swallowed but didn't flinch. "Kris, I'm sorry," she replied in a small voice. It sounded almost exactly like the way she'd said *I'm sorry* two years ago, when she'd first asked me to move out. "But I don't want to have that dream again. Do you?"

No, but— The words disintegrated in my mouth, leaving nothing behind.

Yuri clapped his hands, as if that had settled it. "Okay, then. Let's do this. Everybody, get a piece of paper from someone else; Leah, give me your pencil, I'll get pens for the rest of us..." Of course, he'd remembered the procedure exactly, even while he was scoffing. Before I knew it, we were all seated around the table again, and Trevor, at Yuri's order, was setting a timer on his own phone under the steady stare of Yuri's camera lens. Yuri took his seat, practically rubbing his hands in glee. "You know how this goes, guys. Draw the door. Concentrate on it. And open yourself up to see what comes through." He nodded to Trevor. "Go."

Trevor started the timer, then bent his head to his paper. So did Leah and Yuri. I put my pencil on the paper but sat still, fully intending to draw nothing, write nothing. Okay, I'd scribble the pencil around meaninglessly a little, just to make it look good, but—

My mouth dried.

From what I'd been sure were completely random muscle movements, the cartoon-simple shape of the door—rectangle, tiny circle—had somehow emerged. I couldn't take my eyes from it. My hand cramped; my fingers hurt; my forearm ached. The pencil scribbled across the page. The door seemed to be blurring in and out.

Not real, I thought fuzzily. *Think of something real but faraway. If he's coming to where he thinks you are, show him something different. Send him on.* I tried to conjure up places in my mind that I knew I'd never seen, even to recognize on TV: Boise, Cleveland, Saskatoon. Minsk. Aachen. Beijing. Locations that were nothing more than a name and a vague direction.

But the problem is that the more you try to imagine what's too unfamiliar to conceive, the more your own familiarities snap into place in the gaps, like a default reflex you can't control. The nameless city becomes your own city; a shapeless street becomes a road you know. Any building becomes your building... or your friend's. The corridor becomes an all-too-recognizable hallway. And as the shadows pour down that hallway, surrounding the silently walking figure, its hand lifting to the door to knock, the more your head wants to turn from the paper door to the real one, even while part of you is desperately screaming not to look up, not to look, not to—

Trevor's phone went off in a flurry of electronic chimes. I jumped. Across the table, Leah looked like she wanted either to burst into tears or throw up. Yuri shook his head, seeming to snap awake. "Whoa," he said. "Okay, I'll read mine first, then we—"

A knocking came at the door. Not loud, not heavy-handed; polite, almost diffident. Yuri scowled. "Fuck *me*, go the fuck away," he muttered. When the knocking came again, he repeated himself, this time in a shout: "Fuck *off*, asshole!"

The knocking only continued. Yuri rolled his eyes. I stared at him, trying to get enough breath into my lungs to ask him: couldn't he *see* it? The shadow, coagulating thickly around the edges of his front door, like tar seeping through cardboard? Couldn't he feel the cold in the air? But I couldn't even get my hand to move as he rose from his chair and strode towards the door. Leah was whimpering. Trevor stared at me like a kid waiting for his parents to explain something he didn't understand. Yuri reached the door, grabbed the knob, twisted it, and flung it open.

There was nobody there. And simultaneously all the shadow, all the chill, it was all gone. I could move again. Breathed easily. The absence of fear felt almost like being drunk. Yuri looked down the outside hall, then blew out an exasperated breath. "Well, that was—" he began, turning around.

The doorway behind him went night-black. Something reached out of the darkness behind him, seized his shoulder, and pulled. Yuri flew backwards like a stuntman on a wire and vanished, the void that swallowed him gone in the same instant. The door hung open. The hallway was empty.

I sat there still, same position. Couldn't move a muscle. Leah was the one who went white. Trevor was the one who vomited.

I don't think it ever occurred to any of us to call the police. We couldn't have told them anything they'd believe, obviously. But worse than that, we couldn't have told them anything *we'd* believe. Every 911 call ever made boils down to one of just two messages: *Help me please* or *It's not my fault*; both at once. Problem is, neither of those were true. They still aren't.

Nobody could help Yuri, any more than they could help us. And it *was* our fault.

Trevor cleaned up his sick while Leah had a sobbing breakdown on the couch. I replayed what Yuri's phone had recorded, over and over, but the lens hadn't been pointed towards the front door. Again and again, the knocking came; Yuri scowled, swore, shouted, then got up and walked out of frame as the three of us stared after him; his last, almost-inaudible half sentence; and then, the reaction—Leah swaying, me frozen, Trevor doubling over. It was nearly hypnotic. I only came out of it when Trevor tapped me on the shoulder and told me he was walking me and Leah home.

We had to leave the apartment door unlocked, of course.

I don't remember much of that walk. I barely remember Trevor in the door of our apartment, insisting that it was no problem at all to crash on our couch, and Leah pushing him out, sounding too tired to be either kind or harsh. I remember huddling up under my blankets the way I hadn't done since I was eight. I *think* I remember Leah lying down next to me, but she was gone when I woke.

The day crawled by. My manager called once, asking if I was feeling better; I told her no and tried to feel touched when she sounded worried. In the afternoon, Trevor sent me and Leah several e-mails from his office address, carrying multiple links and attachments. I read them without replying. The final message's subject line had degenerated into all-caps begging, and when I saw it was addressed only to me, not Leah, I deleted it unread. I spent some time looking at the photos and videos of Yuri I still had saved on my phone, trying to think what I'd say when whoever eventually went looking for him started to ask questions.

The light from the windows inched across the floor and faded away. I sat in the deepening gloom. Listening. Every hair on my body stretched out, feeling for a chill in the air.

I am coming.

It was mostly dark when Leah finally got home. She waved a sheaf of paper at me as she came in, apparently unsurprised to find me waiting on the couch. "I printed it all out," she said. "Everything Trevor found. What do you think? It makes a lot of sense to me, I have to say."

"I don't know," I said. "If this is something we... we *created*, just out of our minds with that exercise, why don't we have control over it? Why can't we turn it off?"

"Well, we haven't exactly tried yet." Leah flipped on the lights, came over and sat down beside me, shuffling through the papers. "That Reddit discussion thread, about how to destroy tulpas—"

"Where they all say you just have to stop paying attention to them? How's that been working for you?"

Leah put her hands on her knees and breathed deeply. "The post near the end," she said, when the color had faded out of her face. "It says one way to actively dissipate a tulpa is to force something into its definition that's essentially a self-contradiction. Like, if you create an imaginary friend, you have to visualize it doing something nobody you call a friend could ever do, like stealing your ex, or... or something like that. And then when it can't believe in itself the way it was built to, it falls apart. It literally melts down from the cognitive dissonance."

I snorted. "Yeah, and there are other posts that say the only way to kill a tulpa is to kill whoever created it. Are we buying into that too?"

Leah flushed again. "No! Look, Kris, all I'm saying is that it's worth a shot. I mean, have you got any other ideas?"

Now who's throwing everything back on who? I got up and went to the window, glaring out at the traffic whooshing by outside on Bathurst Street; my legs burned. "We could leave," I said. "Just pick up and get out of here, go as far as we can. See if that makes a difference."

"'We?'" Leah replied.

It was my turn to flush, abrupt and fierce. I opened my mouth to snap *That's not what I meant*, not at all sure what I *had* meant... and coughed out the taken breath in a gasp, heat draining to cold in an instant. "Oh, Christ," I gulped, staring across the street. "Oh, shit—*Leah.*" I pointed, amazed to see my hand was shaking. "Do you see that? Tell me you *see* that!"

"See what?" Leah had raced to my side, squinting through our images in the glass. "Hang on—" She dashed back to the door, turned the lights out. Darkness dropped over us. The black figure across the road, a silhouette huddled in the corner of an alley, became sharper, seemed to loom closer out of the dark. Leah returned to the window; I felt her stiffen. "Oh, shit," she breathed. "Kris, what do we do? What do we *do*?"

Good fucking question. I tried to pull my brain back into one piece. "We could try going out the back door of the main house," I said, voice hoarse. "We'd have to hop the fence, sneak out through the property on the other side, but..."

The figure pushed one hand back awkwardly over its head. Pale hair glinted momentarily in a flicker of the streetlight. And my terror collapsed so completely and quickly into exasperated rage it almost made me puke. "Oh, fuck *me*," I said, yanked the window open and stuck my head out. "*Trevor! Get your ass over here!* " The black figure jerked; the hat it had been wearing fell off, and Trevor hunched down to grab it as if ducking out of a sniper's line of fire.

"What the hell were you thinking?" I bellowed at him a minute later on the doorstep of our building. "Were you fucking *trying* to scare us into a heart attack?" Trevor seemed to shrink as I kept yelling; Leah looked like she wanted to say something but couldn't think what. "This is not a fucking game any more! We don't have time for this kind of stalker bullshit—!"

"I *wasn't...*" Trevor's voice cracked. "I'm not *stalking* you guys, Kris, God! I just... I just want to make sure you're *safe*, OK? Both of you! You're, like, the only people on this planet I give a shit about at all, and if I lost you, I don't... I don't..." He trailed off, swallowed liquidly and scrubbed one hand across his face, not looking at me. "You never answered my last e-mail," he finished. "I tried to say it all in there. But you never answered."

Fuck. Of all the times for Leah to be right. I couldn't decide whether to laugh, cry or scream. "You give a shit about us?" I asked instead. "Fine. Then fucking *listen* to me and get it through your head: Leah I don't know about, but I am very definitely Gay All Day, and you know that thing about 'if this was the last minute before death would you at least kiss me goodbye?' Hate to say it, man, 'cause you're my friend, and I love you, *but not like that*—this probably *is* our last minute, and, no. Never. Not ever. Please, just... go the fuck home and think about it until you get that."

Trevor stared at me for a long time, his eyes wet. "I... can't," he finally whispered, so quiet I could barely hear him. "I'm scared, Kris."

I sighed, too exhausted for any more anger. "Yeah," I said. "Me too. So come in if you want. But no more of this shit, okay? That's done."

Trevor only nodded, staring at the concrete steps.

I want to say his silence worried me, as we got him set up on the couch to stay the night. I want to say I was thinking about him at least that much. I want to say I was thinking about anything at all but the sick dread pooling in my stomach and the sounds outside our apartment's front door.

I want to say that all I felt when I went into the bathroom in the morning and saw Trevor hanging from the showerhead, a pair of Leah's hose serving as a noose, was what anybody would feel: shock, horror, anguish, pain. Rage at the pointlessness, the selfishness. Grief like a hole chewing its way through your gut, even before I read his note through streaming eyes: *It took all four of us to make it. Maybe it needs*

all four of us to keep going. A tulpa dies when its maker dies. Maybe this will break the
chain. I'm sorry, Kris. I can't think of any other way.

I only ever wanted you to be safe.

I was sitting on the cold bathroom floor, note crumpled in my fist, muttering
between dry sobs: "Oh, God, Trev, fuck you. *Fuck you*, Trev. God, God..." when Leah
came in, and started to scream. Which finally gave me something else to think about
besides the sickening, contemptible truth: in that first moment of comprehension,
what I'd felt, more than anything else...

... was envy.

There wasn't any way to keep the cops out of it this time, though nobody official
acted like an asshole. You figure the people who handle this sort of thing learn to
tell the fakers from the genuinely traumatized pretty quick most of the time. Not
that that's exactly consoling. I remember one bad moment when one of the uni-
formed officers gave me a narrow look, like something about my no-I-didn't-have-
the-slightest-idea-but-he-*was*-in-therapy answer didn't ring right, but he didn't do
anything except give me a card and tell me to call him if I thought of anything else.
Leah had cried herself into unconsciousness before anyone had even gotten there,
leaving me to handle the clean-up.

After everything was over and everyone was gone, I went into Leah's room and
sat at her desk, waiting. For a moment I thought about lying down beside her but
couldn't bring myself to do it. The urge didn't last long anyway. Eventually, she
woke up and looked at me, and I knew the truth the instant I met her hollow, red-
dened gaze.

"He's still coming," I said.

Leah only nodded. "He was... I recognized the street. It's in Windsor. I grew up
there. I could smell the fog..." Her voice was raw, a wreck of itself. "This isn't... I don't
think we made this, Kris. Not completely. Maybe we gave it a shape. But this thing—
it's something else. From somewhere else. I think, maybe, it's been looking for a

door for a long time." Her gaze dropped to the bedclothes. "And we gave it four of them."

"And wrote it a fucking set of directions," I said.

Leah frowned, sitting up. "Wait. What if—what if that's it? We wrote its path out for it. Who's to say we can't write its ending the way we want?" Suddenly energized, she swung her legs off the bed and leaned forward to grab my hands. "This whole thing started as a story. Maybe if we want to finish it, we have to *finish* the story."

I stared at her. "Finish it, like... how? Just write him going away?"

"Why not?" With what was now almost manic enthusiasm, Leah leapt up, dug her dream journal out of her box, and slammed it down on the desk in front of me. "That's my book, so you'll have to write it, but we can do this right now! Come on, come on..." Unable to find words to argue, I let her swivel me around, took the pencil she shoved into my hand as she flipped the journal to a blank page. "Okay. Go for it. Draw the door and write the ending."

"This can't..." But my hand was already moving. Same door as before: rectangle, circle. I closed my eyes and saw shapes move in the blackness. Saw one shape moving slowly, steadily, coming nearer. Leah was muttering in my ear: *The road goes ever on and on, and the traveller must follow, no stops, no destination, no visits; no one waits to welcome him, only the endless road, leaving all other souls behind, untouched, safe in the light, safe in the light, safe in the light as he disappears forever—*

"*Jesus!*" My entire arm suddenly cramped in vicious agony, driving the pencil across the page so hard it tore through the paper and snapped in half. Leah yelped, jumping back. I wrung my hand, feeling blood seeping from my gouged knuckles. "Fuck! Okay, that didn't work."

"No. No, of course it wouldn't, that wasn't an ending, that was just a copout." Leah grabbed the book, flipped to another page and yanked another pen from the desk drawer. "It's a journey, right? Journeys have to *end* somewhere." She sketched a door of her own, this one no more complicated than mine, and paused. "We have to send him somewhere. Somewhere a person couldn't survive; somewhere we *know* nothing could survive." She looked at me expectantly.

I shrugged, at a loss. "Underwater?" I said. "I don't know! Um, underground. Buried." Leah nodded, scribbling furiously. "In space. In the center of the sun... Wait! No, he wants his door. I don't think we're gonna keep him away from it."

Leah stopped writing and drew a shuddering breath. She never did give up. I'd loved that about her once, before I'd hated how it meant she never let a fight go until she thought *she'd* won it.

"Doors," she said. "That was how it happened with Yuri, too. Maybe—maybe *that's* the key. Not the words. The door." I gaped at her as she turned to one more blank page and, glancing defiantly at me, drew a different rectangle: this one wider than it was tall, with no knob on it or anything else.

"You want to put him inside a wall?" Terror drove through me like freezing water forced down my throat. "No! No, goddammit, Leah, if you do that it's only going to make every wall a door! He'll be able to get in *anywhere!*" I leaped forward and dragged her away from the desk, into the middle of the room, holding her by the shoulders as I cast around wildly. "Oh, Christ, he's close, isn't he? He can fucking hear it in our *heads!* Don't think of him in the walls! Don't!"

Leah shook her head. "No, shit, you're right, you're right..." She closed her eyes, taking deep breaths, half-determined and half-dismayed. "Not the walls," she muttered, fists clenched. "Not the walls, not the walls, not the—"

She stopped, staring down. I followed her gaze.

Two shadows stretched out in different directions from her feet.

Leah's head snapped up, eyes wide, breath sucking in. "Oh, shit, *Kri*—" was all she got out, before two massive arms made of something that looked like molten tar exploded out of the floor, wrapped around her, and jerked her back down into it. Under. Through. *Away.*

So that was three days ago. I've been working on this ever since, on Leah's laptop.

I told my boss I wasn't coming back to work, after which I unplugged Leah's landline and turned off both her phone and mine. There was a banging on the door yesterday that sounded like a cop's knock, but I just stopped moving and didn't say anything. After a while it stopped. I haven't eaten much or slept much. Strangely, when I do sleep, I don't dream.

And now you know why you shouldn't ever have started reading, whoever's reading this. Because he gets stronger the closer he gets. If you know about him, he knows about you. The only thing I can think of is that if enough people learn about him, he'll be—I don't know—maybe dispersed somehow. Like a drop of ink disappearing in a lake. I want to believe that, because I don't have anything left to think about the alternative.

And maybe if all I do is give him more people to... to take, he'll be grateful enough that whatever he does with me, whenever he *does* come for me, maybe I'll at least end up where Leah is. Wherever she went. Wherever Yuri went. I want to hope maybe somehow Trevor will be there, too, but I don't know how reasonable that is—

Reasonable. Jesus Christ. I just wrote the word *reasonable*.

Maybe I should have tried harder to make this story unreadable, unbelievable. Forgettable. But that's the trick about forgetting: you can't ever really choose to do it. You can only wait and hope it happens. Sit in an empty apartment, breathing as quietly as you can. You can try to unfocus your eyes. Try not to read. Try not to recognize words. Try not to put them together.

Try not to think of water.

Try not to think of darkness.

Try not to think of the inside of your wall.

Try not to think of the inside of your own body. Of the inside of your own head.

Try not to think of anything.

Try to think of nothing.

Look Up

 HERE IS NO *way to love that is not, in some way, an echo.*

So, there's a family gathering you're invited to attend—not the family you know, but your dead father's family up north. The celebration of their eldest member's name-day. "Eldest," said the girl on the phone, one of your endless list of cousins on that side, with a very audible capital "E." And your mother readily admits she never felt accepted by them, always an outsider, never truly welcomed into the heart of their clan... but this isn't about her, is it, really? *You* have *to go*, she tells you. *When else will you get the chance?*

You're not sure you want to. Actually, you're sure you *don't* want to. But you don't want to disappoint her, either.

Or your Dad, she'd tell you, if you ever said this out loud—but Dad doesn't matter, not since you were five. He went away. He went away, and he died.

Went away... back up *there*. And died.

Which isn't his family's fault, you suppose. Just an accident—a storm, black ice, some weird confluence of events, nothing predictable. A semi jack-knifed, there was a pileup, his seatbelt failed, and he went through the windshield, straight up and out, like Superman. So far, they didn't even find him until almost everybody else was accounted for, his spilt blood frozen solid.

But this is the truth: He wouldn't have been there at all if not for them, for *that* particular bunch of insular North Ontario Latvian hicks—the ones half your DNA comes from, who you haven't met more than... well, never, in your entire fucking life. If *his* last name hadn't been Godsmanis too.

Just like you wouldn't be here now if *yours* wasn't.

Let me tell you a story, Youngest.

Once upon a time, long past, there was a land, my land. My blood's hunting-ground. It was dark yet fulsome, cold yet high, well-stocked, and difficult to penetrate. The pine-trees grew everywhere, needles sharp-sticky, exhaling their scent into the air; the stars stared down, pitiless, bright pins in an endless black sky. No human maps could contain it. What was done there stayed secret, however bloody, unseen by any eyes but mine.

It was... beautiful, so very beautiful. My home, my treasure, my charge, and keeping. I gave it everything and took everything from it in return—this is the price one pays to rule. A true king always buys his throne with sacrifice, and gladly.

I sat on a pile of my ancestors' bones there, stacked high, all those others of my blood who had died for the land, again and again: burnt skulls and boiled ribs, jaws and teeth and empty eyes, cauldron-cracked femurs and gnawed-clean vertebrae with all of it painted in fresh flowers and veined green, a midden-heap left to mulch beneath ancient ivy. We were willing to die, I and they, raised to it from birth, but we died only to keep our land ours, no one else's... an act of taking and retaking, never of giving. The visible sign and seal on a thousand years' worth of ownership.

Being a king meant something very different then.

My land and yours. All of ours. This new place is only its shadow, a mere mockery, wind over emptiness. A hollow tree still smoldering from the inside-out, long after being struck by lightning.

But now we return to you once more, in a car, whirring steadily along—more a van, really; too small to be a truck, too large to be anything else. One of those steel boxes with four-wheel drive for off-roading, big enough for you (the only available backup driver, which makes you ten times as nervous), your mother (who doesn't drive anymore at all, since recent LASIK surgery left her night-blind), your stepbrothers, and your stepbrothers' girlfriend and boyfriend. Because neither of them were going to let you meet these weirdos alone, but why not make it a date? They love to camp, unreservedly, Fergus and Emmy, Steve and Stu. Steve and Stu even met in Forestry three years back, halfway up the same Pacific Redwood tree.

They want to support you on this journey, however difficult it may turn out to be... to shield you with their love. And you love them too, naturally enough, this false family of yours—why not? They are, after all, the only one you've ever known.

Going north, the landscape alters as the road narrows, highway to rural route to seasonal route to a long, winding passage through endless overhanging branches, the visible slice of sky slowly narrowing, darkening, long before dusk comes rolling in. Up past Timmins, as far away from Toronto as you've ever been by car—seven and a half hours to get there, past nothing but rocks and trees, trees and rocks, bar the occasional six to ten-building "towns" sprinkled on either side of the dusty asphalt.

Fergus drives because he doesn't trust anyone else to; Emmy and your mother haggle over the stereo system, trading songs from Emmy's iPod to ones from your mother's favorite trip CDs. Stu and Steve sit furthest back, murmuring and poking at each other over the divider together like a couple of giant kids.

While you ride shotgun, silent, leaning your head against the passenger-side window and trying not to think about just how little you want to be here.

Who are these people to me, exactly? you wonder. *Who* can *they ever be? Nurture trumps nature, surely; genetic testing doesn't prove shit. Either we're more than the sum of our parts or we're just... fucking robots dropped at random into this world, pre-programmed by our own biology, and free will's a goddamn myth.*

The very thought makes your chest tighten, makes you hug yourself over the seatbelt and practice your yogic breathing, straight down to the diaphragm: ten counts in, ten counts out, start over. Shut your eyes and watch the bright fragments of random thought tumble past behind them, flickering far too fast to connect into any sort of narrative as you fight down the sick clench of fear, of *wrongness.* Trying not to worry over just how far every fresh kilometer takes you from what you know as home and failing miserably.

—Aija, your mother says, tapping you on the shoulder. —Where'd you go, baby?

You open your eyes slowly. Did you fall asleep? The last thing you remember was the car's dull hum through your molars, the glass against your cheek, Lord Huron playing "Meet Me in the Woods"; a little on the nose, but there you go. And then, just—

(black rushing wind, black sky, the smell of pine)

(wings around you, wrapped tight, frail and smooth as a beetle's split shell)

(and a beat in your ears, inside *you...* liquid, secret. Somehow, somehow)

(familiar)

Back in the car, you blink and squint, dream sliding away from your gaze like a film. Like a snake's inner eyelid.

—I... don't know, you tell her. And look away.

I am sorry, Youngest?

Ah. How can I know so much about you, when we have surely never met before? Well. The echo you dreamed might have told you, had you listened longer. But I will give you a hint. We be of one blood as well, you and I.

Trees and rocks, rocks and trees. The road slopes down, then up, blasted straight through granite thirty feet deep, pink-gray with glinting mineral speckles scattered her and there, topped with dirt and foliage. A smell of pine seeping in through slightly cracked windows, like darkness; reflective spots flashing by on the kilometer-markers, speed-blinking, throwing back the headlights' shine.

The next-to-last time you stop to pee, it's been so long since you've seen even a roadside store you just tell Fergus to park on the gravel; the car hasn't even fully stopped before you're leaping out, dashing headlong between the nearest two trunks, fumbling with your fly, to squat and let go. Reach out one hand to steady yourself as you pull your shorts back up, hoping your underwear would catch whatever might be left, only to feel your palm land smack on a sticky, pungent resin-clump, a clot of pine-sap oozing out between bark-slabs rough as lizard-scale.

On return, both headlights bear hovering, clustered haloes of moths and tiny stinging gnats that break from their orbit to swarm you, attracted by the sweetness gluing your fingers together.

—Aija, get in! Mom yells, muffled behind glass. —We've still got two hours' drive, and there's horseflies out here! Horseflies, blackflies, just plain flies—

As you slam the door, Steve and Stu are already chiming in, drawing an approving snort from Fergus, as Mom and Emmy just roll their eyes: —*"Oh the black... flies, the little blackflies, always the blackflies no matter where ya go..."*

—Yeah, real cool, kids, you throw back, snapping your seatbelt shut. —What is this, summer camp? *"Oh, they built the ship Titanic, to sail the ocean blue... and it was sad when the great ship went down, to the bottom of the—"*

—*"Uncles and aunts, little children lost their pants,"* Emmy and Mom reply, crossing over mid-air with Steve and Stu completing the previous verse: —*"...I'll die with the blackflies pickin' my bones in north Ontair-eye-oh-eye-oh, in north Ontair-eye-oh..."*

—Maybe that guy'll already be dead by the time we get there, you can barely stop yourself from muttering—but is it a guy or a girl? Somebody too withered to identify by sex at all, probably, older than hell and from almost as far away, shipped halfway around the word for a party they can barely understand. You picture them curled in a wheelchair, joints knotted-fragile, skin like rotten lace, barely able to whisper. Will they even speak English?

—Eldest, you say to Mom out loud. —Is that some sort of title, you think? Like, uh... a tribal elder, or whatever?

In the rear-view mirror, you can just see Mom shake her head. Replying, as she does: —I don't think so, honey. More like—the oldest person still alive? In the family, I mean.

—Dad's family.

—*Your* family. We've been over this already, Aija. Remember?

Well, yes, you think, not quite sighing, eyes on the dashboard clock as you rub your hands together, trying in vain to wring the scent of trees' blood from your sticky palms: how could you forget or ever be allowed to? This accident of DNA, tying you to a hundred people you don't know, who don't know you; this dead man's love-gift, posthumously marrying you to a name whose meaning you barely understand. Godsmanis—it sounds Greek, you get that, but it really is Latvian. You looked it up. Godsmanis, meaning not so much "man of God" as "god's man," with the god in question left very much unspecified, seeing how Latvia was Christianized far more recently than the rest of Europe. Not to mention... more violently.

(I could tell you all about that, Youngest. And I will.)

The road stretches on, empty for miles yet, both in front and behind. Above, the wind whips faster through the trees, kicks up dust, in pursuit of your wake. It smells you now, just like the gnats, the moths, the flies. It knows you better than you know yourself as yet.

(I say *it*, of course, and mean me. Obviously. For he is *not* the eldest, in fact, that creature you speed to meet, let alone *Eldest*. Since I alone hold that honor even now.

(That part of the story I will save for when we meet, however; face to face, if possible. Much like all the rest.)

It's not more than half an hour after that before you arrive, though even Fergus has to drive slower now, picking his way through the forest-shrouded dark. At last the gravel road dissolves into a flat, dew-damp field surrounded on all sides by trees, an angular black cabin of improbable size dominating its rough center, flanked by a sea of tents; two long, single-story wings spread out asymmetrically, windows ablaze with light. Something like two dozen vehicles scattered pell-mell all over, grass tire-tracked, ground here and there into mud beneath chained wheels. Off to one side, a beacon-size bonfire roars: black silhouettes circle it, a crowd you can hear from here—talking, laughing, singing, some barely-recognizable English woven in among a harsher, older tongue. Stars drown the sky overhead, the half-moon brighter than you've ever seen it back in Toronto.

Fergus whistles in awe. —Holy sheep-dip, he says. —Just park anywhere?

—I guess! Mom replies, shrugging. Over near the fire, people are already pointing, waving, calling out what you assume must be greetings. One heads your way. Mom puts on her best smile, the one she only uses when she's nervous. You wish it seemed more reassuring.

Insects shrill beneath the fire-crackle, the wind through the trees; unfamiliar smells, or lack of smells. Your headlights tiny and nude in the greater night, which looms large enough to drown in.

(*Ah, but what a very small forest this is, to frighten you so,* I think, almost loud enough for you to hear me; *How so?* I hear you wonder in return, as yet unaware where the idea comes from, and chuckle—*only look up, Youngest,* I think back, smiling to see how you cannot quite keep your chin from rising. *Can you see the sky?*

(*Of course I can.*)

(*Well, then.*)

Perhaps you wonder how I know all this—what you think, what you fear? Well, more easily than you might imagine, though I see you, as well—from nearby, with others' eyes, if not my own. I am closer than you dream, Youngest.

Ah, but I have lived a long time, and have always been the best-studied one I know, long before books were printed on paper. Yet do not ever believe them when they say I had my family's best interests in mind, educating myself; there was never any better reason for me to hoard and pore through words, written or otherwise, than power, a love of secrets. Study was just another branch of magic.

Even the Vikings had caught Christ by the time they reached us, at long last; they thought to save us through slaughter, to baptize us with blood. But not *my* blood, no. Never us.

The things I did, spells I laid... they saved my land, yes, but for me alone. You see? So, *I* would be its only hunter left roaming, and my people only *my* prey.

Still, things change, no matter how long one fights them. Our kingdom vanished slowly, eaten away, piece by piece and bite by bite; I shrank with it, trapped by my own castle's confines, its stones laid over what had once been my temple's sacrificial altar. They lost all I had given them, these ingrates my spawn spawned; forgot their own heritage, what their blood once meant—and owed. Our kingdom vanished, eaten, forgotten. And I was lost as well, in turn.

I am still lost.

Too long have I haunted these foreign woods like a moth, weaving webs in the trees, dug deep in this stony land every winter to freeze like a toad, a hundred-year locust. To wake each summer barely knowing where I am, let alone *who*. Oh, and how tiring it is to know oneself unloved, when love has always been the only seasoning that makes one's choice of food palatable!

Yet with your coming, Youngest, I feel I may finally make a place for myself, even here. I may finally have found reason to.

The man who emailed you, Uncle Mikus, turns out to be younger than you'd feared: only in his forties, and insists on being called Mike. He didn't blink for a second when Stu and Steve emerged holding hands. Within ten minutes, seeing how wiped out you were, he was shepherding everybody inside the house, doling out rooms. Yours has a peak like a chalet's roof, all bark and logs, apparently with housekeeping to match.

—Are those spiderwebs? Mom asks, staring up. —God, they're *everywhere*. I won't sleep a wink.

—Uh huh, you reply, and shut your eyes, immediately falling back into the same dream as before, from a great height. Every detail identical, though the sleep itself is deep and surprisingly restful.

Which is why it comes as such an unpleasant surprise to wake with the stink of wood mold everywhere, seeping in even through the heavily varnished wooden walls and floors. Your sinuses creak like a stuck door. It takes ten minutes under the hottest shower you can stand before your head finally unblocks enough to allow you to blow your nose, sneeze out a gush of mucus leaving your ears popped and your temples aching.

—Can't sleep in here again, you tell a dark-haired girl your own age who finds you snuffling over and over into a wad of toilet paper. —I'm allergic, to—all this.

The girl frowns. —The woods?

—Wood, generally. And pine, probably. All that sap and stuff.

—Like I said: the woods. The girl takes you by one arm, frown skewing to a grin, surprisingly bright. —C'mon, cousin—there's coffee boiling, and meat, so much meat. And red eggs. We'll feast all day, then drink all night. You might as well start things off right.

—I'm Aija, you offer.

—Oh, I know; everyone knows. You can call me Ezti.

Coffee helps, black and sweet. You manage a nod and smile for most of the people you pass. Mike and Ezti seem to be the exception in this crowd, who mainly look like they'll never see sixty again, though they return your smiles cheerfully enough. You're relieved to spot Mom, Mike and the rest of your family (your *real* family, you don't quite admit to thinking) out on the porch and find your way out to them; it turns out to face the pond, which you have to admit glimmers beautifully in the morning sunlight.

—So how late are we going to have to stay up tonight, anyway? Steve is asking, as you sit down at the table. —What time zone is he in, over there?

—They're on summer hours right now, so eight hours difference, says Mike. —The Eldest won't be awake earlier than about noon, so the plan is to start the Skype call 'round three in the morning and go for... well, basically, long as his stamina holds out. He's something like a hundred and ten years old, so that won't be all *that* long.

—Your Great-Aunt, uh... Inese?... said he was turning a hundred twenty-five, Emmy puts in, to you. —At least, I *think* she did.

Mike laughs. —Great-Aunt Inese has trouble remembering her own birthday, Žēlite, he tells you. —But don't tell her I said that. When he uses your real name, the one only Dad could pronounce, for the first time he sounds like the rest of the clan; it shocks you silent, making his eyebrows cant. —Ah, but you prefer your nickname, don't you? Sorry, Cousin Aija.

—Aija's a *nickname?* says Stu, looking genuinely astonished. Then adds, as Steve jabs him hard in the side: —Ow, man! And... Zhaleetah? That's beautiful. Why wouldn't you use that?

You shrug, awkward. —Too hard to spell. I got tired of explaining where the accents go, let alone how they sound.

—Most of us choose a British name for school, Mike agrees. —You look tired, though

—Long trip, strange bed. You know.

—Plus, she's got allergies, Ezti chimes in helpfully. You wince. —Why don't we put her in Strādulis's RV, Mike? He wouldn't mind, much. Besides, it'll be easier talking to the Eldest with some decent sleep under her belt.

—Oh, I don't...you start to protest, only to have them both hiss you silent. —No no, it's settled, Ezti continues. —I'll tell Strade. Mike, you help with the bedding.

—I can do that, Mom says quickly.

—Aha, perfect. Come this way, Mrs. Grigor.

Melanie, you think but don't say, watching Mom's lips move, equally silent, probably wanting to put in Fergus and Steve's Dad's name. But she follows Ezti dutifully past an old woman carrying a steaming platter of sausages who starts dishing it out to everybody, neatly, without being asked. She has maybe five teeth left in her friendly, lopsided grin. Your stomach twists.

—Ezti wasn't kidding about the meat, I see, you mutter to Mike, who laughs.

Later, but not by much, you fall into sleep. And dream, again:

Black wind through black pines. Cold air, black skies. No stars. A warm rain falling, black only in transit. Stick out your hand, palm up: yes, child, just like that. It will be red to the eye, moving closer, and to the tongue? Sweet, not salt. Taste it, please.

—*You're* the one won't use her true name, the old woman standing in the door of Uncle Strādulis's RV says, staring down at you as you open your eyes later that evening, after a few hours' nap; a different one from this morning, more teeth and less smile. Her voice is sandpaper and ash, completely at odds with the ruddy, winter-apple look of her pudgy face and body. Great-Aunt Inese? —It was *her* gave you that habit, hé? *That* woman, Grigor's widow. I knew she'd never be able to manage it.

Your face flushes, red-hot. And: —That *woman* is my mother, lady, you find yourself snapping.

—Ho! Slow down, mad cow. She smiles widely, eyes sparkling despite their heavy cataracts; does this count as hazing or flirtation? —Yes, I see it now; you *do* look like him after all. Come meet your elders.

—Can I put my pants back on, first?

—If you insist.

Deep twilight now, purple sliding from gray to black, stars pricking back through the mist. The bonfire seems twice as big as it did last night 'til you realize it's actually been joined by two smaller fire-pits; beef and pig-laden spits turn over banked coals on the one side, while a camp-sized pan of sausages sizzles next to a cauldron-full of eggs boiling in beet-juice on the other. Further on, you see people lighting sparklers and dancing arm in arm, two concentric circles bending in and around each other, like a human Moebius strip. They're singing too, Latvian first but English after, as if translated for your benefit—an eerie droning choir at base with occasional, added harmony rising and falling like kangling screeches above it, hyoid-bone flute skirls.

The king is buried, stamp him down
The king is buried, stamp him down
Under the dirt, under the ground
É, ééé, éééééé...

We killed the king and stole his gold
We spilled his blood to keep him cold
We broke his crown under the mold
É, ééé, éééééé...

—What king are they talking about? you ask, as she pulls you headlong across the yard by one hand, forcing you to stumble over wet grass to keep up. Then demand, when she doesn't answer: —And why the hell does everyone want to meet *me*, anyways? Caught between flames and cold air, your skin feels tight; the heat hasn't drained at all, keeping both cheeks bright, pulsing, as if infected. —None of you know *me* from shi... from anything.

The old woman doesn't look back. —You're right, we don't, and that needs to change. So the Eldest tells us.

In the house's main room, Fergus will tell you, Mikus has already spent close to an hour just plugging his laptop into the large-screen TV and aiming its camera just exactly so at the couch set facing it. Ezti's waiting with the rest, doling coffee to what looks like the clan's oldest members, still flushed from what you assume to be a turn at the dancing; she smiles at you and nods: *Cousin.* And if the old lady wasn't watching, you might not be so careful to nod back, but even as do, you can't quite help the tail-end of it from turning into a jaw-cracking yawn.

The old lady pauses, looking at you more appraisingly. —Bad sleep, Grigor's girl?

—My name is Aija.

—Your name's Žēlite, but that's no answer. Well?

—Bad dreams, you admit, then hesitate, not wanting to remember. Changing the subject, instead: —You know, I don't even know what that means, Zhaleetah.

—Žēlite. "Aija" is something different entirely, to rock, to lull... like a cradle, like a baby. Žēlite, though...

—...is "long-suffering," believe it or not, Ezti puts in, taking your arm; she moves herself between you and the old lady, gently allowing you to grab back onto the family you came here with. —Medieval, but Christianized. Before, you see, we named people after objects, natural things: Bear, apple, cherry tree. Then the Church came, so priests made up new names for us based on the virtues they wanted us to have, like Dievmīlis for God-lover, Strādulis for hard-worker, or even Skaidrīte—

—You know a lot about it, obviously, Mom notes, cutting her off. —Is that your field, linguistics?

—Ha, no, I'm just fluent; went back over there last summer, made money teaching English. Like you could, Aija, if you wanted. It's not *that* hard.

And you doubt that, but know enough not to say so, surrounded by all these others; you're quite clever, yes, when called upon to be so. As I somehow knew you would be.

(For I am *very* close now, Youngest. Perhaps you can hear me where I lie, far under the earth, my fingers drumming as these fools dance outside, singing songs once made in mockery of a danger they no longer remember to fear. Perhaps you can feel the shiver of my approach even through miles of timber and muck, fallen piles of needles lifting slightly beneath the trees as I crawl upwards, like a soft, gray eddy. Or perhaps not.

Soon enough it will not matter much one way or another.)

The Skype screen's still sitting empty when Inese asks you about your dreams again, so it's as much boredom as anything else that finally gets you talking—that and Ezti's patient, good temper as she translates for all the wizened, decrepit listeners. It's surprisingly gratifying, especially when a surge of interest immediately arises after you start describing the way that the dream you had on your way up—

(black wind, black pines, black stars)

—and the dream you just had now, in the van—

(warm red rain, falling)

—almost seemed like different parts of the same one. One nameless gnome pokes his neighbor and jabbers to Ezti, eyes wide.

—Uncle Lācis says it sounds like that dream someone always has when they come up here, Ezti translates. —The one just like this story his mother—no, his mother's mother—used to tell, about, um... a king who studied black magic, read things he shouldn't have, so he grew wings by mistake. And flew.

—The better to hunt us from above, hé? Inese snorts. —Because people aren't birds, but if we were, we'd be birds of prey.

—Wings? asks Emmy. —Like... with feathers?

—Maybe, Mikus agrees, then snaps his fingers. —Or like a bat's, maybe? No, no... a beetle's. Wasn't that how Gran told it?

Ezti grins. —Exactly. He used to swoop down at night and snatch people up, close one pair of wings around them and use the other to fly away with, fast. Then suck them dry and spit out the rest.

—But if he had beetle-wings, he wouldn't have hands to snatch with, right? Stu argues as Steve just watches, goggling. —Just... like, what do bugs have? Pincers? But maybe six of them, right, 'cause bugs have six legs...

—Dude, that's ridiculous, Fergus objects.

—Oh yeah, dude, 'cause *that*'s the most ridiculous part.

—Hey, man, don't slag on my big sis's Dad's culture, okay?

But: —Fah, don't be foolish, Inese spits. —They grew out of his back, his wings, so he had hands like anyone else. Claws, though. Long claws and long white fingers too, each with many rings. He'd take both their hands in his, fold them close in his wings like a cloak—pretty girls, pretty boys. Always the prettiest. He'd shut his wings and float upwards, kiss them all over then bite them all over as well. 'Til the blood fell down like rain... hot, red, salt. King's rain, they called it.

—Like a vampire, Fergus manages, after a long second.

Mike shakes his head. —No, more like... hmmm. That bird, what's its name? The one that hangs other birds on thorns.

—Butcherbird, says Steve; —Shrike, answers Stu, at almost the same time.

—Yeah, that. Cause he hung them far up, from the pines, to soften. Like a larder.

Another of the elder cousins bursts into excited speech, which Ezti translates as fast as she can. —Cousin Imant says he heard the King was like a fish, the one without bones, teeth in a circle, all around, like ...The old man bares his false teeth in a circular rictus, as Ezti mirrors him, reflexively.

—A lamprey? says your mother, drawn into the story despite herself.

Imant nods, vigorously. —*He'd bite a hole,* he says, through Ezti, —*and suck out what he needed: blood, meat, everything. Nothing left but a skin bag full of slurry. Then he dropped them, broke all their bones in pieces. They went flat, left a stain where they landed.*

The old man grins, as nearly everyone else cringes in disgust.

—Ugh, that *is* ridiculous, says Mike, laughing. —Gran never got *that* graphic!

More interjections come now, fast but subdued, as if what the speakers are coming up with startles even themselves; Ezti does her best to keep pace. —*I heard he was a lord, not a king—but there were many kings back then.* —*I heard he made himself a crown of bones.* —*No, I heard they made him* wear *a crown of iron, heated in the fire. They were going to burn him, but the minute they touched it to his head he began to fly, up through the smoke into black, the gathering storm.* —*I heard he was an outlaw, disinherited, who made a family out of deserters and camp followers. And he called himself king as a joke, so that whenever they killed and stole his name, they could say: We do the king's business.*

—When *was* this? you interrupt, at last, feeling half-drowned.

Inese waves a hand. —Oh, long ago. During the War.

—Which one?

—Who knows? One lasts a hundred years, another two hundred; one never stops at all. Every war is the same. She pauses. —Still, we are free of him now, in any event. This is what matters most.

—Wait, so, let me get this straight, says Fergus. —Was this dude a king or wasn't he?

Inese shrugs. —What gives royalty? Power, and blood; power *in* the blood... but before all else, a man becomes king by proclaiming himself king. He gives himself the name, and he changes to fit it. She sits back, folding her arms as if to declare the discussion finished, and for a few unspeaking seconds it seems like it might be.

Until the first gnome—Uncle Lācis?—says something else, almost too quietly to hear. Everyone looks to Ezti. But as she opens her mouth, instead of her voice, an accent thick as black molasses emerges, gusting surprise through the room like a draft. The old man himself, rasping:

—He smell *our* blood, they say. From up high, down underground... everywhere. Because our blood... *his* blood. That is why he hunt us.

He sits down, carefully, and now the silence truly does seem unbreakable—until it's broken by nothing human. The shrill *chirrup* of the Skype screen coming alive makes everyone jump.

Here we go, you find yourself thinking, without knowing why.

And here we go, yes: A little further, now. Up first, then down. Into the dark sky, the black wind, the weeping pines. Into the deep earth, the black stone, the bones and meat and blood. That place where we all come together. Do not be afraid. You do not have to be afraid. Open your eyes and wait.

Hear the false king hang himself with his own words, he who wanted to be Eldest. He who never *will* be, so long as I still live.

So long now.

I could never have known how long forever really is.

"Old" isn't enough to describe the face on the screen, or even "ancient." "Mummified" might come close if it weren't for those dim glints sunk deep between crumpled eyelids, boiled colorless by a mix of LCD pixels and firelight. When the Eldest's tongue flicks out to moisten what used to be his lips, it's a dull gray-purple, like liver; his scalp shines tight to the skull, waxed tissue-paper melted over bone, while the rest of his face seems weirdly slack, unable to register any sort of recognizable emotion—not welcome, not exhaustion, nothing.

What comes out sounds like a gusty sigh rather than speech, punctuated with the occasional phlegmy groan, but Ezti listens carefully, eyes narrowing.

—The Eldest tells us he's, uh... so happy to meet you, Aija, she begins, carefully. —That it's been too long since he's seen, um... Grigor's face.

You exchange a glance with your mom: *No, eh?* But Ezti just nods, gaze still riveted by the Eldest's mouth, afraid of getting lost. —Um, Aija—Žēlite—the Eldest welcomes you to our family at last... *his* family, the first line. From the old country, the place Grigor left to come here, like the Eldest, um... told him not to. There's an awkward pause. Slowly: —Where *you* should come back to, now, because... Grigor can't. Before it's too late.

Now it's your turn to stare along with the rest of your family. —Um, 'scuse me? you manage, finally. What's he mean by *that,* exactly?

Ezti glances at Inese, who throws Mike a scowl, who literally mime-slaps his forehead for what has to be your benefit, a classic Homer Simpson *d'oh!* —About the package, sure! Forget my own head if I didn't...Trailing away, Mike scrabbles in his jacket for a heavy manila envelope and hands it to you, looking sheepish; obviously, he's been in on this from the start. Like the whole fucking rest of them, probably, with their stupid fairy tales about shared dreams, their ridiculous outlaw-wizard-king bat-bug-vampire stories...

Mom, Fergus, Emmy, Steve and Stu gather around as you open it up, page through; it's in English, but all legal documents full of Latvian names, impossible to parse. —What *is* this?

—Inheritance papers, Mike says. —Property deeds, bank accounts, investment holdings, staffing contracts—the house the Eldest's calling from, even. Would've gone to Grigor, but... He shrugs. —You're the last direct heir, Aija. When the Eldest passes, it's all yours.

The Eldest snarls, and Ezti winces. —*If* you fulfill conditions, she adds, hastily.

—What conditions? Mom beats you to the question by half a breath, only that. —Not that I'm not overjoyed to know Aija's taken care of, but...

Now Mike looks away as Ezti draws a breath, but it's Inese who gets there first. —She has to go home, she says, matter-of-factly. —Say she will, here and now, in front of us all: accept her place as heir. That's tradition.

—To fucking *Latvia?* Fergus blurts out, but Mom shushes him, vehemently. Then begins again, "polite voice" arching just a tick higher, as she does: —Well, listen... I'm certain Aija feels flattered, but we couldn't possibly commit to a

European trip before we'd had these papers looked at or at least checked out how much it would cost or...

—Not your blood, woman, snaps Inese. —Not your business!

You turn on her twice as fast, almost before Mom has time to flush. Hear yourself ask before you've even thought twice about it, in a voice you hardly recognize: —What'd I *tell* you, lady? Lay off my mom or you can just mail this whole package back and tell your Eldest to shove it up his—

—Be *quiet*, girl! You don't know what you do, what you're turning down...

—You're goddamn right, I don't, you snap. I don't know anything, about any of you: what this bullshit even *is*, let alone why you waited so long to ask me up for one of these funky little... shindigs of yours if it mattered so goddamn much! What I *do* know, though—I wouldn't even *be* here right now if Mom hadn't asked me to come in the first fucking place!

—That woman... Inese starts, as the Eldest tries to interrupt, letting loose with another burst of Medieval proto-ur-Latvian, or whatever. To which you find yourself literally bellowing back: —*Melanie! Her* name *is Melanie!*

This time, however, it's Steve playing peacemaker, looking up from the papers, which he's been studying: —Calm down, Aija, okay? It's a year and a month there, basically. Sign a bunch of shit, get "fluent" or whatever, come back rich. Plus, you never have to come back *here* again, you don't want to... that's good, right?

Ezti's got her eyes on you now, pleading, mouthing something you think might be *it's not so hard.* You're already upright, though, just about ready to kick the coffee table over and huff the hell out; Mike grabs for you again, but you shake him off, slipping past Ezti to take your mom's hand, show exactly where in this madhouse your true loyalties lie. Replying: —Yeah, you know what? I don't think so. If you people can't respect the woman who raised me as much as the man who left her alone to do it, then seriously, to hell with you, and *you*, and **you**—

—It's not about money! Ezti cries, voice sounding just strange enough to derail your rage, for the moment. —It's about safety of all our families—the first line, us, you. And, Melanie...

You feel your mom give another start at the sound of her own name, said in such a pleading tone, something sparking between them that you don't quite understand—yet. While on the screen, now you look closer, something in the Eldest's loose, trembling face betrays the truth: it's *not* outrage at being defied he's feeling after all. That unrecognizable emotion lurking underneath? It's fear.

— ... the Eldest says he knows Grigor told you everything—that he made you give your word to keep Aija away from here. Grigor told him. So why, having done that... did you break it?

For a moment, mom keeps on staring, blankly. Then she shivers, and suddenly, you know *exactly* why. Because—

(*She didn't believe it, no. That's right.*)

So few seldom do, these days, even if they came from places that knew better. Even if they've grown up hearing the stories, singing the songs. For it only takes a few generations to create Canadians out of Godsmanises, you see, too happy, healthy and irreligious to care if those myths their mothers whisper at night were ever based on anything but lies.

It's Ezti's pretty face which starts to change first, strangely enough, as the ruin of a man who let your grow up in constant danger growl-hisses on, behind her: a slow, dreadful shift, confusion slowly giving way to realization, then disbelief, then terror.

—*No,* she breaks out at last to no one in particular. —Oh no, that can't, that's impossible; that just *can't* be true. Stop, don't, oh holy Christ that's stupid, no no no *no*—

The crowd is mostly up as well now, even its least able members, muttering amongst itself, repeating whatever Ezti just heard; more cries rise here and there outside, some of them even in English: —*See the sky? Better get inside, before it...*— *Wait, what the hell was that? Somebody start their truck up?* —*Not thunder, too far down for that, it's more like... like...*

Inese flinches, as if she's been slapped; she flumps down next to Ezti, who begins to weep on her shoulder. And simply hugs her, gently, whispering to herself: —It *can't* be true, not anymore; Eldest, did you lie? *Could* you? To *us?*

Sure he could, probably, you think. *But about what?*

Mom's hand abruptly fists itself in yours, hard enough to hurt. —This... was a mistake, Aija, she says. —I'm *so* sorry. A mistake to come here, for all of us: we have to go, we're leaving. Fergus, go start the car—no, Emmy, leave the luggage, it doesn't matter! We have to *go, now*—

Fergus blinks, bewildered. —But mom—

—*Fergus,* just *GO!* mom shouts, and he does; mom matches him, dragging you with her, while Emmy, Steve and Stu struggle after, Steve still clutching the papers. You leave the laptop squalling, Ezti weeping, Great-Aunt Inese muttering. Mike trails you for a step or too, trying to apologize, but she ignores him, throwing the door wide: lets in the night, the yells and shrieks, even as the room behind you all erupts into similar tumult. Noise ahead, noise behind, noise all around—but it's not just revelry now, is it? It's panic. People running to meet you, running past you, trying to cram themselves back in where you used to be, through the still-open door.

The bonfire's gone, pit sodden, flames long-snuffed. Above, clouds circle and strange holes open at random like blinking eyes, potential tornados. It's as if the night itself is turning inside out: harsh, blood-warm rain; lightning spears; the smell of burning resin. Mold in your eyes, sharp enough to draw tears. Fergus has the doors open already, and Mom practically throws you inside, slamming the door behind you. You're still blowing your nose as you scream past the dancing field's gateposts.

—Jesus, Mom, what the hell? Steve says, from the back seat. —Maybe we should stay, at least until it clears—

Mom shakes her head, twice. —*No.* Look, I'll explain on the way, but for now we just need to—

A splintering crash from the meeting-house's direction cuts her off, plus an explosion of fresh screaming: shock and horror, wordless pain, unanswered prayers. Is that one Ezti or Mike? At the same time, all the lights go out, everywhere, except up above—storm-light wavering, liquid, boiling clouds back-lit by electricity. Black over here, then silver (a hidden moon's reflected overspill?), and then... red. Warm, salt, red.

You and everybody else freeze stiff when the next sound reaches you, locked rigid, straining to see through a windshield full of blood: great random whip-cracks, sails snapping in wind. And along with that, another, even worse—like nothing you've ever thought possible. It spikes your ears 'til the screams resume, just bestial raw agony; 'til they choke at last, devolve into gurgles, moans, unspeakable wet tearing sounds...

The car skews sidelong and stops, dead. Fergus revs it again and again: nothing. —Fuck! he yells as you grab for the door, pop Mom's and grab *her,* pulling you both out into the dark; she has Emmy in an armlock on the other side, the boys taking up the rear. The storm blinds you, churned mud and gravel underfoot, so wet and cold your teeth start chattering. You can't help but look back even as you power forward, *just* able to glimpse what's left of the house's roof gaping open, snapped timbers upreared into the churning sky. A lightning strike flash-bulbs to show Uncle Strade's RV on its back, belly similarly eviscerated; must've hit the gas-tank, because something goes *foom!* Which is how you then see everything else in snatches: Fergus and Steve's faces, blown white, holding a bloodied Stu up between them; the meadow between them and the house full of shapes, some crawling, others still. And something else, something like a great black kite flashing down past one of the running figures, first there, then gone: both gone, and *upwards,* far too fast to track. Leaving nothing in their wake but a smell of meat both raw and cooked, and—

(oh God, blood)

Not just blood-rain or rain like blood, but *blood*—whole sprays of it, whole funnels. Whole red twisters of it leaping up into the air, chasing that *thing*'s wake, waterspouts spinning skywards from some mud and gore-polluted sea.

Mom screams at you then, breaking the spell, snapping your face back forwards. And you run, run, run, run, run.

Of course you love them, your false family, as I've said—why would you not? But you could love me too, or grow to; of that, I'm certain. I am not so old I cannot remember love.

For here is wisdom, Youngest—the sort your father might have told you, perhaps, if he hadn't driven quite so fast on the way back home from his own conversation with my betrayer, conducted over the telephone. Are you listening?

The old kings held our land by one simple tradition, dating back to long before we had words to explain it—a trade: life and freedom for good harvest, victory, safety. Each ruled only until the next came of age, at which point they allowed themselves to be killed, our blood's price re-consecrated by blood. For it is a fierce love we have for each other, a ruler and his ruled—they would eat *me* alive as well, if they could, as many have. My books told me how kings used to live only a year or less, depending—for since the land is the king and the king the land, whatever happens, or doesn't, must surely be the king's fault. This is the price of glory.

I saw a small tribal king pulled down once when I was a boy, at my own mother's instigation; saw how they tore him apart and roasted him, ate his meat instead of the harvest they'd lost, then burnt his bones to ash and broke his skull beneath their feet until it was nothing but shards. I remember them scraping his name away, too, so no one would ever tell his reign's sad tale... or remember kings can be killed at all, no doubt. So they could keep it secret knowledge, passed down from seer to seer, forest-speaker to forest-speaker.

Until I became heir, that is, upon my older brother's death; something never planned for by anyone. I, with my books and my studies, alone in my forest hut, mapping the invisible world's parameters while my followers slaughtered and stole from his—an outlaw cult-master, a heretic, even by pagan standards.

I loved my brother, much as we disagreed. So, I did not think to kill him by letting loose a plague to free us after we were captured. Nor did I reckon his warband so foolish as to burn me for it, either—did they simply *forget* my place in line, more direct to the last source than his sons' would ever be, with their war-prize mother? His death gave me power my rituals never would, the oldest power we knew. And I...

... I made myself more with it, more than the forest-speakers ever thought possible. Something no one would ever be allowed to pull down or forget.

You run: Off the road, through the trees, into the woods. Until the slaughter behind dims down but the wind blows harder, rain softening the ground, making you slip and slide. Branches tear at you. Needles in your hair, palms bark-abraded, sealed with sap. Your mom beside you, weeping. When you fall, you fall together and roll down into a ditch where you crouch, soon joined by the others, hugging and shivering as you try to stay still, stay quiet. But she never stops whispering, cupping, one hand over your ear, as if she thinks it'll hold the words in.

—I loved your dad, Aija, she husks. —More than anybody else I ever knew, even Fergus and Steven's... huh, *God*. And I only ever broke that one promise to him because he was already gone. I never really believed what he'd told me, but I'd never have done that if he was still alive.

—I know, Mom. I know.

—I just, I wanted you to know where you'd come from, you know? she goes on, like you didn't even speak. —To know who you were. I thought you *deserved* to know.

You let out your breath, long and slow, hoarse with congestion; take a moment, rain pelting down in bullets, like nails. Shut your eyes, retreating for one brief second into the dark of your skull, hot and black and pulsing. Then reply, simply: —What a very... Canadian way to look at it.

Mom shudders, covering her face. —I'd've promised him anything, she says, muffled. —I thought I understood. People run away from their families all the time! But that old man was right, I fucked up *bad*. I wasn't even supposed to let them know you exist.

—But that doesn't make sense! Why would *he* go back to see them if it was dangerous? The night he—

—Honey, *I* don't know! Maybe he thought he could get them to leave us alone or something. But then the accident happened, and, and...

She trails off, into choked sobs.

—Then Mikus called, right? Fergus growls. —And he didn't *sound* nuts. And it was twenty years ago, so you thought, what, Mom? Maybe Grigor was the crazy one, all along?

—Damnit, you weren't there! Mom flares. —I loved Grigor, but Christ, Fergus, *you* wouldn't have believed it either! All this bullshit about his bloodline, this fucking monster *king* of theirs, what was I supposed to think?! She covers her head with her arms, shoulders shaking.

Emmy nods. —I mean... they were okay, those people. Normal. That old lady was pretty rude to you, but besides her... She trails off, buries her head in Fergus's shoulder. Says, muffled: —Oh shit, what's it matter? What the hell do we do now?

No one knows. And the silence stays unbroken, 'til you hear what you almost don't recognize as your own voice, asking: —Did Dad tell you what they wanted, though—with him? Or me?

It takes her a moment to answer. —Never anything straight out. But those stories they told, back there, before the Skype call, they made me remember... what he said. And the way, how they—how the OPP found him, after the crash—

—How?

—...in the trees.

—The *trees?* Like—like what?

Her voice cracks, deeply; she scrapes the rest out slowly, like it hurts. As... I suppose it must.

(Though I barely remember it, Youngest. Truly. And I would—I *will*—apologize.)

Butcherbird. Shrike. The one that hangs other birds on thorns.

Stu blinks; Steve gags. Emmy's eyes widen, and Fergus's mouth goes slack, like he's about to puke. You don't blame any of them.

—You were *five years old*, Aija, Mom cries, as you stare, feeling your own stomach twist. —I couldn't tell you that! Not about *him*.

You shut your eyes. Perhaps you see him, Grigor, last of the old potential heir's heirs. He could have taken my power from me, if he'd known how.

As their not-Eldest once discovered he could not—when he found me sleeping between generations, between meals—and tried to.

For the stories are not untrue. I did prey on them from above, indiscriminately, when I first became what I am—for years, perhaps for centuries. But slowly, I regained who I had been when they touched that red-hot iron crown to my head, even after all the spells I'd spoken, the rituals I'd performed in my brother's dungeon, when my followers sacrificed themselves (as always) to my need. I came to my family's seat in human form once more, or as much so as I might manage; I called upon the not-Eldest of that time, the potential heir to whom I would never give *my* blood, to deal for our land's future before it lay empty and fallow.

Knowing, if he was anything worth his salt—or more like my brother than me at the least—he would agree to pay tribute each new generation; let me take the true-born heir up into the sky and deed the family's table-head to whoever came next in line, so long as *I* agreed to hibernate for most of the next cycle. To dig myself deep and stay there, 'til the next true-born heir came of age.

I kept my part of the bargain and more. For centuries I fended off outsiders, kept us secret, kept us safe. No one laid claim to our land, believing it somehow poisoned, though its fields grew green and its forests dense, its treasures just as precious as any other kingdom's; no one dared steal our children for soldiers or slaves or force us to marry our beauties away, fearing the stain of our heritage would spread. And even when some fool let the Christians in at last while I lay dormant, since they continued to feed me, I continued to keep my word... until this last betrayal. Until their not-Eldest, your Grigor's great-great-grandfather, made sure that I could not.

Yet—even now I cannot fault him. For I, too, had broken my word in a way. You see, after such a long time of drinking nothing but my kin's blood, I found I had lost all taste for any other kind. So, all my protection has been, in the end, nothing more than a butcher's care for his stock.

I regret not regretting it more.

Ah, but look at him now, that last pretty boy's ruin, who always wanted to hold what remained of our lands by *his* name's power, not mine. For he could hold nothing, of course; two world-wide wars have taught him better since. But he could lie to them and did tell them he'd managed to kill me when all he'd done was to find me where I slept and gently cleared the earth away from my cocoon and made a box around it, plank by plank, then locked it tight and sent it on, staying behind. Grigor's father he lost, and Grigor's father's father. Grigor he could not keep either, not when the walls came down and the world grew so much smaller, so much easier to travel. Age has betrayed him, though, at last; he should have stamped my tale out for good, made sure no one would ever know it to tell you, having forgotten I might still be listening. Better never to speak, since all words are invocations, used correctly. Far more so than any prayer.

I woke alone. I did not know where I was. I broke the damp wood easily, dug my fingers deep into dirt and sent out my call, gathering my own blood back to me—but when those who answered smelled less of me than of themselves, I slept, for lack of any better option. Sometimes those same creatures came and built fires above me, danced and drank, sang songs that reminded me who I once was—but it was not enough to rouse me, beyond the sharing of a dream or two. None of them were of *me*, really. None of them were *mine*.

Then your father came, and I heard him, I smelled him. My ecstasy knew no bounds. I exploded up out of the earth, a thousand-year locust shedding its shell. I caught him up out of that car of his, drank his blood and hung him on a tree. And in his blood, I saw the one he wanted to save from me, the one for whom he willingly paid this price. I saw *you*, Youngest.

I knew you would come eventually.

It has been hard to wait since then, starving. Which is why I rejoiced when I heard you wonder who these people were to you and who were you to them? What could you possibly share?

Blood. My blood kept us alive, all of us—and them, those others, the ones I was sent to. It always has.

But with you here now, I have no need of any of *them*.

I can hear how the beat of your heart changes as you reason your way through what little you know of this. Asking the air, slowly:

—So Dad was scared they wanted to take him back to Latvia, feed him—or me—to... that *thing*. But it's over here now; must be. All that back there, my dad... that was *him*. The ki—

Yes, Youngest, a voice hisses in answer from even further inside your ear, your tympanum's taut drum. *And here I am come at last to meet you. Look up.*

Let me tell you my name.

The night splits open to either side of you, that same roar, that whip-crack; a tornado-eye cluster opening above, a lightning-strike arcing down and splitting as it comes, almost fractally, to fan the trees which shelter you. Hundred-foot-tall pines go crashing down on either side like a huge, green fan opening, a sheaf of wheat scythed in one gigantic, invisible blow. Great sweeps, impossibly precise— unnatural, too, since nature's never this clean. All of it *targeted.* And every tree falls away from you, away from your family, as the six of you leap up as if you're al- ready on fire. None of you are even scratched.

The realization only makes you scream louder.

Your heart's beat speeds to match mine as I circle above, an echolocation, mir- rored click of blood calling to blood, Oldest to Youngest. The me in you reflected, reflecting the you in me.

Love is an echo. Blood itself is a spell, whether words be written in it or no.

I was made what I am by less.

It was hunger drove me to change myself this way, a lust to confirm owner-ship, the firm and greedy belief no one should have what is mine but *me*—not even the direct line, my choicest morsels. That to attempt to cheat me should invite punishment, swift and brutal. That those who rise deserve to come swooping down once more whenever they want, carrying off whatever—whoever—takes their fancy. For the right of kings is absolute, I hear, even self-made kings. And all kings are self-made.

But I think I might have been wrong in my beliefs or become so. Yes, Young-est, after a thousand years, I—even I—have begun to think that change is possible. Necessary, even.

Prove me wrong.

That great black wind circling above, tighter and tighter, lifting needles and peb-bles, dirt and dust—the whole sky narrows, slosh-screaming, a hurricane sea. Green tinge to the clouds now and the glassy air behind, sheet-lightning like creamy jade, behind the red rain's purplish deluge. Their cover lost, a horde of wet gnats and stinging blackflies boil and eddy between droplets, turn tight cor-ners in on themselves again and again, flocking like tiny starlings; you feel blood come to your skin everywhere unclothed, pore-blossoming, to lift and gutter up-wards. Portents, omens; you could read them, if you knew the language. Proof of his—

(of my)

—approach.

And the king swoops down, as advertised, hovers close enough for his boot-tips to touch mud—ancient leather like peat bog mummy-skin, dirt-encrusted. And from here, you see he looks as if he's still burning: a coal statue, black with veins of red and curls of black smoke swirling off him, all over—some hanging down like hair, some blowing back like wings. Eyes like liquid metal. But still the traces of a handsome man left, even all these centuries later; fine bones and an elegant skull still set with hammered iron, its age-blackened spikes grown deep into a band of scar. The long-fingered hands with too many rings to count, nails hooked like a crow's, reaching out for yours.

And his voice inside you, echoing, cavern-deep. Saying: *I know you, Youngest, if only from your father's memories, or the dreams we shared. So, I swear on myself to spare those you feel for, not to slaughter them in front of you or make them my larder... Ezti lives yet, and Mikus. That rude girl Inese too, for all her lack of courtesy.*

I could have torn your car in two as you fled, hurled it off the road, crushed your mother, her spawn, and their concubines like eggs. Instead, I saved those I had to save to save you.

For there is only one sort of death fit for me and mine.

Fergus has one of Mom's arms, Steve the other—they don't need to see you raise your hand to hold her back. Emmy is crying. You think Stu might be in shock. *You*'re probably in shock or should be. But—

(maybe not)

He looks at you, and you look at him. Black wind through where the pines used to be. Red rain falling. And the pulse, *your* pulse, skittering like a bird's, a bat's, a bug's. You watch that spot where his jugular should be flutter, keeping visible time with your own—so fast and light for something unspeakably old, so terrible and calm.

—You killed my Dad? you ask him, this *king*. No preamble; he doesn't deserve one. *Not* my *king*, you think, cold as this mold-stinking storm of his. *Not* my *god*.

He nods, slightly. *I did, Youngest.*

—My name's Žēlite, asshole, you tell him, your tone not changing. —Žēlite Godsmanis, Grigor's girl.

Yes, Youngest. I know.

You nod. —Uh huh. And my friends call me Aija, my *family*, but I guess... I guess that's not you, so fuck it. What the fuck do you fucking well want from me, Your Majesty?

You.

What a lack of surprise.

His mouth opens. You can see the inside glowing, his burning palate, black opal needle-teeth. It gives off a heat you can actually *see* deform the air in front of his lips, night around him suddenly seen through wavy, seventeenth-century glass. His breath comes out as sparks, and his voice, his real, outside voice... well, it probably hasn't been used since long before Vlad Ţepeş was still up and impaling. Sounds like it anyhow.

—I want you, he says, slowly, as if each syllable costs him—and Christ, but you hope it does. —To be... mine. My own. As you... should be, being... heir.

Your lips curl, and your stomach flips again, hard enough to hurt; a bit like trying to repress a guffaw, though you sure don't feel like laughing. —"Yours," huh? Your *meal*, you mean.

—No, not that. My... He pauses. —This tongue is odd to me, the words—no, wait, I know it now. The word I want, is...

(*queen*)

No trust here, nor choice. You can't look back, not and think of the people he left all over the meadow, in the wreck of the house—your relatives. How they must have spun, caught in his whip-crack draft, twisting apart. How they must have torn all over and bloomed from inside-out like blown flowers, if flowers were carrion.

You go with him, it'll still happen, but not to Mom. Not your brothers. No one you have to know, if you don't want to. And besides which...

... an unchanging thing that wants to can't help but fascinate on some level. Most especially so if it looks like *this*: some demon prince, some fairy tale made flesh, whose both sets of black smoke wings abruptly snap out kite-stiff in obvious peacock display, showing off what's underneath to matrimonial advantage. All iridescent scale grown into armor, jewelled chitin and breastplate shell, set off here and there with a weird, rough-woven rag of what probably used to be some pretty fashionable shit, back in the Dark Ages. You can see gold and silver threads unravelled to stitch through his hide in random gleams, glam prison tattoo-style.

Queen, huh? you say, stepping forward, and let the current between you take over, tune your shared DNA radio to a channel far too loud to let you hear your mom screaming for you to stop. *Sure beats finishing my thesis all to hell, I guess. But how do I know you won't just drop me?*

He considers, or seems to; hard to tell, even at this distance.

I mean, I already know you're used to getting what you want. Say you get hungry again or bored...

More sparks trace his lips' curve, a sinister black grin as those molten eyes slant, approving. *Oh, but I do not expect to tire of you so soon, Youngest. Not when I have never before met... or made... my like.*

You are a scholar, are you not? Well-read, restless. You love deeply; you have rage. We have all this in common, you and I.

I could teach you much, if you would let me.

(If.)

That old "free will" scam again, you think, own lips twitching; *destiny trumps destiny, my ass.* And open your arms to him before you can reconsider, so wide both your shoulders crack.

His answering hug burns, almost unbearable; one wing-set twines you both, pulling you in tight while the other flaps just once, whipping you both up into the sky so high and fast you barely have time to feel the lack of oxygen before his lips seal over yours in a circle, lamprey-teeth latching on. It hurts, so much you go numb—your eyes squeeze automatically shut even on the storm below, the earth's curvature, the rim where atmosphere meets space. Yet you can still see your family's desperate, craning faces wink and fade, somehow, in your mind's eye. You can still count every tear on your Mother's cheeks.

You might learn to forget them, Youngest—Aija—if you wished. All manner of things are possible, or may be, now we are together...

Yeah, sure; magical powers, monster queen, blah blah. *"All things" but one,* you think, hoping they had sarcasm back then. *Now shut up and do your damn thing, before I just let go.*

As you wish, he tells you, sucking in. And starts to drink.

The numbness moves further down your spine, along your limbs; a toxic swoon, lids falling open as your eyes roll back, and he folds you closer still, cloak-wrapped. But here an odd memory-flash intrudes amongst the lessening grief, so quick it barely registers, as one heart-pump drains your blood into him while the other replaces it with something utterly ancient, venomous, cold: Ezti in the kitchen, offering you red eggs boiled in beet juice, her smile the single best thing you saw tonight in retrospect. Remembering how Dad used to say girls give them to boys, at Easter—one's an insult, two not much better; three is just all right. Four, that means *you're a rich idiot, so I'll consent to be your wife.* Five, you are the one I've waited for all my life. Come here now and take me."

There's nothing about what's happening now that should make you laugh, and yet.

The cocoon he spins around you both drifts back down by degrees, gravity-tugged, 'til impact wakes you both once more; you tear your way out and further down, into the earth to wait for dark. When you feel the sun sinking you open your eyes to find your grave already filled in, yourself laid out on top with your head in the true Eldest's lap, as if he's been watching you sleep. And the night, falling all around you... the night is strange and bright and singing like nothing you've ever heard or seen or felt. It smells so good it makes you hungry.

You feel different, he says. Not a question.

Um, you agree. Then ask, without moving your lips—your wings unfurling as you stretch, claws out, your new eyes molten: *What the hell* was *your name before you were king, anyhow?* To which he simply smiles again, amused...

... and tells you.

THE CHURCH IN THE MOUNTAINS

Part One

The bus up only ran every three hours, and the girl arrived on the Greyhound from Toronto just as it was pulling away. It was 4:00 PM, so she had to wait outside the post office in Descant, at the mountain's base, shut since 2:30; she stood shivering next to a lamp post with no shelter, suitcase at her feet, watching the sky darken. No gloves, so she stuck her fists deep inside her pockets, knowing it wouldn't be enough. The wind was cold but damp, blowing steadily from the north; her Walkman kept her company for almost two full hours, music finally starting to buzz and elongate as the batteries lost charge. At which point she turned it off and gave herself over entirely to the truth of where she was—these shuttered windows and empty buildings surrounded by woods that cracked and sighed, peeling signs for discontinued products, the general wind-touched silence.

By the time the bus finally came back down and wheeled around to park, a little snow had already begun to fall.

Once on the bus, she watched her white hands slowly turn pink again, trying not to grunt in pain. When they'd warmed enough to let her doze, she leaned her hot forehead against the window and fell into a thin, gray version of sleep lit by flickering, brightly-colored dream-flashes, too disconnected for full narrative: What she could only assume might be fragments of memories, cut here and there with something far less explicable—the feel of having her once-long hair washed in some dark-panelled bathroom, a dim bulb swinging naked up above, drawing her gaze like one faint twilight star; Mom's frail-skinned hands at her temples, their touch gentle and sure yet too-familiar smell of rosewater moisturizer enough to make her stomach lurch, immediately reminiscent of a childhood spent in a near constant state of anxiety. Or that strange set of stained-glass windows blazing with reflected sunset light near the back of the church they'd prayed in together every evening, set three steps back in an apse or nave just past where the statue of the Madonna cast her eyes up to Heaven, fake tears made from varnish pearl-sparkling on either cheek.

We won't go back, Mom had said that last time, just before they'd left. *Never. I promise, baby; I promise.* But apparently, that must've been a lie—by omission, if nothing else.

The bus pulled up at the church's front steps, jolting her awake. That the first person she saw under its cracked sodium-yellow porchlights was her aunt came as no surprise.

Ten years, she thought, nodding to the driver on her way past, suitcase in hand. *Ten years away from here, out in the real world—half my whole damn life. Enough time to forget almost every detail of this place, wouldn't you think? And yet.*

"It's good you're here," her aunt said, voice creaky and dull as ever, a blade dragged on stone. Her whole head was covered by an incongruous-looking 1970s-era turban hat in some dull, metallic gray fabric, hair tucked so far up underneath she looked bald. "I didn't know if that number was yours or not, when I called—or if you'd come at all, even once you knew, so thank you for that. It makes things so much easier."

Carefully: "I came for Mom."

"Oh yes, of course. Obviously."

Behind them, the bus pulled away almost without a sound, snow muffling its wheels. Her aunt moved aside with an odd sort of flourish, letting the door behind her fall open, and waited for her to come forward, up the steps. To step through into darkness, the church's interior.

Less a classical church than a converted meetinghouse, she recalled that much, now she strained to, hesitating at the bottom. Her aunt lived upstairs in what might have been considered the sacristy; she and Mom had lived further up in the attic, smelling of wood-rot and mothballs. There'd been a skylight too, usually kept shuttered... but here she suddenly found herself gripped by yet another memory-rush, so keen it was like she was right there again for just a fraction of a second, caught fast in the moment like a webbed-up fly. The image of herself craning high, head so far back her throat hurt, to stare through its slightly warped glass into a passing storm's laid-open heart: all swirling sleet and pelting, freezing rain, an endless spiral with gravity either suspended or overturned inside it, going both up and down at the same exact time. And then—

"How much do you remember, I wonder?" Her aunt's voice reached her slowly, as though over great distances, thrumming less in her eardrums than in her bones. "From when you were last here, I mean, with her. With *us*."

"Almost nothing," she tried to lie, wishing it was true.

Her aunt's gaze slid her way sidelong, studying her closely: those mud-colored eyes, so level, so opaque. "You do remember *me*, though, I think," she said at last, smiling her comfortless version of a smile. To which the girl soon found she had no answer at all.

End Part One

Hmmm, pretty good so far. You know where it's going?

Nope.

You never mention her name, either.

That's 'cause I don't know it. Yet.

Oh my Lord, another At The Mercy of My Muse bullshit artist. So just make one up, dude—placeholder the bitch. It's all she she she, break it up. Hard to track, otherwise.

Hold your water, asshole. It'll come to me.

Process queen, Jesus Christ.

Dude, fuck you. Later, gator.

[Thumbs up emoji]

Sharla closes out, shuts her laptop and turns to Ned, sighing. "Ever find yourself remembering stuff you know can't possibly be true?" she asks, to which Ned just shrugs, not bothering to look up from his phone. "All the damn time, according to Les," he replies, scrolling down further. "You know... like if he was gonna call me, if we were supposed to get together, whether or not blowjobs are cheating..."

Sharla shakes her head. "Nah, that's not what I meant. I mean—things you think you saw once somewhere, like on TV or whatever, when you were a kid; spooky shit, disturbing, real nightmare fuel. Only you can't tell if you actually really did see it, looking back, or somebody just told you about it, and it got inside you that way... if you even just *dreamed* it, maybe. Like the whole thing actually came from *you*, only you can't remember how, or why."

This last part makes Ned glance up at last, eyebrows raised. "Oh, Christ. Are we talking Satanic Panic here, honey? Recovered Memory Syndrome?"

"Fuck, Ned, how old you think I *am*?" Adding, off his laugh: "But that'd be real life, though, right? Not a movie, or TV show..."

"Sure. Okay, well—you've already tried praying to the Church of Google, I assume."

"Yup. No joy, though."

"So, tell me about it, then. Walk me through."

"Uh..."

Here she pauses, wondering how best to begin. Would be easier if he took it more seriously, probably, but talking to Ned's like talking to the wall at the best of times, which sort of helps. So, in the end, she simply opens her mouth and lets it spill out, unedited: the full weirdness, fifteen years' worth, all in a lump. Memory and fiction, so tangled together they might as well be inextricable.

"I think I must've seen it on TV, sometime in the 1990s," she says, slowly, trying her best to conjure context from its earliest traces. "Like... when I was up in Barrie, maybe, with my grandmother? And she was asleep, so I was watching it with the sound down really low, so it was hard to hear what anybody was saying. I remember thinking I knew from the first moments on that this was something I wasn't supposed to see, something for grown-ups, so I already had my hackles up—I was on point, trying to keep an ear out for Gram if she woke up so I could snap it off and go see what she wanted. But it began with this girl getting onto a bus and going up through the mountains on this really narrow, winding road, barely wide enough for traffic one way, not the other. Lots of trees, dark and getting darker and with this really creepy music over it too—weird and cold, some kind of hymn. And I felt like I'd be able to recognize it if I strained, but it was transposed into a minor key and played on a Moog synthesizer or something..."

"Like the beginning of *The Shining*," Ned suggests. "*Dies Irae, dies illa...*"

But Sharla shakes her head. "No, it was older, like a folk song—rougher, weirder. And in English too. Damn, I can almost hear it—"

"All right, fine, don't get snagged. So... at the top of the mountain, there's the church?"

"Just like I wrote, yeah. The church, her aunt..." Sharla pauses again. "Man, that chick put the fear up inside me for sure. Eyes like a snake, this bulgy kind of forehead, and like almost no eyebrows. Plus, it's not like she doesn't care about that girl or she's just a cold kind of person—she *hates* her. I mean, she's polite, but it's boiling off her. Like you'd be afraid to be in the same room if you were the heroine."

"And she's nobody you recognize, right? Not an actress you could just look up."

"Nope, she's nobody—kind of familiar, but you totally can't tell from where. That's why I always assumed the show must be Canadian."

"Huh, good guess." Now it's Ned's turn to pause and frown, thinking. "Where'd you try tracking this thing down again?"

"Oh, you know—bulletin boards here and there, stuff for horror fans, collectors. Did you know there's a whole Facebook page devoted to this 1980s CBC Radio show called *Nightfall*? Been a bust, though. I even tried summarizing it on WhatWasThatShow.com, but all I got was a bunch of weirdos."

"Imagine my surprise. Weirdos like how?"

Sharla sighs again. "Like... one guy accused me of spying on his dreams, said he was gonna find out where I lived and beat me up if I didn't stop?"

"Wow, florid. Well, maybe you should try somewhere else for a change... less film-related, more WTF-related." Sharla raises an eyebrow. "Paranormally inclined is what I mean."

"Shit, Ned, c'mon. This is a brain fart, not some sort of haunting."

"Hey, a haunting doesn't have to just be a ghost or rattling chains, a spooky old house, whatever—it could be a memory, an idea. The very definition of a haunting is something that keeps on coming back to you again and again. Right?" Adding, when she doesn't reply: "This place called CreepTracker.org's always been my best bet for the super-strange stuff."

"Since when's that been your thing?"

"Hey, man, I get strange sometimes—you just don't tend to be the person I tell about it. Now gimme your phone."

That night, before Sharla lets herself open up her writing group's homepage and start hammering out the story's next section, she spends a few moments scrolling around on the site Ned sent her. CreepTracker.org's a dicey place on first glance, to put it mildly: jam-packed with improbably, unprovable single-witness reports on apparitions, hauntings, all sorts of SFFnal oddity. She isn't sure exactly how Ned can think any of these obsessives would be likely to help her track down a phantom TV show, 'til at last she trips across the thread labeled TRUTH IN FIC-TION—PARANORMAL ACTIVITY VS POP CULTURE, which seems to have been around since 2009, carefully maintained by the site's manager, who's sepa-rated all its various components out into a header post full of sub-thread links. Many of these tend to begin with someone asking *Is this movie/TV show based on RL?*, which sounds promising.

Ghost of servant girl climbs invisible stairs, one reads. *Could be the Windhouse on Yell, or Nigel Kneale's* The Stone Tape, someone—a guy screen-named euan100—replies, posting a grainy screen-grab. *Can find it on YouTube usually.*

Steps are invisible, the first commenter repeats, more patient than Sharla might be.

*Windhouse on Yell, then. Here's an article—*The Guardian, *not* Wikipedia.

Resisting the urge to click through, Sharla keeps on scrolling: *Scary face at window, Skin in a box, u kno this 1?* A lot of them start off with jokers or trolls, but euan100 often ends up getting involved halfway down; she watches him identify more fragmentary images and stories, cross-referencing "real" rumors or anecdotes with easily IMDb-checkable movies and TV shows in ways that are always interesting, even when they don't come to much. One thread's actually about *Nightfall*, believe it or not.

"Love and the Lonely One," 1980, season one. Based on an urban legend called "The Anatomy Student Prank."

ur shittin me

Nope, look it up: California Folklore Quarterly *p. 45 line 13, "Campus Legends," June 1978. It's a variant on "Joke On The Janitor," where two students connect a cadaver to a car battery, jolt it to make it sit up when the janitor comes in to clean—he has a heart attack and dies, haunts the dissection room forever after.*

It's his tenth or eleventh entry that makes her decide, though—the one where he gets his debate on over whether or not CityTV did a series of late-night horror shorts around the mid-1980s. *You're thinking of* Night Walk, *on Global—three hours of hand-held cam POV shots through downtown Toronto, suitable for insomniacs and potheads. City ripped it off in 1986 as* Night Ride, *shot inside a car, but neither show had the budget for scripts or even a narrator. Just a whole lot of smooth jazz and repetitive hypnagogic imagery.*

So, she sets fingers to keys, rattles off a new post: *looking for show from my childhood, 1970s or early 1980s. maybe anthology series, half hour format, spooky shit? dead mom, girl home from university, a church in the mountains. more detail on response.*

"'Spooky shit,' Jesus, Sharl," she mutters out loud. "That could literally be anything."

Still, any answer's better than none, if only to find out if she's been ripping something off, too, without even knowing it. If there's a bit more tweaking and filing off of serial numbers to do before she can really call this tale she's been pulling out of herself—word by word, inch by inch, weirdly painful and weirdly not—a tapeworm teased from her own mental stomach.

She wants to know, one way or the other.

She wants an excuse to keep on writing so she can finally see how it ends.

Part Two

The house was already full of people, most of whom looked familiar to her, though only vaguely. Her aunt cleared the way, cutting her a path—a murmur in the ear here, head inclined, voice low; a gentle touch or a stroke there, her fingers lingering all too briefly on their forearms, shoulders, cheeks. The girl followed behind at her heels, stride too short for comfort, subtly blocked on every hand— her aunt always there before her, no matter which way she turned. A long table stood against the far wall, spread with food nobody else seemed interested in touching: every stacked plate was empty, cutlery and glasses similarly untouched. The girl's stomach rumbled.

Outside, she knew, true night would have already fallen along with the snow, come down thick and fast and purple black in two long folds, neat as curtains. No light to mark the horizon anymore, trees having long since blended together into a single, many-branched shadow, impossible to penetrate.

"You'll remember Cousin David," her aunt told her, guiding them together; "Sure," she agreed, knowing damn well that she didn't. "Nice to see you again."

"You too," he replied, briefly pressing both her hands in his in a way she was sure was meant to seem comforting, but just felt clammy. "Not that it wouldn't be more welcome under better circumstances..."

"I understand. Thanks a lot."

"We were all so surprised when Miriam—when your mother—came home. So shocked when... what happened, happened."

Not as much as I was, the girl wanted to say. But he was already moving away from her, waved off; her aunt slipped back into place beside her, beckoning yet another relative near. Which was how it went for most of the rest of the evening, every interaction carefully curated aside from that moment when her aunt orbited away to check on something—the music, maybe? Because it *did* change just then, almost in mid-phrase, sliding from plaintively generic piano into something a bit more exotic—deep thrum of cellos over drums so lightly beaten they scratched rather than pounded with some single woodwind yearning overtop, hoarse as a calling voice...

The sound of her own name, repeated, was enough to wrench her back to the current conversation. Whichever latest cousin this might be, wrinkling her brows at the girl in mild surprise, and asking, hesitant, as she did—

"I just... you don't believe in *anything*? But you grew up here. That doesn't make any sense."

The girl widened her eyes, tried to look interested rather than annoyed. "Look, what's it matter *what* I believe? I'm not—one of you, anymore. I left, remember?"

"You came back though."

"Yeah, for Mom. That's the only reason. And I'm sure not staying."

Perhaps a bit too harsh, that last part, in context. But her cousin simply nodded slightly, understandingly, which had the unfortunate effect of annoying the girl even more. "I understand. But... don't you want to think we *go* somewhere when we die? Don't you want to think your mother's somewhere right now, looking down on you?"

No, the girl thought, her eyes drawn back once more to that recessed door which led into the chapel itself, the church proper, its frame outlined in darkness so thick it looked half ajar, even though she knew—remembered, at any rate—how her aunt always kept it locked during functions. *No, I don't. I don't want to think that at all.*

The last guests filtered out by one in the morning, headed for home, for sleep. The girl found herself helping her aunt clear up, wrapping the funeral meats and stowing them away for later in the church kitchen's huge refrigerator.

"She wasn't *just* your mother, you know," her aunt suddenly told her, tone almost conversational, but not quite. "She wasn't reborn when she had you, made over, a blank slate. She was *my* sister first, always."

"I know that."

"Ah, but do you really?" Her aunt smiled, thinly. "I doubt it."

The girl paused, choosing her next words carefully. "Look," she began, at last. "I know I was an accident—"

"Is that what she told you? You were a *mistake*."

"That's one way to put it."

Keeping her tone agreeable yet firm, projecting the implications without stating them outright: *Let's not fight, please—try to believe that I do see your grief, acknowledge it, share it. But if you really think yours is more painful than mine, I guess we'll just have to agree to disagree.* Her aunt, however, didn't appear to find the girl's self-censorship admirable or respectful enough not to challenge. "Is that all you have to say?" she demanded.

The girl sighed. "What do you *want*, exactly? Me to apologize for being born?"

"It's far too late for that."

"Yeah, all right." She turned away, not looking back. "Well, if we're done here, I think I'm just going to go up to bed—"

But here her aunt's hand stopped her, laid directly over her heart—the girl glanced down automatically, shocked to stillness by the sudden contact, only to realize her aunt's fingernails were so much longer than she'd previously seen: curved, strong, barely touched at their tips with a hint of red polish, a French manicure straight from the guillotine's steps. "No," her aunt told her. "Not yet."

"Let go, please."

"Not until I've had my say."

Not much recourse, really, unless she wanted to get physical with her only living relative—start a struggle, throw a punch. Knock her to the floor, then run out into the night, the falling snow, and keep on running.

As a rational being in a rational world, however, the girl sat down instead; shrugged her aunt's hand away, crossed her arms, as if warding off its return. "I'm listening."

Her aunt drew herself up again, full height, turban gleaming in the kitchen's soft, old-fashioned lights. "Your mother..." she began. Then, correcting herself: "My *sister...*"

"Yeah, we've established that. What next?"

Her aunt paused. "She made a promise," she said eventually. "When she was about your age, she promised to—do something. Made a vow, before us all. It couldn't have been easy, but she did it. We were so proud of her."

"Uh huh. But she didn't keep it, am I right?"

"...No. She didn't."

"She went away. Had me."

"Had *you*, and *then* went away."

"Same difference. Or—isn't it?"

Another pause. "No," the older woman said, at last. "This promise was... powerful. No way to confront it except either to give in to it, the way she always should have done, or to flee. And she chose the latter path, for *you*."

The girl laughed, drily. "Gotta say, I'm a little surprised that that surprises you."

Her aunt stared her down. "She was our hope. Now we have none, unless..."

"Unless...?"

"*You* do what she wouldn't: take up the vow, do what was promised. Carry it through."

"But I don't *believe* in your—"

"It doesn't matter; the vow applies all the same. And besides... you were born here, weren't you? You have our blood—her blood."

"This is fucking insane." The girl rose, brushing her aunt's taloned hands away, impatient. "No, seriously—even you have to know just how crazy this sounds, right? I don't even know what you're talking about, and I don't want to. I came here for Mom, that's all: pay my respects, close the door. Then I'm going back to university the very next chance I get after the funeral, and *you can't stop me*."

She watched her aunt's snake-eyes narrow under invisible brows, that tight gold band bulging above like some ancient, ill-cast crown. "Oh?" was all she asked, to that.

That night, the girl dreamed she went into the church alone, drawn by the sound of singing. Her mother's coffin was in there, open, her mother laid out as though for a viewing. She looked radiant, as much so as a corpse *could* look, but the church itself was full of flies—huge and black, massing and clustered at the corners of that odd stained-glass window, the three martyrs in their glory being burned at the stake before a stern-eyed judge. It was enough to make the girl wonder if her mother had actually been embalmed. Was their buzzing the music she'd thought she'd heard?

Feeling that flutter of fear once more, that urge to keep on running. Yet her eyes returned to the window, backlit, its story blazing forth, all those illuminated details she couldn't remember noticing before. How the martyrs wore tabards over their naked bodies in true auto-da-fé style, with candles in their bound hands and high, peaked dunces' caps on their heads. How at least one of them—the one set highest, in honor above the others—seemed to be a disinterred corpse, half-rotten, his only partially bandaged jaw gaping darkly open against the flames.

Our faith's founders, she heard her aunt whisper behind her, from the shadows. *You remember the stories, don't you? They prepared the way. They kept their promises.*

The coffin's side bumped her stomach then, making her glance down into it. Her mother's painted mouth could just be glimpsed burning inside like a brand.

You could kiss her, at least, her aunt said, reprovingly. *Show your love like a good daughter.* So just to prove her wrong she leaned down and did it, pressing those cold lips hard 'til the paint smeared, blood-like, all over her teeth. Until her mother's dry tongue slipped out to meet hers at last, like a worm, and sent her scrambling back, squealing, into her dream-aunt's arms.

Seconds later the girl woke sickened, sat upright, spasmed to the left-hand side as though genuflecting... and puked, headlong, into her own open suitcase.

End Part Two

"Okay," Ned says, putting the Starbucks cups down on the table, "you remember how the BBC thought it was a great idea to just erase a bunch of their earliest video recordings rather than archive them, to save money? Like old black-and-white *Doctor Who* episodes, and stuff?"

"Vaguely, sure. Why?"

"Well, maybe that's what happened here, except with the CBC. Or wherever."

Sharla sighs. "Why the fuck did I ask you along on this again?"

"'Cause you're meeting some dude from the Internet, and you don't even know what he looks like. Plus you're scared he's gonna turn out to be some sort of weirdo." As she shoots him the side-eye: "Weirder than *me,* I mean. Weirder than that."

"Heaven forbid."

Ned throws up his hands, fluttering slightly: "Oh, all the bloody saints and holy martyrs preserve us, yes! Wait a minute, though... sounds a bit too much like your story, right? That window."

"I don't think those people were meant to be saints, Ned. Or martyrs."

"Yeah, maybe not. Then again, you could get burnt for a whole hell of a lot of different stuff, you know, back in the day: being a Jew, being gay, being an apostate. That's a Christian who renounces Christianity."

"Uh huh. Or maybe they were exactly what they looked like."

"Barbecue?"

Sharla can't quite repress a shudder. "Witches."

Turns out, euan100's a woman—girl? A youngish person who reads like a girl anyhow, with a pink-tinged buzz-cut and a gigantic army surplus camo jacket over pegged black jeans and faux-Doc Martens covered in rhinestone stars. Sharla doesn't think she's ever worn anything quite this interesting, at least not since high school, when she used to favor a high and brimless black felt mandarin hat with a rotating set of junk-store brooches pinned to the front.

"You sharlajones@gmail.com?" they ask, huskily.

"Yeah, that's me. This's Ned. He's here in case you try to kill me."

Ned raises his hand. "Hi."

Which gets them both the side-eye from under mascara-rimmed lids. Moments later, though, they're ensconced in the corner, going over euan100's tablet—a bunch of Wayback Machine screenshots, interspersed with what looks like clone-phone snaps of physical materials in some sort of library. "Spent the morning down at the National Film Archive, or what's left of it after that Silver Nitrate Film Project fire last year," they tell Sharla. "But I think I actually might've tracked this thing of yours down, believe it or not."

"Seriously?" Sharla isn't sure exactly how she feels, hearing that. "I was genuinely starting to think I'd just made it all up."

"No, that's almost never the case—not that I've found anyway. I mean yeah, sometimes people have dreams where they're watching something, but the stuff they're watching always sort of slips and slides around, goes through weird jump-cuts or two or three characters suddenly becoming one character without the watcher even noticing 'til after they wake up, all that. Those types of dreams are almost never as linear as this story you've been writing..."

Sharla nods automatically; then the words penetrate. She stiffens. "Wait a minute, you've seen my *story*? How the *hell*—?!"

"Don't take this personally, but once I stalked you on Facebook, then found your group on Slack. Your Sharepad password was really easy to guess."

Sharla glances over just in time to see Ned hide his smirk behind his palm and gets the immediate urge to punch him, hard, in the shoulder. "...okay," she says, instead, after a moment. "So, what is it I've been remembering having watched exactly?"

"Well, it was never called 'The Church in the Mountains,' for one thing." Euan100 scrolls and swipes, taps on another photo: Looks like a page from a reference book, somewhere between textbook- and coffee table-sized. "*A Cool Sound from Hell: Canuxploitation Basics, from Quota Quickies to the Tax-Shelter Era*—the guy who wrote this went through U of T for film studies, then self-pubbed this on his way out. He's got the best collection of CanCon one-offs I've ever seen, even if two-thirds of them are still on video, which kind of sucks, for a couple of reasons."

Ned: "Those being?"

"Well... he's super-paranoid, so if you want to see any of his shit, you have to go to his place. And his place is, um..."

"Not so great?" Sharla suggests.

"That's putting it mildly." A pause. "But I guess you'll find out."

As euan100 guides them over to "the guy"'s place, which plays out in stages—first you have to call the dude, then wait for him to call back, then negotiate, moving from coffee shop to Internet bar to Tim Horton's and back again as you do—they fill Sharla and Ned in, in pedantic yet thorough fashion. "*Nighttouched*, that's the title of record," they begin. "They filed copyright in 1978. It was originally supposed to be an anthology film, like Hammer and Amicus used to do—four segments, thirteen to twenty minutes apiece, plus a frame narrative to thread it all together."

"Like *V/H/S*, right? Or *XX*."

"Yeah, except every part of this was made by the same dude, a really obscure director out of backwoods Ontario—at first some people thought he was David Cronenberg working under an alias, doing a bad Bob Clark impression. But no, he was just this guy from Your Lips who rode the Hollywood North tax shelter gravy train for a year and a half, maybe two—rumor was he got his start-up investment money from his psychiatrist, instead of his dentist or his real estate agent like most of those hacks. The end product ran an hour forty, perfect for the grindhouse circuit, something to play against hardcore pornos back when Linda Lovelace and *Deep Throat* gave them some 'mainstream' popularity. But when the production company couldn't find a distributor in the States, they decided they might as well just chop it into sections and dump it on late-night or early afternoon TV to keep their CanCon quota numbers up in between American simulcasts."

"So, *not* your classic success story, I take it," deadpans Ned.

Euan100 shakes their head, mouth in a wry twist. "Guy only made three movies, this one included, but apparently that was enough. He got blackballed, forever—couldn't even get a job laying down gaffer's tape or making 'Hot Set' signs, let alone another chance in the director's chair." They pause, then, not quite lowering their voice, as though they think somebody aside from Ned and Sharla might be listening. "Arthur Fogwill, or maybe Fogwell—I've seen it spelled both ways. That was his name."

"Blackballed for *what*?" Sharla knows Ned probably wants to know, so she asks it first—payback for the smirk, thanks very much. But that only makes euan100 hesitate a long moment more.

"Being... odd," they reply, finally. "Believing stuff. *In* stuff."

Ned, impatient: "*Like?*"

"Well, like... like the stuff he put in that part of *Nighttouched*, basically; the part you're remembering. Or that's the rumor. The guy I know, the one who wrote the book, says he interviewed Fogwell's girlfriend at the time, and she told him that Fogwell told *her* he shouldn't have put that part in at all—he said it was a story his family used to tell, something personal, a secret. She asked him whether he was afraid of being sued or something, and he just laughed; 'My folks don't watch a lot of films,' he told her. 'They're kind of against it.'"

Sharla nods. "Yeah, all right, makes sense—Anabaptists pretty much think the movie screen's like an open gate to hell, and there's Mennonites or whatever all over, up around those parts. Lake of the North, etcetera."

"Like Paul Schrader's family," Ned agrees. "Or Patricia Rozema's."

"Well, Ms. Girlfriend didn't think much of it at the time," euan100 continues. "Not until *Nighttouched* tanked and Fogwell disappeared." Another beat. "Like— literally. I mean, *gone*. Like nobody's ever figured out where he went since then."

"Anybody ever bother looking?" Ned asks.

Euan100 just shrugs. "Back to Your Lips, maybe—there's a *lot* of mountains near there, plus a *whole* lot of churches. One of 'em burnt down almost right after that, actually, in 1979. Cops thought it was maybe some sort of Canadian Jim Jones deal, mass suicide by fire long before the Order of the Solar Temple did it over in Quebec, but... that kind of thing's a little hard to prove, you know? After the fact. 'Cause human ashes look pretty much like any other kind of ash once it's all mixed together."

And then, just as Sharla opens her mouth to ask for more, their phone rings again—a texting app tone, this time. Euan100 breaks off and stares down, thumb moving furiously, before finally glancing up once more.

"He'll see us now," they say.

Part Three

The girl couldn't remember ever having gotten drunk enough to try and tell her friends at university where she and her mother came from—the mountains, the church, her aunt's apartment, the attic. That basement where she and the other kids had studied every weekend, smelling of chalk-dust and incense. That terrible window, blazing at the dead end of that dark and tiny hall.

"Your mother," her aunt began once more, next evening, as they got ready for the memorial service. "When she went away, it was like the heart went out of me—of us all. She was our saint-to-be, our faith's cornerstone. Oh, we say our prayers still, perform our rituals, but it's no good, and we know it if we're honest. Even when we pray in the old language, from the Book, the words themselves taste like ashes in our mouths."

"Cousin David doesn't seem to think so," the girl observed.

Her aunt just laughed, bitterly. "Cousin David's a fool. His faith's never been anything but childhood yammerings grown up, at least so far as it takes to wear a man's pants instead of a little boy's. He's never once in his whole life understood the full truth of who we are and what we do... or wanted to."

"And what's that, exactly?" the girl asked, not turning. Her eyes stayed on the mirror, her own body, her mother's wedding dress hanging off it just slightly, an ill-fitting glove. *It's the nicest thing we have,* her aunt had assured her, carefully unwrapping the yellow-tinged tissue paper she must have cocooned it in whenever she'd stowed it away at the very back of her armoire, so old it tore slightly as she peeled it away. *You might as well wear it tonight, while your other things go through the wash.*

"If you don't remember, I certainly can't tell you." Her aunt threw one of those narrowed glares her way again, forcing the girl's reflection to meet that silvery, mercury-poisoned gaze. "I can only give thanks she never truly became one of them, no matter what—she did admit that at the end, to me, if no one else. *That* much, she spared us."

"One of who?"

Her aunt hissed, turban-band contracting. "*Them,*" she repeated, as if the question itself was too ridiculous to merit more elaboration. Then added a moment later, unwillingly, the word eked out like a curse: "A *Christian.*"

"What?"

"You heard me."

Her favorite phrase, the girl thought, feeling a queasy wave envelop her, wrack her head to toe; her head swum for a second, eyes coming ever so slightly unfocused. "But..." she said, hesitant, before pausing for just a heartbeat or so, to recuperate. "...I thought *you* were Christians," she concluded, finally, and watched her aunt's face twist.

"No more than you are," her aunt replied, flat—then swerved to one side and spat on the floor, thumb slipping fast between her first two fingers, fisted against implied insult. A tiny puff rose from the saliva: dust, the girl could only assume. Even though it looked much more like smoke.

Left alone in front of the glass, the girl spanned her own waist with her hands, palms down, finger spread; admired the dress's fineness, its ancient sea-silk trim, gold lace spun from *byssus,* those lemon juice-soaked filaments harvested from metre-long pen shell bivalve mollusks. She thought of pictures she'd seen of the Aegean, blue waves under fierce gold sunlight; white sand, seagulls crying. Far away from any place she'd ever known, and old. Primordially old.

Hadn't Mom told her stories about how the Three built their first church by the seaside, in some part of the Mediterranean? They'd already been running from something by the time they'd gotten there, of course, same as ever: an endless persecution always climaxing in massacre, fire after fire after fire, the tearing down and sowing over with salt of every other place of worship that'd come before. The more the girl thought about it, the more she seemed to recall the most distant of these places had been not churches at all, but temples.

Wherever we shed our blood, that's where we put down roots, always, her aunt's voice had told her down in the basement, the other kids sprawled all around her, chewing their pencil-ends in boredom and waiting to be told how to fill in their workbooks' blank spaces. *Their hatred gives us power, that's what they'll never understand—how our deaths themselves are sanctifying because we give up our lives happily, gratefully, in tribute to our founders' glory. That whenever they murder us, our graves become our churches. That we are, in fact, our own sacrifices.*

Time and again, her aunt had told them, proudly, they'd resigned themselves to the cycle: Be cast out, suffer, die, regroup and then move on—until, at last, it had simply become too hard to sustain. Which, the girl could only assume, was when they'd finally taken on protective coloration.

Behind her eyes, the window blazed: The Three, these black saints, all too willing to proclaim themselves monsters and burn for it in order to draw their persecutors' eyes away from the rest of their flock, their blood. From those left behind.

How could I have ever believed this place was a real *church—sacred, holy?* the girl wondered, obscurely angry at her younger self. *How could I ever have thought this place could be my* home?

These stories the sect she'd been born into told themselves, these faint, vain excuses for a pattern of magical thinking stretching back centuries: they were what her mother had been raised on, her aunt. What *she* would have been raised on had they stayed.

She hadn't, though. And she had Mom to thank for that.

You think telling your fear will make it go away, the girl thought, looking at herself in the mirror. *But it doesn't.*

Maybe that's just what makes it come true, all the faster.

End Part Three

It's weird finally putting a face to a name Sharla only now remembers she's seen for years on handbills all over downtown. Though the Collector himself actually turns out to be the exact opposite of what she might have imagined beforehand had she thought about trying to—some neck-bearded senior citizen version of *The Simpsons'* Comic Book Guy, maybe, wearing sandals in winter and an extra-large cartoon-themed Hawaiian shirt, pumping halitosis-flavoured BO their way with every breath. Instead, euan100's vaunted expert is a small man of indeterminate age, eyes hidden behind classic John Lennon granny-glasses and sleek head shaved bald, pumped as hell under a tight black turtleneck. He stands aside with a flourish, letting them into an apartment whose walls are covered in floor-to-ceiling shelves crammed with videocassettes, some still in clamshell cases or cardboard sleeves but most blackly naked, marked only by hand-lettered labels. More tapes than she's seen anywhere, ever, aside from the back rooms of Suspect Video (dead twice over, of revered memory) or her childhood neighborhood's local Blockbuster store's aisles.

The plastic-metal smell of dust-choked heating vents exhales itself everywhere, reek of fading, dried-up Magic Marker ink undercut with an acrid hint of old ozone, all reminding her strongly if counter-intuitively of the one time she visited U of T's rare book library: Forgotten stories, obsolete media, secrets... a furtive vibe, half challenge, half warning.

The Collector turns those blank lenses on them, arms crossed, fingers drumming on one elbow. "*Kane,*" he says, voice high enough to crack slightly. "*Citizen Kane.* Inspired by whom?"

Sharla and Ned exchange a frown. "Uh, William Randolph Hearst," says Ned, a strong note of *Duh* in his voice.

The Collector nods. "Cronenberg's first film."

Ned scowls at the ceiling. "First like *really* first?... okay. It's either *Shivers*, or *Rabid*, or—"

"Nope," Sharla corrects him, snapping her fingers. "I read the script in a collection, from Faber & Faber: *Stereo,* 1969. About telepathy."

The Collector nods again, smiling. Sharla squints, straining not to catch her own face staring back at her in tiny, circular duplicate. "Founder of the National Film Board."

"Mate, c'mon—John Grierson. Bloody try harder."

The Collector glances over at euan100, who shrugs, and seems to relax; he turns for a shelf nearest the doorway, hand darting out without a glance, seeming to pluck a tape at random from the barely organized jumble that fills it. He weighs it a minute, like he's trying to judge how hard he'd have to throw it to break it. "Got this off a guy who taped it off of City-TV back in their *I Am Curious (Yellow)* days, when they ran on Swedish softcore and bad 1960s Hong Kong movie dubs," he says, finally. "The timestamp says 3:09 AM to 5:00 AM, which seems long, but that's because there's commercials. The good part is that the sections themselves run pretty much intact, though the framing device gets a bit mangled. Gotta take what you can get, though, when you're dealing with The Lost."

This last bit comes out in a tone of high significance, consonants popping to imply capitalization, and euan100 and Sharla exchange a look, silently agreeing to just let that shit go by. Ned, however, hikes his brows and asks, with equal emphasis: "'The *Lost*'?"

"You know... lost films, lost TV. Stuff that falls between the cracks. Stuff that's not supposed to exist."

"'Cause they got erased?" says Ned, shooting a *told-you-so* glance at Sharla, who glowers in return. The Collector nods.

"Exactly. Though in this case it was intentional."

"Yeah, heard about that," says Sharla. "They wanted to save money, BBC-style."

Surprisingly, this gets a headshake rather than another nod. "Most of this stuff, sure—but not *Nighttouched*. Not *anything* Arthur Fogwell was involved with. Those got thrown on the pile deliberately, because someone at Meteor Films—maybe a whole *bunch* of someones—wanted to make it look like Fogwell'd never made anything for them at all." Off Sharla's baffled look: "Meteor was the company that funded all three of Fogwell's movies, plus a bunch of other crap, equally obscure; they started off doing nudies, then got into sexy crossover appeal thrillers for the international market—pay a recognizable American 'star' to sit center-stage, then most of the rest of the money goes to boobs, blood and stock footage. Fogwell was their one and only sideline into horror, but they ran into trouble with him almost immediately."

"Why?" asks euan100, leaning forward. Sharla realizes they're as drawn into the story as she is; this must be a part of the tale even they haven't heard, as yet.

The Collector shrugs. "They wanted another *Black Christmas*, he wanted to make *The Brood, Part II*. But he wasn't really up to delivering either, far as I can tell."

"So—" Ned clears his throat. "—what *was* he up to delivering? We've come all this way, let's see it." He nods at the tape and then at the VCR-DVD setup in front of the guy's TV, a huge brown vacuum tube box that looks like it dates from the '70s. The Collector scowls slightly, like he's thinking about taking offense, but euan100 touches his knee and he subsides. Sharla wonders for a second if they're sleeping together.

Abruptly, the Collector swivels and leans down, popping the tape into the VCR. The whirring *ch-clack* as the tape sockets home—a sound as familiar as a school-bell, for all it's been close to ten years since Sharla heard either—silences the room instantly. The Collector yanks the TV's power switch on and sits back into a nearby chair, beckoning them to do the same; "Your segment's already cued up," he tells Sharla as she, Ned and euan100 drag their own hastily-located seats forward (a trio of peeling 1960s vinyl-topped aluminum-frame chairs that all look like they were bought second-hand from the same decommissioned diner), the screen gradually warming to life. "*Not* one of the American 'star' ones. You're welcome."

But Sharla's too intent to notice his snark or to care.

Goes without saying she's never yet been able to recall what "the girl" looks like, but... there she is anyhow, absolutely, waiting for her bus at the bottom of the mountain road, familiar as some relative known mainly through photos in a well-thumbed family album: rubbing her hands, breath gusting white, flakes sifting down all around her as the sky dulls and dims, the shelter light's sodium glare intensifying steadily to lend her a cruel yellow halo. Yet every color's just an implication, even the brightest, conjured as they are from different varying shades of brownish gray.

In Sharla's story—her dreams—the angles obviously aren't there, boldly canted as a series of E.C. Comics panels, or that popping, verge-of-skipping 1970s grindhouse grain with its incessant parade of hairs flickering across the projectionist's trap, its barely-there in and out fade, its intermittent cigarette burns. The credits come up wavering slightly, a trademark stamped next to its sectional title, like in Ti West's *House of the Devil*; "What Your Mother Owed," it calls itself, just as euan100 implied, not "The Church in the Mountains" at all. The sound's exactly the same as she remembers, though: artificially realistic ambient noise mixed in-studio and laid in afterwards, submerged by increments even as the soundtrack music comes up overtop like a warped, tinny echo, a half-melted wax cylinder recording...

"Jesus," Sharla hears herself whisper, dimly. "It *does* exist, after all."

From her side, she hears Ned draw a shaky breath, equally impressed, and annoyed to be so; "I guess," he agrees, eventually. Then adds, like he's whistling past a graveyard: "So what's that make what you've been writing all this time, then—fanfic or straight up plagiarism?"

"Shut the fuck up, Ned," Sharla tells him, not turning, as euan100 shushes them both.

"She's the one who sued him, y'know," the Collector puts in at almost the same time, apparently not considering his own added commentary track any sort of distraction, just as the bus draws up to its destination. "That actress, there. She's the whole reason Fogwell became a pariah."

Sharla traces his pointing finger's angle back to the screen, where girl and evil, turban-wearing aunt are facing off at the Church in the Mountains' cramped front portico. "The aunt, or the main character?" she asks.

"The girl."

Back past Ned, euan100 snaps their fingers, as if suddenly connecting the dots. "Oh, uh huh—the hypnotism story, right? I thought that was just a rumor."

The Collector hits pause, image freezing. "Nope; court sealed the records, probably because she was underage, but I finally found them in the back of a storage locker belonging to the kids of the guy who was Fogwell's lawyer at the time—they rented it to store all their dad's crap in after he died and were still gearing up to sort through it all when I showed up. They were happy enough to let me save 'em the trouble." He smiles to himself at this, like he's a *Criminal Minds* cast member or some shit. "Anyhow, that girl—"

"Whose name was?" Sharla prompts.

"Like anybody really gives a shit?" Off her glare: "Okay, okay... Harris, Regina Elaine, folks called her Reggie. It was maybe her third film at most, first as a principal, and right after they struck set for the last time, she just *went off* on Fogwell in public—right in the middle of the wrap party, is how I heard it. Accused him of all sort of weird stuff."

"Like?"

"Oh, like... one day, apparently, she was having trouble doing the exact thing Fogwell wanted her to, fucking up so bad they went through ten or more takes in a row, so he closed up the set—tells everybody but the cameraman, the sound guy and the key lighting dude to take a super-long lunch. Then he takes her aside and turns down all the lights, orders her to shut her eyes, then tells her the 'real' story behind the script—the same way his family used to tell it to him, unexpurgated, to improve her performance. Supposedly it worked, but she said afterwards she felt like he must've hypnotized her or something, because she started having these terrible nightmares almost every night, to the extent she had to get shit-faced drunk just to go to sleep at all. And then she started going off into 'fugue states,' like low-grade epilepsy or whatever, with at least one full seizure where she bit into her own tongue—but never on set, that was the weird thing. Always when she was somewhere else, at home, with her family and friends. So even though nobody in the cast and crew could back her up, she had plenty of witnesses to proceed with."

"Doctors' testimony?" euan100 asks.

The Collector nods. "The whole nine yards. And that's why Meteor blackballed Fogwell, because they didn't want to get involved in a prospective court case, let alone a kidnapping/murder investigation—"

"Wait, wait," Ned says, head snapping up. "A what?"

Both the Collector and euan100 turn his way, as if choreographed. "No, it's true," euan100 tells him. "Reggie Harris disappeared long before Fogwell—just didn't show up for court, her first day of testimony. And when the cops went to check her apartment there was nothing there aside from a creepy plastic angel statue on the windowsill and a dead fly next to it, so big it looked fake. I've seen photos."

"Meteor fired Fogwell the week after," the Collector agrees, "right after he finished *Nighttouched*'s first cut. And he said he was gonna sue them for back pay, not to mention all the footage that didn't make it in, but luckily enough for them, he just sort of... went away, after that. Went away without telling anybody he was going to, beforehand—not his friends, not his girlfriend, no one. And never came back."

A pause, then—a general pause, a long pause. Like none of them knows what the hell else to say.

"Can we watch the rest of the movie now?" is all Ned can apparently think of, at last.

Part Four

The girl came down the stairs in her mother's byssus wedding dress, her aunt a step or two behind, shadow falling across hers and snuffing it the same way she'd snuffed out a candle with two tongue-wet fingers a million times or more—close to the wick, at the flame's white heart yet stinging only slightly, to send up a dim, gray flume of smoke. And the church was full of congregants, of course, exactly as she'd expected it would be; all the same people who'd come to her mother's wake plus many, many more, so many more than she ever could have remembered from her childhood here, all those years she'd worked so hard to forget.

There was nothing but darkness outside, and inside, lit dishes of oil lining the windowsills and long tables. Even the stained-glass window looked dead. A dim film of night overlaid atop it all, twilight-occluded, spreading up from the floors and down from the ceilings and in from all four walls at once to hang in her lashes like cobwebs, like a storm gathering at the corners of both her eyes.

"This way," her aunt said, though she surely must have known it wasn't as though the girl had to be told. And she took the girl's hot right hand between her own two palms, so smooth and cold, to pull her along all the faster.

Chanting on every side, from every pew. The Old Speech rose up like a wave, harsh and guttural, sweeping her along—up the center aisle, up to the front, where her mother's coffin waited. She felt the taste of that dream-kiss in her mouth once more and spasmed, wanting to sick it back up, but her aunt only pulled all the harder.

"Keep going," she told her. "Sharla, keep *going*. For your mother's sake; for all our sakes. You're not done yet."

Sharla sucks in her breath so fast she almost chokes. Beneath his tiny lenses, she can see the Collector's eyes widen. "That didn't happen," he blurts out, before he can stop himself.

Ned: "*What* didn't happen?"

The Collector hits pause again, backing away, shaking his head. "I mean... it didn't happen like that, last time I watched this. It was a while ago, but I have an eidetic memory for this kind of shit, and that was *not* what that woman called her, back then. That was *not* her name."

"Sharla, you mean?"

"Well, what the fuck *else* would I mean, man? Who the *fuck* has a name like *Sharla,* anyhow?"

Once more, euan100 lays a hand on the Collector's arm, as if hoping the pressure will calm him; they glance over at Ned, who glances over at Sharla in turn, who isn't looking at any of them. Whose eyes are still riveted to the screen, paused or not: that same flickering image, Reggie Harris being pulled along, her (hypnotized?) eyes rolling back in her head. The aunt and her congregants, the mother's open coffin. That black, recessed window, its vivid colors gone, hanging over all.

"*My* name is Sharla," she points out, without turning.

The Collector blinks. "Well," he says, after a moment. "That doesn't make any goddamn sense at all."

Sharla nods, like: *I know, right?* And—

—when they reach the coffin's side, the girl looks down to see her mother's face exactly how she remembered it last, save for the fact that because she's been washed of her usual make-up, every part of her seems suddenly the same color: all dull yellow-gray, from the lank strands of her hair to the folds of her crooked nose, her shut eyes, her shut lips. As if she's been turned to sandstone, pores like a thousand tiny points of shadow, or carved out of soap; an effigy, a monument, herself to herself. It makes the girl's throat close up just to look at her.

"Repeat after me," her aunt tells her, nails digging in. "'In your name, better late than never, I fulfill my mother's promises. In *your* name, I so vow.'"

The girl pauses, licking numb lips. "Whose name?"

"It doesn't matter—*say* it, Sharla. 'In *your* name, I so vow.'"

"I... in your name, I..."

"'So vow.' *Say* it, girl."

"...I... so vow."

At the sound of it, spoken out loud, the entire congregation gives one loud, hoarse common sigh, a blade-rasp over whetstone. Her aunt opens her dark-painted mouth wide enough to bite someone's heart out, just tasting it.

"Ahhh," she says, happily. "At last."

Onscreen, the church darkens further, oil-lamps guttering; offscreen, something considerably closer pops and fizzles at the corner of Sharla's gaze, like heat-lightning—the rumble of a breaking storm, so low it's felt rather than heard. Euan100 looks 'round, startled. "Hell's that...?" they begin, but Ned shushes them silent even as he waves a palm in front of Sharla's face, other hand taking hers.

"You okay?" he asks. "Sharla, babe, you're scaring me. Are you *okay?*"

But Sharla's gaze is still locked upon the TV, her whole world dimming to that single point, this moment, those images—watching it finally all play out the way it always has, inside her head and otherwise. Watching things reach their climax.

"That's *never* been her name, goddamnit," the Collector puts in, from beside them both, his tiny whine of a voice less angry now than frightened. "*Never.*"

"Shut the fuck *up*, man, nobody cares. Sharla?"

"I'm all right," she manages, through lips that hardly move. "Won't be... long, now."

"You don't *look* all right, man; I mean, screw this crap. I think we should—"

"*No*, Ned, 'sokay. 'Salmost... over."

Just watch.

Watch the girl behind that flickering convex screen—that girl, Reggie, Sharla— as her eyes fix and dilate, as the pain begins furling up and outwards: a split seed, a flower, a promise long-planted; a prayer from the Book in the old language, exhaled from every cell at once. As she feels each word well up like blood behind her teeth, then miserably fails to cough the sentences they string together to form back out, in turn. *Wherever we shed our blood, that's where we put down roots, always. Whenever they murder us, our graves become our churches. We are, in fact, our own sacrifices.*

(*Every image is a story, every story a door, most especially those tales you aren't supposed to tell at all, outside the walls of your family home*—those in particular, as even Arthur Fogwell must have known, eventually. *And doors open both ways, always.*)

Watching, watching, watching as first the girl onscreen spasms and hugs herself, then Sharla does the same—as they fall headlong together into gathering darkness, shadow tumbling down all around like a set of blackout curtains. As time's drapery twitches forward and then aside once more, a blended-over jump-cut, a stitch sewing one moment to another.

Ned is yelling somewhere, close yet far away, muffled behind all the sudden weight of a thirty-year lag made flesh, a ritual at last fulfilled. And Sharla thinks she can almost hear the Collector, too, still denying it all through shock-slack lips like: *No, this isn't... this isn't right; what the hell did you* do, *Sharla, Reggie? Fogwell, what did you DO?*

Nothing very much at all, she knows, yet something all the same: something very old and very, very new. Some crazy flash of night-black inspiration, obsession, possession by some god-genius-devil—doesn't the word "genius" mean a guardian spirit, anyway? A lunatic Hail Mary pass, reinvention of some obscure ancestral mystery thrown spiraling into the future; a ritual enactment just waiting for the right mind to socket home into its core, like a tape into a VCR. Waiting to snare its—victim? priestess?—with dreams twice-removed, memories just vague enough to tantalize and mesmerize, like a pitcher plant luring in an insect; a locked gate, awaiting only the proper key.

To slide in... and *turn.*

And when the curtains draw back, the hardwood floor and ozone-plastic smell of the Collector's apartment are gone, replaced by cold, gritty stone, snow-damp air candle-lit and pain, pain, *unbelievable* pain. Some deep instinct beyond conscious awareness half-recognizes it—the agony every woman who chooses to give birth inherits, core-deep, all-encompassing and *pulsing*, swamping her entire body in rising and ebbing tides. Sharla writhes, so lost in hurt her attempt to scream only dribbles out as a tiny, echoing whimper.

Through anguish-slitted eyes, she can barely see her impossible surroundings: the church, almost exactly the same as that faux-Gothic set Fogwell had built forty-odd years ago yet so much larger, its ceiling vanished into shadow. Rawer too, from the cracked stone floor to the black-gapped windows; the stained-glass burning scene is holed by starburst fractures now, though that rotted corpse-king-saint still looms high atop it. There are no pews, no candle-racks, no statues; every lamp is empty, and the only light comes from a single thick candle embedded in its own melted wax atop the altar on its dais. Wind through broken glass is the only sound.

Ned is gone. The Collector and euan100 are gone. *Color* is gone—she doesn't know if it's the pain, or some subliminally thick dust in the air or drug given off from the candle, but everything from the floors to the walls to her own flesh looks... *coarser*, grainier, faded and yellowish. Like—

(*like the film*)

And then she realizes that even her *clothes* have changed. The jeans, t-shirt and jacket she wore to visit the Collector have melted away, replaced by a long, mustard-golden dress so thick with layered embroidery it looks like it should weigh far more than it does; only the silken, tissue-thin lightness of the fabric lets her breathe. But most horrifying of all, it *fits*—fits as if made specifically, for her own wedding.

Then another wave of pain rolls through her, and she contorts, terror taking on an altogether new dimension. Because this *isn't* childbirth, impossible as that would be—it doesn't roll through the womb, downwards and out. This agony, she dimly grasps, thrusts *upwards*, between her shoulder-blades; the unbalanced weight of something growing along her spine, stretching the skin to tearing. And—she can feel it *moving*. Inside her.

Oh Jesus, oh Christ, please help me—

More thought than speech, airless words between bloodless lips, yet *somebody*'s offended; Sharla can hear the harsh hiss of indrawn breath from up above as a single finger—hot and hard, skin a faint dusty rind over burning coal—lays itself across her mouth, urging her to *ssshhh.* "None of that," a cracked voice orders. Sharla's barely able to move her head, straining to see where it comes from. And then, all of a sudden, there's a woman-shape kneeling over her, ash-skinned and husk-withered, black eyes dry as two stones beneath her charred turban's moldering band.

(*the aunt*)

"That *name*... not ours, not Yours..." Here the aunt's fixed gaze flicks downwards, sparkling, as if remembering a long-lost loved one. "Anathema, unclean, unfit for this place. Our place." She closes crepey lids and sways, for a moment looking like she might keel over right here. "Yet he spoke truly, after all: that boy, the apostate's child, his faith so much stronger than we knew. Better to seed our grave, we thought, so others could rebuild... but we were mistaken. And now, that plan of his—our time, our moment, caught here inside his looping tale—is come."

That boy. Sharla's body twists and jerks, outside her control. "*Fogwell,*" she rasps.

"Yes."

For a moment, the pain lessens, dropping to something only marginally unendurable. Sharla cracks her eyes open further, manages to inch slightly around. Behind the aunt, standing in serried ranks, she abruptly finds she can make out rows of black-robed figures, their garb so dark she'd mistaken them for shadows. Hoods cover most of the faces, but she can see the occasional, gray-bearded jaw or pursed winter-apple mouth; their breathing is harsh and rapid, like they're bracing themselves to cheer or scream.

Sharla sucks in another moan, fumbles for the crone's hand; surprisingly, the woman lets her take it, stands still without complaint as she grips it hard and bears down, straining to get the question out. Demanding, at last: "*Why?*"

The aunt cocks her head, birdlike. "We didn't know," she says, sounding almost pleased, like an Evil Overlord given a chance to monologue. "We thought he mocked us, you see; mocked our faith, by reducing it to fodder for some shadow-show, some circus. These tricks of technology you find so familiar were very... strange to us, difficult to reconcile. So we took her, then him, suffered them to come unto us as the First Three once suffered..." Her dim, blank stare rises to the broken stained-glass window. "Scraping their heresy away by degrees, burning it free before letting the fire spread further to take this place, ourselves, all of it. Because we thought all our works here were lost, that the attention he'd thrown our way would bring *them* down on us once more; better to die ourselves, in our own time and way, than risk that. And the girl didn't understand at all, of course, dying in useless pain like some animal, some slaughtered lamb; a Lamb of God, as that bloodthirsty Christ of yours would have himself known. But Arthur, my traitor sister's son—I truly do believe *he* believed, now, considering the result. That even amongst *you people,* he still recalled enough to be driven by our words, our truth, our vision..."

... the First Three in their window, burning; this church, an ash-box reliquary, a skull inset in pearl; his mother's byssus dress, the one we buried her in. All fragments crushed and recombined to make an imago of his bloodline's cult, a fresh image, fit to birth us into this century. Into your—

(our)

—MY world.

Sharla doesn't have to hear the explanation to know it intimately, to hear it in her blood, reverberate. To see it forming in her brain's buried underside, where Fogwell's fragment has apparently always lodged, replaying itself over and over: a stye in God's eye, a splinter lodged deep, spinning scar tissue. Building steadily up and outwards through her for almost all her whole life long, 'til she finally put it into words designed to spread the infection as wide as it could go, deforming reality around her. Fished in first Ned, then euan100, then the Collector—

A fresh crest of pain, hazing Sharla's vision over; she wails and flops, turns facedown, sweat-wet and wracked all along her burning spine, coughing out a sob. Half-starts to ask *why me?,* then breaks off, knowing there'll be no answer— that she's not *special,* not her. That there might have been others over the years, though probably not more than fifty, thirty, twenty... because let's face it, this is Canadian film we're talking about, Canadian TV. Which means there's only so damn far it could ever hope to *go,* even after all this effort.

Thinking, at the very, very last, her face too rictus-set to laugh: *Should've moved to Hollywood, you* really *wanted to proselytize, you boutique fucking heretic...*

And that's the saddest part of all, in context, as the aunt lifts her hands towards the altar and cries out in some incomprehensible tongue while her congregants call back their response. No warning posted to ignore; no transgression being punished: Sharla just glanced up when her Nana failed to change the channel, put her attention—along with other people's, eventually—where most people wouldn't. Just stayed interested enough to push a bit too hard on the fold between forgotten and remembered secrets, wearing a hole so something could seep through. Just enabled an act of creation, destruction, rebirth.

With that thought, a final rip opens itself wide, inside her; Sharla feels the skin of her back give way with a snapping, tearing sound, her shriek so high it razors through her throat. The mass inside her lurches, shifts, spills out into Fogwell's aunt's waiting hands, some hot alien liquid too slippery to be blood gushing over the stone floor. And the church itself seems to howl its triumph, as all her pain abruptly washes away, dwindling to nothingness.

Is that a baby's cry? So far away, so high above, it's hard for her to tell. Sharla bends one hand back, feeling for the wound, eyes squinched against potential agony—but the skin that meets her fingers is only raw, no worse than a peeled sunburn. Shreds of byssus peel away in every direction, torn by that swelling, wrenching spasm; the layer of skin sealing in... *whatever* just came out of her is already shrinking, drying, shedding away in strips and scraps. Sharla manages to roll back over, gaping up at the aunt, who has risen to her feet. Something slimy-pink bawls and wriggles in those withered arms, the only sound in a sudden, reverent hush; the aunt smiles blissfully down, half overjoyed, half awed—and the fact that what she's staring at looks like a perfectly ordinary human baby is, somehow, the most unnatural thing of all.

"Thank you," the woman tells her, almost gently, before turning to face the congregation, lifting the fruit of Sharla's pain high. "And now, She is here," she proclaims. "Now the Days of Blood and Water come again. Now the Restitution comes. Now all will once more be set right." Cradling this thing she holds close, then, her voice drops into a low murmur, shaping that atonal, meaningless language of theirs into a soft, repetitive refrain as she walks away. One by one, the black-robed worshippers follow, some taking up the song in her wake, some of them quietly weeping.

Sharla wants to close her mouth, but all her strength vanished with the pain; she's weak, so weak. She can barely remember to breathe. *Wait,* she wants to scream after them, as they file out the door. *What about me?* But she can't get more out than a hiss, lost in the chant. She can't move; the ancient yellow dress, once so light, compresses her into the floor like a lead blanket. Her eyes blur, vision dimming.

"*Come... back...*" she husks as the heavy wooden doors swing shut, close with a *boom* whose draft snuffs the altar candle, plunges Sharla into cold and silent dark. A darkness complete as the final frame in a movie—

—a straight cut, smashed to black.

Distant Dark Places

Y MARCH IT'D been six months since I'd last seen Jong, and I was almost getting used to being alone, potentially forever. Then Brom came by my apartment.

"I found her," he told me; blurted it out the instant our eyes met, with no explanation as to who "her" might be, and none needed. Then added, hastily: "Maybe."

"Maybe?"

"Well... look, I don't want to get either of our hopes up too high, but... even if this was anybody else, someone I didn't have a personal connection to, I'd be ninety per cent certain, right out the gate. Eighty-nine, at the very least."

"That's eleven points out, Brom."

"Eleven points is damn good in our line of work."

He was right, and I knew it; I'd done enough work myself on similar investigations to understand how tracing a person through their digital footprint or finding echoes of said footprint inside of other people's tracks was like trying to catch a ghost in a sieve. That's what you designed and implemented algorithms for, these 21st century spells we both trucked in, fast enough to do your intelligence picking and sorting for you, but useless without a human being—like Brom or me—to interpret the results.

Statistics, analysis. The chaff inside the grain.

Jong wouldn't mind us trying to find her that way, I thought. She'd think of it like looking for stars in the seemingly empty places of the night sky, panning through the parts of the spectrum no human could see unaided. Then organizing what you found into constellations, an invisible zodiac, and naming them after whoever'd gone missing: Brom, me, Jong; the Statistician, the Reporter, the Astronomer-Physicist. The Friend. The Lover Left Behind.

The Zealot.

Brom hadn't gone looking for Jong intentionally, since we'd both already agreed we knew better—yet there she'd been, nonetheless, emerging abruptly from the middle background of a story he'd been researching for his internship at Last Things, the global cult-watch site. Though really, that's a far too visual turn of phrase; what he meant was that he'd *heard* her or thought he might have—caught the faintest of Jong-related rumors, the trace-echo of her words repeating through the interstices of someone else's like resonance. Nothing concrete at first, not even a blurry screengrab from some darkened room or one more figure at the edge of a crowd, slightly turned away, unnamed and faceless to anybody but the ones who supposedly knew her best.

"There's this intersectional drift between prepper groups and intelligent design advocates we've been tracking, lately," Brom told me, spreading a sheaf of printouts across the kitchen table between us. "Like hardcore environmentalists but on a more... cosmic scale, you know? Science Is God types. Probably started with people who got cut from SETI for being way too into the whole idea of an alien invasion, but it's more grassroots, now—second or third-gen, closer to home, and *considerably* weirder."

"Elaborate."

"Okay, well—most of the groups we monitor have some sort of Armageddon mythology going on, right?" I nodded. "Yeah, and a lot of them have plans to kick the final conflict off, too, 'cause that's a cult-builder's stock in trade: predict the apocalypse, wait for it to occur then get pissed off when it doesn't, purge, regroup, repeat. But that's more the prepper side of things, whereas the cosmic side, they just have to *stay* with their predictions once they've made 'em. 'Cause there's no possible way they could affect any of the stuff they're talking about, right? Not directly."

"'A long time ago, in a galaxy far away'," I said dryly. "Can't ever make Halley's Comet swing back around any faster, no matter *how* hard you chemically castrate yourself."

"Exactly. But there's one faction I kept running across in the sub-thread chatter, so I chased mentions 'til I tripped across a few direct statements. They call themselves the Theia Collect."

"And?"

He pushed a printout my way, eyes still on mine. "Read for yourself," he said.

This was weeks ago, of course. But here, right now, in Croniston—by the very shore of Hudson's Bay itself, in the northern-most part of North Ontario—time is already running backwards; night blooming up rather than falling, revealing itself like a stripper redressing, the black behind the blue. And on a quantum level, I guess it's probably *been* night since the universe began, at least everywhere outside that still point where everything used to be all crushed together, pre-Big Bang; the same night, even, or close enough for jazz. It's just that the spaces between things kept on getting exponentially longer as everything we know and everything we don't furled outwards from the blast, with darkness rushing in to fill those ever-widening holes, like surf on sand. Energy neither created nor destroyed, yet riding a wave which will one day finally exhaust itself enough to start going backwards—entropy always rendering the universe's component parts progressively slower, progressively colder, 'til Endless Empty rears up at last to repossess it all.

That's not science, Jong would've protested, had I ever told her this. To which I would've simply replied: *Good thing I was never the scientist in this relationship then.*

One way or the other, though, that permanent night underlying the sky's illusion has always been there, whether seen or un: every night the same, everywhere. Day has only ever been a facade, a lie agreed upon. It never could have lasted.

Now time turns, stitching the sky back together, and scary as the thought might be, I find I very much want to see what... exactly... the last veil to be put back on will turn out to be, once this long dance is finally done. What we'll be left with by the end.

If anything.

That old Joan Jett song really does say it best: *love is pain.* We open ourselves up to its pure potential, full of hope and horror; take that ultimate leap of faith and pray for the best, suspecting—expecting—the worst, and we are only ever very rarely surprised in that respect. So yes, on one level I'm responsible for this hurt I "let" Jong give me, but she's the one who chose to do so in the first place; to give herself to me, then take herself away again. And I wasn't *wrong* to gamble that she wouldn't, or stupid, or weak—it's sad, but it's not my fault. Like any other act of impending galactic cannibalism performed in distant dark places, it has nothing whatsoever to do with me.

This is true too: Every wound makes an exit or an entry; loss tears channels in us all through which things rush either out or in, bound on tides of guilt. We become conduits, and grief becomes a game we play in dark rooms, giving false names, pretending we're someone else. A lie we'd probably even kill for, if challenged on.

Jong was always going to abandon me. Not that she would've thought of it that way; I know that now, conclusively. For her, entropy was the sole constant underlying everything. She studied it, professionally and otherwise—liked to think the universe's true beauty lay in how it was mainly held together by its own ongoing decay.

Here's a little story, for example, of the existentially dreadful kind she so often used to tell me: the sort of cosmic fairy-tale people in her field love to swap, fun, new, unprovable scenarios calculated to deform our received ideas about time and space. Like the astronomical term *spaghettification*, used to describe how an object plummeting into a black hole might stretch out into an infinitely long tube, which inevitably strikes much the same black comedic note as the "fact" that when a rock thought to be a meteorite turns out to be terrestrial, astronomers call it a meteowrong.

Oh, and I can hear her now, words reverberant through flesh, whispering directly into my breastbone. Curled in my arms and should be sleeping, but instead, she's... well, probably not *trying* to creep me out about outer space as a concept, so much, but definitely succeeding. Hard enough I might never be able to watch *Interstellar* again.

Look up, Sid. In the eastern sky, there's a constellation called Eridanus, named after the water flowing from Aquarius's amphora, a river of stars. Nothing much on its own unless you go deeper, switch spectrums, shift over into the range of perception we humans can never access unaided by technology. That's when you'll notice that in between these stars, there's a place where the background radiation turns cold.

Now, to our eyes, all the oldest spots in the sky only show up as darkness, no matter how much we stare. But this spot in Eridanus is even darker, made up of some of the oldest light in the universe, dating right back to the Big Bang. Imperceptible to humans, it's so dim it only shows up as microwaves on our long-range sensory arrays—not a glow of microwaves, either; just a blush. A slightly shallower sort of night.

This Eridanus gap is enormous, roughly a billion light years across and mainly made up of just nothing, emptiness. No planets. No stars. One theory is that it's a void where no galaxies exist; such areas have been recorded before, a predictable part of the known universe. If the cold spot is a void, though, and could be confirmed as such without us having to waste a thousand times the span of human history to travel within observational distance, it could change our whole understanding of what's allowable, our entire model of reality.

It might even turn out to be a place where some part of a parallel universe intersects our own.

And what's the point of that *particular piece of trivia, exactly?* I'd ask, to which Jong would simply shrug, soft hair kissing my clavicle as she turned her head in the hollow of my arm. Replying: *Does everything really have to have a point to be worth something to you, Sidionia? That's a pretty sad way to live.*

Always drawn to the creepiest possible parts of outer space, the black holes and the pulsars, the gas giants and the Kuiper Belt fragments, country-sized chunks of ice elliptically orbiting so far beyond our sun's reach it's like they've been cut loose to drift forever before reappearing at mathematically-predictable intervals, pulling comet-tails made from who the fuck knows what behind them. Event horizons and vanishing points, gravitational anomalies and quantum freaks. All the phantom planets this physics-haunted universe can provide.

There was a book she used to pore over, back when we first met—*Speculative Science,* she called it. It asked questions, then spun scenarios about possible variations on Earths that might have been: what if the Moon didn't exist, or Earth had *two* moons or was a moon itself to some much larger planet? What if a local star went supernova or our axis started to tilt, if we were hit by a comet, a meteor, a black hole? What if we cooked or drowned or blew away? Or what if—worst of all—the hundred million random coincidences that supposedly combined to produce life on our planet had simply arranged themselves another way?

So, like I said: Jong was always thinking about endings, ours very much included. They excited her. 'Cause every new beginning comes from some other beginning's end, as the old song says.

I'm almost sure that prospect never struck her as sad, let alone avoidable.

This world is broken, the Theia Collect's manifesto began. *It was born that way. Things are not as they should be, and we know it. You know it.*

Why do we do the things we do to each other, to ourselves? Why are we never satisfied? Because, in our heart of hearts, we know there's already a hole at the heart of everything. Because, on some intangible level, we understand that we are part of something that was never meant to be.

It can *be fixed, however, if enough people are willing. What was sundered* can *be made whole again and fresh and new. Paradise on Earth, literally.*

And all we have to do to earn this redemption is be willing to not only cooperate *with our own extinction, but to also take an active hand in* jump-starting *it.*

I was frankly starting to wonder what part of this vaguely off-putting ideological pitch reminded Brom of Jong in particular, when the text made a sudden swerve into science mode, snapping it into focus—began to talk about the Big Splash, aka the giant-impact hypothesis. That's the theory which posits Earth's Moon might have formed out of the debris left over from an indirect collision between Earth and a protoplanet called Theia, an astronomical body the size of Mars, approximately four and a half billion years ago in the Hadean eon, some twenty to a hundred million years after the solar system coalesced.

A protoplanet is a large planetary embryo that originated within a protoplanetary disc and has undergone internal melting to produce a differentiated interior, Jong told me, once, in the very thick of it—more of her very particular version of pillow-talk. *Thought to form out of planetesimals that gravitationally perturb each other's orbits and collide, gradually coalescing into dominant planets.*

Oh, uh huh, I managed, in return. Making her laugh enough to slow her down but not even vaguely stop what she was doing, continuing, as she did—

No, seriously: sounds far-fetched, I get it. But in the inner Solar System alone, there's three protoplanets that survive more-or-less intact to this day—Ceres, Pallas, and Vesta, all previously classed as asteroids. 16 Psyche, one of the largest bodies in the Belt, is thought to be an exposed iron core of a protoplanet, one that got its outer rocky layers stripped off after a hit-and-run with some even bigger object. And very recently, astronomers finally made the first direct observation of a protoplanet forming in a disk of gas and dust around a distant star.

Her hands were busy, and it was getting hard to breathe. But I made myself grit it out, nonetheless: *Oh yeah? When was that?*

February 2013, she murmured in my ear. *A nice little Valentine's Day gift for scientists everywhere.*

So, this was the reference the Collect had chosen to name themselves after, suitably enough. And as for why the theoretical protoplanet in question was called Theia, well: the tie-in wasn't a huge surprise, given the Greek mythological figure after which the Collect had chosen to name themselves: Theia was a Titan, one of Cronus's bunch, precursors to the eventual pantheon of Zeus, his siblings, and children. She was also the mother of Selene, goddess of the Moon.

The evidence mounts year by year, the printout continued. *Consider that the Earth's spin and the Moon's orbit have similar orientations; consider that lunar samples indicate the Moon once had a molten surface, even though the Moon has both a relatively small iron core and a lower density than Earth. The stable-isotope ratios of lunar and terrestrial rock are also identical, confirming a common origin...*

So far, so persuasive, at least at first glance. Most new recruits probably wouldn't know much about the established counter-arguments, I guessed—like why the Moon's rocks seem to have lost all their volatile elements or why there are three minerals found there that aren't found anywhere on Earth (armalcolite, tranquillityite and pyroxferroite). Or why Venus, which definitely experienced giant impacts during its formation, has no moon at all. Classic rhetorical tricks I'd seen employed in a dozen manifestos just like this one: state possibilities as certainties, ignore what doesn't fit, and hope nobody thinks to ask the right—or wrong—questions. Classic Jong.

(*You can't just bend the facts to fit your own vision of things,* I'd told her on more than one occasion. *This is science, not poetry; it's supposed to make sense.* To which she'd simply laughed, replying: *How much of reality have you ever known to make sense, exactly?*)

Well... not a lot, granted. And probably less even than that, given how easily much of the rest of it, all objects and forces invisible to the naked eye, can be categorically reduced to things we've been forced to agree to take on faith.

In the end, we're all just ghosts in decaying meat-suits, chained to this planet by forces we can't hope to quantify, let alone control, the printout said. *Only the names change—what we once called God we now call gravity, and what does that get us besides a creeping suspicion we must be utterly, infinitesimally unimportant, especially when compared with the rest of the universe? Nothing.*

We were small before, of course. But at least when we gave what we could never understand a god's name, we could still delude ourselves that we were loved by unknown forces, huge and invisible, yet supportive, not malign. Or we surely wouldn't be here at all.

Suddenly exhausted by it all, I shook my head and sat back, meeting Brom's eyes directly. "Yeah, I'm not buying it," I lied. "What is it these people've even *done*, so far, to get them on Last Things' radar?"

"Not much, thus far, but the company they keep's pretty indicative..."

"Of what, all eating the same fruitcake? Not a crime, and Jong's not a *joiner*, never was. We both knew her better than that."

His gaze didn't waver, making me oddly proud. "*Tell* me that doesn't sound like her, Sid, especially at her worst. Make it convincing."

I sighed. "Okay, sure... I could *maybe* believe she'd been made into a figurehead for some movement she didn't even know about, like other people just started taking her ideas and running with them. But 'jump-start your own extinction?' The fuck would that even entail?"

"You want the Coles Notes version?"

I wanted to say no, as he could probably tell.

"Just fucking tell me," I said, finally.

Here's what I know or think I do: I loved Jong to the best of my ability. I believe she loved me. But while for me, the way I loved her felt immediate as a disease, some kind of infection, the sort which changes you forever on a cellular basis—a kind of emotional chimerism, as though she had distributed herself throughout me so completely it made us all but indistinguishable to anyone without a high-grade electron microscope—it's possible, in hindsight, that the way she loved me was... different, as she and I are different. That it had to be.

Could it be, I wonder now, that she loved me the way she loved any other natural phenomenon, at an interstellar remove, from great, dark distances? That in fact, she might have needed that sort of space between us, in *order* to love me? And that from where I am now, from where I've always been, whatever love she felt for me won't be fully visible for at least another million years?

Always separate, *separated*, even when we lay together entwined with her tongue in my mouth, an oyster in my shut jaws' shell. Or even whenever, after great expenditure of soft, slow patience, I managed to finally coax her far enough open to force my way inside, for both our pleasures.

This world is *flawed,* I might've argued, if she'd ever thought to ask me, *maybe even broken, but beautiful nonetheless, inside and out. Why would you ever* want *it to end, especially when you already know it will?*

But maybe that's where the illusion of control comes in, right? Prospectively, like any other suicide. Choose the manner and moment of your own death and you're finally rendered free of time, death, fear; Prometheus stealing fire, Christ harrowing Hell. For that briefest of all moments, you become your own personal saint, savior, god.

To make the same choice for everybody else, however... well, that's just murder. On a global scale. Not something I'd have considered Jong capable of, even taking the longest possible view: her eye was elsewhere, always. The planet we both lived on was temporary at best to begin with, hardly worth the effort to bring to its own long-foregone conclusion.

But then again, maybe there'd been a lot about Jong I hadn't known quite as well as I'd always assumed I did.

The Collect had been talking to Seth's Hands, Brom explained, a pan-Abrahamic ecological activist outfit who operated up and down the East Coast. Last Things had tied them to a bunch of weird happenings, running the gamut from corporation-targeted property damage and theft to potential murder via product interference; a joint ATF/FBI operation had finally managed to track down and trap about half of them on an estate in the Thousand Islands recently, snapping them up before they had a chance to scrub their laptops.

"The ATF knew Seth's Hands stole a bunch of army-grade explosives sometime in the last two months," Brom continued, "and the FBI found evidence they sold it off to various other groups—anyone who'd promise them they were going to use to it to 'protect' the Earth... or 'remake' it, a couple of messages imply. And one of those latter groups must've been the Collect."

"How'd you know that?" I asked.

"They paid with moon rocks."

I surprised myself by laughing. "Of course they did." Less than a thousand pounds total of lunar mineral on the entire Earth, either brought back from U.S. or Soviet missions or harvested from cast-off meteorites, and all of it supposedly catalogued to the gram—yet somehow, this crew manages to get hold of enough of it to swap for *explosives*. "Jesus, didn't they realize how much that shit's worth? I mean, *Jong* would know."

Brom shrugged. "Honestly, that's probably why she did it. Ten to one it was trying to fence the rocks that let the FBI home in on Seth's Hands in the first place."

I shook my head. Jong as apocalyptic cult member was hard enough to believe. Jong as some kind of criminal mastermind, buying weapons, coldly exploiting patsies and setting them up for the fall? No. Not *my*—

—*"yours," really, Sid? But was she ever?*

"Why the hell do they want explosives, anyway?" I asked, stifling the thought.

Brom put a hand over his eyes. "What do groups like this ever want that stuff for? Blowing up buildings or power plants or SWAT teams when it's Waco time. I don't know. Neither did the guy from Seth's Hands when the ATF quizzed him on it. What he *did* know, well..." He squared his shoulders uncomfortably. "That's kind of why I'm here." He slid a thin manila folder to me, not looking at me this time. I opened it, and an invisible hammer punched me in the gut.

The top sheet was an 8x10 black and white photo of Jong hurrying down some nameless town street with a heavy backpack slung across one shoulder, caught looking over the other, dark eyes wide and alert but unafraid. Then again, I'd never seen her afraid that I knew of; I couldn't even begin to imagine what that might look like.

Cheekbones maybe a little more prominent, hair shorter, more ragged. But still her. Always her. My throat hurt.

"Sid?"

"You could've warned me," I said, at last, and forced myself to flip the photo over, moving on to the next few pages: a short interview transcript, participants named only by initials. "This is the Seth's Hands guy?"

Brom nodded. "You probably wanna cut to the chase. Last couple paragraphs." Adding, as I did: "No, I never heard of Croniston either, and I don't know why she'd want to go there. According to canada.gov it's the northernmost populated point in Ontario, less than a thousand people—if she was looking for someplace she wouldn't stand out, that's not it."

I took a deep breath. "Are the Feds looking for her?"

"They want to. What I heard through Last Things, though, was that the op which caught all those guys, it didn't go as well as the news says; lost them a lot of goodwill with the OPP, plus there's some extra jurisdictional head-butting going on now. So, there's probably still time, if... well, you know."

"Get involved?" I suggested. "Chase after her, track her down—get there first? See if she'll listen to me, or us, when we tell her exactly how fucking close she is to a treason charge and some officially-deniable black site jail-time?"

Brom shrugged, uncomfortably. "Yeah, all that. If you wanted."

Him fairly projecting at me, silent: *So... do you?* And me just thinking back at him, equally wordless: *Well, that's a stupid question.*

All of which he could see on my face, I'm pretty damn sure. Which would probably explain why he didn't seem all too surprised when I closed the folder, pushed it back to him, and stood up.

"We're gonna need to do some prepping ourselves," I said.

If there was one thing my time with Jong taught me (beyond the fact that I am clearly *not* "just confused," as my parents always wanted to think, but very firmly gay, gay, gay) it was this: the universe is both far larger than we can ever under-stand and weirder than we can imagine, its possibilities almost endless.

The Earth-sized exoplanet 55 Cancri E, for example, located about forty light-years away, is more likely than not almost one-third pure carbon, making its core a single giant diamond worth nearly thirty *nonillion* dollars (that's a one with thirty zeroes after it, or a thousand *trillion trillion* times global GDP). Gliese 436b is an ice planet so close to its parent star it's constantly on *fire* but doesn't melt be-cause the planet's gravity is too strong to let it liquefy.

On the planet HB 189733b, it rains glass sideways, constantly. HD 188753 has three suns, so if you could stand on it you'd have three shadows, a sunset always in progress no matter where you looked. Wasp-17b is twice the size of Jupiter but half the mass and orbits in the opposite direction from its star's spin, which all previous planetary formation theories claim is impossible. And Gliese 581c... in some ways, that's the weirdest of all.

It's one of the few candidates we've found that might be able to support life, I re-member Jong telling me over dinner, on an early date. *Except that it orbits this tiny dwarf star, and it's tidally locked, which means one side's constantly bombarded in killing sunlight, while the other's frozen in darkness. Buuut*—and here she leaned forwards, eyes gone all flirty—*there's a tiny area in between the halves that's just the right tem-perature to support life, so long as you never stepped out of it. You wouldn't have night or day; the skies would be red, and if there were any plant-type lifeforms, they'd be jet-black instead of green, because they'd have to use infrared light for photosynthesis. Still, it* is *possible, and possible is just...* how *many points on the curve away from probable, again?*

More than you think, I told her, deadpan. To which she just grinned, as though she'd suddenly remembered a really good joke.

Did you know we actually sent a message *to 581c in 2008, Sid, just on the sheer chance there was somebody on site to answer? Like the world's longest-range game of Ding Dong Ditch ever.*

Nope, I did not *know that. So... what was it?*

Oh, math and music, insects and angels; standard first-contact bullshit. But given it's supposed to get there around 2029. Even if there is *anybody home, we wouldn't hear back until 2050—kind of an academic issue, at best. Just thinking about all the things we haven't found yet, though, out there...* I can still see her lick her lips, still feel the stab of desire that sight clawed out of me. *Almost makes it worth going on, day to day. You know?*

I looked up everything she told me, later; all of it was true, or true enough—impossible to prove, at any rate, or disprove. Like so much else.

So, keep that in mind, why don't you, when your reflex skepticism starts kicking in, as it probably will; about Jong, about me. About... everything.

Croniston wasn't an easy place to get to, not that I'd really thought it would be. Between arranging time away from our jobs, figuring out exactly how to reach a town hundreds of miles from the nearest airport and planning what to do when we got there, it took longer to get underway than I liked. In the meantime, I surfed all the news-aggregator and environmental underground sites I could find for any mention of those uncaught Seth's Hands fugitives, let alone the Theia Collect, and got only the usual quasi-tabloid clickbait about inexplicable magnetic anomalies, record-high tides worldwide, full moons making people behave even more nuttily than usual. I looked up Croniston, trying to figure out what Jong could want there, and found nothing beyond the same official government paragraphs Brom had: a mostly Greek immigrant-descended population of farmers and fishers, so disconnected from the rest of the province no bus ran there more than once a week. It wasn't until we were in the air, two and a half weeks later, that Brom paused while flipping through the papers he'd brought. "Huh," he said.

"Huh what?" I asked, not looking round.

"You ever heard of something called the Omphalos?"

"Sounds like a Dr. Seuss character. No."

"Funny." He shoved some of the pages under my nose: a Wikipedia printout. "In Greek religious iconography the Omphalos was the 'navel of the world', its geographical and spiritual center; there was this whole tradition of marking places like that with stones—Delphi most famously, but a bunch of others—"

"Delphi, like Oracle of Delphi?"

"Yeah, yeah. But it was also what they called the stone Rhea gave Cronus, so he'd swallow it thinking it was Zeus—Titans, just like Theia. There was a sacred artifact at Delphi they said was that exact stone; they'd anoint it with oil, bring it out on special occasions. And a number of others as well, used by more obscure cults and sects... so this is what I'm wondering." Brom pointed out the window, as if he could somehow target the town over the horizon from twenty thousand feet. "Here we've got this tiny town full of people fleeing the Turks, leaving around 1820 to settle in Canada, but nowhere near any of the big cities; they end up here, a thousand miles from everything, like they want to keep something hidden, something safe. Think about the town's fucking *name*, Sid!"

I did and got it a second later. " 'Cronus-town'?"

"Or 'Cronus-stone', maybe. Whichever." Brom scrabbled through the pages stacked all over his dining tray. "Come *on*, I had it just a second ago... "

"Yeah, okay, so Dan Brown conspiracy theories aside, what exactly are you 'wondering,' Brom? What's all this got to do with Jong?"

"Because there's a part in the Theia Collect manifesto that I kinda skimmed the first time, when they were talking about their Big Splash theory—ah, here it is." Brom pulled out a ream of dog-eared, corner-stapled paper, packed densely with single-spaced text, and flipped to a page somewhere in the middle. "They talk about how they think the Theia protoplanet didn't just break the Moon *off* from the Earth when it collided; they argue here that it actually split in two *itself* and merged most of its mass with both new bodies."

Theia could have been thoroughly mixed into both the Earth and the Moon, dispersed evenly between the two, I heard Jong murmur, in the back of my head. *That'd explain why the Moon's radioactive signature is almost exactly the same as Earth's...*

Sure, I remember answering. *Or there never having been any protoplanet in the first place, let alone one called Theia—that'd explain it too, right?*

I could still feel her smile in the dark, curving against my skin. As she'd replied: *Oh, Sid. You're no fun.*

Yeah, well; sorry I have difficulty appreciating the inevitable heat death decay of the universe in all its vast cosmic beauty, especially late at night. Let alone how most things we think we see apparently just aren't there, anymore...

I know, it's hard. But think about it this way: The memory of everything that was there will live forever, somewhere. That's how I prefer to think about it.

I remember swallowing at the thought, sharp enough to hurt. *That really doesn't help, actually. That sounds* worse.

Why?

Because... I reached for an answer, found none, sighed instead. Concluding at last, after another long moment: *Because some shit should be over and done with, permanently. That's what being human's for.*

That same smile, then, if a shade sadder. *Ah, but you and I know better, Sid, don't we? We're both scientists, after all.*

Nothing is ever really done, is what she probably meant; not on a cosmic level. And...

... not otherwise, either.

"So, they claim to have analyzed places on Earth where the mineral makeup's supposed to be similar to the Moon," Brom continued, unaware of any of this. "And wherever the overlap's high enough is supposed to be a remnant of the original impact point. Or... eruption point."

I snorted. "After four and a half billion years of plate tectonics? You could argue just as persuasively for any point on Earth you wanted."

"I know. Best kind of cult teaching, the unfalsifiable kind—the kind you can't prove wrong." Brom closed the Collect's manifesto and looked at me somberly. "But point is, what if they're taking the idea of 'navel of the world' literally? Maybe they think Croniston is at one of these impact points, or on its edge, or something; you remember people used to think all of Hudson Bay might be one gigantic Precambrian impact crater..."

"Yeah, but Jong told me they'd disproved that years ago, I think. Not that it matters." I shook my head. It kept hitting me anew, the sheer *wrongness* of Jong having taken up with these kinds of people, her stygian imaginings being made into excuses for petty bloodshed. "So, you think Jong's bringing the moon rocks to one of these impact points, so the Collect can do… what? Open a connection to Zeta Reticuli? Summon Zeus or Cronus or something—oh, Jesus, I can't even say this shit with a straight face." I turned and leant my head against the window, laughing in dry, shallow hitches that felt uncomfortably like sobs.

I heard Brom swallow; felt him pat my hand awkwardly. "It's not important," he said after a second. "Let's just find her. Take care of the rest of it when we—"

The plane's cabin lights flickered. He broke off. "Okay, *that* wasn't disquieting at all… Look, Sid, I—" Another flicker, sharper and longer; an electronic *bing* as the seat-belt sign went on. Brom gulped. "Sid, I think you might want to put on your—"

With a shockingly loud *BANG,* the plane bucked in midair; I yelled, mostly in surprise, as I bounced nearly a foot out of my seat. The cabin filled with screams of fear. I scrabbled to lock my belt, only half aware of an unintelligible voice probably instructing us to shut (the fuck) up and calm (the fuck) down over the P.A. while the plane juddered and jolted under me. Then the lights went out and didn't come back on. Oxygen masks fell from the ceiling. I grabbed one and put it on as Brom just sat there, eyes wide, knuckles white on his armrests; the screams spiked, and in the sunlight coming through the window, I could see the plastic bag attached to my mask pulsing in and out with my gasps.

Jong would find this funny as hell, it suddenly occurred to me, if I died by sheer bad luck in a plane accident, days before finally seeing her again. And thinking that, somehow, I found myself laughing too—breathlessly and silently into the mask, as my guts pushed upward into my chest.

Summing up: We all survived, obviously, mostly because we had a really good pilot, an older plane without a lot of electronics, and had already been on approach to the airport. That made us luckier than about a dozen other flights in the air over northern Ontario that day. Brom and I sat for hours watching the one working passenger lounge TV, a montage of talking heads from CNN to Fox bloviating about death statistics and crash damage and lunar magnetic events until it all became a numb blur, while checking our phones every ten minutes and waiting for service to resume.

Eventually it did. Airport clerks got their systems up and running; we were able to pay for a motel room to wait in 'till our rescheduled bus got there and went outside to hail a taxi. Planes sat lifeless and deathly silent on the tarmac, the gray air above empty, aside from fog. Though it wasn't particularly cold, it took all my willpower not to shiver. "Never realize how much noise an airport makes 'till it isn't there anymore, do you?" Brom remarked quietly, but I didn't answer. It didn't seem worth it.

I dreamt that night about a lake like a boiling black hole, whole expanse of water surging and frothing below a moon so impossibly close and huge that it filled the sky, its light nearly blinding; hollow cracks zigzagged across that moon's surface like lightning, while a tornado of stone and ripped-up trees whirled furiously from ground to sky. And at the bottom of that tornado, somehow untouched, a tiny figure stood, looking up: Jong, I could somehow tell, even at this distance. Smiling; awestruck; happier than I'd ever seen. Like Saint Teresa of Avila, transfixed with the sight of God.

Then: something huge and round and fiery emerged with dreadful lethargy from the lake's fevered center, steam shrieking off it as it boiled black water away, rising up and up and up. Its surface roiled, red-seared, misshapen, like a malformed egg, a worm-infested organ, embryo of some aborted chthonic god. Lifted yearning towards the falling, shattering moon, as all around it the earth tore apart in seismic convulsion, no end to it; just grew and grew, organic, a lump of world-marrow oozing from the same hole the World-snake had once burrowed through our planet. Yet still Jong stood beneath, arms outspread and unmoving, weeping in rapture.

I'd never seen Jong cry, before—not in real life. The thought alone was enough to start the dream dissolving. But then, as though cued, Jong looked around. Smiled through her tears. And *beckoned* to me, just before everything faded out, with me left staring up at the ceiling of my darkened motel room, greasy sweat cold on my skin. My stomach in convulsion, sour, like I'd been screaming.

Brom glanced at the knapsack I'd carried with me all the way from Toronto, shaking his head. "Still can't believe Reese actually let you guys take some of that stuff."

I shrugged. "Ever since the ROM shut down the Planetarium, they haven't really done anything with what used to be inside. Plus, it's hard to say no to the OPP... and I kinda played on how pissed off Reese still is, too, about the way Jong left."

"Right," said Brom. "'Cause *you're* not at all. Pissed off."

I let that pass. "The guy I've been emailing says he'll meet us tonight in the pub at six—only the one in town, so no need to worry about missing each other. When we get off the bus, you call your OPP guy and confirm everything's a go. After we take buddy through the whole haggling song and dance, he'll want a sample away for testing—I'll give him the idea myself, if he doesn't think of it first—so when he leaves the OPP guys will follow him, then grab up whoever he leads them to, which'll hopefully be the rest of the Collect, including Jong. After which..." I let myself trail off with a casual shrug, hoping Brom would take that as confident certainty rather than an admission I didn't actually know what I was going to do.

Brom only nodded, glancing at the bag I'd tucked down by my legs. "Hey," he said, suddenly. "You've got the box with you, don't you? Could I..." He leant forward. "Can I see it? Them. Just for a second."

"Touch a piece of the moon, huh?"

He shrugged. "Me and Neil Armstrong, yeah. Wouldn't you?"

"Guess not. I mean... I haven't."

He stared at me, so I sighed, and hauled the thing out. Reese had given it to me in a dark green metal cashbox with a combination lock, so it took me a minute to get it open; when I did, Brom straight-up gaped. Trying for diffidence, he stirred his finger through the contents: a layer of silvery-gray dust and gravel studded with larger jagged stones, black and gray, dun and brown, sparkling here and there—indistinguishable from anything you could scrape off a Hawaiian beach, to my eye. But Brom took a deep, unsteady breath, like he was fighting to control himself. "Wow," he finally said.

"Yeah, wow," I repeated; perhaps more harshly than I needed to, but the smell of the stuff turned my stomach for some reason. "Just remember what we're actually planning to do with this shit, in our worst-case scenario."

"Right." Brom watched me close the box, lock it, put it back in my knapsack. "I can hope it doesn't come to that, though, right?"

"Hope away," I said, flat enough to make him wince again. I ignored him, signaling the waitress.

The advantage of boring plans is that they tend to work; simple is almost always best, because it's simplest. The disadvantage is that when they *do* go wrong, they do so in ways it never even occurred to you to think about.

Croniston was one of those towns you could drive through in two minutes, one if the three traffic lights happened to be with you. The bus let us off at the main intersection around four o'clock; the sky was still gray, air cold and damp, buildings weathered as if by sea-salt. After we got settled, I killed time in my room surfing the 'Net on my iPad, though the motel's wi-fi kept dropping out intermittently—more fallout from yesterday's solar storm was the headline du jour, or whatever the fuck it'd been: Amazon and eBay screaming about lost profits, thousands of airline cancellations, people suffering hallucinations and fits over the continent's entire northeast quarter. I remember wondering if I should call my parents, yet somehow never quite getting around to it. There wasn't enough room in my mind for more than one person by then.

Brom and I hit the town's single pub at ten to six, though it was less pub than taverna: low-roofed, with yellowed plaster arches and scuffed wooden tables, air inside smelling of garlic and spices and anise. A couple of men in denim jackets sat in the corner, eating in silence. I tucked my knapsack under my chair and ordered Turkish coffee, amused by the idea of people escaping everything about the Ottoman Empire except its cuisine.

I was still smiling when Jong sat down across from us, dropping her own backpack with a thump. "Hi, Sid," she said, cheerfully.

As if it *hadn't* been more than six months since we'd seen each other. As if the last time we'd seen each other I *hadn't* been fighting to keep from breaking down, brain screaming as it tried to think of how to beg her to stay without looking like I was begging, because that would only send her out the door all the faster. As if everybody else who might have missed her, looked for her, wept over her, during those intervening months might as well have not existed.

It was like ripping a bandage off a half-healed wound, so fast the pain sent you into a whole new level of shock; my fingers froze solid, not allowing me to drop the tiny coffee cup I held, while Brom actually choked on his, spraying caffeine. Jong laughed as she ducked aside, grabbing a napkin. "Jeez, Brom, breathe much?" She wiped her face. "God, you guys haven't changed."

"No," I managed at last, hoarsely. "No, Jong. *I* have."

Jong's grin faded. "Yeah," she said eventually, gaze holding on mine. "I get that, Sid. But let me ask you this: If I'd drawn it out—told you everything I'd learned so you could spend two months thinking you were watching me go crazy, then six more torturing yourself over me anyway—would that really have been better? Be honest."

I wanted to punch her, to scream. Instead: "I always knew you were crazy, bitch," was all I answered, hoarsely. "Never cared about *that*. Still... I'd've thought I meant enough to you, you'd at least give me a chance to try and change your mind."

"Oh, God, Sid." Jong slumped. "What do you think all this *is?*"

Brom blinked. "What?"

"C'mon, Brom. You're good, but you're not *that* good." Jong shook her head. "I knew you were looking for me, months back; talked the guys in the Collect into buying their shit with the moon rocks, 'cause I knew that was exactly the kind of flag that'd pop your search algorithms. Then I talked them into going for *this* deal, because I knew you'd already be running a sting on it, and I don't need them anymore. And I came here myself, because ..." She trailed off. For the first time since I'd ever met her, she actually looked unsure of herself.

(*...I wanted to,* my brain supplied, silent. Though that was probably wishful thinking.)

My hands had curled into fists without me realizing it, head throbbing. "If you tell me you're here to *apologize,*" I began, in a whisper, then stopped, having no idea how to finish the sentence.

"No." Jong stared at the table, her own voice low. "No, you can only apologize for things you honestly wouldn't do again, given the same situation. This is... well, I guess it's an invitation."

I coughed, incredulous. "To—what? Join the fucking Theia Collect, save the world by murdering it? Bring back the protoplanet through the Omphalos or whatever half-baked occult astrophysics shit you're selling new recruits this week?"

"It's *not* half-baked—or 'occult shit', either, really. Just a level of science nobody else's really put together yet."

"Except *you?*" Brom challenged. "You're the only one who can stop this happening, so we better let you go—that it?"

Jong threw me a smile, wryly intimate; I recognized the look she reserved for people being particularly stupid, and *almost* returned it, before remembering how angry with her I still was. "Nobody's *stopping* anything, Brom. The only option is how we come out of it." Without warning, she reached over and took my hand. "Which is what I came here to ask. Look, I know—" And here, shockingly, her voice broke. "I *know*... how badly I hurt you, and how you can't possibly grasp that it—that it was necessary. Or *why* it was. But I hope *I* meant enough to *you* you'll give me one more chance to prove it."

She swiped at her eyes once, hard, then let go of my hand and sat up. "This is how it's gonna go," she continued, all businesslike. "I'm gonna take the pack with the rocks, and I'm gonna walk out of here. I'm driving the red Civic, outside; the license is BCXT 401, you want to give it to the OPP guys." She indicated the two men at the other table, with just the barest twitch of her head. "Then you can follow me to where the Collect's holed up, let the cops do their thing. Pick them all up, and that. After which... you'll know when... you'll have a chance to follow me somewhere else and see what it's all about, finally. If—you know. You want."

Bending to grab my pack, she hoisted it over her shoulder, eyes still on mine. "We'll be in touch," she said, pitching it loud enough that the OPP officers could hear, and walked out without looking back. I sat there staring at the tabletop, barely aware that Brom had twisted to watch her go until he turned back to me as the door closed, mouthing: *What the fuck, Sid?!*

The *fuck*, indeed.

No chance for a response, though. The OPP guys jumped to their feet and hurried after her, one of them beckoning us on impatiently; Brom groaned through gritted teeth and got up too, half-dragging me along in his wake. I let him. The words replaying over and over in my brain, same way they had when Brom had asked me pretty much the same thing, more than a month ago: *If you want. If you want, if you want, if you want.*

Did I?

"Holy *shit!*" blurted one of the officers, staring upwards; I looked up as well, immediately realizing why. The few people out on the street were all similarly riveted, eyes to the skies. The clouds had burned away; in the deepening twilight, the horizon looked as if it had caught on fire, rippling curtains of blue, green, pink and violet chasing each other back and forth in utter, terrifying silence. The temperature had plunged, and the air had gone freezing, bone-dry, stinking of ozone and static. When my breath came out, in a great streaming plume, for half a second I thought I could see sparks inside it.

Brom, to himself: "*That*'s not good."

The taller OPP guy hit his partner's shoulder, hard. "Get your shit together, man! It's the fucking northern lights, that's all. Come on." He jogged across the street to their unmarked car while his partner glanced back at us reluctantly, clearly wanting to ask the same question Brom and I had already exchanged with a single look: *Northern lights?* This *far south of the Arctic Circle?* But there wasn't time. Jong's car was already near the end of the street, halfway out of town.

We drove.

The OPP officers tailed Jong with professional skill, always staying a hundred yards back, though on an empty road after nightfall that wasn't exactly difficult: even Brom could have done it, or me. The road wove northwards through dense black forest, even skeletonized as it was from winter, Hudson's Bay's ice-sluggish waters intermittently visible on the right, flaring with the aurora's reflected fire. After about forty-five minutes, the Civic's red taillights turned left off the main road onto an ascending gravel driveway, disappearing into the woods. We cruised past, pulling over maybe a quarter mile farther on.

Presently, after a few terse radio orders, another six black-and-white patrol cars pulled up; the plainclothes officers got out to meet them, uniforms putting on body armour and loading weapons. Then suddenly, all seven vehicles were rolling up the gravel laneway, black leafless branches scraping by on all sides, to emerge onto a flat lot before a dilapidated farmhouse. Under the aurora's weird light, the police swarmed the house in a perfectly coordinated ritual dance, pulling ragged-looking people out in pairs and trios, body-slamming them to the ground.

The Collect cultists all looked more bewildered than anything, like they just couldn't believe this was happening. Like they'd been sold out. I had to admit, I knew the feeling.

That Jong wasn't amongst them, meanwhile, should come as no surprise.

It certainly didn't to Brom or me.

You'll know. That's what she'd said, so Brom and I were on the alert, looking for signs. We didn't have to wait long—or watch too hard, either, as it turned out. No Morse-code flashlights from the woods, no flares going up; Jong just tapped on the window of the car, startling the shit out of both of us, then turned and walked away into the woods carrying my backpack. All in black, completely outside any headlights, she would've been completely invisible to the cops.

"God *dammit*," Brom gasped, pressing his chest. "Where the fuck is she—Sid! The fuck're *you*—?!" But I closed the car door on the rest of his sentence and flung myself into the forest, not thinking about anything except catching up. Arms up to shield myself from low-hanging branches, I soon realized I was stumbling uphill, that the ground wasn't as uneven or undergrowth-clogged as I'd expected— had to be a trail, equally impossible to see, only negotiable by touch. I followed it up the slope as the OPP vehicle lights fell away, leaving me in pitch blackness, straining for any trace of Jong: her footsteps, her breath. The rustle of her passage leading me ever forward, while Brom stumbled to catch up behind.

All another part of Jong's plan, I thought: Lead the cops back here, leave the house within minutes, wait motionlessly in the dark outside, then duck neatly out from under their noses while they swept up the rest of her discarded pawns. My breath hitched in my chest again, as much from rage as fatigue. Christ, I was so *fucking* tired of running after this woman.

So, stop, said something cold, deep inside me.

I slowed, holding onto a tree and blinking away tears, trying to steady myself.

Turn around. Go home.

Jesus, I could, couldn't I? Fuck "closure"; closure was for sane people, dealing with other sane people. Fuck Jong's one more chance—she'd had it, back in that restaurant, where she could have behaved like a person instead of some maniac street preacher, tempting me out into the wilderness to show me... well, what? Some convergence, some black miracle? The place where science turned into magic, and vice versa?

She doesn't love you or care you love her. Bitch doesn't even know what love is, besides something that doesn't show up on any scope.

I was actually in the middle of turning around—hoping against hope to find Brom standing right there instead of probably blundering off in the exact opposite direction—when the radiance of the aurora borealis suddenly blazed up like orbiting spotlights; the night sky vanished, drowned in an exploding cyclonic storm of blue and green lightning, crackling 'round a central column of luminescent St. Elmo's fire that struck what looked less than two hundred yards away at the top of the hill: a luminous tornado touching down, God's moving finger writing a name on this world that was far too old to read, far too big to stop. A roar of wind smashed over the woods, nearly loud enough to deafen, and before I knew it, I was already in mid-sprint, hair lifting as I ran, as though the whole hill had become one giant Van de Graaf generator.

I found Jong knelt in the clearing at the top, my knapsack at her feet, shading her eyes with one hand while her own hair stood on end, throwing sparks. Scooping out handfuls of moon-dust and rocks with the other, throwing them straight into the conflagration, same way an engineer feeds a boiler's fire. The stones disintegrated in mid-arc, light-eaten, fireflies crisped by a tree-sized zapper.

As she bent down to scrape out the last of it, meanwhile, she finally caught sight of me, swaying at the clearing's edge. A delighted grin broke over her face. "*Sid!*" she cried over the roar of the wind. "You came! So scared you'd bail on me, 'cause you had every right to, but you *didn't!* You didn't. *Thank* you, just thank you, so—very—"

"The fuck *for,* exactly?" I called back, watching her face fall at my tone. "What *is* this fucking shit? And for Christ's sake, don't say—"

"—the Omphalos?" she filled in. "Mmmm... can't really help you there, Sid. Because..."

(... that's just what it is. Exactly.)

So here's Jong's thesis, I can only guess, looking back on it now from where I was then: If what Theia once was became equally Moon *and* Earth, then if you found the place where the Moon tore itself free and threw itself up into the sky—gravity reversing, time running backwards and forwards at once, in that moment of prime creation, which might have lasted millions of today's years yet passed like only a second's semi-blink—and fed enough moon rocks into it, admixed Earth and Moon 'till their humors re-balanced themselves, then... would what had been done become, somehow, undone? Would the world and its satellite break down to their component ingredients, ready to intersect and form something entirely new?

It's a spell, of course, not a formula, let alone a recipe. But there has to be something cooking at the heart of it, the iron core all set aglow with possibility, waiting to be stripped of its upper layers and the troublesome viruses inhabiting them. Took them to this particular spot, the place where all three planets intersected and altered each other's development forever—creation's ghost, the scar, the Omphalos, center of all—then could you make the one place on Earth that's mainly Theia? The divided materials would fuse together again, reforming a planetary embryo, a potential Theia which would rise and separate from the Earth, making everything go back to the way it once was. The marrow of the world, the hole the world-snake once slithered out of. An egg would form, then start to hatch.

This isn't *science, Jong,* I want to tell her once again, with extra emphasis. *No sort of science at all. Do this, baby, and you'll never be able to call yourself a* scientist *again...*

Huh. But then again, do this—as she *is* doing right fucking now, right with me watching—and none of us will able to call ourselves *anything*, really. Not for very long.

In the woods outside Chroniston, Ontario, on the shores of Hudson's Bay. Time running backwards, forwards, backwards. I watch reality rewrite itself, trying out possibilities, trying to find another way; watch Jong feed moon rocks down the hole, watch what was sundered reform itself. Get my shit together long enough momentarily to hit the switch and set off that small-bore charge Brom and I booby-trapped the box with, back in Toronto—and for an instant, I think it's worked. I think we're home free, apocalypse deferred. Can just see Brom himself blundering up over the ridge, close enough to wave, a look of baffled hope on his sadly open face ...

... but no: too late, it always was and always will be. The cloud of moon-dust starts to swirl about on its own accord, rises from the box's shattered ruin and eddies back inside the Omphalos, quick as dirty water down a drain. A critical threshold, crossed. Theia reforming, whole, like Athena from Zeus's skull; it rips free, throws itself back out into the dark, knowing what was the Moon will slam back into this scar where it once ripped away in turn, crushing us all. That the Earth itself will become a lump of uncooled lava, an anti-life elemental soup, before drifting away, back into the sun, with a smash and a crash and a crush.

And everything will become as it once was, amen. The way it should have always been, had sheer blind chance not intervened.

Not science, no. Nothing like. Yet I can't stop being who I am, even now. Can't stop... wanting to know. To see. To witness.

I want that, above all. To see and be destroyed by it. Find a hole and fall into it, go down deep deep deep, and never stop. Never stop falling. And in that endlessness will be my end, an ouroboros knot, forever tied and untying. No heaven, no hell. Just the circuit, eternally casting off energy, the sparks that move this awful world.

Because the light's all right for most work—most folk. Safer, for sure. But sometimes dark is good too, in its own way; *necessary*, if only for cover, protection. Protective coloration.

Sometimes, even, depending on who you know yourself to be... dark is better.

I look at Jong, so happy in her insanity, and think, *I can bear anything, I believe—however unlikely—so long as I have you at my side*. And knowing, even as I think it... that I do.

Up above, I watch ghost constellations reform. One by one, in the night's empty places, dead stars are coming back to life and turning back on, blooming like wounds in darkness. Brightening the sky 'til it disappears, every one of them a hole ripped through to some other possibility, leaking light.

"Isn't it beautiful?" Jong calls out, eyes on the sky; *You are,* I want to say, but don't.

"Yes," I reply, numbly, knowing it'll make her happy, or keep her happy, until the end. If literally nothing else.

At least we'll be together, I think, not knowing if it'll be the last thought I have.

Forever.

Worm Moon

By the time the Worm Moon rises, you will already have been aware of its approach for far longer than a month. This is not *their* Worm Moon we speak of, after all; the false one, the sham, a mere matter of phases. This moon—*our* moon—does not come tied to any month or linked to any human season. It rises in cold, wet darkness, from under snow and stones, so slowly none of them can even feel its approach. It rises on the other side of that dead place you and they pretend to share, the face turned always away from the sun, of which they can only ever see half.

The dark will be opening wide soon. You will rise to meet it, emerge from this meat suit they make you wear, slick and filthy. Disgorge yourself, at last. Be fulfilled.

Locusts only have to wait seven years to find fruition; we wait far longer, work far harder. This is why all that lies Below loves us far more than anything Above.

You don't remember being born so much as just crawling your way up out of the earth, shell cracking to shuck itself and slip back down into the dark, the muck, the wounded, gaping soil-mouth. Your thin new human skin slapped by cold air as you wriggled free, slimy and goose-pimpled all over, into the fire's weak light. You thought you would never be warm again.

Cold blood is the best sort of blood for the long sleep, congealed like anti-freeze. You could lie lost under three feet of ice and still survive, every part of you re-organizing itself from roe to egg, egg to pupa, pupa to nymph, nymph to larva. Larva, which means mask, the false face over the true.

This face, *their* face, over you.

Twenty-four hours before the Worm Moon's arrival, you'll already know it's on its way. This will give you just enough time to gather all the bits and pieces of this life you've made for yourself here—amongst them, unseen, unheeded—and fold them up like a soldier's coffin-flag. The knowledge will come to you at the height of an indrawn breath the very moment your throat turns hollow and starts to bell, a blown-into reed swollen with potential speech, too large for your own hand to fit around. Your larynx will vibrate, a struck skin. Then the note will sound in your gut as you force the air back out silently, biting down, creating an undertone rather than words or song. It will taint whatever comes out of you next, lending it a vile, hungry shade.

Maybe this will happen while you're at rehearsal and the choirmaster will call halt, unaware you're the culprit; he'll spend the next ten minutes trying to figure out what went wrong, reframe the line he's been teaching you, make sure it doesn't happen again. To fix things. And you'll just stand there and let him while the other choristers blame each other, blame themselves. No need to point out their mistakes.

It's their business, not yours, after all. Not really. You are not part of this, of them.

You never have been.

Drive until the lights dim and fade, then turn off into the woods, and park. Leave it all unlocked; nothing here means anything. Your feet will find the way. Take off your shoes, your socks, and stand with bare soles on the cold, hard, wet earth. The snow will melt beneath your feet, becoming mud, bringing you closer and closer to that thin rind of stony soil overtop what really matters. And as your toes turn blue, then gray, then black, the pulse will rise. You will feel it in what would be your marrow, if only you had bones.

When you've finally reached the right place, you will open your mouth, inhale. Cold air will coat your throat and settle inside your lungs. Every hair on your head will prick up. The blood in your veins will whirl and congeal, separating, black from red. Close your lips and blow.

Eventually, something will answer.

Out here, the Moon rises tiny and dull, a pebble off a dead man's eye. Out here, every stone—however fragmentary—is made from our mother's bones.

You will be met in the woods. So many more of you! You never knew. So many of them older. So many with drums.

(No one taught you how to make drums, you may think. No one taught you anything. You have been alone all your life. You will not know who to blame for this. Not that it matters now.)

Some of you will turn your drums to ground and beat them. Soft, soft, hard, harder, harder, hardest. Pound and pound. Match the heart which beats at the world's core, that bubbling volcanic rhythm. That liquid, glottal roar.

Here is how it will happen at last:

Your blood will rise as the moon does, blackening your veins to make your feet, your fingers. Making them writhe.

The dark will open, wider than your mouth by far. An empty, gaping void, aside from the Worm Moon above.

Your pores will open as the blood keeps on rising. As it noses out from each pore in your face like a fine filament of night, spinning itself together, thickening into a web, a sort of beard, fringing your mouth like whiskers. Thickening until it reaches out like fingers. Like the fine fungus that grows on some corpses' faces, a pallid mask, deep down under the ground.

Straighten, squirm, let your skin snap. Let it ruck off. Leave it behind.

You won't need it anymore.

Split yourself in two. Make a friend.

Cut a long slit in their spine and crawl inside, face-first. Wear them like a coat.

It will not warm you.

You will not want it to.

Fall and slither, spreading slick slime along the dirt, the carven furrow. The seeding trace.

Spore. Spore. Spore.

Plow and plow. Seed it under. Bury it deep.

Wait seven years and look! New yous.

All the while, the pulse will deepen, become louder. A crack will form and open wide, rippling with the beat. Inside the crack, more wetness, more cold. More you.

Something looks out, eyeless. Something noses the air.

Come down, it seems to say. And so you will.

(You always do.)

All you will leave in your wake is a hole.

But:

Nothing is perfect.

Not even this, for all it's simpler in its own way than anything you watched the meat-bags do. All the things you finally tried, more from boredom than curiosity. If there was surprise in its ending, it was only in how much more pain he seemed to feel than you did.

It wasn't like you weren't grateful. After all, it was his books, his endless monologues about work, which set you on the hunt.

You read about arcane names like *Gliocladium* and *Eurotium chevalieri* and *E. repens*—midwife organisms between rot and rebirth. *Ascomata* and *conidia*, the words thrilling in your skin like a thousand pictures anatomy never had. Read about the cycles of the moon and the web of all the invisible life that spun to its pattern. All of it mulch for the strange fruit of your epiphany.

All of it which led you here, now. With the others.

Writhing in the dirt.

Changing.

If only you'd read just a little bit more.

The Moon's road isn't perfect either.

Its elliptical path, the faintest degree out of circular true, sways it nearer and farther as it travels, like a pendulum. Humans have a dozen names for how these oscillations synchronize with orbital facings: *supermoons, micromoons, blue moons, wolf moons, blood moons* for the reddish umbra of a full lunar eclipse. All of it pointless, harmless poetry, you'd always thought.

But it means that not all moons are created equal.

And that every cycle has its reset point.

Something's wrong, you think with the closest thing left to a brain you have. *Something's—not right. Not... right.* Whatever those words can mean now.

A sea of black earth churned up by a hundred slick, viscous bodies, white-capped in the moonlight by the shreds of what was once skin. Stirred to a near-froth by the remains of limbs, by fogs of a thousand spore-laden tendrils. The metamorphosis you'd ached for in every cell. Except... your reach, your ache, is not pulling you down or outwards.

But in.

Plasm entangles with plasm, knotting at the molecular level. Hands—or the remains thereof—grip hands, fusing like tree roots, melding into singularity. Pseudopods dance and mate. Your memory drowns in the orgasmic, irruptive rush of a hundred other souls, dissolving into the imperative common to you all: Transformation. Rebirth. But not separate, as you'd expected.

Together.

You thought what you'd wanted was metamorphosis. To become what you should have been all along. You were so certain you knew what the final form of your cycle was. Not the details of its shape, of course. That didn't matter. What it *meant*.

You'd wanted freedom.

But that is not the nature of this stage.

If you had the neurons left to remember it, you would know that this is called the *hypogeous sporocarp*. The fruiting body. A thousand-foot-wide tangled web of wormlike, mycelial tissue, woven through the earth, flickering with the last sparks of the previous cycle's memories. Collecting the genetic information of every bipedal pedipalp's life, collating it, rebuilding it into eggs like a wasp hatching young in its own flesh.

The last, supreme irony: *This* is the sexual stage of the reproductive cycle, a corpse-bed from which new yous will incubate—new, but not *you*. One generation to a bio form, and the species reboots. It survives. You don't.

This is as close to what the one you left behind truly wanted from you as you could ever give him. Too bad he'll never know that if he ever does come seeking you, only to find what you took instead—the car, clothes, whatever else. A discarded shell.

A seven-year locust's pupa-larvae, left behind, as the self—the molted, bright-winged, buzzing seed—drifts free.

Nothing is visible now above the surface of the soil except the remains of clothing; abandoned drums; here and there half-buried flashlights, still alight, slowly fading. Leaves rustle in the wind.

A watcher might see the earth between the trees move, faintly, as if the forest floor itself breathed. Then the Moon passes behind clouds and is gone. Leaving only—the dark. Above. Below.

Inside.

HALLOO

A VOICE IN the dark, that's how it starts, when you don't even think you're listening – words breathed breathless into darkness, in a whisper, never returned. A voice made from your own blood's secret echo, like waves: that endless hissing surf, the sea inside every shell. They disappear into its open, black maw, eaten alive, one by one by one.

Hello?

Are you there?

I can't—

I need to talk. To someone.

Can anyone hear?

If you hear me, please say. Please.

Tell me, please.

I can't—

I need to speak. Need to – tell somebody. To tell them, tell them...

... what I've done.

Winter makes you want to sleep all day, even when you've already slept just fine all night–just fine but not enough, obviously. You never feel fully awake. Each time the year turns, the sky just seems to gray out, color draining, and there's a sudden sensation of pressure everywhere at once, pulling you down. Like if you actually bothered to go outside once in a while, you'd fall through the sidewalk and just keep on falling, all the way to the Earth's hollow, kindling core.

"It's just Seasonal Affective Disorder," Mom tells you, dismissively, over the phone. "Lots of people have it; you could go to the doctor for that, get some pills if you wanted."

The underlying implication always being if you really cared to, wanted to make the effort, to put yourself out. Because: *It's no big deal, Isla – no bigger than anything else you complain about anyhow.*

"She's a bitch," is all Amaya says when she comes home that evening, for neither the first time nor the fiftieth. To which you can barely raise enough energy to agree beyond a hollow-sounding laugh, four cups of strong-brewed coffee notwithstanding.

"Uh huh," you reply. "I come by it honestly. And in other news, water still wet, icecaps still melting, the president still a tool. Plus, gravity still sucks."

"You need a vacation, babe."

"*We* need, you mean."

"That too."

But it's not like either of you have that sort of extra money, so the next weekend finds you both still hanging around watching Home & Garden TV in your underwear together, exclaiming once more over the sad fact that every house-hunting couple in North America apparently wants an open-plan kitchen with stainless steel appliances or hooting at yet another pair of idiots who seem utterly convinced they'll be able to live the rest of their lives in a three hundred square foot tiny house on wheels without killing each other (or their kid or their dog or their two kids and two dogs).

Mom rings just as *Flip or Flop Atlanta* comes on. "My Stratford student tenant defaulted," she tells you, without even a hello first. "I need you and Anna—"

"Amaya."

"—that *girlfriend* of yours to go up and check if there's damage. She has a car, right?"

You glance over at Amaya, her eyes still on the TV, trying to figure out a lie Mom might believe: It's in the shop after an accident, she lent it out to friends, it got stolen. But you can't, so:

"... yes," you have to admit, at last.

"Well, perfect."

Hardly. But there isn't much to say, not really; the Festival's on, so Mom offers free tickets to *Twelfth Night* to sweeten the pot.

"Plus, we can stay as long as we want to after," you say to Amaya, as she–no big Shakespeare lover–groans slightly. "If the place isn't too wrecked, I mean."

She frowns. "You expect it to be?"

"Not really. Mom's usually pretty good at picking the Waterloo students who're least likely to hot-box the bathrooms or set up some sort of off-campus brothel or whatever."

"Except for when they run off without paying rent," she points out.

"Yup."

The Stratford house is always cold; that's what you remember most about it. It was your grandmother's, Nan's, once–the only place she'd ever lived and ultimately where she died, barricaded against the outside world amidst piles of filth and mail-order delivery boxes full of rhinestone jewelry bought off the Shopping Network. When you helped Mom break the front door down almost ten years ago, the soundtrack from Camelot had been playing on endless repeat from a boom box in the living room. You still remember hearing "If Ever I Would Leave You" coming faintly through the walls, counterpointed by Mom's breathless sobs, and the splintering thud of sledgehammer against wood.

The place looks a whole lot better this time around, thank God: no bodily fluid-stained carpet, no peeling vinyl wallpaper, no nicotine-yellowed ceiling paint. Mom's designers have tricked it out in what the HGTV people would no doubt call a "beachy, rustic" sort of color scheme; all light blues, bright whites and sandy accents, hardwood floors milk-washed to brighten the space overall, while mirrors gleam from every corner. Of course, this is the part of the house reserved for theatergoing "guests" and seasonal vacationers booked through Airbnb, while the student tenants–and thus, for the time being, you and Amaya–always occupy the apartment in what used to be the basement. Which might have been insulting if it wasn't just a confirmation of something you've known ever since you told her

Amaya's gender: on some level, Mom doesn't really consider you family anymore, let alone guest bedroom worthy.

"I kicked a hole in this door once, you know," you tell Amaya in front of the kitchen door that leads down to this place you're both supposed to check, clean and (maybe) repair, fishing out the master keys Mom gave you years ago. "Nan was livid when she saw; Mom had to pay to get it filled in, and she made me get a second job so I could pay her back. See, right there? You can almost see the seam."

Amaya frowns prettily. "Why would you do that, though?"

"God, I don't remember – wanted to get down there for some reason, but it was locked, and I got pissed; I was probably on the rag or about to be. Story of my adolescence."

"Yeah, yeah; whatever, babe. You're one scary lady, all right."

"You don't even know."

The lock finally yields to the key, and the door opens. The stairwell beyond is black.

There was a time in your life, and not actually all that long ago, when you didn't want anything to do with darkness–you were raised in it, just like your mom and hers. All of you used to live there, both together and apart, as if it was your shared home address.

They say scent carries memory and vice versa, and that might actually be true. For yourself, there are certain smells you still loathe on contact, smells that fill you with terror: the rose-scented hand cream Mom used during those first few years after the divorce, for example, when you moved into a nightmare-nest of a house three streets over from where she, you and Dad once lived. On its own, it was nothing special, but at the time, its very atmosphere seemed to signify and embody the violent death of everything you'd known up to that point. Even now, you can't help but flinch whenever Amaya slicks her dry, flaking elbows with something squeezed from a tube, at least until the scent (almond, lavender, some combination of the two) reaches you.

You were always "finding things to be afraid of" when you lived there, as Mom used to put it: the grates full of dust, through which distant voices always seemed to be whispering; the upstairs bathroom, with its painted-shut window and its high, cold toilet. The constantly knocking pipes, like Morse code messages sent from behind the walls. Like something trapped in plaster, frantic to find – or make – a way out.

Fear is anger turned inside out, Dr. Lavin told you later on. *And maybe that's where this rage that haunts you comes from, Isla, have you ever thought of that? All these tantrums, these destructive fits, the disassociation afterwards... You want to explode, to go off like a bomb. And then, when you see what you've done, the fear takes over, wiping your mind. Making you forget all about it.*

A lot of people do things they feel bad about, after, you replied. *But they remember them, still; they can't forget, no matter how much they try. Why am I different? What's so special about me?*

She shrugged. *What's so special about any of us? Things are as they are. I'm just here to make sure you understand yourself well enough to forgive.*

She'd never said who you were supposed to forgive, though. Yourself, your dad, Nan, your mom–all equally unlikely prospects in the end.

"That's weird," Amaya says.

You're cleaning out the basement, going through the closet, and amongst all the crap there's a bottle you're almost sure you've never seen before. It's pearly, frosted, vaguely translucent–more blue than white. You can't see through it. Raised letters on the side: Atwood's Jaundice Bitters, Moses Atwood, Mass. There's a cork in the top, almost rotted through.

"How old you think this is, exactly?" Amaya asks.

You shrug. "Old," you reply. "Like... turn of the century? The twentieth century, I mean."

"'Jaundice bitters.' The fuck are those?"

"Heroin, probably, or morphine. They put that shit in everything."

"*Laaaauuuuudanummmm,*" Amaya intones. "*Ab*sinthe."

"It'd be green if it was absinthe."

"Yeah, I guess that's right."

Amaya starts to up-end it, and you suddenly feel the urge to reach out, blurting: *Oh, I wouldn't do that.* No idea why. But you know better than to say shit like that out loud (these days, anyhow), so you don't.

So, the last of the cork falls out, hits the floor and skitters, instantly gone. And when you hold the bottle back up to blow across the top, trying to make her laugh, the flute-like note it produces is lower than low, so soft it's barely audible, a mere murmur. It hisses.

Like blood in your ear, your inner ear. Like the sea.

Amaya claims to like it, so you stand the open bottle carefully up on what will hopefully become the next student tenant's bedside table, planning to lose it somehow before you leave for home. Then you snap the light off and lie there beside her with eyes wide open, staring into nothing. You're not sure when you fall asleep.

Later that night, though, you dream you're walking down a long, empty beach. Sand squeaks beneath your bare feet, a slippery, volcanic shade of black. The tide is coming in somewhere to your left, the surf a repetitive shussssssh sound, half lullaby, half warning. Still, you just keep on walking forward, only stopping when you feel something frail about to crack under the sand as you step down.

It's a shell, half-buried. You brush it off, turn for the waves, let one wash it mostly clean; it is nacreous, pale to transparent in places, curled beautifully in on itself like the abandoned home of some long-dead giant snail. You raise it to your ear, and hear—

That voice, faintly echoing out of a darkness you can almost see, more red than black; not night, not some windowless room, some closet. Interior in every possible way. You feel it in your chest, your clenched jaw, the delicate facial bones set humming, pulsing, aching. As though, the more you think about it, it's somehow coming from inside...

(you)

What I did, I have to tell, please listen—
Are you there? Can you hear me?
Anyone, I need
need
please

It's been too long since you were last here to remember much of the place, so distinguishing what might be theft or damage from what's just age and change is a lot harder than you'd expected. As a result, you still aren't done with the basement apartment by the end of the next afternoon, at which point it's time to get ready for the theater–off to the Avon for the promised *Twelfth Night*. It's excellent as always.

It's only walking home afterwards you remember how quiet this town is. You're used to sirens, shouts, airplanes, car alarms, never-ceasing traffic, streetlights lining every block. Stratford at night in winter, the two of you walking arm in arm past a river already dammed up to prevent freezing damage to its bridges, all icy mud rather than gently flowing water, with the swans, ducks and geese safely housed away until spring... Well, it's not exactly "quiet as the grave," but it's no place you'd ever particularly want to live. Which you know because–as you tell Amaya–you've done so.

"It was back when my Nan was still alive," you explain, eyes skewing to keep watch on the pools of shadow bracketing your path. Your breath plumes in the frigid air. "My mom and I had a... thing, and she threw me out, so I didn't really have any other choice–I came up here, got a shit job, paid Nan rent. Just lucky it was between semesters, I guess."

"You lived down there?"

"Yeah, for almost three months. So, some of that stuff in the closet probably used to be mine." You pause, disengaging to blow on your hands, numb even through thick wool gloves. "I'd have thought she'd thrown it all in the trash by now, considering, but no. Christ, she was an odd old broad."

"How so?"

"Well, things eventually blew up between us, like always. I mean, you could practically time it–there was always something. Like... I listened to music too loud, or I flushed the toilet too many times during the night, woke her up. Or I must've been sneaking up and stealing her food out of the fridge, which I very much was not doing, because all she ever ate was shitty casseroles made out of, like, two cans of Campbell's stew mixed with a box of Kraft Dinner, heated up in the microwave. Oh God, the stink of it. It was like living in a greasy-spoon."

"So, she was a bitch, too, is what you're saying."

"A bitch who birthed a bitch, who birthed another bitch in turn. The blood breeds true."

Amaya suddenly stops, turning. "She locked you out," she says, dots connecting visibly. "Your Nan. Changed the basement door lock so your key didn't work, with all your stuff inside. That's why you kicked a hole in the door. Wasn't it?"

"You got it." A sigh. "She was out, at the Legion Hall–same dance every weekend, all these busted-up human wrecks sitting around listening to swing music and flirting. Used to dress up and everything, like Betty fuckin' Grable."

"But she knew you still had a key to the front door?" Amaya tilts her head. "Wasn't she afraid you'd return the favor? Smash her stuff up or something?"

"She didn't care." You shrug. "On some level, I think she knew everything in her half of the house was total shit... and besides, so what if I wrecked it? She had insurance."

"Wow." A slow, bemused headshake. "Babe, don't take this the wrong way, but sometimes I'm amazed you're as sane as you are."

For certain values of "sane," you consider replying, then change your mind. Innocent Amaya. Kind Amaya. Who knows so much less than she thinks she does, including about her current topic of conversation.

A swell of love lights your ribcage, and from the back of your mind you hear Viola's speech from tonight's performance repeat itself, those glorious iambic pentameter lines–Viola as Sebastian, a woman playing a man written to be played by a man playing a woman, wooing Olivia the way she wishes unperceptive Prince Orsino would know to woo her. So breathtakingly beautiful, no matter who it's meant for.

(*My mother used to recite this to me at night before I went to sleep,* you wanted to tell Amaya in a whisper, earlier. *Gave me* The Collected Works of Shakespeare *for my seventh birthday, so I could read along. She was understudying the part at the time, and guess how many years it took me to figure out I was mostly there to take her on her lines? I mean... actors, right? This is what I got, instead of fairy tales.*)

"Make me a willow cabin at your gate

And call upon my soul within the house.

Write loyal cantons of contemned love

And sing them loud even in the dead of night.

Halloo your name to the reverberate hills

And make the babbling gossip of the air

Cry out..."

"Sometimes I'm amazed, too," you say instead, and slip an arm around her waist.

The key is finding a non-destructive way to release stress, Dr. Lavin told you. *I promised you when we started this journey together that I wouldn't press you for more than you were ready to give–because I have to tell you, Isla, it's been pretty obvious you've been holding stuff back.* To which you'd said nothing, because there was nothing you could have said without lying.

Which puts us in an awkward position, Lavin went on after a pause, not sounding awkward at all. *You need to express the issue underlying your stress, but you don't have anybody to whom you feel you can do that safely yet. I might become that, eventually, but*— A shrug. *Fortunately, your subconscious mind isn't nearly as fussy as your conscious. A purely symbolic action may very well help as much as anything more explicit.*

Like what? you asked.

A ritual. Get yourself a container–a bottle, an empty spice tin, a small fabric bag you don't use anymore, so long as it's something unusual and striking. Then tell your story into it, with as much detail as you can, and close it up: cork it, wax it, tie it shut. Put it somewhere you can't get to it again afterwards and forget about it.

That's therapy? you finally said, once you realized she was serious. *Doc, no offense; that sounds like fucking witchcraft.*

Lavin shrugged again. *A lot of what people called witchcraft is based on exactly these kinds of psychological techniques,* she'd said. *Sympathetic magic, metaphor, whatever–but if it works, who cares?* She leant forward, holding your gaze with hers. *Just promise me you'll try it. Please.*

So, you did. You went home, found that huge cowrie shell your dad once sent you from Australia, furled and blushing like a fine-toothed *vagina dentate*, brought it up to your lips and breathed your worst behaviour in, over and over. You didn't get rid of it, though, after. It's at home even now, hung on the wall of the bedroom you and Amaya share in a gold-rimmed glass display case your mother once got you, right next to your other family relics–driftwood and coral, a tiny box full of baby teeth, a bleached-out tin button impressed with a snapshot from 1974 (Mom, Dad, you at maybe six, posing just like a real family on a day out to Toronto's Center Island fun-park, even as your relationship hovers on the ragged edge of dissolving).

Most importantly, however, Dr. Lavin's crazy-seeming idea actually did work. Does still. Always has, the shell absorbing your words endlessly, holding your secrets like a cup that never spills over. Because that rage-fire's dimmed somewhat since you were a teenager, but it never entirely dies.

Yet still, as long as you have somewhere to put it all, you're okay.

So far.

Sometime in the very early morning darkness there's that voice again, reverberating, setting your skull's shell ringing. Whispering, murmuring—

Did something, oh, I...

—are you there?

... something so terrible, so unforgivable, I have to tell, must—

Are you listening?

Is anyone listening?

Amaya's half out of bed before your posture registers–slumped over, elbows on knees, hands holding up your forehead. "Oh, baby, you barely slept again, did you?" She doesn't wait for an answer before she bounces to her feet. "Give me a few minutes, I'll make coffee."

You listen to her chatter in the kitchenette, wondering how you managed to fall in love with a morning person, 'til your iPhone chirrups. You pick it up and groan. Who else? And you don't dare ignore a FaceTime call this early in the morning; that'll just make it worse when you finally do reply. Pulling up whatever reserves of energy remain after last night, you tap ANSWER.

"Hi, Mom."

Amaya glances at you, instantly silent–she's learned the hard way to stay off your mom's radar. For her part, Mom seems a little more relaxed than usual: early morning fatigue, maybe.

"Isla. Don't tell me I woke you."

"Nope, I was up already."

"Hmmm. Well, I just wanted to see how things are going—"

"See for yourself," you tell her, sweeping the phone around, grateful and annoyed in equal measure as Amaya skips hastily out of its sightline. "One more day maybe. The play was great, by the way."

"Oh, I'm sure you earned it. I appreciate that this was an inconvenience..." Mom's eyes narrow, staring at something behind you. "Oh, God. So that's where that went."

"Where?"

"That horrible bottle you bought at the Weekend Market, the one you used to keep in your room. Smelled like rotten vinegar." She gives an affected micro-shudder of disgust. "I never could tell whether you genuinely didn't notice or just claimed you didn't; should've guessed it might have found its way up to Nan's. You two always did like that... stuff."

"Antiques?"

"Old things. Junk. Like the useless beach trash your father used to mail you every year instead of money, full of all that muck—"

A flickering image of ripping brown paper away from a box and opening it teases you, of pouring sand from the cowrie's inner folds back inside its packaging, purest white-blonde and apparently ground from the cracked wrecks of even tinier shells, every grain a new skeleton. As right in your inner ear, meanwhile, you almost think you can hear that most recent dream's voice murmur, telling you to break it off, don't take the bait for once, just hang up on her, Isla—

(You'll feel so much better if you do)

"Mom," your mouth says, curtly, "I have to run–still got that last bit of stuff to do, remember? We'll get back to you."

"'We?'"

"Amaya and me. You know, my *girlfriend,* who I live with? Who's here cleaning out Nan's crap too, for free, just because she loves me?"

Mom frowns, dismissing all of the above with a single flick of her brows: not now, not yet, not ever. "Well, when exactly will the two of you—?"

"When it's done, Mom; talk to you then. Bye."

A finger stabs hard on red, and the screen goes blank. To your left, Amaya resurfaces from under the kitchenette counter, filter and coffee-tin in hand. "That sounded... different," she says, eventually, to which you simply shrug, spasm-quick.

"I'm done tiptoeing around her," you reply, not turning. "Especially when she keeps pretending you don't exist."

"Huh, well... some people might call that a blessing, considering."

"And some people might call it an insult, ten years' worth at least, ever since I first tried coming out to that bitch only to have her completely ignore me: *oh that's very interesting, Isla. Will you be inviting any of your little college friends home this Thanksgiving? That nice boy Randy, perhaps?*"

"Babe, you're getting yourself all upset—"

Just be quiet, Maya; pour yourself a cup of that fucking awful coffee of yours and shut up. Don't talk about things you couldn't possibly hope to understand.

The same faint whisper, even lower, now barely thrumming through your marrow:

yes, just like that, that's good, yes

(*oh Isla, yes, that's perfect*)

"Agree to disagree," is all you say out loud, cool enough to wound. And walk away, back up into what used to be Nan's domain, mounting the rickety steps through a spill of memories let loose, like you're breasting some awful tide, submerged and struggling as the current bears you inexorably back, years peeling away like skin until at last you see clearly what you once thought you'd never have to think about again, so clear it hurts—

Should've known that cork was far too fragile to last, shouldn't you? the murmur asks, sweetly. *But the bottle was cheap, at the very least... cheap enough, anyhow.*

You see it blink open in your mind's eye now, blue-white, where a shaft of sun from the door catches it on the edge of one of Mom's favorite Sunday Market tables: lit up from within, what's left of its original glaze gone silvery, come away here and there in patches like glue worn tissue-paper thin. Remember paying for it with a random handful of change, three dollars and four two-dollar coins, the weight of them suddenly so palpable in your palm it makes you start to sweat. It seems frankly impossible you could ever have forgotten–that the bottle belonged to you once, along with anything you might have left inside it. That it still does and always will.

The frosting, like a bubble, a slow pocket of time. It didn't just appear there in the closet; you put it there, cork in place, certain you wouldn't see it again. And what was it that attracted you to it in the first place?

Sometimes, things simply suggest themselves on sight. Objects find their own utility.

Here comes your mother's voice from years before, meanwhile, overheard through a half-closed office door, younger than you ever recall her and angry in the way only someone terrified can be, biting the words off like poisoned threads: *Don't you dare tell me those quacks at the Clarke Institute have it right, Doctor–that my daughter's an... early-onset child schizophrenic, a psychopath, for Christ's own sake. That she's mentally goddamn ill.*

Isla's angry, Mrs. Decouteau, Dr. Lavin replies, maddeningly calm as always. *Abandoned by one parent, pathologized by the other... You've got your own stresses to deal with, I'm sure, but those aren't my problem, except in terms of how they manifest through Isla's various behaviours. What she needs most right now is to let herself forget the ways in which her fits of rage cause her to let you down–forgive herself for them, eventually, if she can. But that will never happen until you learn to stop pressuring her.*

She'll only come to terms with what she does when she's pushed beyond her limits. When she's ready. Not at my convenience or yours.

(Or hers.)

The next night you have another dream entirely, lying silent next to Amaya, who's curled away from you with her pillow tucked over her face. This time there is no beach, no shell, no voice. Just Nan's house the way it used to be back when you lived here, however briefly.

She's already gone out and left a list of things for you to do behind: one of those weird scrawled, barely-legible ones she used to tape to the basement apartment door before you came up in the morning. But this time the house is full of animals you've apparently agreed to look after, a random bunch of pets that Nan–animal-hater that she was–would never have owned in the first place: cats, dogs, birds, rats. Plus, some sort of thing you can't even begin to recognize, something truly awful, unnatural... long and hairless, with a ferret's slithery body but the head of leech or lamprey, all mouth, no teeth. And it's going around swallowing the smaller animals down whole with its jaw unhinged like a snake, as you watch, horrified.

And you want to interfere, but you don't want to touch it for fear it'll turn that fierce appetite your way before you can–too afraid your disgust will take over and make you beat it to death with a skillet, then having to explain that to Nan afterwards, too revolted by the idea of having to take responsibility for its actions or your own lack thereof. Because Jesus, it's not *your* pet, after all...

Which is exactly when you notice it's shitting as it swallows, of course, but also giving birth at the same time, as messily as possible–all these tinier versions of the same animal sliding out onto Nan's spotless vinyl-tiled kitchen floor slimed head to toe with crap, stinking and spilling, humping and squirming. The sound of this horrible, unknown creature panting, grunting in painful effort, its very pain repulsive. The fucking *smell*.

It makes you want to scream, to set the house on fire. Makes you wake up crying so hard you think you're going to go blind, choking and shuddering as Amaya bolts upright, cringing away when she tries to hug you. And teetering throughout on the ragged edge of some memory too painful to access at all during your waking hours. Of something, something, something so bad—

"I need to tell you about what else happened after Nan threw me out," you begin, later that morning, as Amaya glances up from her smartphone's screen.

"Your mom blame you for *that*, too?"

"No, actually. No, she was... occupied... with something else, back then. Someone else." You swallow, throat dry.

"The boyfriend she didn't marry."

"Mmm. Which kind of worked out for me, as it happened, but anyway. Not the point." Your hands work against each other, massaging the knuckles as if you can already feel the arthritis both Mom and Nan have probably passed on in your genes. "You see, I didn't just go straight home."

Amaya tilts her head silently, patient as always.

You make yourself go on. "Nan locked me out of the basement; I kicked a hole in the door, but I couldn't get it open. Still, I wasn't going to leave everything I cared about behind–so instead of leaving, I went into her room and hid under her bed to wait for her to come back. Just lie there 'til she was asleep then sneak out and get the new keys off her ring, that's all I was thinking... all I think I was thinking. But—"

The darkness and silence of Nan's bedroom, stinking with overflowing cigarette trays, thick dusty air, talcum powder–then at long last an opened door, stumbling steps, clothes dropped to the floor, a body settling back onto the mattress, so frail the box spring barely creaks. Wait 'til the light goes out plus an hour more, counted by heartbeats, breathing slowly through your nose, before finally slithering out, straightening up. Tiptoeing to the dresser and the purse left there, open far enough for you to rummage through it, your own silent anger outlining every shadow like it's boiling out through your pores, a radiation-sickness halo—

From the bed, there's a sudden sickly gasp as Nan jolts upright, eyes bulging, too disoriented to recognize the threatening black shape in the corner as her granddaughter: that rigid-backed thing already turning on her, its mouth gone square and teeth bared, eyes hateful enough to scald. *You'd probably scare you too,* you remember thinking, if you could see yourself: *good, good. You* should *be scared, you horrible old*—

But here the gasp is cut off by a squeal, then a thick, disgustingly hoarse rattle; the sound alone's enough to choke your horribly happy pleasure at her fright right off at the root as Nan's gaze glazes over, one eye skewing and mouth going slack on the same side, face half-melted. Makes it swerve hairpin, locking into the same track Nan's fear continues to plunge downhill on as she slumps over, settling into a permanent lean, with you all the while thinking, equally terrified: *Oh God, what happened, what did I* do?

(that *voice,* coolly: *You know, Isla*)

"A stroke," Amaya says, out loud. "You frightened her into a stroke."

"That's right."

"Okay, well, um... that's really, really bad, obviously. But it was... that was an accident, babe."

You snort. "Fucking her brain forever just because I wanted my specific pile of crap back? Yeah, I can see how you'd like to think so, and me too. But no."

"Oh, c'mon, Isla! I mean, how could it not be? There's no way on earth you could've known that would happen, and—well, she survived, right? I remember you saying. Your Nan didn't die until—"

"Five years later, right. And how do you think she was all that time, Maya? I know I told you *that,* too."

You see her stop and take a breath, thinking. Hearing your voice in her head, maybe, recounting Nan's subsequent downward plunge into dementia, paranoia, sheer outright insanity. How she went from simple bitch to raging harridan in what seemed like zero to sixty, only to let her house degenerate into a human rat's nest so bad it had to be almost entirely gutted and rebuilt from the studs after she died.

"*I* did that," you tell Amaya, perversely glad to hear the words out loud. "Me. I knew something would happen when I moved in with her, just not what—"

"Yeah, but you thought it would be a blow-up or a fight, something you were actually responsible for. As opposed to her just chucking you out for nothing, because she was a bitter, verge-of-nuts bitch–your mom squared, basically. Because she's where your mom gets it from."

You shake your head. "I was a guest. She let me into her home, and—"

"Hey, you need to *stop*. That is not your fault."

"Oh baby, it is my fault, and more than you know. More than even I remembered, up 'til now."

Back in the bedroom, you watch Nan's expression distort like a fist-crushed clay mask. Obscenities explode on a cloud of spit, too fast and slurred to make any sense–yet you know you've heard them all before already, more snidely, more subtly. And here's the primal raw hatred version, flayed and bleeding: how you're worthless, unlovable, a monster who'll make nothing but more monsters, a waste of time and breath and life. How everything you've ever dreaded is true, and worse.

You should feel sorry, and you do. Guilty. You do.

It also makes you hate her, more than ever.

You pick up Nan's keys from the floor and leave the bedroom; her ranting doesn't change or stop, not even when you close the door on her. You unlock the basement door and go down to collect your belongings, as much as you can take in a single trip, and—

(this is the part you don't tell Amaya, because)

(well, it sounds *crazy,* even to you)

—you see the Jaundice Bitters bottle by your bedside, its silver patina glimmering in the dark; stare at it a moment, before making the decision. Then pick it up, work the cork out carefully. In a series of whispers, tell the empty air inside the bottle what you did, feeling the story slip from your shoulders as you say it aloud–slip out and down, inside, settle at the bottle's bottom. Shove the cork back in with your last word, hard, to keep even the faintest shred of it from leaking back out. Go over to the closet, move as much of the stuff inside as you can, make a hole; lifting the bottle up to the top shelf seems to take disproportionate effort, let alone shoving it in, far as you can.

The minute you let go, though, it's like you've already forgotten it. Like it was never there.

(and here we go back to reality, the agreed-upon version)

You shut the door, hump your things back upstairs, toss Nan's keys onto the living room floor and leave without looking back, front door cracked open to the cold, cold night. Don't even bother calling 911 'til you're at the bus station.

Amaya's taken your hand at some point during your story, studying you closely; she waits for a pause long enough to suggest you've finished, then swallows. Begins: "That's—God, Isla, I'm so sorry that happened to you. I can't even imagine how that feels."

You gawk. "I don't... Were you *listening*? I don't think you really heard what I—"

"Of course I did, and it sounds traumatizing, to say the fucking least. But I still think you're blaming yourself too much for what happened, especially after all these..."

"The paramedics could have got there faster, maybe could've... done something, I don't know. But I didn't let them, because–well, I hated her, okay? Always. So that's on me."

"She sounds legitimately hateable, babe. And you were young–younger. You're not that person anymore."

(*Oh no?*)

"Maya, you really don't get it, do you? I'm responsible for weaponizing her craziness, then walking away, knowing Mom would have to deal with the result. And now I know it again, I'm *glad*. I *knew* how bad her health was, what a sudden shock could do to her—"

"Goddamnit, *no!*" Amaya so seldom interrupts you at all, let alone this forcefully. That surprise is enough to stop you. "Strokes don't work like that, Isla; it could've happened at any time. It's even odds you had nothing to do with it at all–

and even if you did, A) being angry isn't the same as legal malicious intent and B) it sounds like she damn well deserved it!" She stands, eyes blazing. "So, if you want forgiveness, then fine, I'll give it to you! Good enough?"

"That easy, huh? You 'forgive' me, and I'm just supposed to feel better?"

Amaya's fists tighten. "What I'm saying is, there's nothing to forgive. The only person in this house who thinks you did something wrong that night is you."

(*And yet.*)

You almost turn your head this time; the impression of a voice is so strong. But Amaya clearly hears nothing.

And yet, what? you wonder. Is this only that secret, constant worm of doubt, the one that fears Amaya's only ever been humouring you? Or is it something—

(*some one*)

—else?

"I'll always be 'that person'," is all you snap back, however–quoting her savagely, throwing her own words back in her face–before you can think not to. Watching her flinch and feeling like flinching yourself but walking away again instead: down, this time. Back to the basement, half-lit with daylight seeping in through the shades, with the bottle's furtive gleam. To which that murmur behind your eyes replies, just as simply: *Yes.*

You will.

Amaya's voice reaches you through the basement bathroom door now, barely audible over not just the shower's roar but also that hiss, that thrum, that oceanic back and forth building inside your inner ear, your skull, your entire pounding body. The one that meets every fervent pledge of love and support she makes with its own litany of self-fulfilling prophecy, advice you don't even want to hear, let alone follow...

Just listen, keep on listening.

You promised to help me, Isla.

Don't be afraid, you'll like it.

You'll want to.

You'll feel so much better once you do.

Remember: Amaya thinks she knows, but she doesn't–she never will. She can't. She can't, can't ever be allowed to know.

(*how bad you are, have always been, how awful*)

(she'd stop loving you if she knew, and that would just be...)

I'd rather die, you think. And hear something sigh in pleasure, somewhere deep inside: *Yes, exactly.*

Exactly.

"Baby, come on," you think you hear Amaya plead, from so much farther away than through three inches of door. "Come out of there, Isla, please. Everything's going to be okay, I promise you."

You clear your dry throat, raise your voice just a bit. "You should go, Maya. I don't want to..."

"Don't want to what?"

"Doesn't matter. Just... go home, all right?"

"I don't—"

"Christ, can you just trust me for once? Go *home,* Amaya! Why won't you just *go home?*"

A pause, during which you can almost see her draw her breath: so determined, so loving. So innocent.

"You couldn't make me go home, Isla," she says, at last. "Remember? I'm here for you."

Staring down at the razor in your hand, one leg half-done, you wonder exactly how best to pop the blade inside out without letting Amaya know what you're doing, so you'll never have to shave the other one. So you won't have to worry about hurting her or hurting yourself. And hearing it still, all through these breathless seconds–another voice in yet another room, then in this one, then inside you: *go here, do that.* Telling you how nothing you've done in the years since you bottled up your crime and left it behind has meant anything, if it can all be wiped away so easily; telling you how no one ever really changes, how even that stroke you gave Nan simply broke the mask she wore and let what was always inside spill out. Telling you–oh so plausibly, rationally, soothingly–how if she really knew you at all, that friend of yours, she'd surely want to kill you, too. So...

... kill her first, then kill yourself. Leave the house empty as your sin-catching bottle.
It only makes sense; you know it does.
But: Goddamnit, no. NO.
I won't, you think. *Not that, not ever – not to her. And you can't make me.*
Oh...
... can't I?

By the time you finally come out, hair still wet, she's already asleep. So, you creep back upstairs, lock yourself in Nan's former room, crawl under the (new, clean smelling, only slightly dusty) bed and lie there with eyes wide open in the dark, looking up. Like you're trying to count the bedsprings.

All at once, you find yourself aware of something scurrying in the darkness, a lithe, wet scuttle. Is it that thing from your other dream, shitting its slimy-blind progeny out everywhere it goes? So, you roll out once more, up on all fours, teeth bared. Follow the sound more than any movement, its nailed feet clicking fast towards the bedroom door, and scrabble just as quick at the handle–twisting it to and fro, hard enough to strain your wrist–before finally throwing it open, stumbling out into, not the hall, but that long, black beach under a silver-glazed sky. Mica and volcanic grains beneath, gray blue above, pale smears of cloud like the peeling patina under raised letters, J-A-U-N-D...

There's a plop to your right, a watery swish as that thing immerses itself in the surf, speeding away. Something buried bruises your heel as you step back. Another shell?

No. A half-circle, then a stem, then the rest. You scrape away sand from every side, freeing it, and raise up the result.

The bottle.

On impulse, you raise it to your lips. Breathe across the rim like you're testing a flute, light but long, evoking a low, pale note–then inhale once more without thinking, only to taste that same note in your mouth like a lover's tongue or a drug's first hit, narcotic, numbing. Feel your lungs start to ache with that rush and whisper: *Who are you?*

You, the voice replies, or seems to.

(You're almost certain.)

Who?

You.

(*I am you.*)

That voice in the dream, in the dark. That voice.

It's yours, you realize. Oh God.

It always was.

Anger is a ghost. Guilt is a ghost. This confession is a ghost.

You are a ghost.

You are your own ghost.

And here you recoil, throw the bottle into the sea, the incoming waves. But all at once you can see the sky is tightening, and you start to see through it to a bent, warped reflection of your room. You yell, pound on the bottle's sides as it moves inwards, crushing you down into a mere flickering light. And as you shrink, the world outside gets clearer–you begin to perceive what you're looking at, that smeary room (the basement), that smeary figure (yourself). Standing over the bed, occupied by Amaya. Holding a knife.

On the bedside table, the bottle starts to move, to slide, to fall, to crash. Inside the falling bottle, you feel yourself start to wink out.

This is when you'll wake up, you can already tell, looking down on the self-made pattern of your own ruin. The room will be dark, dark enough it takes your eyes a moment to adjust. Staring up at you is Amaya, the one you love so much your heart hurts, with her red mouth open and teeth beginning to pull apart, her soft black pansy eyes gone wide and hard with terror.

Did you really think love would save her, or you? A girl like you, everything you've done, allowed yourself to forget you've done... What sort of love do you think you deserve, hmmm?

(That's right: none.)

Outside, "you" smiles back at "yourself," glass-trapped, bottle-bound. Forever trapped in that one bad decision, a still-time pocket bounded only by the bottle you whispered it into's deceptively fragile sides. Forever stuck in a moment you can't remember well enough to get out of, until it breaks...

...or you do.

Oh, you should not rest
Between the elements of air and earth,
But you should pity me.

Cuckoo

OWN THE CROOKED street, up the crooked stairs, then through a band of darkness and up once more, into the pallid light of flickering fluorescents—one for each door, dimming by degrees, like dying stars. Mine is two from the end on your left, next to the garbage chute. The address is accurate; you do not need to check. Knock, and I will answer.

Just that way, exactly. And... here I am.

Perhaps I do not look as expected. Perhaps this is what keeps you on my doorstep, hesitant, wary. You pictured something else—some*one* else, another sort of person. Less odd in composition. Taller.

Well, we cannot always help the way things are, sadly, not even such as I, with my skills—I cannot use them to alter such trivialities as appearance, at least not my own. For this is part of the deal, you see; a price we pay, my kind, in return for being able to work change on others' behalf. You might call it ironic.

Not me. I come from somewhere older, somewhere colder, somewhere *else*. Where politeness is not simply social, but essential. Where it keeps you alive.

For example: once upon a time, in my own place, payment was far less metaphorical: instead of simply agreeing not to do ourselves the same services we offer others, we cut away bits of ourselves and buried them like seeds, then watered them with bowls full of blood, to see what would grow. The results were always interesting.

Or so the stories say. I have not tried it myself.

Not yet.

But let us keep to the matter at hand—come in, mother; father, you too. Shut the door behind you, please. Do not be wary. Nothing here can hurt you, not any more than you have already *been* hurt. Sit down.

You want something. Someone told you I might be the one to give it to you. So... tell me. Tell *me*.

Ah, do not cry, mother. There is no need.

Speak.

You show me a picture, taken on your phone. You play me a video. You tell me your story haltingly, taking it in turns. When one is overcome, the other takes up the tale, filling in details that sometimes contradict, but only slightly. Only as much as memories often do.

He will not speak, you tell me. *He will not sleep. He will not eat what we tell him, when we tell him. We do not know if he loves us.*

This creature, with a face made from both your faces put together. But how much is there of you inside him really? You cannot tell, even now, after all these years. You simply cannot tell.

Does he laugh? Yes, sometimes.

Does he cry? Yes, often.

Is he angry? Probably. As you would be, were you he.

He was born huge, with grasping hands and bleak, bulging, old man's eyes. He has wrecked your chances for more children, mother—not so much through physical damage, but because you fear to make another like him. The odds are high. You have seen the studies: more likely than not, they say. Better not to try.

And how long, father, since your wife has taken *you* in her arms, instead of merely weeping over your recalcitrant offspring? I know better than to ask, especially since your eyes give the answer. This is his fault too, you believe.

He sits in your home, this stranger, taking everything, giving nothing back. Stealing your sleep, your food, your happiness. The same way I sit here nodding, perhaps—polite, as I am to all my guests. This is only sensible in business.

Would it surprise you just how often I have heard this same sad tale? For how seldom we get what we wish for in this life! Never the right house, the right job, the right car; not the right husband, nor the right wife. And children, ah, children... most difficult of all things to get right, it sometimes seems. Judging by *my* clientele at least.

When I ask you to name your wants directly, you hesitate. It is hard to say the words, I know. Harder still to carry them inside you, heavy as a stone, a shell formed over years, grown tight yet brittle 'round some unhatched foulness.

Well, do not feel you must ask me directly if it hurts you to do so. I know the answer already, after all. It is always the same.

You want the child you thought you had a right to, before this one came instead. The child from your head, not the one you gave birth to. You want the dream, the child you think you would have had, if only...

Oh, if only.

Still: driven mad by ceaseless crying, sleepless with guilt and self-hatred... who among you would not take such a chance, if it was offered? Who among you has not had that same thought yet failed to act upon it, only to do something far worse? Magic or murder, a choice that is no choice. No choice at all.

You cannot be blamed. Surely you will be forgiven, if only by each other.

Never doubt I know the word you most fear to speak, father, perhaps because you still do not quite believe it, even though you dared to seek *me* out—me, and my kin. Shall I say it out loud, since you cannot? Or would that disturb you further?

Very well, then: *changeling.*

In the tales, these creatures are interlopers foisted on unsuspecting humans through trickery, slyly slipped into unsuspecting human parents' cradles by those who are not human... goblins, trolls, fairies, punishing when you will not or cannot. Those who exist, apparently, merely to dispose of *your* leavings.

Be good, or the fairies will take you: slander to cover up the truth of the matter, a story agreed upon after the fact. And if you disagree, let me point out that even if we did indeed "steal" your rejects now and then in the past, since we cannot even enter into your houses without invitation, an invitation must have been issued in order for that to have happened. Who is it you think must have done that?

Or perhaps these changelings are simply babies, whose parents deny them because they fall short somehow, fail to thrive, reflect badly on those who birthed them. So, the parents name them creatures in disguise, unworthy of care; alien, other, a stone sown amongst seeds. The one bad apple that sours every crop.

Yet tales also tell us how *some* still manage to love them, these fiends in disguise, even after the mask has slipped.

In Bettna, for example—many years ago—when a peasant's wife had her first child, her mother knew not to let the fire in the child's room go out until it was baptized. But she was obliged to go home, and during her absence her daughter forgot to stoke it. Embarrassed, she did not tell her mother what she had done but laid another on the ashes of the first.

During the baptism the child cried lustily, and afterwards, it became so greedy it devoured everything that came its way. The parents, being poor, were in danger of being eaten out of house and home. Only the grandmother knew what to do. She helped her daughter build a fire in the bake oven, put the changeling upon a shovel, then had her pretend that she was about to throw it in.

Immediately, a little woman rushed up, tossed the original baby in its crib, and grabbed up her own—the changeling—instead. "I would never treat *your* child so badly or think to do it such harm as you threaten mine with," she complained before vanishing.

Have you tried this method yet, to find out whether the child is truly yours? Just as well, I suppose; those at Social Services do tend to frown on such things. On no account will they let you hang a suspect baby in a basket over the fire anymore or lay it at the crossroads so a dead body may be carried over it, so it might vanish, and the real child be returned. Why, they will not even allow you to touch it with hot iron or pierce its lying hide with needles! Such are the vagaries of civilized society.

In another era, once you had rid yourself of the changeling through either threat or trickery, you might then seek your *true* son out wherever my kin had hidden him. Like the brave Irish smith who entered a certain hill on a certain night, carrying with him only a Bible, a knife, and a crowing cock. He knocked and was let in, stuck his blade in the door's jamb to prevent it closing once more upon him, then quickly found his stolen boy working at a great forge, ceaselessly and silent. Demanding his child's freedom, the smith brandished his Bible, to which the boy's captors simply laughed. But that woke the cock, who crowed long and loud, convincing them day was dawning; they therefore threw both smith and son back out of the hill, slamming the door behind.

For a year and a day, the smith's boy hardly ever spoke, doing nothing, still as a stone. But at last, watching his father finish a sword he was making for some chief, the son suddenly exclaimed: "That is not the way." Taking the tools from his father's hands, he fashioned a weapon the likes of which had never been seen before. Thus, smith and son were kept in constant employment, their fame spread far and wide, and they lived very happily with one another.

Some odd boys and girls do have similar talents, I hear—though often not so practical, unfortunately. For children are seldom forced to earn their own keep in these too-soft times, let alone pay back the cost of their upbringing.

Ah, but that reminds me: who looks after this child of yours as you sit here, mother, father? Someone, I hope. I hope you did not simply leave him at home, mistakenly believing he will be fine so long as there is food, water, television. Thinking that because he cannot say he does or does not care when you are present, he cannot possibly miss you.

This curse-child. This thing of darkness you do not acknowledge yours.

Since you have none for him, it pleases you to believe him incapable of love—a sweet equation, and possibly even true if you are lucky. But who can know, truly? Who of us here or elsewhere?

No, but please: do not look to *me*.

There are many other children out there already, I might gently suggest, any of whom you could easily replace this unbearable son of yours with. Your world is full of them, parentless, as you believe yourself childless—lost, stolen, hopeless, seeking, trapped. Children to whom you would not be just parents, but saviors. Whose love you would be assured of forever, given the debt they knew they owed you.

Oh, but you do not want *them,* do you—someone else's leavings, another broken thing, another potential mistake. A child you might actually have to *pay* to take possession of, merely to replace the defective child who came to you for free.

And now you are crying again, mother, while you sit gritting your teeth, father: angry at me yet too courteous to show it, I have no doubt. Seeing how you are so obviously a gentleman, and I only... what I am.

Well, I apologize. I meant no insult, so am not insulted in turn. And no, this does not mean I will *not* do what you ask of me, either.

You came to me because you were told I have treated with certain powers in the past, gaining continued access to them, if not influence over them. Which is true for many of my blood, stretching back to that time when we still lived in our own place; a mark we bear on our skins, our souls. The same visible trace of strangeness that kept you caught on my doorstep until I invited you in—signs of kinship with both those that made us and those who made *them* in turn.

They can be called, not commanded. Never that. Their attention, unlike mine, cannot be bought with money alone; they require more. Much more. A price I will establish, and you must pay to its fullest before we can proceed any further. And then—

Oh, one of them *will* come, never fear. They are idle, so it amuses them to pretend to serve us; it is a game they cannot play alone. And they will give you what you want, but what they give you will not be *your* child. None return from where your child will have gone by then. You will get something—flesh and blood and bone—which moves and speaks and seems to love, yet truly loves nothing except your own ruin and confusion.

Do not say I have not warned you.

They cannot take him sight unseen, however, my relatives... my kin. You must bring him to me—to us. Only then can it be done.

I will wait, obviously. I have no other place to be.

Sometimes I consider the cuckoo, evolved to lay eggs in other birds' nests—brood parasites, your scientists call them. Less known, however, is the fact that most cuckoos keep their own children and raise them, just like other birds. We do not know why the opposite scenario occurs, only that it does on occasion. Is it genetics alone that drives them to ensure their young survive and thrive through masquerading as another species, piggybacking on the deluded kindness of strangers?

Myths aside, the presence of cuckoos is not *always* detrimental. Horror stories about "real" chicks starved and pushed from nests are mainly untrue; cuckoo-bearing nests are more likely to thrive, overall, than those without. The chaotic strength of hybrid vigor proving nature yet once more so wonderfully odd, so essentially unknowable.

Must every child you do not want become a cuckoo too, through sheer necessity?

Besides which: do you truly think your children so precious we have to *steal* them anymore, when there are so many surplus humans to go around? When you treat each other like garbage, expecting us to treat you like gold? What is it you suppose makes you so special, exactly?

Or perhaps you still believe every odd child must be one of ours from the start, stolen secretly, replaced. How stupid we would have to be, in that case—to make such a bad replica, one so easily spotted. Our magic must be truly degraded.

Why would it matter if it was "your" child? Do you know what happens to these unclaimed children? Any one of them could be "yours." But you want only your own flesh and blood—that or a version thereof.

Selfish, willful, like all your kind. Ask yourselves: why would we have ever needed your rejects in the first place, except to amuse ourselves by turning them into mirrors that reflect you, not the way you see yourselves, but how *we* see you— cracked, bent, ridiculous? As iron spread across the world and fenced us in, drove us underground to squat inside cold hills and use glamor to conjure luxuries from leaves, twigs, mud... all we had was what you allowed us, what you deigned to give us, the scraps from your table, your endless feast. What you threw away, our way.

Oh, but that won't happen here, not to *you*. How could it? You, so different, such a different case. Entirely.

Do you not think that we—I and those others, the creatures we descend from and their kin in turn, the glorious and dreadful things we serve—must grow somewhat weary by now, mother, father? Of performing the only function your iron-bound world has left to us? Of taking the children you deem too broken for you to be bothered to love?

But who am I to tell you that child you long for doesn't exist and never did? That the child you have is the only one you are entitled to? Who am I to be so cruel?

Well, life *is* often cruel, even for good people, the best sort of people. But this is what money is for, I hear.

Mother, father—I do not use your names, you will notice. I never have or will. If you told them to me, I have already filled that place in, covered it over; I do not *want* to know them, not even long enough to forget them. You and you are only one more, one more, one more. You are all the same.

So, we will fix terms now, discuss payment. You will bring me the boy, say your goodbyes or not, depending on whether you believe he hears them, and then whatever happens next... will happen. Even I cannot say for sure what that will be. For I am not *one* of them, after all, not truly—no more than you or him. No more than anyone.

And yet...

...let us imagine, just for one last moment, that I was not always as I am— *what* I am. That perhaps *I* was an unwanted child once, sullen, angry and sleepless, always crying. That perhaps my parents came up these very stairs to deal with someone much like me, yet not me. That perhaps I was given away, changed, worked upon, altered until my own mother and father would never recognize me again, not even if they stood in this same room once more. That perhaps all... this... is simply what is left.

I would not be able to tell you, if so; those would be the rules of the game, if this was one. Not even if I were *him,* come back through time to tempt and try you. It is not impossible; magic can do all things if it can do even one. It might be I was given one chance to persuade you *not* to give me up, to stop you from making a terrible mistake. To solve my own soul-murder before it can happen.

Perhaps we have been here before, all of us, over and over again. Right here in this same moment. Right now. And perhaps you have never been persuaded. Perhaps you have given me up each and every time, consigned me to the underhill, the open forge, the wrack and ruin of a humanity you could not recognize when it was right in front of you, crying for love you thought me incapable of feeling. Crying out forever to *be* loved by those who should have cherished me for what I was, not what they wanted me to be.

How would you feel then, mother, father? Would you make the same choice for your own child still? Would you still give him to me, to give to them? Would you feel it worth the price you might pay, knowing the result?

No, I am not surprised. Not even disappointed.

You understand you must sacrifice the child you have for the child you want. I see that. Very well. But what if I told you I could not, in fact, promise that what you got would be what you wanted, after?

Still, you would have *something*. Something else. For better or for worse. Which is all anyone can ever promise, really, magic or no magic. To anybody.

Shall we begin?

ABOUT THE AUTHOR

Formerly a film critic, journalist, screenwriter and teacher, **Gemma Files** has been an award-winning horror author since 1999. She has published two collections of short work, two chapbooks of speculative poetry, a Weird Western trilogy, a story-cycle and a stand-alone novel (*Experimental Film*, which won the 2016 Shirley Jackson Award for Best Novel and the 2016 Sunburst award for Best Adult Novel). She has two new story collections from Trepidatio (*Spectral Evidence* and *Drawn Up From Deep Places*), one upcoming from Cemetery Dance (*Dark Is Better*), and a new poetry collection from Aqueduct Press (*Invocabulary*).

GRIMSCRIBE PRESS

CPSIA information can be obtained
at www.ICGtesting.com
Printed in the USA
LVHW100706190822
726322LV00005B/6/J